CHANGE OF LEADS

BOOK SIX

DEEDS OF THE PAST

THE NAVARRE LINK CHRONICLES

CHANGE OF LEADS

BOOK SIX

DEEDS OF THE PAST

A. K. BRAUNEIS

First Printing: 2026
Printed and bound in the USA
ISBN: 978-1-7335920-9-3

Two Blazes Artworks
710 Terry Lane
Selah, Washington
USA

www.twoblazesartworks.com

Cover art and design by A. K. Brauneis.

Dedication

To my husband, Paul. Though often shaking his head at my chaotic creativity, he has always been there with his love and support throughout this whole process. Love you, Babe. You're the best thing to come into my life.

To Peter Deuel. Although gone from this Earth for many years, he was, back then and still is, my creative inspiration.

Acknowledgments

Where would I be without Westerns? Movies, TV, books—they were all my sanctuary, my private world where I could go anytime and disappear into a world filled with fun and adventure.

Jimmy Stewart, Audie Murphy, and Ben Johnston, to name only a few, kept my eyes glued to the screen. Wagon Train, Wanted Dead or Alive, High Chaparral, Lancer, and my all-time, forever favorite, Alias Smith and Jones. Westerns were abundant when I was growing up, and I'm sure I watched every movie and most of the TV series out there.

Charlie Russell. Oh my, what an influence he had, and still has, on my creative endeavors. Attending the Out West Art Show in Great Falls, Montana, has become one of the highlights of my year.

Max Brand was my favorite Western author, and though I read books by others, his were the ones that kept me coming back.

Today, I watch most of the new Western movies that hit the silver screen, supporting a genre that has lost its way but is struggling to make a comeback. At the very least, these more recent westerns have been entertaining, but there are a few that stand out as gems: Silverado, Dances with Wolves, Appaloosa, Open Range, Hostiles, and yes, I did enjoy Cowboys and Aliens.

I thank all these creations and the many people who helped produce them for giving me a love that has lasted a lifetime. Now, here I am, writing my own western series, and enjoying every minute of it.

For those people in my life now who have helped me along the way, I would like to thank:

Lisa Baird for the many hours she dedicated to proofreading this manuscript, and for her knowledge of legal proceedings and terminology

S. Whyment for her support and contributions towards character development.

Eric Hotz for his technical support. For someone like me, who is computer illiterate, his advice and assistance have been invaluable.

Also available on Amazon

ICE: Prelude to the Navarre Link Chronicles
ISBN 978-1-7335920-3-1

THE NAVARRE LINK CHRONICLES
Change of Leads: The Lost Shoe
ISBN 13:978-1-7335920-0-0

THE NAVARRE LINK CHRONICLES
Change of Leads: Aftershock
ISBN: 978-1-7335920-1-7

THE NAVARRE LINK CHRONICLES
Change of Leads: Dangerous Games
ISBN: 978-1-7335920-4-8

THE NAVARRE LINK CHRONICLES
Change of Leads: Departures
ISBN: 978-1-7335920-5-5

THE NAVARRE LINK CHRONICLES
Change of Leads: The Way Out
ISBN: 978-1-7335920-6-2

THE NAVARRE LINK CHRONICLES
Dinner at The Elk: The Outlaw Years
ISBN: 978-1-7335920-8-6

THE NAVARRE LINK CHRONICLES
Change of Leads: Deeds of The Past
ISBN: 978-1-7335920-9-3

Prelude

These stories were first written for the Alias Smith and Jones fanfiction sites. When I decided to publish them for the general public, I rewrote much of the storyline to make it my own. There are times when I still second-guess myself and feel that I should have changed even more of the background to disassociate from the original series.

Those of you who remember the series will find the storyline familiar despite my efforts.

I intended to explore those dark avenues our mind travels along that ultimately convince a person that taking their own lives is the only course open for them to escape a life that no longer holds any joy.

My mother took her life in 1967 when I was ten years old. Then, in the wee hours on the last day of 1971, the lead actor in Alias Smith and Jones, Peter Elstrom Deuel, also chose to leave this world in a similar fashion.

I think I was too young to fully understand the consequences of my mother's passing, but Peter's death was devastating. In a way, I think it allowed me to process the loss of my mother, which I had not been able to do previously. I was hit hard by the passing of two people who had chosen this drastic and irreversible way of escaping their unhappiness.

Forty years later, I discovered the joy of writing through the fanfiction sites. After writing several short stories, I realized I needed to do more. It had become apparent that suicide was not uncommon; it was simply hidden away as something that people chose not to talk about.

I realized I needed not only to talk about it but also to write about it. So began the journey that has extended far longer than I could have ever anticipated.

My objective was to combine the characteristics of the person Peter Deuel with those of the TV character Hannibal Heyes, thereby creating a whole new, complex personality.

I knew Hannibal Heyes very well, but getting to know Peter proved challenging. He'd been gone for over 40 years, and whatever I thought I knew about him came from the fanzines of the 1960s and '70s—hardly a reliable source.

Thanks to two separate biographies titled “Pete Duel: A Biography” and “Pete Duel: A Biography Second Edition” by Paul Green, I was able to get a glimpse into Peter’s complex and often contradictory personality.

I was also fortunate to meet a close friend of his from the ‘60s, and she was kind enough to share many of her memories and personal photos from that time.

I cannot pretend to know Peter as well as his friends and family do, but at least I was allowed a glimpse into his tumultuous life. By combining those aspects with the light-hearted and cheeky character of Hannibal Heyes, I believe I have developed an antihero in Napoleon Nash who is likable, flawed, infuriating, and often contradictory, just like the inspirational Pete Duel.

Volume Six: Deeds of the Past

Dedications 5
Acknowledgements 6
Prelude 8
Shadows 13
Announcements 29
Fourth of July 45
The First Sign 65
Baby Steps 73
The Visit 87
The Test 103
A Gathering of Friends 113
Into Danger 127
Coming To Terms 139
Cause and Effect 153
Set in Motion 175
A Family Torn Apart 197
The Great Deception 221
Buck Up 247
A Lost Love 259
Conflicts 281
Confessions 299
Topeka 307
Working For a Living 317
The Long Chase 331
Home Again 347
A Trail of Blood 361
Full Circle 377
Combined Forces 393
Kidnapped 405

Preview 411
List of Characters 413
List of Governors 415
About the Author 417

CHAPTER ONE
SHADOWS

Arvada, Colorado
May, 1889

Leon and Karma galloped across the landscape in a joyous exhibition of flight and freedom. Only when he was riding his mare did Leon feel that he was unencumbered and completely without constraint. She was his freedom from the invisible shackles that still bound him, and from the anchor that weighed him down with the rules and conditions of living life on parole.

This was glorious.

The spring day couldn't have been nicer, and the breeze, fresh and filled with sunshine, whipped his old hat off his head, causing it to fly along behind him, attached only by its stampede straps.

Karma felt good; she had missed her human. And though life at the Rocking M had many pleasures and bonuses, having her human back with her again was worth all of that, and more. If he asked her to leave this sanctuary, leave her children, and ride the transient trail again, she would have done it without question. Now that he was back with her, she remembered how much she had missed him before the image and scent of him had faded away. But now, they were together again, no questions asked, no grudges held. They were together again, and she was in her glory.

After two miles at a full gallop, followed by three more miles at an easy, swinging lope, Leon pulled his mare down to a walk. They settled into a pleasant ride across the meadow, drinking in the greens, the blues, and the yellows, the sun, the grass, and the great, cloudless sky. Leon asked her to halt, shading his eyes against the sun, and squinted into the distance, not quite believing what he was seeing.

He rode closer, but it didn't help to clarify.

There was a table ahead, covered with a red-and-white checkered cloth. There were two chairs at the table, with one being occupied by a man whom Leon could not quite make out. This whole strange arrangement was set out under a large willow tree, and there was a gurgling brook running by them, inviting the horseman to come and join in.

Leon rode closer, then, stepping down from his mare, he approached the table. The man sitting at it turned and smiled at his friend.

"Nash! About time you showed up. The steaks are gettin' cold."

Leon's face broke into a huge grin, and he gave the man a heartfelt hug, right where he sat.

"Doc! Doc, it's been ages. How are you?"

"Well, I'm still dead, but other than that, I suppose I'm fine." Then his expression dropped. "I'm a little disappointed in you, though."

Leon felt hurt settle into his chest.

"Disappointed in me? Why?"

"C'mon, sit down. Have a beer. I know that's your favorite. And there's a nice steak for ya, too. Dig in."

"Yeah, okay." Leon sat down to the meal, but he was still feeling hurt and didn't really want to eat. He took a small gulp of the beer and couldn't help but smile. This beer tasted good, unlike most of the beer he'd been drinking lately.

He sighed and looked to his friend again.

"Why, Doc? What did I do?"

"It's not what ya did, Nash. It's what ya haven't done."

Leon furrowed his brow. Doc wasn't making any sense.

The older man saw the confusion and continued to explain.

"You ignored what I told ya. I told ya it was Carson, that fucking prick, who murdered me, not Boeman. But you let outside pressure convince ya that our last meeting was all just a delusion due to ya bein' so close to death an' all."

"Yes, well ... I know, Doc." Leon felt like a schoolboy who was being reprimanded for misbehavior. "I just ... I thought they were right. And the more I came back to the land of the living, the more that conversation drifted away, until it did seem like it had just been a dream. I mentioned it to my lawyer." He perked up as he pointed this out, hoping for approval.

Doc tutted and shook his head. "Yeah, but as soon as he suggested that you were loony bins, you backed off. It's not easy, ya know, tryin' to get these messages to ya. Then you just ignore 'em as bad dreams!"

"Oh." Leon was contrite. "I thought that's all they were."

"What do I have ta do?" Doc demanded. "Write it all up in a goddam document and get your lawyer to sign it before you'll sit up and pay attention!?"

Leon hung his head.

Doc took pity on the younger man's discomfort and came down a notch or two.

"It's not like I'm askin' it for me, Nash. That goddam, son-of-a-bitch has got to be stopped. I'm not the only person he's murdered, and he's gonna do it again too—you can bet your goddam talisman on that!"

"I know, but there's no evidence," Leon pointed out. "He always covers his tracks, or Mitchel did for him. I wouldn't know where to start."

"You wouldn't know where to start?" Doc was incredulous. "The great Napoleon Nash wouldn't know where to start?"

Leon hung his head again; this was not going well.

"Of all the goddam, fuckin', lame excuses I've ever heard," Doc cursed. "All I ask is this one little favor from you, and all you can say is, 'I wouldn't know where to start.'? Sheesh."

"Yeah, yeah, okay," Leon grumbled. "I guess that was kind of lame."

"Hmm." Doc was in a snit.

Leon leaned back with another sigh.

"So, you're sure it was Carson who did it?"

Doc did not honor this question with an answer and simply glared at his friend.

"Yeah, yeah, all right, Doc. I suppose . . ."

Suddenly, the surroundings changed, and the beautiful, spring day was no longer in evidence around them.

Leon felt a chill go through him, not just from the lowered temperature, but from the fear that now clutched at his heart and threatened to stop his breath.

***

He was in that dank, cold chamber again, hanging from the ceiling by his arms. His shoulders felt as though they were on fire, and he struggled as he yelled, trying to break free. The fear and the pain overwhelmed him, and he knew he was going to pass out.

Then he spluttered and choked. Gasping for air, he opened his eyes and saw Carson sneering at him, the emptied cup of water still dripping in his hand.

"Wake up, Nash," Carson growled at him. "How do ya expect ta learn anything, if ya keep passin' out on us?"

Carson laughed and slapped him hard across the face, causing his suspended body to swing against the rope.

Leon screamed his rage and agony, trying to fight back, but he was helpless.

Carson sneered at him. Then the guard had a pillow in his hands, and he turned away from the inmate to glare down at something on the floor.

Leon looked closer and saw that it was Doc who lay there in an ever-expanding pool of blood. He clutched the gaping wound in his side. When he saw Carson coming toward him with murder in his eyes, he started calling for help as he tried to scramble out of the way. But he was too weak.

Carson moved toward him, then, kneeling beside the helpless man, he slapped him hard across the face. Doc tried to fight back, but the blow stunned him. The guard pushed the pillow down on top of his victim's face and leaned into it.

Leon screamed.

He fought against the rope; he fought against the air, trying to get to his friend, trying desperately to help him.

"No! No, Doc!" He cried and screamed, fighting like a man possessed, until he felt the muscles and tendons in his arms and shoulders snap and break free as his joints pulled from their sockets. His head exploded with the light, and he screamed out his torment . . .

***

"Napoleon! Napoleon, wake up!"

Leon lashed out at the light burning his eyes. He gasped for air as he scrambled away from the presence in the room. He had pushed himself up against the headboard of his bed, the blankets clutched around him as he tried to get away.

"Napoleon, it's all right," said a gentle voice behind the blinding light. "It was just a bad dream. Wake up."

Leon breathed in great gulps of air, his heart pounding so hard, he was sure it would burst from his chest and force blood to break through his eardrums. He was shivering, bathed in a cold sweat, and shaking like a leaf.

The blinding light mellowed as Jean set the lantern down on the side table and adjusted the flame so a soft light now filled the bedroom. Leon looked at her, still clutching the blanket and gasping for air. But he was awake now, and he knew who she was, and he knew where he was. He began to calm down.

He breathed a sigh of relief as Jean smiled and put a gentle hand on his arm.

"Are you all right now?"

Leon nodded. "Yes," he gasped out. "Sorry. I ... didn't mean to wake you."

She sat on the bed beside him.

"You didn't wake me. I was already up. I couldn't sleep and thought I would make some tea." They both heard the kettle on the stove start to whistle. She laughed. "See? Why don't you join me? A cup of tea might just be the ticket."

"Yeah."

She smiled again and patted his knee. She stood up, and leaving the light there, made her way into the kitchen to tend to the kettle. Leon could hear her striking up another light in there and then begin putting out the tea service.

He took a deep breath and gave himself a few more minutes to calm down. He rubbed his eyes and ran his hands through the stubble that was the beginning of his hair growing back. He groaned quietly.

"Oh, Doc. You're gonna keep on haunting me until I get the message, aren't you? Well, you can stop now, because I think I finally got it."

Then, just as he had done at David's place, he pulled on his socks, and, grabbing the blanket, he wrapped it around himself just as much out of modesty as for warmth. He took the lamp with him and padded quietly out to the dining table and sat down.

***

Jean joined Leon from the kitchen, carrying two cups and the teapot on a tray, then set them on the table. She embarrassed him with yet another of many heartfelt hugs. Then, sitting down beside him, she poured the tea.

"I hope you don't mind," she said.

"Mind what?"

"It has occurred to me that both Penny and I give you hugs every time we see you."

Leon smiled. "No, I don't mind. I'm not really sure how to respond to them, but it actually feels kind of nice."

Jean set the pot down and slid a cup to her companion. "It's just that we're so glad to have you home again. We've missed you. Being able to hug you, I suppose, helps to reaffirm the fact that you are actually here."

Leon chuckled; it sounded foreign to his ears. "I know what you mean. You and Penny have my permission to carry on giving hugs."

An expression of concern crossed Jean's eyes as Leon picked up his teacup, his hand still shaking.

"Do you have those nightmares often?" she asked him, gently.

"Almost every night," Leon admitted, then sent a glance to the door of the first bedroom. "I'm surprised Jack didn't wake up."

"You didn't make much noise," Jean assured him. "As I said, I only heard you because I was already awake." Leon nodded acceptance. "Do you want to talk about them?"

Leon sent her a quick, self-conscious smile, then contemplated his teacup again and accepted the inevitable. "They vary." A hand came to his mouth as a soft cough escaped him. "Often, I'm going through the punishments again, only worse. If that's possible. The reality of them was bad enough. But in the dreams, I'm actually being pulled apart, and it's just . . ."

He stopped as a tremble went through him, the fear clutching his throat. He took a deep, shuddering breath and ran a hand over his stubbly head.

Jean tried hard not to be too much of a mother. She sat quietly, waiting for him to continue.

"Then the other dream I have, over and over, is about the doctor out there who was killed. Those dreams are so real, I swear they're actually happening." He blinked his eyes against the burning that often accompanied memories of his friend's death. "I'm not sure what to do about them."

"How do you mean?"

Leon looked at her, concern and confusion in his eyes. He took a deep breath and went for it.

"We all know that it was an inmate named Boeman who murdered the Doc—we saw the assault. But now, Doc is coming to me in my dreams, insisting that it wasn't Boeman, but the senior guard, Carson, who killed him, and Leon twitched a smile, preparing to be ridiculed, "and the Doc wants me to prove it and get justice for him."

"Well," Jean poured more tea, "dreams are very strange things. Most of them don't mean anything at all; they're simply reactions to what has been going on in our lives and in our waking thoughts. Like those punishments. But others can be quite vivid, and they tend to stay with us when the regular dreams fade away. I'm not sure what those dreams mean, if anything. Perhaps it's simply your own doubts nagging at you. Maybe you know something about it that you don't know you know." She smiled. "If you know what I mean."

Leon nodded.

"Remember the day of your arrest?" she asked him.

Leon's mouth hardened for an instant, and a great sadness passed over his features.

"Yes."

Jean put a reassuring hand on his arm again.

"Remember what I told you about Penny?"

Leon sent her an enquiring look.

"About her premonitions?" Jean clarified.

"Oh, yes," Leon nodded. "Yes, I remember that now."

"They came true, didn't they?" Jean pointed out. "Not only in the way she hoped they would, but also her insistence that she and Jack had something important to do together, some quest, or mission. Well, obviously, that mission was saving you! Getting you out of that horrid place was always on her mind, always her motivation. She did a lot to support Jack throughout those years, encouraged him to keep going, even on those occasions when he felt like giving up on the legal system and simply coming to get you. She's still determined to stay after the Board of Directors, to bring about some reform. Perhaps she and that guard will end up combining forces."

"Warden," Leon corrected her.

Jean's eyebrows rose in question.

"Kenny is the warden out there now." Leon clarified.

"Oh, of course!" Jean laughed. "I had forgotten that. So many changes."

Leon hardly heard her; he was contemplating his teacup.

"I owe Penny a lot," he murmured. "She accomplished so much more than I ever would have thought possible."

"Yes, she did," Jean agreed, pride in her daughter shining through. "But the point I'm trying to make here is that there is so much more to who we are, and what we are capable of, than we understand. I can't explain Penny's premonitions, but there is certainly no denying them. It's the same thing with these dreams you're having. Just because you don't understand them doesn't mean there isn't something to them. Perhaps it is worth looking into. At the very least, you could talk to David about it; as a doctor, he might have a better understanding of these things. I don't know."

Leon sighed and took another drink from his cup, his expression thoughtful.

"David does seem to have certain insights into a lot of different things, but," he shrugged. "I don't know. I seem to be burdening him a lot these days."

Jean laughed. "He lives for things like this! I don't think I've ever met a young man with David's sense of compassion for people. It's as though he feels that he's not fulfilling his purpose in life if he isn't helping someone." She patted Leon's arm again. "I wouldn't worry about 'burdening' him, Napoleon. He just might be able to help you. If not with the dreams themselves, then at least, in letting you get a good night's sleep."

"I'll drink to that."

***

The following morning, Jean and Penny were up early, getting everything ready for the family visit the Marsham women had so eagerly anticipated.

Cameron was also looking forward to his eldest daughter visiting them. Not only to reassure himself of her continued well-being after the difficult birth, but also to meet his first grandchild. This was a special day for everyone.

The train from Denver had arrived late the previous evening, so the young Granger family, along with Josephine, had stayed at the hotel for what remained of the night. The next morning, Cameron hitched up Monty and drove into town to pick them up and bring them out to the ranch. David and Tricia Gibson would also be joining the gathering for the belated welcome-home party, so it would be a full house.

Everyone was excited. Like Christmas and the 4th of July, all rolled into one.

Leon had spent the morning brushing Karma and getting re-acquainted. He had forgotten how soothing it could be to stand quietly in a barnyard, on a warm spring day, and simply spend time with his horse. To add to this serene picture, the new barn dog, Cassie, was also in attendance and was stretched out in the sunshine, snoozing and daydreaming, with the occasional flicking of an ear at an early fly.

Leon was still occupied with this pleasurable pastime when he heard the jangle of harness and the clop, clop, of horses' hooves coming down the lane informing him that the beginnings of their company had arrived. He stepped away from his horse and glanced down the roadway, then smiled in anticipation.

Both buggies arrived together; the Marsham/Granger brood in one conveyance, and the Gibson party following in another.

Sam appeared to take hold of the second horse's bridle, while Leon closed in on Monty until Cameron stepped down from the driver's seat and took over.

"Napoleon!" came Caroline's high-pitched greeting. "How wonderful to see you." She was practically jumping for joy as she rushed over to him.

"Leon," Josey was a close second. "Haven't you gained any weight yet? You still look like a drowned scarecrow."

Leon grinned as both ladies were instantly upon him, and the hugs and kisses reigned supreme. He laughed with their contagious high spirits.

"Hello, Caroline. Hey, Josephine," he greeted them back. "Ohh—it's so good to see you."

It was then that Steven joined the group, and Leon looked up from the gaggle of female attention and noticed the small bundle that was being gently carried in the proud father's arms."

"Oh," Leon breathed a smile. "Is this Rosie?"

Both Caroline and Steven beamed.

"Yes," Caroline radiated love. "Come and meet her, Napoleon; she's so precious."

Leon stepped forward and, gingerly taking hold of a corner, peeled the swaddling blanket away from the infant.

Then, much to Leon's surprise, Steven settled the little creature into his arms. Before Leon had a chance to decline the honor, he found himself cradling the baby and looking down into a quiet, chubby little face, accentuated by tiny, clenched fists.

Large, blue eyes stared up at him as the newest member of the family took in every detail of his face.

Leon grinned, and with his free arm, he gave Caroline an embrace and kissed her on the forehead.

Caroline put her arms around her friend and hugged him close.

"We were thinking of calling her 'Napoleon' if she had been a boy, but then, for a girl we thought ... Napoleona . . .?"

"Ha!" Leon laughed, "Don't you dare." He smiled at Steven. "She's perfect just the way she is."

Then Leon glanced at the house and met his partner's eyes.

Jack stood on the front porch, watching this exchange and smiling with pleasure. It did his heart good to see Leon surrounded by friends and family, and so obviously enjoying himself and feeling like he belonged.

The two friends locked eyes for a moment, then Leon again gazed down at the infant in his arms.

He gently stroked her face and then, just as Eli had done to Jack five years before, little Rosie responded by emitting a huge yawn and clamped down on the finger with her tiny fist. She refused to let go.

Leon couldn't look at her long enough to take her all in. He seemed lost in a world all his own, remembering the last time he'd held an infant girl in his arms and thinking how beautiful she was.

Then Jean hurried down the front steps and, hoisting her skirts, ran towards the group.

"Oh, you're finally here! Where is she?"

Leon turned to show Jean that he held the infant.

Jean stopped when she got to them. Her hands came up to her mouth as a tear threatened to slide down her cheek.

"Oh, good Lord. She is beautiful. Let me hold her."

Leon grinned at Jean's excitement, then dutifully lowered the alert infant into her grandmother's arms.

Rosie's little fist let go of Leon's finger and attached itself to the new digit as her attention was diverted from Leon, and her wide, blue eyes stared up at her grandma.

"Oh, Caroline, she's beautiful," Jean gushed. "Hello, Rosie. Welcome to the family."

Rosie gurgled up at her and almost looked like she was going to laugh.

"Look, she has her grandpa's nose," Jean laughed. "Oh my, what a precious little girl. Come along, Caroline. She must be hungry after her long journey. Let's get you settled while Penny and I finish preparing lunch."

With that, Jean strode away with the baby, confident the new mother would follow.

Caroline sent a quick smile to her husband, then followed along behind her mother, while Steven hurried to catch up.

Leon watched them go with a knowing smile on his face, then looked up to find himself locking eyes with Miranda. She and the Gibsons had arrived right behind the Grangers and exited their buggy just in time to witness the exchange between Leon and the infant.

Tricia and David were busy talking with Cameron, since they had already been introduced to the new arrival. But Miranda had hesitated and found herself mesmerized by this 'con man' who seemed so entranced by the new little life form.

Realizing that she had been caught staring, Miranda smiled and then looked away. She felt confused. From the descriptions that others had given her of this man, she had no idea what to expect so she had created her own conception.

Despite Jean's affection and David's concern for the ex-outlaw, Miranda imagined him to be either a boisterous lout or a quiet, smooth-talking confidence man trying to weasel his way into her trust.

Or, perhaps those were just the images she had conjured up for herself to stay safe from him.

Whatever the reason for her preconceptions, this man was quite different from anything she had imagined. That first night, when they arrived from Laramie, she had been caught off guard by his genuine demeanor. She had been all prepared to dislike him. He was an outlaw, having done time in prison. He could not possibly be likable; he could not possibly be vulnerable.

She was not some flighty maiden who was easily impressed. She was a widowed woman who was well aware of men and their seductions; she had prepared herself not to be taken in by him. But then, he had looked so flustered over the mistaken identity in the Gibsons' kitchen that she felt her heart go out to him. But that wasn't 'love'—certainly not. She wasn't looking for that yet. It was simply compassion.

But when he had taken her hand and looked into her eyes, her heart had skipped a beat. The moment seemed an eternity, and she looked at him and didn't see a bald-headed, scrawny ex-convict or a slick, overbearing con man. What she saw was a gentle soul and warm heart, and though she wasn't quite ready to accept it, from that moment on, she was lost in him.

And now, again, she had been caught staring.

She quickly turned away and followed Josephine into the house to see if Jean needed any help preparing the meal. There was always plenty to do to keep the ladies busy while the men stood around chatting. Always plenty to do.

***

The midday meal was an unqualified success.

Penelope and Caroline sat down on either side of their friend and were very attentive to him with gentle touches on his arm and making sure he had enough on his plate. Occasionally, there was even an all-out hug from the side, filled with smiles and fondness.

Leon wasn't sure how to respond to so much physical affection, but eventually he simply accepted it. Occasionally, he sent a self-conscious smile to Steven or Jack, knowing that these were their ladies, who gave him so much attention. But neither of them seemed to mind. In fact, Jack himself was grinning and couldn't have been more pleased with the support that his partner received from the two young women.

Steven didn't seem to mind either, and though he sent the occasional glance to his wife, he spent much of the time talking with Cameron and David. These two gentlemen, along with Jean, were very patient and supportive of Steven as he struggled with his obsession over his new daughter. It was all the young man seemed capable of talking about.

Tricia, Josey, and Miranda floated through the conversations at the table and joined whichever caught their interest at any given moment.

Tricia and Jean enjoyed listening to Steven talk about his new family, but Josey and Miranda found it hard to relate and joined Penny and Caroline in talking about the horses, the ranch, and the upcoming dances. Josey was constantly cajoling Leon into eating more, since his appetite still seemed lacking despite the excellent meal, whereas Miranda enjoyed listening to the flow of the conversation.

After the meal was over, and the clearing up quickly dispensed with, everyone broke up into groups and carried on with conversation. Coffee had been put on, and things seemed to be settling down into a quiet afternoon.

But, of course, when children are present, pandemonium is bound to break out sooner or later, and sure enough, the three youngsters started expressing their negative views.

It began with Nathan and Eli quarreling over a favorite toy, then escalated when the baby cried in protest at the angry tones. She was also tired and more than ready for her nap.

Leon found this all a little too much, too soon, and with a freshly poured cup of coffee, he discreetly made his exit to the front porch and settled into one of the chairs. He appreciated the warm affection and loving support he was receiving here on this day, but it all felt overwhelming.

He sat back in the chair with a deep, contented sigh and took a sip of coffee. He smiled as he savored the strong flavor of it, secure in the knowledge that his taste buds were finally getting back to normal. Maybe he could enjoy a nice juicy beef steak right about now. Time to have a talk with the chef; this was a cattle ranch, after all.

The day was perfect. Not too hot, but just warm enough to be pleasant. Leon smiled to himself. He knew he still had a long way to go to recover from the ordeals of his incarceration, but, at least when he was awake, he knew that he was a relatively free man. There were conditions to his freedom, but he could live with those, for now, anyway. It was a whole lot better than the alternative.

One of the barn cats appeared out of nowhere and jumped up onto his lap.

This event startled Leon, but he quickly regained his composure as the feline began to purr and knead his leg. He smiled and scratched the cat behind the ears, and it leaned into his hand and assisted with the rubbing.

"Ouch! That hurts, you know," Leon commented as the kneading became more intense.

But the cat only purred louder and demanded more attention.

Funny thing, Leon mused, *cats never used to come up to me.*

His smile held a hint of sadness when thoughts of Mouse invaded this moment. He was surprised at how much he missed her.

Then he heard the screen door open and close, and the cat made an instant dash for cover. Leon glanced up to see who was joining him.

Miranda stopped short, almost spilling her own coffee in her consternation at intruding on another's privacy.

"Oh. Napoleon. I'm sorry. I didn't realize you were out here."

"That's quite all right." Leon smiled as he rose and offered her his seat. "Please, sit down."

"Oh, don't be silly," she said, waving him aside. "Sit back down. There are plenty of other chairs here."

And to prove the point, she grabbed another chair, pulled it over, and sat down beside a grinning Leon.

"I hope you don't mind," she continued. "I didn't mean to intrude on you, but I'm not used to all this noise. I never had children of my own, and I even find Nathan a bit tiring at times. So, to get all three of them going at once! It's beyond my bearing."

"No apologies necessary." Leon's smile conveyed his pleasure. "Why do you think I'm out here?"

Miranda settled back in her chair and, taking a sip from her coffee, she contemplated the man sitting next to her. She had no idea what to make of him. Even the descriptions from people who knew him well were full of contradictions and ambiguities, which had helped her form her earlier conclusions about who he was.

But now, once again, her fantasized impression of who he must be was being dashed. She found herself drawn to him. Her eyes always sought out his features whenever he was close by, and her heart quickened when he met that gaze.

But she was afraid of the attraction as well; she was still in mourning and didn't need any complications.

There was a strained silence for a moment, and both focused on their coffee.

Leon, normally confident around women, found himself unsure of the next move. He knew he was attracted to her, but he didn't know if he was ready to pursue it. His encounter with the upstairs gal in Laramie was too fresh in his mind, and he was scared to death of making a mockery of himself again.

Finally, he picked a topic he thought was safe.

"The Kid tells me that you're a widow," he stated, trying to be casual, then instantly regretted the remark as being far too personal. He didn't know Miranda very well and hadn't come to realize that to her, nothing was too personal.

She, however, had focused on something else.

"The Kid?" she asked, slightly confused. Then she made the connection. "Oh, you mean Jack."

Leon smiled; sometimes it was fun to put his nephew down a notch, even if Jack wasn't aware of it.

"Yes. I mean Jack."

"Nobody calls him 'Kid' here, well, except for your friend, Josephine. I've heard her call him that when she's frustrated with him," Miranda commented. "I've only just recently met him, but it sounds odd to me, calling a grown man 'Kid'. But if it's what you're used to."

"No," Leon assured her. "Like Josey, I only use it when I want to get a rise out of him. Most of our acquaintances from our previous profession still call him that, but he hates it for the most part. Which, of course, makes it all the more fun to throw at him once in a while."

"Well, both of you seem to have more names than royalty," Miranda observed. "It's just a matter of picking one you like and sticking with it. And to answer your question, yes, I am a widow."

"I'm sorry," Leon responded. "I didn't mean to pry."

"Oh, pry away," she told him. "Everybody here knows it, anyway. It's not like it's a secret."

Leon smiled again. Another sip of coffee.

"How do you like living here in Arvada?" he finally asked her, thinking this was probably a more suitable question to ask someone whom he hardly knew.

Miranda smiled at him and sat back with a sigh.

"I do like it here," she stated. "I wasn't sure at first; it's quite a bit smaller than what I'm used to. But the people are very nice." Her smile turned to what might have been called "shy", if Miranda could ever be considered shy. "And the more people I meet, the more I like the town." And she sent him a coyish look, her manner turning flirtatious even though she had insisted she wasn't interested.

"That's nice," Leon responded, the subtle hint going right over his head. He really wasn't in top form these days. "So, do you think you'll stay?"

"I think so, yes. I'm already looking around for a place to buy. I've been staying at Miss Hardcastle's boarding house, but I still seem to spend most of my time at Trisha and David's place. So, I think it's probably time I got my own residence. I suppose that means I'm staying."

"Good," Leon stated, his deep dimples accentuating his smile. "Give us a chance to get to know one another."

Miranda smiled in agreement.

Then the screen door opened again, and Cameron poked his head out.

"Here's where you two have gotten to," he observed. "C'mon back inside. Something important is about to happen!"

"Oh!"

Leon stood and offered his hand to the lady.

Miranda was pleased to accept it, and the two of them entered the house together.

CHAPTER TWO
THE ANNOUNCEMENT

The children had all settled down, either to play or sleep, and the adults of the gathering were standing around the table again. Cameron took down a bottle of "the good stuff", while Jean discreetly got glasses ready. Penelope and Jack stood at the head of the table, both looking nervous, but pleased.

As soon as Leon entered the room, Jack met his eye with an intent gaze.

Leon nodded back as the thought occurred to him, *Oh, I already know what this is about.*

Everyone was in an expectant silence. This had been a long time coming.

Jack nervously cleared his throat and took hold of Penny's hand.

"Well, now that you're all here," he began, "we have an announcement ta make. I know we've waited a long time for this, and some of ya," a glance to Leon, "didn't mind tellin' me that I was takin' too long. But certain things had ta happen first, and well, now they have. So, with Cameron's and Jean's permission, I have asked Penelope ta be my wife, and she has graciously accepted my offer."

A collective sigh of relief went around the table, and then everyone came forward to congratulate the couple with handshakes, back slaps, and kisses on the cheeks.

"Finally!"

"This is wonderful. When is the big day?"

"Oh dear," came Josey's voice from the crowd, "another wedding to plan; a best friend's job is never done."

"It's about time," David said. "I was beginning to think you were never going to get around to it."

"Well, come on, everyone," Cameron began pouring spirits into the glasses, "A toast to the happy news, and the happy couple."

"Here, here!"

Everyone gathered around and helped themselves to a glass. Leon procured two and handed one to Miranda, who smiled at him with sparkles in her eyes.

He then grinned at his partner; he was genuinely pleased for him, but a little anxious as well. Things were moving ahead quickly now. So many changes, so many new relationships, that the ex-convict felt his head spinning. This was going to change their lives, and though it was bound to happen, sooner or later, and Leon had pushed his nephew toward it, now that it was happening, he couldn't help feel a little scared about what this might mean for him. He was also a little jealous.

He felt a gentle hand on his arm, and he glanced down to find Miranda sending him a quizzical look.

"Are you all right?" she mouthed, quietly.

Leon nodded, not realizing he had been that easy to read. "Yes."

Then Cameron called the room to attention. "I'm sure everyone in this room is acquainted with the history of these two fine, young men we have living with us now." He sent smiles to both Leon and Jack. "Who would have thought that their unexpected visit on that cold Christmas, nearly ten years ago, would have brought us all here to this place, on this day. We knew, way back then, that you were family—both of you. And, like with all families, we've had our ups and downs." This was met with some chuckles and head nodding. "But now, we stand here at the announcement of Jack and Penny's betrothal, and I could not be happier. Indeed, both my daughters have chosen well. Penelope, I could not be prouder of you. You have grown into a beautiful young woman, and I still marvel at your tenacity and your wisdom."

Penny smiled at her father, fighting tears. "Thank you, Papa."

"And after you're a married woman, I still expect you to keep the books here," Cameron reminded her. "Goodness knows we would probably go under if it were left to me!"

This comment was met with more laughing and head nodding. Everyone knew that Penny was the one with a head for business.

"Jack, it was a little shaky at first, I have to admit," Cameron continued, "but you've stayed the ground, and you've proven yourself, over and over, to be worthy of my daughter. I won't say welcome to the family, since I just stated that you already are family, so, perhaps I should say that I'm pleased you decided to make it official." Cameron raised his glass. "To Jack and Penelope, on the occasion of their betrothal!"

Everyone raised their glasses and clinked as many as they could reach. Congratulations made the rounds again.

"Ahh, I'd like to say something, if I may," Leon requested.

Everyone quieted down, and all eyes turned to Leon.

He smiled nervously and could feel Miranda's hand gently squeeze his arm. He wondered, fleetingly, why that made him feel comforted.

"Well," he began, with a deep breath, "I'm happy for you, Jack. I know you both waited a long time for this, and I know why you waited. I kept on telling you not to, that you should get on with your lives, but deep inside, I suppose I'm glad you didn't listen to me. You were always there for me. Even when I pushed you away, you kept coming back, and I want to thank you for that. You're the best friend a man could have."

He turned to the young lady who held onto his nephew's arm, "Penny, you have a man there who can be just as stubborn as you are, just as tenacious, and just as loyal and true, and I want to thank you from the bottom of my heart. You have no idea how scared I was that he was going to wind up marrying one of the 'downtrodden' folk! Thank you for stepping in and preventing that disaster."

Everyone laughed.

Jack grinned at his uncle, shaking his head. Trust Leon to come up with that one.

Leon raised his glass. "To Jack and Penny, two of the best friends a man could ever have."

More clinking of glasses, along with congratulations and back-slapping, and then everyone started to mingle.

Penny came straight to Leon and hugged him.

"Thank you, Napoleon," she said. "I'm so pleased that you're here with us now, and that you'll be at our wedding."

"Thank you," Leon responded. "You had a lot to do with bringing all this about, and I'm never going to forget that."

She smiled and hugged him again.

Then her sister, Caroline, called her from the other side of the room.

"Penny! Come on. We want to see your ring."

"Oh yes, of course!"

With a quick kiss to Leon's cheek, and a squeeze to her betrothed's arm, she hurried over to the group of females, and the high-spirited admiration began.

Jack turned to his partner and shook his hand.

"Leon, thank you," he said. "Are you okay with this? I know it's a lot ta take in all at once."

Leon waved Jack's concerns away.

"No, I'm fine. I'm happy for you."

"Leon?"

"Hmm?

"The 'downtrodden' folk?"

"Well, you always were one to take the needy ones under your wing."

"Ha! Naw. I think I'm done with the needy folk for a while."

"Good."

"Ah, Napoleon," Miranda broke in on them, "I think I'd better do the supportive woman thing and go admire Penny's ring. I'll see you later."

"Oh yes," he smiled at her, "I'll look forward to it."

He glanced around again and found Jack grinning at him with a wicked sparkle in his eyes.

"What?" Leon asked him.

"What!" Jack laughed again. "Don't give me that; I'm seein' sparks."

"What?" Leon tried to sound innocent. "You mean, between Miranda and me?"

"Uh-huh."

"Oh no ... I mean ... no. That's nothing."

"Uh-huh."

David joined the partners and shook Jack's hand.

"Congratulations, Jack. Nice to see it all finally coming together."

"Yeah, David. Thanks."

"Any ideas on the date?"

"Ahh, can't say as we've really discussed that part yet," Jack admitted. "Probably later in the summer."

David nodded. "Summer weddings are always nice." He took a sip of brandy, then looked at Leon. "How are you holding up, Napoleon? Jean tells me you're still having those bad dreams."

Leon slumped. There was no keeping secrets within their tight circle of friends. Still, he had planned on talking to David about it anyway.

"Jean knows about your nightmares?" Jack asked.

"Well, yes," Leon admitted. "She walked in on one of them the other night."

"What?" Jack was instantly alarmed. "She didn't touch ya, did she?"

Leon frowned, wondering at the concern. "No. She woke me up with the light from the lamp."

"Oh, good." Jack was instantly relieved.

"Yes," David agreed. "It's not wise to touch someone who is having a nightmare. The person who's asleep could think that you're part of the dream and lash out at you."

"Yeah, no foolin'," was Jack's caustic remark. "I found that out the hard way."

Leon and David both sent Jack a questioning look.

"Did you wake Napoleon up from one of his nightmares?" David asked him. "By touching him, or shaking him?"

"I don't remember that," Leon commented.

"That's 'cause ya didn't wake up!" Jack informed him. "Ya damned near choked me ta death, and ya were asleep the whole dang time."

"Oh." Leon swallowed and paled slightly.

"Aw, jeez, Leon, I'm sorry. There I go mouthin' off again. I wasn't even gonna tell ya about it."

"I'm sorry," Leon said quietly. "I didn't mean—"

"I know ya didn't mean to." Jack put a hand on Leon's shoulder. "You were asleep. That's why I wasn't gonna say nothin'. And I shouldn'ta."

"No, actually, it's a good thing you did," David assured him. "It's important that you know how serious these nightmares are, Napoleon. It's not surprising you're suffering from them, but I think you still need to talk about them. Get it out in the open. I'll be finished with my rounds in the morning tomorrow. Why don't you come by after lunch, and we'll talk."

Leon looked reluctant but accepted the offer anyway. "Yeah, all right, David. I'll come by."

"Good! We can work on your shoulders then, too."

Leon groaned; he'd walked right into that one.

"Well, it's probably time we headed home," the doctor announced, then downed the rest of his drink in one go. "I need to collect the two ladies and track down the wayward son. Jack, again, congratulations. I won't say you'll make a fine couple, because you already are that. It's just nice to see it all coming together for you."

"Yeah, thanks, David."

The two men shook hands, and David went off in search of his wife.

Jack and Leon locked eyes.

"I'm sorry, Jack," Leon apologized again.

"Naw, Leon. C'mon," Jack assured him. "Everything's all right. And I learned a real valuable lesson." He wrapped his arm around his uncle's shoulder and steered him toward the table. "Have another drink, on me; we're celebratin'!"

"Yeah!"

***

Colorado
Summer 1889

As warmer days took over from chilly nights, Leon began to feel more like his old self again. His hair was growing back, even to the point where Jean had to cut it to keep it from taking over his head. He was slowly putting on weight, too slowly according to some, but still in accordance with who he was. And though he had not been able to finish his first piece of steak, he had enjoyed it immensely.

Cameron kept him on light duty only, with chores such as tending the barn and livestock. Much to Leon's surprise, he didn't mind the work. He wasn't getting tired as quickly as he had when he'd first started helping. The horse stalls that used to take him all morning to clean now took him only a couple of hours. He could feel himself getting back into condition, and the warm, summer days made working outside a pleasure, especially when he could take time out to spend with his mare.

The bond between them hadn't needed any time to re-establish itself; it'd been there right from that first day of his return. Even in the mornings, when Leon would enter the barn for the first feeding, Karma's nicker of greeting was just as much for his company as it was for the anticipated meal. She'd nod her head as he approached her stall and nibble on his buttons and breathe tickling whiskers into his neck. He'd laugh and stroke her head while whispering endearments to her.

She was in her glory, and with her, he was slowly beginning to heal.

***

"How are things goin' between you and Miranda?" Jack asked while they were out mending fences.

Leon shrugged. "I dunno." Then proceeded to bang a nail into the post, securing the wire in place.

The two men sat in the grass along the fence line, tackling a particularly nasty tangle of barbed wire and getting it all straightened out, so it could be reattached to the post.

Karma and Gov happily grazed close by, with no intention of going anywhere.

"What do ya mean, ya don't know?" Jack pushed. "You've been seein' her, haven't ya?"

Leon shrugged again. "Yes. Sort of. Casual like, you know."

Jack put down his hammer and sighed, feeling frustrated with his friend's ambiguity.

"Well, the Fourth of July dance is comin' up quick. Have ya asked her to go with ya?"

"No."

"Why the hell not?"

Leon cringed, then shrugged again. "I dunno. Do you think I should?"

Jack looked at him, dumbfounded. He still had a hard time dealing with this new 'Leon'. He wasn't used to his partner being so insecure and undecided about issues that the pre-prison Nash would have had no trouble handling.

"Yeah, I think ya should ask her," he finally stated, trying to keep his tone neutral and his frustration hidden. "You like her, don't ya?"

"I guess."

"She obviously likes you," Jack stated, "so, what's the problem?"

Leon busied himself with beating up a nail.

"Leon—what's the problem!"

"I dunno." Another shrug. "It's just ... I don't think I'm ready yet."

"What's there ta be ready for?" Jack asked him. "It ain't like you're gonna ... you know. Not on a first date. It'll just be fun. You'll see. We always have a good time at the Fourth of July dance. Everybody will be there. And believe me, if you don't ask Miranda to go with ya, there's a couple of other fellas who wouldn't mind, I can tell ya that."

"Really? Maybe she'd rather go with someone else."

"Leon! Just ask her, will ya?" Jack pushed him. "Let the lady decide for herself. Okay?"

"Yeah, okay."

"Good! Glad we got that settled." Jack went back to untangling the wire. "Maybe after that, we can go visit Kenny and his family. You wanna do that next month? You up ta that?"

"Yeah, I suppose." Leon sounded nervous about it. "I'm not looking forward to reporting in to that Sheriff, but if Kenny can let him know beforehand that we're coming, and why, maybe he'll be nice about it."

"Good. I'll send Kenny a telegram ta let 'im know, and we'll see 'im. We can meet up with Taggard too, if'n ya want. You can meet his wife."

"They'll be coming to your wedding, won't they?"

"Yeah, I expect so," Jack confirmed. "But that ain't until the end of August. Don't ya want ta meet Martha?"

"Yes, of course I do. Of course. It's just ... yeah, of course I do."

Jack frowned and sent Leon a look, but Leon ignored him and busied himself with the banging of nails.

***

Later that week, Leon was sitting in David's office with his shirt off, and his jaw clenched.

"Try to breathe, Napoleon," David advised, yet again.

"I know. I am trying. Is there ever going to be a time when this doesn't hurt?"

"We'll get there," David assured him. "It took a long time for Jack to heal up, but he's doing well now, isn't he?"

"Yes, he is."

"We'll get you there, too. It just takes time."

"Hmm."

"You're looking better," David noted. "You've put on a little weight and are getting some muscle back. How are you feeling? Have the nightmares eased off at all?"

Leon sighed as David rubbed salve into the now-sore muscles.

"Not really," he admitted. "The sleeping draft you gave me does help, and it seems to calm the worst of the nightmares down, but I'm still getting them."

"Dr. Palin still haunting you?"

Leon gave a sardonic laugh. "Yes! He's been getting downright insulting, too. I don't know what to do about it. My brain doesn't want to go there. Whenever I think back to that day in the infirmary, nothing makes sense. If it was Carson who killed Doc after we left, I don't know how to prove it. I have nothing to go on."

"Hmm." David thought about it. "Is there anybody else who was there who might know something more?"

"Yes," Leon told him. "Harris. He's the one inmate who actually escaped during that prison break, and nobody knows where he is. A couple of our friends are looking for him. Oh—well, Malachi. You remember him from the prison?"

"Oh yes," David nodded. "That odd little man, who always seemed so happy."

"Yes," Leon concurred. "Well, apparently, Jack and Steven Granger are paying him and, well, an associate of his, to track Harris down. But he's gone to ground, and he's not too likely to give himself up for this. Palin was nothing to him."

"Given the right incentive, he might be willing to talk," David pointed out. He noticed Leon's hesitation in giving away too many details, but decided to ignore it. Some things were best left alone. "If your friends do find him, perhaps some agreement can be reached in exchange for any information. You never know."

"I suppose," Leon mumbled, his natural pessimism coming through. "Well, we're going to visit Kenny next month. Maybe he'll have some ideas."

"Yes. He strikes me as a very resourceful individual," David observed. "I'm sure he'll be of help. In the meantime, though, you still need to take things easy. Don't push yourself too hard. You have a lot of things to adjust to here, and your dreams are letting you know that you're still trying to deal with it all. One step at a time. Okay?"

"Yes. All right."

They both heard the front door opening and women's voices coming down the hallway.

"Sounds like the ladies are back from shopping," David announced.

Then the sound of thump, thump, thumping of little boy feet, running toward the office, met their ears. This was instantly followed by the door banging open, and the little boy himself appeared.

"Papa! We're home!"

"Yes, I heard," David commented.

Nathan saw the visitor and brightened up even more.

"Uncle Nap'on! We're home."

Leon smiled at him. "So I see."

Nathan's childish brow furrowed, and he pursed his lips.

"Wha's those lines on you' back?"

"Nathan, what did I tell you about coming into my office?" his father interrupted. "What are you supposed to do?"

Nathan looked contrite, shuffling his feet. "I suppose ta knock first, and then wait 'till you say 'okay'."

"That's right," David told him. "I'm with a patient now. You go back to the kitchen and help your mother. Uncle Napoleon will come out and see you when we're done."

"Yes, Papa."

Looking at the two men from under his brows, Nathan reached up to grab the door handle, then closed the door as he backed out of the office. Instantly, the reprimand was forgotten, and the thumping of little boy feet could be heard heading back toward the kitchen again.

"Momma want help?" the distant query drifted back to them.

Leon chuckled.

"Sorry about that," said David. "Curiosity before manners, I'm afraid."

"He's a fine boy, David," Leon told him. "No need to apologize."

David grinned.

"Okay, I think we're done here for now. Put your shirt back on. We can go for a week now, before your next treatment."

"Oh!" Leon was pleased about this.

"Just remember to keep up with the stretching," the doctor

reminded him. "That's important."

"Yes, I know," Leon commented dryly. "Jack won't let me get away with forgetting about it."

"Good!"

***

Leon tucked in his shirt and followed David out to the kitchen. Then, he felt awkward when he found himself in Miranda's company again. He smiled at her and looked away, biting his lower lip.

"Find anything interesting?" David asked his wife.

"Maybe," Tricia answered him. "We went to look at that nice little cottage down on Creek Road. You know—the one the Mulroneys have for sale? I think Miranda likes it."

"Yes," Miranda agreed. "It's perfect. I think I'll go speak with the seller tomorrow and see what we can arrange."

"Well, good," said David. "That is a nice little place, and close enough to be handy. If you need me to sign the purchase papers, let me know. I'll be happy to do it."

Miranda smiled her thanks and nodded. A heavy silence followed this, and Tricia exchanged a quick look with her cousin.

"Ah, David," Tricia commented as she took Nathan's hand. "There's something we need to talk about—in your office."

"Now?" David asked with a creased brow. "Don't you think we should—?"

"Now, David," Tricia repeated.

David was confused until he glanced at their guests and noticed they were both giving him awkward looks, and he finally got the message.

"Oh! Yes, of course," he stammered. "Ah, we'll be right back. But not too soon—just…"

"David!"

"Yes—coming!"

Leon and Miranda were suddenly alone.

Leon frowned when he caught himself fingering the brim of the new hat he held in his hands. This was such a dead giveaway that he was nervous.

Miranda smiled at him.

Leon coughed, then cringed at the second dead giveaway.

"Well," he began, "it's nice to see you."

"Hmm." Miranda nodded politely.

"You're thinking of buying the Mulroney place?"

"Yes. I think it would suit."

"Hmm." Leon took a deep breath; this was ridiculous. "So… are you planning on going to the July 4th dance here in town?"

"I had hoped to," she answered, pointedly.

"Oh. So… you've been asked?"

"No. Though I sense the wolves circling."

"Ah," Leon nodded. "Would you like to go with me? To save you from the wolves, that is."

"Well, it's about time," she responded with a smile. "I was beginning to think I was going to have to go with Hershel Rowlens, just to be able to get there at all."

Leon snorted, then quickly put a hand to his mouth to cover it up.

"Well, Hershel's not a bad fellow…"

"Right!" Miranda countered. "He's five years younger than I am, has no front teeth, and smells like he only bathes for the holidays."

Leon chuckled again, then tried to put on a straight face without really succeeding.

"So, I take it, of the two of us, you'd prefer to go with me?"

"Of course!" she assured him. "I was wondering what was taking you so long."

"Oh, sorry," Leon grinned. "I wasn't sure if you'd want to."

"Well, that's why you need to ask, isn't it?" she pointed out with a twinkle in her eye. "It's the only way to find out. That's always been my motto; if you want to know something, just ask."

"Yes. You're quite right," Leon agreed with a relieved laugh. "Good."

Then he stopped smiling as he became trapped inside her dark blue eyes. He felt as though he couldn't breathe. It scared him; he wasn't sure if he was ready for this yet. But she was so pretty, and he knew that he found her—enticing.

He stepped toward her and slipped his hand around her waist, bringing her in close to him.

She didn't resist.

He could feel his heart pounding, and his fingers going numb. He didn't care; he'd come this far, and he was going to see it through. He felt her body press up against his chest, and he held her with his eyes.

He leaned in and kissed her on the lips. Full, soft, and moist—and gentle.

She kissed him back and held him in that embrace for what seemed a long, long time.

He hadn't realized that he had closed his eyes until he opened them again, and then he pulled away from her.

Her eyes opened, too, and she smiled. Sweet and gentle.

Leon felt his heart flutter, and he took in a deep, shuddering breath.

"Ahh… I'll see you on the Fourth, then," he said lamely.

"I look forward to it," she agreed. "Perhaps even sooner."

Leon swallowed, then regained some of his composure.

"Yes. Perhaps. Goodbye, for now."

Leon left the doctor's house, leaving Miranda standing alone in the kitchen. She put a hand on the back of one of the chairs to steady herself, and with her other hand up to her breast, she did the best she could to breathe again.

This was unexpected.

She had hoped that Napoleon would ask her, but she hadn't been prepared to feel such passion from just a simple kiss. This was frightening; this was happening too fast. Oh dear—this was happening way too fast. But wasn't it glorious?

***

That evening, after supper, Tricia and Randa were busy cleaning up the kitchen while David had retreated to his office to bring the daily paperwork up to date. Nathan sat at the table, coloring his pictures and paying little attention to anything else.

"So," Tricia nudged her cousin. "I've been nearly bursting all through supper. What happened?"

"When?" Miranda teased.

"You know when," Tricia laughed. "Did he finally get around to asking you?"

Miranda smiled. "Yes." Then she made a face, like; *Oh, oh—now what?*

"It's about time," Tricia commented. "It is what you wanted, isn't it?"

"Yes," Miranda agreed. "But now that he's asked, well, I have to admit, I'm rather nervous. Isn't that silly? It's not like I'm a maiden. It's just that—I never saw myself getting involved with a... a...scoundrel!"

Tricia smiled slyly.

"Scoundrels can be fun."

"Well, yes, that's true," Miranda agreed. "But he's such the opposite of William. William was an upstanding citizen—a solid businessman. He was respected. Oh, my goodness. He must be spinning in his grave right now. I've actually accepted an invitation to the dance with an ex-outlaw! A convict—a con man. Oh dear." Her thoughts then became reflective and a little worried. "How will I know if he's conning me? If he's putting on an act? I remember reading about his trial and how everyone said how good he was at manipulating people. Top of the game. How will I know if he's being honest with me?"

Tricia dropped her teasing and listened to her cousin's concerns, realizing this truly troubled her.

"I admit, I don't know Napoleon well," she said. "All I can go on is what others, who do know him, say about him. Cameron and Jean are not foolish people. They would not allow either of those men into their home unless they trusted them. They certainly wouldn't be allowing Jack to marry Penny if they had any doubts as to his character!

"And did you notice?" she continued, with a smile. "At the dinner last week, Jean was being so supportive of Napoleon. You can tell; she loves him very much. And even Cameron, who is no man's fool, treated him like a long-lost son.

"I don't think you need to worry about Napoleon deliberately trying to deceive you. And besides, it's just a dance! Go—have fun. There's no need for you to rush into anything. Then, if he does turn out to be a scoundrel, well, we'll just hook him up with Isabelle."

Miranda laughed at that.

"Yes, of course. You're right," she said. "I'm getting way ahead of myself and worrying over nothing. It's not like I'm in a hurry to get married again. I have a lot of time to pick and choose." She sighed and smiled, a little dreamily. "Still, he is very attractive, especially since he's put on some pounds. I can see a woman being drawn into those warm, chocolate eyes of his, and never wanting to come back out."

Tricia smiled at her cousin. It sounded to her like Miranda had already gone past the point of no return.

CHAPTER THREE
FOURTH OF JULY

Arvada, Colorado
July 4th, 1889

The big holiday came upon the small community quickly. Everyone hurried through their morning chores so they could be in town for the afternoon festivities.

Cameron and Jean had no intention of staying for the evening's dancing, but they agreed to do their fair share of babysitting. Sam's mother and Tricia's folks also took on that role, so the younger adults could have a fun night out on the town.

Sam hitched Monty between the traces of the four-seater buggy while Jack and Leon got their own horses geared up and ready to go. After a quick cleanup from chores, Jean and Penny slipped into their colorful summer frocks and chose a bonnet to match.

The four men also changed into lighter, summer-weight trousers and shirts, and tried to slap the dust out of their everyday hats.

"Thank goodness, it's not windy today," Jean commented over her shoulder, as she tied her summer bonnet. "Last year was a bit trying."

Penny chuckled. "It was entertaining, though. I lost count of how many bonnets and hats went flying across the town square."

Jean laughed. "It was a sight. Just make sure your bonnet is tied securely. You don't want to lose this one, it looks so pretty on you."

"Yes, Momma."

And off they went. They made a stop along the way, so Sam could pick up his own family. When they pulled into the yard, Maribelle already had Sam's mare, Ginger, hitched to their buggy and ready to go.

Sam jumped down and took control of his mare's head while Maribelle, Merle, and the two children, Beth and Todd, climbed on board.

Jack and Leon could have picked up their own pace and arrived in town before the buggies, but it was too much fun staying with the group. The laughter and banter between the two families were enough to keep them all together and entertained.

Besides, Jack liked to keep Penny in his sight. After their forced separation, he couldn't get enough of watching her and her antics. She got more beautiful every day, and he still couldn't believe his good fortune.

Once they arrived in town, even the horses picked up their feet and held their heads high. Flags flapped, and banners stretched across the main street, while groups of people crowded the boardwalk, window shopping or waving and calling out greetings to everyone they knew, which was just about everyone.

Leon was thrilled. He'd been concerned that the crowds and noise would bother him, but he experienced the opposite. His face split into a grin as people he barely knew called out his name and waved a greeting. He had family around him, and he was beginning to feel part of this town now. He was in his glory.

Both buggies stopped by the town square to let passengers off so they could find a picnic table big enough for their expected group.

Eli and Todd joined up and instantly ran off to play with a group of boys already engaged in a game of tag.

Beth felt the tug to join them, but since she decided she wanted to be a lady, she opted to stay with the group to find a table. She and Penny, though they differed in age, shared many interests and hobbies and had become friends.

The men moved off towards the livery stable and hoped there would still be room for their horses. Eric always did good business on these holidays, so he made sure all his stalls and paddocks were in good repair and available.

The establishment got a bit crowded, but with lots of hay available, all the horses got along fine. There was always a minor upheaval as new horses were added to the group, but a squeal and a fake strike usually established the order, and they all settled in to eat.

Back at the town square, a high-pitched shout from the center of the park caught the ladies' attention. They spotted Josephine jumping up and down by a large table and waving at them.

Jean and Merle laughed.

"She certainly stands out in a crowd," Jean said, waving back.

"Indeed." Merle rolled her eyes. "She is a force, all right. I swear, I never thought I could enjoy the company of a woman in her profession, but it is hard not to like her."

"What profession is that?" Beth asked.

Jean and Merle exchanged smiles.

"Let's just say she likes to entertain," Jean told her.

"Oh." Beth shrugged. "There's nothing wrong with that."

"Josephine!" Penny greeted her friend as the group approached. "Thank goodness you got here early. I don't think we would have found a table for all of us if you hadn't."

"Oh, phaw," Josie waved it off. "All we had to do was put two tables together."

"You couldn't have done that all by yourself," Merle said with just a hint of a smile.

"Of course not. I had plenty of young men swoop in to help all for the promise of a dance later."

"Yes, I'm sure," Penny teased. "You're going to be busy tonight."

"No busier than I want to be."

"Have you seen Caroline yet?" Jean asked as she scanned the park. "She and Steven should be here by now."

"I hope they're going to make it," Penny said with a touch of anxiety. "I haven't seen Caroline in ages, and that train from Denver can get crowded today."

"They'll be here," Jean assured her youngest daughter. "Stop fretting."

Then, right on cue, they heard the familiar "Hello!" as the young family came into sight.

Penny lit up with pleasure and ran to her sister to hug her.

Caroline quickly handed Rosie over to Steven just in time to embrace her sibling. Laughing in delight, they draped an arm around each other's waists as they walked toward the group.

"Where is everyone else?" Steven asked as he cuddled his baby daughter. "Still putting the horses up?"

"Yes," Jean said. "We only just got here ourselves."

"We might as well get settled while we wait for them," Josie suggested. "Oh, look! It must be getting close to lunchtime. The music has stopped."

As is often the case, the background music had become so much a part of the festivities that no one paid it any attention until it fell quiet.

The three fiddle players had set their instruments down and were walking away from their covered stage area in search of refreshment. It was going to be a long day and a busy evening for them.

***

As Cameron, Jack, Leon, and Sam walked across the grass towards their party, they nodded greetings to the fiddle players while they passed by.

"Good to see you out from behind the teller window, Tom," Cameron said. "We expect some fine music from you fellas today."

"Don't worry about that, Mr. Marsham," Tom assured him. "It took some doin', but I managed ta drag John and Ansley here away from the merc to help out."

"It didn't take much draggin', as I recall," Ansley stated. "Playin' fiddle on the Fourth offers us a good time. I think we have just as much fun as the rest of you folks."

"We even got Charlie coming later with his horn," John said with a grin. "And Mike with his banjo. They'll get things hoppin' come tonight."

Jack nodded. "I do recall Mike can get quite a tune goin' with that thing. Lookin' forward to it."

***

"There they are!" Penny waved to get the men's attention. "Jack! Papa!"

The men smiled and waved back.

"Any trouble at the livery?" Jean asked as she slipped an arm around her husband's waist.

"No more than expected," Cameron said. "Eric sure knows when he has the upper hand. He's charging double what he normally does, and he's getting it."

Jean laughed. "It wouldn't be Eric if he didn't do that."

"Good point."

Jack sniffed the air, and his attention was drawn to the far corner of the park. A large grilling pit had been installed a few years ago so that outdoor gatherings like this could bring in some commerce to the local meat and produce markets.

"Hey!" Penny pulled Jack's attention back to her. "Is food always going to be your first love?"

Leon walked by and smirked. "Get used to it, Darlin'. Jack would rather eat than do anything else."

Jack grinned but pulled Penny into an embrace.

"Almost anything else," he assured her.

"Oh, you!" Penny gave him a mock slap on the cheek. "Always teasing."

A snort came from Leon, but then he straightened up as he noticed the next addition to their party approach the group.

"Hello, Miranda. You look lovely today."

Miranda smiled and acknowledged the compliment. A teasing remark of, *You mean I don't look lovely every day?* played upon her tongue, but she held it back. Though meant in jest, she knew that Leon's battered confidence might not handle it well. He was still taking baby steps, and she didn't wish to discourage him.

She fell back on the proper but mundane response. "You're looking very handsome as well."

Leon offered his arm, and she accepted it as they joined the main group.

Meanwhile, Nathan had spotted his friend Eli playing with the other group of boys.

He tugged on his mother's hand. "I wanna go play!"

Tricia looked at the other boys and noted that they were all bigger than her son. "The game they are playing looks awfully rough. Why don't you wait until Eli tires of it and comes over to play with you?"

"No!" Nathan tugged harder. "I wanna go play."

"But you always wanted to stay with me at these gatherings," Tricia reminded him. "Don't you want to sit with us?"

Nathan stopped struggling and stood there pouting.

"He'll be fine," Jean assured the first-time mother. "He's at an age now where he wants some independence. Better get used to it. Eli will watch out for him."

"Do you think so?"

Then Eli caught sight of his friend. "Hey, Nathan! Come on."

Nathan brightened, excitement widening his eyes. "Can I, Momma?"

Eli came running over, all flushed and excited with their game.

"It's okay, Mrs. Gibson, I'll watch out for him. Come on, Nathan."

Nathan grabbed hold of Eli's hand, and the two boys ran back to their playmates.

Tricia watched them with concern.

"This is silly," she said, as she tucked a strand of dark hair back under her summer bonnet. "Usually, I can't wait to get him out from underfoot."

"But that's when you're at home," Jean told her as she took Tricia's arm and directed her to the table. "Let him play."

Tricia laughed. "Of course, you're right. You don't seem to have a concern in the world when it comes to Eli."

"It's not that I'm not concerned," Jean told her. "You simply learn how to hide it. The girls used to run me into the ground with worry when they were young. Then I realized I wasn't doing any of us any good by trying to protect them all the time. And the children are safe here. Nobody in this town would dare to bother them."

Tricia sighed as she willed the stress to leave her body. "As long as I can see him, I'll be fine."

"Good."

"Are there any refreshments ready yet?"

"I believe Cameron, David, and Jack are on their way over to the stands now to get some drinks for us all. And to check out which steak they're going to snatch as soon as they're done."

***

Beth approached Leon and took hold of the hand that Miranda did not occupy.

"Will you sit beside me, Mr. Nash?"

Leon smiled down at her. "Of course I will, Beth. How could I turn down having the two loveliest ladies in town sitting on either side of me?"

Beth's face lit up with a smile.

"I think lunch will be ready soon," she stated as she pulled Leon and Miranda in the direction of the picnic table.

***

Half an hour later, the group was seated at the picnic tables, enjoying many of the culinary delights, and the music coming to them from the fiddle players who had returned from their own respite.

Jack sat and marveled at how this extended family unit had grown over the years, with both adults and young 'uns being added as time went by.

The three boys, Todd, Nathan, and Eli, were doing their best to settle, but they were too full of high spirits. Once each had gobbled down a small plate of chicken and potato salad, they asked to be excused and were gone almost before permission had been granted.

"They grow up so fast," Caroline said as she fed her baby from a bottle with a rubber nipple at the end of it. "I remember when Eli was no bigger than Rosie, and now he's there looking out for Nathan. Aren't they cute?"

Jean laughed. "Just wait until Rosie starts crawling. You'll have your hands full then."

"I'm looking forward to it," Caroline insisted.

"I've missed out on that," Maribelle commented in a whimsical tone as she gazed upon Caroline's infant.

"You didn't miss out on too much," Merle assured her. "Fortunately, Rosie appears to be a good baby, but Sam! Oh my goodness."

"Oh, Mother, must we?" Sam groaned.

"You were a little monster!" Merle continued, ignoring her son's protests. "I can't recall how many nights' sleep I missed because you refused to settle. And there was nothing wrong with you. You wanted to be awake, and you insisted that I stay awake with you."

"Yes, Mother."

"So, you see?" Merle patted her daughter-in-law's arm. "Adopting two older children may very well have been a blessing."

Maribelle smiled at Beth, who was busy conversing with Penny. "And we do love them so much. Just as much as if they had been born to us. Don't we, Sam?"

Sam nodded and smiled as he watched Todd play with the other boys. "We sure do. You really helped us out there, Jack. We can never thank you enough."

"Ahhh," Jack waved it away. "Seein' them two young'uns happy and in a good family is thanks enough. Ain't that right, Leon?"

"Hmm?" Leon broke away from talking to Miranda. "What?"

"Seein' Todd and Beth so happy is worth the thanks for me suggestin' adoptin' 'em in the first place."

"Oh." Leon looked at Sam, his earlier animosity toward the younger man no longer getting in the way. "Yeah, it is. Those two youngsters landed in a good place."

Jack grinned, his blue eyes sparkling with delight. He couldn't have been happier. Leon had finally come home, and they were with family—an ever-extending family, and life was good. He could tell Leon was still struggling to adjust to the crowd and to the children running and laughing in their play, but he was trying.

Josephine sat quietly, watching the family circus carry on around her. She was usually the life of any gathering, but not right now. Like Jack, she had been discreetly watching Leon, and it pleased her heart to see him so happy and comfortable with the people surrounding him.

Josie hadn't come to all the holiday outings, often preferring to stay home and entertain her own guests, but this was the first major event since Leon had been released, and she was determined to be a part of it. Indeed, Josey had spent so much time with the Marshams over the years and had become such good friends with Caroline and Penelope that she always felt welcome in their home and in their company.

Then, sure enough, Frans Sorenson, who ran the general store, was taking advantage of the festive spirit by making the rounds, selling popcorn and balloons.

Every child's head in the vicinity jerked up and took note, and all of a sudden, the boys, who had been so busy playing, now parted company and clustered around their own picnic tables.

Todd, Nathan, and Eli were no exceptions.

"Papa!" Nathan tugged at David's shirt sleeve. "Balloons!"

"Can we have some popcorn, Papa?" Beth asked with hope shining in her eyes.

"I have allowance coming, don't I?" Eli insisted. "I'm sure I do."

All the fathers in attendance began digging into their pockets, looking for loose change.

Then the dealing began, with numerous sets of young, eager eyes waiting impatiently for the bartering to conclude. Soon, all the youngsters had brightly colored balloons tied around their wrists, and popcorn was being given undivided attention.

Frans moved on to his next victims.

Things settled down at the Marsham table, and conversation started up again.

"Does anyone have any plans for this afternoon?" Cameron asked the group.

They all looked around, shrugging their shoulders.

"Not really," David said. "Just walk around town and see the sights until the dance starts."

"They have a shooting contest going on," Cameron pointed out. "You interested this year, Jack?"

"No!" was Jack's adamant reply. "I'm gonna stay as far away from any shootin' contests as I possibly can. Goddamn amateurs; they figure just 'cause they shoot a bunch of plates outta the air, suddenly they can take on a professional. I'm stayin' away from those yahoos."

Most people smiled, remembered Jack's first 4th of July encounter, and could appreciate that he didn't want to repeat it. The others, who had not been present, simply accepted his comments as common sense.

Then Leon noticed that the people at their table, facing him, suddenly focused on something behind him. He frowned, then saw Cameron smile and let himself relax. But only until Cameron spoke.

"Good afternoon, Carl. Quiet day, so far?"

"Pretty quiet, yes," Sheriff Jacobs answered, and Leon instantly tensed, realizing from the sheriff's voice that the man was standing directly behind him. "It might get a little crazy tonight, but most of the folks in this town are decent and will behave themselves."

Then Leon jumped and tensed even more when he felt the sheriff place both hands on his shoulders and give them a little squeeze. Leon couldn't help it; the fear welled up in him, and every fiber in his being anticipated a blow. After all, that was always how it came about in the prison; Carson would lay a casual hand on him, and next thing he knew—POW. Life became a nightmare, and pain always followed.

Everyone at the table, even the children, stopped what they were doing and watched the lawman and the ex-convict. It wasn't that anyone present thought that Sheriff Jacobs was going to do anything unsavory; he wasn't that kind of man. But Leon's fear was so palpable that everyone felt it and held their breath.

Jacobs smiled, feeling the tension in Leon's shoulders. "Relax, Mr. Nash. You're acting like you're guilty of something, and all I've done is come over to speak with you."

"Oh yes, Sheriff?"

"Uh huh." Jacobs patted one of Leon's shoulders. "It seems that some of our local patrons at the saloon have been hoping that you would see fit to join in on their weekly poker games," Jacobs explained. "They understand that you probably needed some time to settle in, so they weren't expecting you to come by right away. But seeing as how you have a reputation for enjoying the game, well, they've been feeling kinda insulted that you haven't bothered to drop by and participate."

"Oh," was Leon's only comment. He was both relieved and concerned at this bit of news.

"Now normally, I wouldn't encourage a cardsharp to patronize our local saloon," Jacobs continued," but, apparently, you played a few games here before you were arrested. The fellas have assured me that you were, in fact, an honest and considerate player. They have extended an open invitation for you to come and join them."

"Oh."

Jacobs gave his shoulder another quick pat.

"Just thought I would let ya know. Good afternoon, folks. Enjoy the day."

"Same to you, Carl." Cameron tried hard to stifle a laugh. "Thanks for dropping by."

Leon's knees turned to butter, and he was sure that if he hadn't already been sitting down, he would be on his butt on the ground.

"Phew," he sighed with relief as Miranda stroked his back. "He really had me worried."

He could hear Jack haw-hawing down at his end of the table, while everyone laughed. Those who could reach Leon gave him a reassuring pat on the arm or a slap on the back.

"You don't need to worry about Carl," Cameron assured him. "He's a good man, Carl Jacobs. That's why he keeps getting re-elected as sheriff. You treat him fair, and he'll give the same back."

"Oh brother," Leon mumbled, not feeling too sure about Cameron's assurance just yet. Five years of conditioning was going to take a lot of undoing.

Down at the other end of the table, Sam listened to this

conversation with a guilty knot in his gut. He remembered back to that evening, five years ago, when he had ridden out to the Rocking M with Nash as his companion. Sam had been so disgusted with the ease in which this highwayman had 'tricked' the locals out of their wages, that he had wanted to arrest the outlaw right then and there.

Oh, he had been so naïve. Not only by thinking that he could have taken on Napoleon Nash all by himself, but that he thought he had known who and what the man was, simply by the fact of his profession.

Nash was an outlaw and, therefore, there could be nothing honorable about him, and he deserved whatever justice was handed to him.

Since that time, Sam had occasion to speak with some of those fellas in that poker game, and every one of them, to a man, had felt privileged to have not only that caliber of player join them, but one who obviously had a strong sense of fair play. The game had been for small stakes and was meant just for fun, and though the stranger had ended the evening as the undisputed winner, he had not wiped them all out.

The next day, when they had discovered his identity, the honor they felt had no bounds. They had actually sat down and played poker with Napoleon Nash. This was an experience money couldn't buy, and it was certainly worth what each man had contributed to the pot. There had been no hard feelings, and Sam had imagined an insult where none occurred.

Sam had grown up since then. He sat at this table with his wife and children, enjoying the picnic on this 4th of July, and realized how fortunate he was. He looked down the table at the ex-convict, watching him trying to relax, trying to fit in, but still not sure of his footing.

Sam no longer felt intimidated by him, at least, not in a bad way. He still felt that draw that most people, men and women alike, felt when in his company. The ex-outlaw had that "something" that was indefinable, but was there, nonetheless. Love him or hate him, Napoleon Nash was a man you could not ignore.

Sam smiled as he watched his daughter hug Leon's arm and speak quiet words to him, obviously trying to reassure him after his harrowing encounter with the sheriff.

Leon smiled down at her as she carried on her conversation. He lifted his hand and gently stroked Beth's hair, and then, as though he knew he was being scrutinized, he looked up and met Sam's gaze.

The two men exchanged quick smiles of understanding, and Leon turned and went back to his discussion with Miranda.

Beth went back to eating her popcorn.

***

As lunch wound down, everyone prepared to split up and go their separate ways until the evening meal would bring them all together again.

Jean and Sam's mother, Merle, offered to take care of the youngsters so the young ladies could go and enjoy the festivities.

Caroline was reluctant at first. Not that she didn't trust her mother, but being a new parent, the instinct to protect her baby was still running strong.

Jean smiled and put her at ease, while her sister and Josephine wouldn't take "no" for an answer and pulled her along with the gaggle of females.

The men headed for the saloon.

As usual, there was an opportunity to sample the new homebrews. The locals who participated in the competition all sourced their hops from the same supplier, yet the beers made with those hops were often surprising. The brews at the top of the favorable list were brought in as regular fare for patrons, so everyone felt it was their civic duty to vote on which few would make the list.

Leon was nervous. He always seemed to be nervous these days, and it irritated him, but there wasn't anything he could do about it. He pushed himself to join these social outings, knowing it was expected, and that the more he did, the more comfortable he would feel about them. But it was still a strain, and now he had the added stress of feeling obligated to join the poker game if one was on the go.

He didn't want to; the palms of his hands began to sweat just thinking about it.

It was with a sigh of relief that a glance around the saloon assured him that no games were on the go at that moment. It was noisy and crowded, but everyone was in the festive spirit, enjoying the new brews and the company of good friends. Nobody was in the mood for poker.

As luck would have it, David spotted a vacant table in the corner, and he darted in to lay claim to it. Being tall and slender, he could move quickly through the crowd and pull off the takeover, while the rest of his group took a more cumbersome approach.

Within moments, one of the gals came by to ask what they would like.

"Afternoon fellas," she smiled at the table. "We got six new brews here today for the sampling. Any preferences?"

Cameron looked around the table, but nobody spoke up.

"Doesn't look like it," he observed. "How about we start at the top of the list and work our way down?"

"Fine," she smiled and did a quick head count. "So, six glasses of Harvie's 'Hollow Tree' ale comin' up!"

Leon grinned as she disappeared back into the crowd.

"Is this what usually goes on during the 4th of July festivities?"

"Oh yeah," Jack told him. "This is the best part of the day. Although the dancin' is kinda fun too." His blue eyes sparkled with anticipation of the events still to come. "But this is nice. Make sure ya choose wisely though, cause whatever brew wins, we could be drinkin' a lot of it."

"I don't know if I should vote," Leon admitted. "My taste in beer has been somewhat compromised of late."

"Don't worry about that, Napoleon," Cameron assured him. "You just might discover one here that you really like. There have been some interesting concoctions that have found their way into this contest over the years."

"That's for sure," David rolled his eyes. "Some of it's quite good, but there have been others… I expect to be handing out a fair amount of hangover tonics tomorrow, for those who push it too far today."

"Sometimes I think they judge the winner by the amount that gets thrown away," Sam stated. "The one that gets dumped the least gets the blue ribbon.'

"And on that note," David cautioned the newcomer, "if you don't like the one you're given, Napoleon, by all means, don't feel you have to finish it. You don't want to ruin your palate for one you do like by drinking the ones you don't. A lot of beer gets thrown away at these little contests. It's expected."

"Oh, okay." Leon was grateful for the advice, as he had been worried that he might not keep up with everyone else at the table.

The first round arrived, and they each received a shot glass of the home-made brew. They all raised their glasses in a unanimous toast and took testing sips.

Reviews were mixed.

"Hmm, not bad."

"Not much body to it."

"Nice and refreshing for a hot summer day."

"Would be good for cuttin' through trail dust."

"A nice all-around light beer for a picnic."

"Well, it's wet, anyway."

Pro or con, nobody had trouble finishing their portion, and Leon decided that he might enjoy this after all.

Everyone settled in for the long haul, awaiting the next round.

***

Further along the street, the young ladies of the clan, now unburdened of offspring, made their way to the soda shop and settled in at a lovely, outside table to enjoy some flavored ices. They continued to admire Penny's ring, making her feel special all over again. She beamed with pleasure and excitement and didn't mind at all talking about her favorite subject.

"It is lovely, isn't it?" she reiterated, admiring the ring on her finger. "It truly is an embarrassment of riches."

"Why would you think that?" asked Josey. "Most ladies I know want the biggest ring they can possibly get. Yours is quite dainty."

"Oh, I know," Penny agreed, "but it's so elegant. I can't believe Jack picked this out all on his own, and he must have been saving his money for ages to be able to buy it. It's so lovely!"

The other ladies at the table shared quiet smiles.

Truth be known, Jack had asked Caroline's opinion on the matter, knowing that she would have a better idea of what her sister would like when it came to choosing the ring. Caroline, however, had no intention of bursting the bubble that Penny was floating in and let the matter lie.

She was pleased that her sister was pleased.

"And what about you, Randa?" Tricia asked once the topic of Penny's upcoming nuptials had wound down. "There was more than one lady in town who hoped Napoleon would ask her to the dance. I expect you appreciate the honor."

Miranda sent her cousin a scathing look for putting her on the spot, but smiled with pleasure anyway.

"I still have butterflies," she confessed. "I must admit, I'm a little afraid of him."

"Afraid of him?"

"What?"

"Of Napoleon?"

"You ladies must understand," Miranda explained, "you all know him. But I'm still relatively new here. All I can really go on is his reputation and what I hear from others."

"Isn't that what courting is all about?" asked Penny. "To get to know each other?"

"Well, yes, I suppose it is," Miranda agreed. "But I hardly call one date to a dance, 'courting'."

"It's a start!" Josey laughed. "Besides, Leon wouldn't have asked you if he wasn't interested."

"You've known him longer than anyone here, Josephine," Miranda stated. "Is he an honorable man?"

Josey snorted into her ice.

"Honorable? The man is so honorable, I could wring his neck. I'm not sure I'll ever forgive him for going to prison to protect me. I'm quite capable of taking care of myself, thank you."

"We all know there was more to it than that, Josephine," Caroline reminded her. "Even Steven stated that Napoleon was going to prison anyway, simply for having been involved in that confidence game. The reasons didn't matter. His own attitude, more than anything else, got him on the wrong side of that judge, who then was looking for an excuse to find Napoleon guilty of something."

"Yes," Miranda piped in. "I do recall the articles in the paper commenting on his arrogance and lack of respect for the court. I suppose this is what's worrying me."

"He's changed," Josey commented, and the other ladies who knew him well nodded in agreement. "Some of the changes are for the better, some of them not."

"How do you mean?" Miranda asked.

"He's certainly not as arrogant anymore," Caroline put in. "He was always sweet and kind to us, but there was that other side to him, we never saw until his trial." She smiled reassuringly at Miranda. "I can understand you feeling unsure of him. As Momma says, he can be very masterful at times. But you can tell that it's not there so much anymore. Prison certainly knocked that arrogance out of him."

"Yes. But with it went his self-confidence," Josey added. "You notice how he doesn't offer his opinions now? He also struggles to make decisions. Just what happened here today when Sheriff Jacobs came to our table. I don't think I've ever seen Leon that scared."

Silence settled over the group as the ladies contemplated the truth of that observation.

"Poor Napoleon," Caroline finally commented. "I don't think we can even imagine what it was like for him in there. Even though we've all heard the reports, and Penny witnessed one of the assaults, it's nothing compared to him having to live through it. No wonder he thought about killing himself."

"Oh dear," Miranda commented, suddenly thinking that maybe she was in over her head.

Josey patted her hand, giving reassurance.

"No, no. Leon is nothing if not resilient. I have no doubt that he will pull himself out of this, and he'll be a better man for it. It's just going to take some time. And help from his friends, of course!"

"Oh, of course!" Caroline agreed.

"We'll all help him!" Penny seconded.

"That's what friends are for!" Caroline added. "He's going to be fine."

"Just be his friend, Miranda," Josey advised her. "I think you'll find him to be worth the effort. But don't ask me to describe him to you. This afternoon isn't long enough—that well runs too deep!"

"That's for sure."

"But what an interesting well it is."

"Just relax and enjoy the ride."

"He's going to be fine."

***

The dancing got started right on time that evening, and everybody, save one, was eager to get out onto the cleared town square for some music and fun.

Leon felt trepidation at the prospect and began to regret his impetuousness in inviting Miranda to be his date. This was all Jack's fault. If he hadn't pushed...

There was nothing for it now, so Leon went along with the group and tried to relax and have a good time. They were fortunate again to find a table that would accommodate their party, and the ladies settled in, while the men trotted off to get punch for them all.

Josephine began scanning the floor—or, more precisely, the field, knowing that she would have no trouble finding partners to dance with. All the locals knew her, and many of the young men in attendance hoped to be added to her dance card.

Leon offered to get Josey her punch, along with his and Miranda's, so he was taking a bit more time to return to their table, trying to keep from spilling three glasses, and to keep out of the way of the other partygoers. Then, much to his chagrin, it all became a moot point when he was bumped from behind, and all three glasses ejected half their contents.

Leon pushed down his irritation as he turned to confront the clumsy person, when he found himself staring at a handsome young woman.

She smiled up at him.

"I'm so sorry," she purred. "Shall I help you replenish them?"

"Oh. No, ma'am, that's quite all right." Leon decided to be polite. "It was my fault, and no harm done."

"Oh, please, call me Isabelle," she informed him, and held up a delicate hand for his consideration.

"Oh, ahh..." Leon felt awkward, with both hands occupied.

"Oh. Yes, of course," she smiled and batted her lashes. "Consider our hands shaken."

"Yes, ma'am," Leon smiled. "My name's Leon."

"Yes, I know. I think everyone in town knows who you are."

"Oh." Leon smiled, embarrassed at this attention.

"And I dare say," she continued, "that we are all so pleased to have you returned to us, safe and sound. Many of us stood behind Jack and the Marshams in their efforts to secure your release. I know, for myself personally, I had many a talk with Jack when he was feeling like giving it up, and I'm sure that what I had to say was often all that kept him going. So, in that way, I like to think that I was able to contribute at least that little bit to the effort of securing your release."

"Oh yes," Leon nodded at her. "Well, thank you ... Isabelle. I know I am beholden to many people who are here tonight."

“Well, if you wish to thank me properly, perhaps you can offer me a dance later on.”

“Oh,” Leon felt cornered. “Well… it does seem that my dances are all spoken for at the moment. But if one becomes available, I will certainly keep you in mind.”

Disappointment flashed across Isabelle’s eyes, but she quickly recovered.

“Of course,” she said. “I’ll look forward to it.”

“Evenin’, Isabelle,” came Jack’s voice from behind Leon. “On the prowl early, I see.”

“Oh, Jack,” she patted his arm. “Don’t be such a tease.”

“Uh-huh. C’mon, Leon,” he said, taking a couple of the glasses out of his uncle’s grip. “Let’s get these refilled. Miranda was wonderin’ what was keepin’ ya.”

“Oh, yeah. Thanks.” Leon sent a quick nod to the lady. “Good evening, Isabelle. Nice to meet you.”

“And you.”

Isabelle smiled sweetly and turned to head back to her own table. As soon as her back was to them, she sniffed and then cursed Jack for ruining her fun. She would have to plan a whole new strategy now.

The two gentlemen returned to the refreshment table to refill their glasses.

“That was close,” Jack commented.

“Oh, she was just saying ‘hello’,” Leon assured him.

“Leon, to that woman, sayin’ ‘hello’ is a prelude ta joinin’ her at the church—and I don’t mean for Sunday services, either.”

“Oh. Ha, ha,” Leon grinned at his close call, as they headed back to their table with glasses replenished.

“Just stay away from her until ya find your footin’ again,” Jack advised him. “She might very well attempt ta split you and Miranda up tonight, so just be careful, okay?”

“Yes, I will. Thanks for the warning.” Then they were back at their table. “Here we are. Sorry for the delay; I had a run-in with one of the locals.”

“That Isabelle again!” Josey rolled her eyes. “That floozy. Hasn’t she found some dope to marry her, yet?”

“Apparently not,” Leon commented.

“That woman!” Caroline snarked. “She did everything she could to break up Jack and Penny. She even tried to convince Jack to forget about getting you released from prison. That you were a lost cause and that he should marry her and get on with his life."

"Really?" Leon's brows went up. "That's interesting."

"Yeah," Jack agreed. "She insulted you and Penny all at the same time. I was already gettin' annoyed with her, but that was the final straw, and I let her know, in no uncertain terms, that I weren't interested. That was the last time she tried any 'a that."

"Her pa and brothers aren't any better," Caroline continued. "Even her older sister had to go live with her aunt, just to get away from them. Terrible family."

"Oh. Well," Leon smiled, "I have been forewarned. Thank you."

He picked up Miranda's hand and gently kissed it.

Miranda went all warm and fuzzy inside.

Isabelle spotted the affectionate exchange from across the dance area and grimaced with disgust. Those Marshams really were a thorn in her side. Then her thoughts got interrupted by a gentle enquiry.

"Good evenin', Miss Isabelle," Hershel Rawlins greeted her, "would y'all care ta dance?"

Isabelle smiled at him, then turned away for an instant and rolled her eyes.

Oh blast!

***

A couple of hours later, the dancing was in full swing, and everyone was having a grand old time. Everyone, that is, except Leon and Miranda.

Josephine had breathlessly finished up a whirlwind of a dance with one of her local favorites and was making her way back to their table when she spotted the new couple sitting there in conversation.

Miranda was engaged enough with what Leon was saying, but the occasional whimsical glance at the dance area suggested that she would much rather be joining in on the festivities.

Josey sighed, and shaking her head, she marched right over to the table and grabbed Leon by the arm.

"C'mon, Silly," she ordered him, as she hauled him out of his chair, "It's time you got your feet wet."

"What? No! We were just—"

"Yes, I know what you were just. I could see it from way over there." She glanced down at the surprised Miranda. "You sit tight. I'll bring him right back. I promise."

"No, Josey, come on," Leon protested. "I really don't—"

"Yes, I know you really don't," Josey continued, as she pushed him onto the dance area, "but this is getting ridiculous. Miranda came here tonight to have fun, not just sit there and listen to you prattle on. Now, you get out here, and you start dancing."

"No, Josey. Come on . . ." Leon repeated, showing that he was at a loss for words. "I don't feel—"

"Too bad!" Josey threw back at him. "C'mon, put your arms around me. That's right. Now start moving your feet. My goodness, you'd think you were sixteen again, the way you're behaving. Well, you can do better than that. C'mon, stop shuffling. I know for a fact that you do not have two left feet. Now, put your arm around my waist and take the lead. There! That's better. See? You knucklehead, you haven't forgotten how to dance."

Leon grinned. The music took hold of his mood, and before he knew it, he was floating Josey around the dance floor like an old pro, and he was beginning to enjoy the event. By the time the dance number was finished, his blood was up, and he was flushed and laughing. He felt a bit more like his old, agile self again.

As they headed back to the table, Leon was still grinning.

Josey felt the satisfaction of a job well done as she handed him back over to a smiling Miranda.

Leon took the lady's hand and brought her to her feet.

"I'm sorry," he apologized. "Josey is right; I've been behaving like an old stick-in-the-mud. Would you like to dance?"

Miranda's sparkling blue eyes added radiance to her smile.

"Yes, I would!"

As Leon led her out onto the dance floor, she turned to Josey and mouthed a silent "Thank you".

Josey smiled, then went off in search of a new partner for herself.

CHAPTER FOUR
THE FIRST SIGN

The evening carried on, and as usually happens at these events, everyone in the Marsham party ended up dancing with everyone else, and all had a good time.

At one point, Penny found herself without a partner and decided to take that opportune moment to make a discreet exit to the ladies' loo and be back again before anyone noticed her missing.

It was getting dark away from the lights of the dance area, but she knew the way well enough, even if subtle lanterns hadn't marked the path. She quickly ducked into the small enclosure, did her business, and then made her way back toward the party. She was about halfway there when a stranger's voice behind her stopped her and sent a shiver down her spine.

"Good evening, Miss Marsham," the man's voice whispered to her. "Are you having a good time tonight?"

Penny gasped in surprise and spun around to face the dark silhouette of the interloper.

"Excuse me," she breathed, trying to come off as indignant, "do I know you?"

"No, Miss," came the eerie reply from the shadows.

Then, the first of the fireworks shot up into the air, exploded over top of them, and sent a flash of bright light over the entire area.

Penny gasped again in surprise as she got a fleeting glimpse of the man before her, and her heartbeat quickened in her throat. His eyes were dagger points, and his smile stretched with a maliciousness that caused her chest to tighten. She put a shaking hand to her mouth and involuntarily stepped back.

"You don't know me," he continued quietly, and his eyes narrowed. "Not yet."

Then he was gone, disappearing into the night, and Penny turned and ran the rest of the way back to the company of her friends. She reached their table, breathless and shaking, but she sat down and tried to relax while she waited for the dance to finish. But his final words echoed eerily in her mind, *Not yet*, he'd said. What did that mean?

More fireworks shot into the air, and everyone returned to their tables in anticipation of going out to the main street to enjoy the show.

Jack returned with the rest of their party, but the smile on his face turned to a frown of concern when he saw his betrothed looking pale and shaken.

"What's the matter, Darlin'?" he asked her, putting a hand on her shoulder. "Did somethin' happen?"

"No, no," Penny smiled, not wanting to ruin the evening for everyone else. "Silly, really. I just went to the loo and got frightened by shadows. I'm fine."

"Oh. Okay." But Jack didn't look convinced. "Well, the next time ya wanna go to the loo, you tell me. I'll escort ya, and then ya won't have ta be jumpin' at shadows."

"Yes, of course," she assured him as she leaned into his hug. "It was nothing, really. Just silly me. Come, let's go enjoy the fireworks!"

"Everything all right?" Leon asked, as he, with Miranda on his arm, prepared to head out.

"Yup," Jack told him. "Just shadows."

"Ohh."

***

Main Street was blocked with numerous wagons and buckboards lined along the roadway, with each one loaded with its own array of fireworks.

The crowds stayed on the boardwalks, watching with awe as the light show stretched the whole length of the street from the town square to the mercantile. The horses hitched to the wagons showed their anxiety through tense bodies and white-rimmed eyes, but they stood still in their harness and tolerated the loud bangs and bright lights.

During the walk along the boardwalk of Main Street, Penny held on tightly to Jack's arm and spent much of the time darting glances around her at the various people walking by. Quite understandably, she was skittish, and Jack caressed her arm. "Are you sure you're okay, Darlin'? You're tremblin'."

Penny sighed, mad at herself for not getting her emotions under control.

"I'm sorry. You know how it is when something startles you, but it turns out to be nothing important. It takes a while for your nerves to settle."

"Yeah, I suppose. But you're sure you're okay?"

"Yes, I'm fine." She smiled and leaned against him. "Let's just enjoy the show."

Then, following her own suggestion, the lights and sounds of the festive spirits that continued to swirl about her lifted her spirits, and the memory of her encounter lost its original scare.

She convinced herself that she was being silly. Her family was well known and the wealthiest in the county, so he was likely just someone new in town for the festivities, wanting to connect with the Marshams. He had just been saying 'hello', and it was only the strange lighting from the fireworks that made his appearance so sinister. He would probably come out to the ranch tomorrow to officially introduce himself.

Yes, she told herself. *That was it. I'm just being silly.*

The fireworks display was the best they'd had in years. The flares, lights, and bright colors lit up the sky, exploding with loud bangs and cracks that made spectators jump, gasp, and hold one another. Then, they'd all laugh with nervous excitement and anticipation of more to come.

Leon felt such a thrill! Suddenly, the loud noises and crowds of people didn't bother him anymore, and for the first time since his release, he forgot all about the prison. He forgot about the pain and fear and just lived in the moment, letting himself be swallowed by the excitement, the fun, the noise, and the brilliant colors. His friends surrounded him, and he had a fine woman on his arm. For the first time in five years, he was joyously happy.

Then something happened that no one expected, and yet no one really knew how it had come about or why. None of the witnesses could describe it later, because there was too much noise, too many bright flashes of color, and too many people in the way for anyone to have a clear reckoning of the events.

Penny had let go of Jack's arm in her excitement of watching the display. Her hands were to her mouth with oo's and aahhs, and her eyes up to the sky, watching the lights. Then, she felt herself pushed from behind. She plunged forward into the street, her senses overwhelmed by the loud noises and bright flashes of color. She regained her balance and heard Jack calling her name, but the darkness surrounded her, and she lost her sense of direction. She could hear Jack calling her, but which way was he?

Then, more fireworks exploded into the sky, lighting up the whole area, and she looked up just in time to see flaring nostrils and white-rimmed eyes charging toward her. Sudden light reflected off buckles and bits. Her ears were assaulted with the pounding of hooves, the jangling of harness, and the wild snorting of horses spooked beyond reason. She felt, rather than saw, the bulk of the two animals charging into her, in their panic to get away from the terrifying noise.

She screamed, but more explosions ripped away her voice. She felt the impact of one of the horses just as someone grabbed her arm and yanked her out of the path of the runaway wagon. She hit the ground hard and lay still, the wind knocked out of her, and her senses reeling.

She heard Jack's frightened voice calling to her, and then she passed out and heard no more.

***

When Penny awoke, she was in a strange room and a strange bed. She opened her eyes to slits, but didn't dare go any further than that—her head pounded. She tried to take a breath, but caught herself with the pain that shot through her ribcage. She groaned.

"Penny, Sweetheart ... are you awake?"

"Momma?" It was barely a whisper.

"Yes, Sweetheart," came the beloved voice. "Thank God. Thank God!"

Her mother's face came into view, and a gentle hand touched her cheek. She tried to move, tried to speak.

"Shh," Jean soothed her. "Lie still, Sweetheart. You've been hurt, but you're safe now. We're at David's place. He's taking care of you. You're safe."

"What happened?" Penny's voice was a whisper as her clouded brain struggled to make sense of this. "Where's Jack?"

Jean looked up at Tricia.

Tricia smiled and quietly left the room.

In the kitchen, numerous sets of eyes locked on as the doctor's wife came over to the table.

She smiled at Jack.

"She's awake," Tricia told him. "She's asking for you."

Everyone at the table released a sigh of relief.

Leon grinned and rubbed his nephew's back.

Jack felt like he was going to throw up. He was pale and cold with fear, and Leon had stayed close to him, hoping to give moral support but without suffocating him.

Jack had spent the last couple of hours hardly able to breathe, but now those few spoken words were like a floodgate opening, and he started to shake with relief.

"Can I ... can I see her?"

"Yes," Tricia told him, "But just for a few moments. She's still fatigued."

"Yeah. Yeah, okay. Oh, Leon, thank goodness!"

"Yes, I know," Leon said, and gave him a gentle squeeze on the arm. "Go to your lady. We'll be here."

"Yeah."

Jack stood up on shaky knees and made his way to the bedroom, the same bedroom that he had spent so many nights in, recovering from his own demons.

Leon leaned back in his chair with an exhausted sigh.

Miranda, who was sitting on his other side, hugged his arm and leaned her head on his shoulder.

He smiled, then reached over and patted her arm. "This has been one hell of a first date."

***

Jack stepped quietly into the bedroom and locked eyes with Jean.

She smiled at him and nodded.

David sat beside the bed and had just raised a small lamp in front of Penny's eyes.

She gasped, then squeezed her eyes shut and pulled away.

David shut off the light and set it aside.

"Sorry," he assured his patient, "but I had to check. You're light-sensitive, so I expect you have a concussion."

Penny frowned but refused to open her eyes.

"A concussion? How?"

"A buckboard nearly ran you over," David told her. "Do you remember anything?"

"A buckboard?"

"Yes," David confirmed, then repeated. "Do you remember anything?"

"Is Jack here? I need to see Jack."

"I'm here, Darlin'," Jack gave assurance, then moved around to where she could see him.

Penny squinted at him. She put on a brave smile and held out a frail hand to him. "Hold me."

David stepped out of the way so Jack could take over his place.

Even as he sat down, Jack took Penny's hand in both of his and brought it up to his lips for a gentle kiss.

"You can sit with her for a few minutes, Jack," David whispered. "But that's all."

"Yeah, yeah, okay."

"Jack?"

"Hi, Darlin'," Jack cupped his love's bruised face in his hand. "You look a mess."

Penny smiled, then grimaced. Every inch of her hurt.

"What happened?" she asked.

"Dunno," Jack told her. "One minute you was standin' beside me, and the next ... do you remember anything?"

"Just ... someone pushing me."

"What?" Jack instantly tensed.

"What was that?" David asked.

"Someone pushed you?" Jean asked as she took her daughter's other hand. "Are you sure?"

Penny nodded, then regretted the movement as her head exploded with more pounding.

"My head hurts," she mumbled.

"I'll get you something for that," David assured her. "It will help you sleep, and you need that more than anything else. I'll come in every few hours and check on you."

"Someone pushed you?" Jack repeated. "But you were standing right beside me. I would have known if . . ."

"Jack," Jean's quiet tone interrupted him. "Not now. She needs to rest."

"But if somebody pushed her . . ."

"Not now, Jack. Let her sleep."

"I couldn't see who it was," Penny mumbled as her focus faded and her head lolled to one side.

Right on cue, David returned to the room with a cup full of liquid meds. He hustled everybody out.

"Okay, that's enough visiting," he announced. "The patient needs to rest."

"Yeah, all right, David," Jack relented. "I'll see ya later, Darlin'. I love you."

"Love ... you . . .too."

***

In the kitchen, Tricia put more coffee on. Apparently, nobody was going anywhere for a while.

The two boys had been put to bed in David and Tricia's room for the time being, and Caroline kept Rosa with her while the infant slept.

David joined them at the table and sat down with a sigh. Every head turned his way. He looked up at them and smiled.

"She'll be all right,' he assured the group. "She has a concussion, two cracked ribs, and a lot of bruises, but she should be able to go home in a couple of days."

"Oh, what a relief!" Jean breathed. "My goodness, what a thing to have happen."

Cameron reached over and squeezed his wife's hand. She smiled at him and leaned her head into his shoulder.

David looked around the table.

"Does anyone even know what did happen?" he asked.

They all looked perplexed.

"I didn't even know anything was happening until I heard Jack yelling," Steven admitted.

"No, neither did I," David seconded. "We were all too busy watching the display."

"She said she felt someone push her," Jack informed them. Then he frowned and looked at Leon. "Did you see anyone close to her?"

Leon shook his head. "No. I was looking ahead, at the fireworks."

"I expect that's what this person was counting on," Cameron said. "Nobody would be looking at their companions. You'd all be looking up at the sky."

"Dammit," Jack slapped the tabletop as he recalled the events. "Something else happened this evenin'," he continued, "though, I didn't think nothin' of it at the time, but . . ."

All eyes were upon him.

"You mean, just before we headed out to the fireworks?" Leon asked him. "She did look awfully shaken."

"Yeah," Jack confirmed. "I asked her if somethin' had happened, and she just said she had gone to the loo and been frightened by shadows."

"Penny has never been one to jump at shadows," Cameron commented.

"I know," Jack confirmed. "Like I said, I didn't think nothin' of it then. But now . . ."

An ominous silence settled over the kitchen.

The coffee pot started to boil over.

CHAPTER FIVE
BABY STEPS

Rocking M Ranch
July 9th 1889

Fireworks exploded high in the nighttime sky, raining bright lights down upon the spectators, who gasped and clapped their hands in joyous appreciation.

Leon was walking down the boardwalk, casually watching the show. This was a dream. He knew it was a dream, and when Carson suddenly showed up in front of him, his cruel features accentuated by the flaring lights, the ex-convict was not surprised.

Even at that, a tingling of fear went through him. Then, when Carson grinned and uncoiled the bullwhip, giving it a snap, the tingling turned into a full-fledged knot that squeezed his lungs and grabbed his heart.

"Stay away from me," Leon murmured in his sleep as the dream became more real to him. "Leave me alone—please, just leave me alone!"

Then Doc Palin was there, standing beside Carson, tutting and shaking his head in disgust.

"What do ya mean, 'leave you alone'? I'm lying cold in my grave, and that's all ya can say to the man who put me here? Grab him, why don't you? He's right in front of you. C'mon, Nash, stop bein' such a lily-livered coward—grab him."

Leon looked back at Carson and was just about to take the doctor's advice when Penny came into the picture. Carson had a solid grip on her arm.

"No! No, let her go!" Leon yelled, trying to reach his young friend. "Let her go!"

Carson laughed and shook Penny like she was a rag doll. "Grab me, huh? I dare ya to try it!" He sneered, then gave the whip another loud snap. "How do you think her pretty little back would look, all cut to ribbons? Shall we find out?"

Carson pulled Penny away from Leon. Penny screamed, trying to break free, but Carson had too solid a grip on her.

"Napoleon, help me!" Penny pleaded with Leon. "Help me! Do something—!"

"No! No! Leave her alone!"

"Napoleon, wake up!"

The ground that Leon stood upon began to shake and tremble, as though an earthquake had taken hold of the town, rattling and rolling it until all the buildings fell to pieces. Leon tried to grab onto something—anything, but there was nothing there. He began to fall... falling... down, down into darkness.

His world shook again, and then he was awake.

Jean stood at the foot of the bed, holding up the lamp. Cameron was behind her, gripping the bedpost and shaking it, forcing the sleeping man to wake up.

"Oh, God." Leon lay on his back upon the pillows, but again, he was covered in a cold sweat, and he could feel himself trembling. He ran a hand over his eyes and through his hair. "Oh no, when are these going to stop?"

Jean came forward, and, placing the lamp on the nightstand, she sat down on the bed and took Leon's hand in hers; it felt warm and clammy.

"They do take over your nights, don't they?" she commented. "Would you like some tea or anything to calm you down?"

"No, no," Leon breathed, "that's all right. I'm sorry, I woke you both up."

Cameron shrugged. "After raising three children, that's nothing new for us. Don't worry about it. I'd rather you woke us up than have your whole night disrupted. I'm more concerned with why you're having such bad nightmares. I know David says it's not unusual, considering what you've been through, but still . . ."

"Yeah." Leon trembled, but the coolness of Jean's hands upon his fingers was helping. He took a deep breath, feeling himself calm down. "Is Penny all right?"

"Yes, she's fine," Jean assured him. "She's asleep, downstairs."

She rolled her eyes. "She can't move a muscle without Jack knowing about it and checking up on her. She's fine."

"Oh, good." Leon sighed and leaned back into the pillows. "Jack really can be an old mother hen, sometimes."

"Was she part of your nightmare this time?" Jean asked.

"Yeah. Yeah ... she was being threatened."

"I suppose that's not surprising," Cameron said, "after what happened the other night. But she's fine, Napoleon. Think you can get back to sleep?"

Leon nodded. "Yes. Sorry. Maybe I should have stayed in the downstairs bedroom. I wouldn't be disturbing you down there."

"Now, we discussed this," Jean reminded him. "We all agreed it would be better for Penny to be downstairs, so she could stay in bed throughout the day and not have to worry about tackling the stairs. She's fine. And don't you worry about disturbing us." She patted his arm as she stood up. "Just try to relax and go back to sleep. We'll see you in the morning."

"All right. Goodnight."

"Goodnight, Napoleon."

The couple left the room, taking the lamplight with them.

Leon snuggled under his blanket again, and with a deep, cleansing sigh, he relaxed into the pillow and, very quickly, was back to sleep.

***

The same could not be said for Jean and Cameron.

"Didn't David give him a sleeping draft to help with these nightmares?" Cameron asked as they settled into their own pillows.

"Yes," Jean said. "It seemed to help at first, but now, those nightmares are taking over again. I suppose if he weren't on that medicine, he wouldn't be getting back to sleep at all tonight. Still, those nightmares are taking their toll. Napoleon looked to be improving, but lately, he's simply wearing out."

Cameron sighed, and as the couple lay snuggled in each other's arms, he stared up at the ceiling and tried to make sense of all these strange events that were happening around them.

"And now, his dreams include Penny," he mumbled to himself.

"Yes," Jean heard him and quietly agreed. "There's so much he has to get over. It's as though he's scared much of the time, that he feels threatened by everything that happens, even if it doesn't directly involve him. Here we were all thinking that getting him out of prison would be the end of his troubles, but now, it seems to be just the beginning. What a terrible place it must be. Napoleon didn't deserve that—he just didn't! I don't care what he did!"

Cameron hugged his wife closer. "I know," he consoled her, "but he's home now, and everybody's rallying around him." Then Cameron chuckled. "Even Carl Jacobs!"

Jean furrowed her brow. "Carl? What did he do?"

"Do you really think that little encounter with him at the picnic was a coincidence?" he asked. "Carl could have told Leon about the poker games at any time and certainly didn't have to come up behind him like that and put his hands on his shoulders. No, Carl did that on purpose."

"What do you mean?" Jean asked, still confused. "He really frightened Napoleon. And, like you say, there was no need for it."

"Except that it's showing Napoleon that not every lawman who approaches him is going to be a threat," Cameron explained. "Carl came up behind Leon and laid hands upon him, and the encounter did not result in anything negative or threatening. In fact, it was good news: an invitation to 'join in', to participate. Indeed, to feel free to become involved with the activities the town has to offer. It's still going to take some time, but, bit by bit, Leon will become more relaxed and not expect a blow every time an officer of the law looks twice at him."

Jean smiled and patted her husband's arm. "All right," she conceded, "good point." She became contemplative again. "I wonder why he hasn't gone in to play poker. He used to enjoy it quite a bit. You'd think it'd be one of the first things he'd want to get back to."

"Yes," Cameron agreed. "Jack says he's lost his confidence. He needs to build it back up again. We'll get him there. Ohh, we just need to get him past these nightmares! They're holding him back."

"Or pointing the way," Jean surmised.

Cameron laughed and, giving his wife a squeeze, he kissed her on the forehead. "Yes! Or pointing the way."

***

Later that morning, the day started much the same as any other. Penny still seemed under the weather but was putting on a brave face for the breakfast meal. She could always go back to bed, once she'd put in the effort to eat something.

Leon was in good spirits, though he was overly attentive to Penny and busied himself with fetching and carrying for her, in between swallows of his oatmeal.

Jack watched him with some curiosity and just a touch of humor, thinking that Leon really could be an old mother hen sometimes.

Cameron also watched, but he, at least, knew where the protectiveness came from. Indeed, looking at his daughter, he could see that she was still pale and shaken from her ordeal, and he wasn't sure if all this attention was helping or hindering her.

"So, are you still planning on visiting your friends this week?" Cameron asked the two young men, mainly to draw their attention away from Penny so she could eat her breakfast in peace.

"Ahh, I don't know," Jack said. "I ain't sure I wanna leave Penny like this."

"She's fine, Jack," Jean assured him. "You know, David said she's recovering nicely. All she needs right now is rest—something she'll get more of with you two gone for a while."

"Oh." Leon's smile was impish with his embarrassment.

Jack grinned, then kissed Penny on the forehead. "I guess we have been hoverin' a bit."

"Yes," Penny agreed, "but it's been nice. I'm fine, Jack. You and Leon go and visit your friends; they're expecting you."

"Well, Kenny is." Jack revised the plan. "Taggard sent word that he's been called away, so there's no point in us comin' by ta see 'em. They'll see us at the weddin'."

"Oh." Leon nodded. "Probably better that way."

Jack frowned at this comment but made no mention of it.

***

That evening, Cameron drove the fellas into town and dropped them off at the sheriff's office.

Leon was obviously nervous, but he covered it up nicely and, taking his carpet bag from the buggy, he joined Jack in bidding adieu to their benefactor.

Jack clapped his uncle on the back. "Well, c'mon, Leon. Your first official leave from town. Let's go sign the paperwork."

Leon took a deep breath and followed his partner into the office.

Sheriff Jacobs was at his desk, finishing up the reports and getting ready to shut down the day shift. He smiled as the two men entered the office, then stood to greet them.

"Well, howdy, gents," he said. "I've been waitin' for ya. Figured you'd be in soon, considering the train schedule."

Leon simply nodded.

Jack picked up the slack. "Evenin', Sheriff. Hope we ain't kept ya too long."

"No, no," Jacobs assured him. "I don't usually get outta here before now, anyway. So, come on, let's get this done."

He opened the drawer of his desk, pulled out the ledger, and flipped it open to the first page. Leon's date and time of arrival in the town were written there in black and white, along with his signature.

Now, Leon stepped forward and, taking the pen, prepared to add another date and place to the page.

He licked his lips and hesitated.

"It's all right, Mr. Nash," Jacobs assured him. "Just write down where you're goin' and why, and when you expect ta be back. Then sign it."

Leon smiled at him, feeling silly at the way his own body was betraying his emotions.

Jack watched him struggle, trying so hard to be himself again, trying so hard to be the self-assured individual he had been before.

Leon sighed, dipped the pen into the ink, put nib to paper, and began to write.

Laramie, Wyoming. To visit a friend, Kenny Reece. Expect to be back July 12th, 1889. Napoleon Nash.

Leon took a deep breath and straightened up. A shy smile tugged at his lips; that hadn't been so hard after all.

"Good!" Jacobs declared. "I'll expect ya on the twelfth. If you're gonna be later than that, send me a telegram. That's all there is to it."

"Yeah, okay."

"Have a good trip," the sheriff said, then offered Leon his hand.

Leon stared at it for a moment, unsure, then smiled and accepted it. His grin now was genuine. "Thank you, Sheriff. I'll see you in a few days."

Leon turned to leave, while Jack and Jacobs exchanged knowing smiles. Then Jack turned and followed his partner outside, where they would head to the depot and await the arrival of their train. Jack put a hand on Leon's shoulder as they walked.

"See? That weren't so bad, was it?"

"No," Leon admitted. "Now, all we have to do is get by Sheriff MacPherson."

"Hmm, yeah."

"I hope Kenny let him know we're coming."

***

Most of the train ride to Laramie was spent snoozing by both men. It wasn't the same as a good night's sleep in a real bed, but they felt rested enough by the time the train pulled into the familiar station.

MacPherson was not pleased to find those two particular gentlemen back in his town. He had enough riffraff to deal with, what with the prison being so close. Oh, sure, the inmates came in handy a lot of times for cheap physical labor, but for the most part, they were more trouble than they were worth. The type of folks who usually came to visit them weren't too savory, either.

Still, when the warden says he's expecting these two men, and that they are in town on his invite, well, there's not too much the sheriff can do to prevent it. MacPherson made the wise decision to simply endure the inconvenience.

The scowl he sent them, as they entered his office the following morning, however, did not leave much to the imagination.

"Howdy, Sheriff," Leon greeted the lawman, trying not to let his anxiety show through. "I'm just here to sign in with you, as required by my parole."

"Uh-huh," the sheriff grumbled, "fine. Here's the ledger. Write down the date, who you're here ta see, why you're here ta see 'im, and when you intend ta leave. Then sign it. You can write, can't ya?"

Leon smiled, knowing the sheriff was deliberately trying to irritate him. "Well now, Sheriff, I signed out of this town a few months ago, so it would kind of stand to reason that I can sign back in again."

"Hmm." MacPherson turned the ledger around and read what

Leon had jotted down. "Oh, good. You're leavin' tomorrow. Not goin' ta visit your Sister friends, this trip?"

"No, sir, Sheriff," Leon answered, surprised to find his confidence building with this assault, rather than cringing away from it. He turned and clapped Jack on the shoulder. "My partner here is getting married next month," he smiled, cheekily, "and his intended can't stand to have him out of her sight for more than an hour at a time. So, we have to get back." Leon then fixed a serious look on the sheriff. "But I sure can't think of a nicer town to spend my time in than Laramie, Wyoming!"

Jack stifled a chuckle as MacPherson sent Leon a suspicious glare, not quite sure if the ex-con was being smart with him or not.

Leon smiled as he tipped his hat. "Good morning, Sheriff. I'll drop in again, before we leave tomorrow. You have yourself a nice day."

"Yeah," MacPherson responded, still not sure if there was a double meaning coming at him from somewhere. "You have a nice ... just stay outta trouble while you're in my town!"

Leon's grin broadened as he turned to leave.

Jack nodded good morning to the lawman, then followed in his uncle's footsteps.

"Jeez, Leon!" He laughed as they headed toward the hotel. "Ya might give me warnin' when you're gonna change tactics like that. I thought you was worried about him."

"Yes, I was," Leon admitted. "But once we got in there, I realized that he can't hurt me; as long as I stick to the conditions of the parole, he's got no say. Especially when we're here on invite from Warden Kenneth Reece, himself! It pays to have friends in high places."

"Ha, ha!" Jack laughed in genuine pleasure at seeing his partner slowly showing signs of his old self again. "You're right! You're so right. C'mon, let's get checked in at the hotel and then go get something ta eat. I'm famished!"

Leon smiled and shook his head; some things never change.

***

In the café, Lisa was pleased to see them again.

"Jack!" she greeted her once regular customer. "How ya been keepin'? Why, ever since you stopped comin', we got so much food left over. You gotta promise me, you're gonna help clear out that ole' pantry while you're in town."

"I'll sure do my best ta help ya out with that, Lisa," Jack promised. "In the meantime, how about some steak and eggs?"

"You betcha!" she agreed, then looked at Leon. "Well now, you can't go tellin' me that you're that same bald-headed, scrawny, little ex-con, who pulled my Jack away from this fine eatery. You can't be the same man!"

Leon beamed, his wide smile taking over. There was something about this flamboyant woman that made a man feel good. "Good morning, Lisa. How are you today?"

"Well, my goodness!" She played her part well. "The voice is certainly the same. What a difference a head of hair makes, eh, fellas? I swear, you are downright handsome. You're still awful skinny, though. You sure you're eatin' enough?"

"I'm trying."

"Well, you just keep on tryin' there, Napoleon, cause between you and me, you got a long ways ta go," she smiled knowingly, as she gave him a gentle pat on the shoulder. "I bet you're real ready for that steak and eggs now, ain't ya?"

"Oh, yes, ma'am." Leon's mouth was already watering at the thought. "Medium rare and over easy."

"Right you are! With lots 'a taters, too. Coffee's on the way. Fresh pot should be just about ready." She took a step to leave, then stopped and sent Leon a speculative look. "Ah, you drinkin' the strong stuff yet, Sweetie, or should I make ya a special pot?"

"Oh, no, no," Leon was quick to assure her. "Strong coffee, for sure."

"Good! I knew you could do it."

Then she was gone.

The partners exchanged looks, then broke out into chuckles, and nothing more needed to be said.

Coffee soon arrived, and twenty minutes after that, one of the best breakfasts Leon had ever tasted got plunked down on the table in front of him. He dug in with a vengeance that even Jack had to sit back and admire.

***

After breakfast, the partners headed back to their hotel room for another nap. Then, at the appropriate time, they got cleaned up and headed to Kenny's house, with Jack leading the way.

As they approached the front door, Jack put a hand on his partner's arm to stop him.

"What?" Leon asked.

"Just fair warnin'," Jack said. "You're about ta get bombarded. Sure you're up ta this?"

Leon shrugged. "Yeah, I guess. Can't be worse than the orphans."

"Hmm, I suppose." Jack smiled, and they continued on their way.

Jack hardly had time to get one rap on the door when it was flung open, and eight-year-old Evelyn stood in the threshold. Excited enthusiasm and awkward shyness competed for control of her countenance. She smiled with a huge, radiant grin, her gray eyes sparkling as she welcomed her beloved.

"Good afternoon, Mr. Kiefer," she greeted Jack, then giggled.

"Well, good afternoon, Miss Evelyn," Jack returned the greeting as he took off his hat. "How is my young lady on this fine day?"

More giggling as she smiled up at him, completely lost on what the next move should be.

Then Sarah saved the day.

"Show our guests in, Evelyn," came the suggestion from deeper inside the house.

Evelyn reached up her hand and took hold of Jack's, then began to pull him into the front hall. He went willingly, and Leon followed, hat in hand and a stifled grin fighting for space on his face. He closed the door behind him as Jack retook possession of his hand, then indicated to Leon where they were to leave their hats and gun belts.

They were in the process of ridding themselves of these items when Leon spotted the plump but pleasant-looking woman coming towards them with a smile of greeting on her face and a look of welcome in her eyes.

"Jack, how nice to see you again."

"Hello, Sarah," Jack answered and kissed her on the cheek. "Sarah, I'd like ya ta meet my uncle, Napoleon Nash. Leon, this is Kenny's wife, Sarah."

Sarah smiled warmly up at him.

"Mr. Nash. I'm so glad to finally meet you."

"Ma'am." Leon returned the smile, feeling awkward. "Ah, thank you for inviting us."

"Please, go on into the sitting room. Make yourselves comfortable," Sarah insisted. "Kenny will be home soon. I believe the boys are all out back." Then they heard the screen door banging shut, and the atmosphere in the house changed as the three energetic young men exploded upon the scene. "My mistake!" Sarah laughed. "Here they are now."

The three males in question were upon them, taking up the space in the hallway as the two younger ones rushed forward in greeting.

"Mr. Kiefer—you finally got here!"

"You're here!"

"Hello, Charlie, Alex," Jack greeted them, shaking their hands in turn. Then he looked to the older lad, who was definitely a young man in his own right, and oh so much his father's son. "You must be Connor."

"Yessir," Connor stepped forward and shook Jack's hand. "It's very nice to meet you, sir."

"It's nice ta meet you," Jack answered him. "Your father speaks very proudly of you."

Connor grinned with pleasure. "Thank you, sir."

"And this is my uncle, Napoleon Nash."

All eyes turned to Leon, and there was a heartbeat of silence. Then, all pandemonium broke out, and Leon found himself the center of a greeting frenzy.

"Oh wow—Napoleon Nash!"

"It's really him, in our house!"

"It's an honor to meet you, sir."

"Can you show us some card tricks?"

"Papa says you can make cards dance!"

"Can you show us how to open a safe?"

"Boys—show some manners!" Sarah cut in on the boisterous greetings. "Give our guests the chance to settle in, for goodness sake."

"Oh, yeah. Sorry."

"That's all right." Leon's wide grin took over. "It's good to meet you all."

Then Evelyn, who'd had enough of being overshadowed by her older brothers, took Jack's hand again and started to pull him toward the sitting room.

"C'mon, Mr. Kiefer," she insisted. "Papa said that you can wait in here, and we will give you drinks."

"Offer them drinks," Sarah corrected her.

"Yeah!" Evelyn didn't get the difference.

Sarah laughed it off.

"Well then, if you gentlemen will excuse me. I will leave you in the capable hands of my children while I get back to dinner preparations. We're having pot roast tonight," she informed them, with a twinkle to Jack. "As I said, Kenny will be home any time now, so just make yourselves comfortable."

"Yes, ma'am."

"Thank you, Sarah."

Within minutes, the partners found themselves settled into comfortable chairs, glasses of sherry in hand. Then Connor poured one for himself and Charlie. He glanced at sixteen-year-old Alexander, whose eyes had lit up in hopeful anticipation.

Connor sighed, poured a third serving, and handed it to his youngest brother.

"I suppose it is a special occasion. Just don't tell Father."

Alexander grinned as he accepted the small glass. He took a gulp and then gasped, as his face turned red.

Connor and Charlie laughed at him.

"You're not supposed to gulp it!" Charlie told him. "Sip it."

"Okay," came out as a rasping affirmative, then he went and sat in a corner chair while he got his breath back.

Connor looked at Evelyn and shook his head. "Not for you. You're way too young."

Evelyn sniffed, her little nose raising in the air. "I don't want any. Real ladies don't drink that stuff anyway."

Jack and Leon had to work to keep a straight face throughout this sibling conversation.

Then Jack stepped up to change the subject. "So, Connor, your Pa tells me, you're takin' engineering. Is that right?"

"Yessir, Mr. Kiefer. I'll be starting my final year in September."

"Good for you. Are ya enjoyin' it?"

Connor grinned. "Oh, yes, sir! I've always found it fascinating how things get built. You know, like tall buildings and bridges. I mean, how do you build a bridge across a canyon—or a river? It's amazing what you can do, once you understand the dimensions and the mathematics of it."

"Hmm," Leon took a sip of sherry. "I suppose I never really thought about it that way. I was always looking at the problem from the other end of things, you might say."

Connor regarded Leon and looked him straight in the eye.

"The things I've heard about you, Mr. Nash," he said. "They say you were a criminal genius."

Leon sighed, a look of regret flashing across his dark eyes.

"Don't believe everything you hear people say, Connor."

"But, even my professor at college acknowledges your mathematical ability and intuition," Connor persisted. "He even gave a lecture on how you blew that safe in Denver back in '74. That was a top-of-the-line safe, and supposed to be unrobbable, and yet, you did it. It was pure genius. That's one of the reasons I wanted to meet you. I don't know; I thought maybe I could learn from you."

Leon smiled at him. "You seem to be doing all right. You're already miles ahead of me. For all of my so-called brains, here I am coming up on forty years of age, and what do I have to show for it? A criminal record, who knows how many years on parole, and barely a penny to my name. The best thing you could learn from me, Connor, is what not to do with your gifts."

"I don't think I agree with that, Mr. Nash," Connor said. "My father says you have a lot to offer still. That you've done amazing things already, just on the wrong side of the law, and that once you find your footing, you will do amazing things again."

Jack couldn't help but grin at the comical look of bewilderment that got stuck on Leon's face.

How could this young man, just into his twenties, be so self-possessed and confident?

Leon remembered back to being that age and feeling just as confident in his abilities. But with that attitude had come an arrogance that had gotten him into trouble more than once. But Connor didn't give any indication of arrogance, just a quiet assurance and an acceptance of his own abilities.

Finally, Leon smiled. He liked this young man very much.

CHAPTER SIX
THE VISIT

The front door opened, and the man of the house was home.

Evelyn had been sitting beside her hero, not willing to relinquish her position of honor, that is, until her father arrived.

"Papa!" Evelyn jumped to her feet and ran from the room to end up in her father's arms, welcoming him home.

They could hear the greeting coming to them from the hallway.

"How is my young lady this evening?"

"Good, Papa."

Leon instantly had a knot in his stomach at the sound of that voice, and it took him by surprise. Why was he so nervous? He hadn't done anything wrong, and Kenny wasn't here to reprimand him—this was a social visit. This was silly; there was nothing to be afraid of.

The two men stood up as Kenny entered the sitting room, supporting his daughter in his left arm, while she hugged him around the neck. He smiled as he stepped forward and shook each of their hands.

The first thing that struck Leon was that Kenny was wearing a suit. He'd seen him in a suit before on several occasions, but he had expected Kenny to walk in still wearing the uniform of a prison guard. It took him a second to adjust to this surprise.

"Evening, gentlemen," Kenny greeted them. "Are my children treating you with all due respect?"

"Yessir, Warden."

Kenny cocked a brow at this formal greeting, then Jack distracted him.

"They've been fine hosts," Jack assured him, then added with a twinkle, "and hostess."

Evelyn giggled and hid her face in the nape of her father's neck.

"Listen, Darlin', you and I are going to have to stop greeting one another like this," Kenny complained as he set his daughter down on her feet. "You're getting to be far too grown up a young lady for my back to handle. Off you go now—help your mother."

"Yes, Papa."

Kenny smiled at his guests, as he stretched out his back.

"Oh my! They do keep growing, don't they?"

"Yup, they do, at that," Jack agreed. "I swear, she's an inch taller every time I see her."

"Hmm. Not to mention a few pounds heavier." Then Kenny smiled and put a hand on Leon's shoulder. "How's it going, Leon? You settling in at home all right?"

Leon tried to force himself not to tense up, but he knew his smile showed his nerves.

"Yeah. Okay, I suppose."

Jack and Kenny exchanged a glance, then Kenny nodded.

"Well, we can talk about that later," he said. "In the meantime, just relax. I'll go get changed and join you in a moment."

Everyone settled into their respective chairs again as they heard Kenny's voice drifting toward them from the kitchen, and then Sarah laughing.

Jack always felt comfortable in this house and with this family. Looking over at his uncle, he hoped that Leon would, too.

Leon, however, was distracted; his thoughts were miles away, but were they close enough to be up at the prison? To get his uncle's focus back into the here and now, Jack started up the conversation again.

"So, Charlie," he said to the middle son, "I hear you're gonna be takin' up medicine."

Charlie suddenly looked uncomfortable at being the focus of attention, but he also smiled at being recognized.

"Yes!" He was adamant. "I wasn't sure if I would be able to go this year, but with father getting his promotion, well," he grinned even more and looked at his older brother, "it's going to be great fun."

Connor laughed.

"Yes, great fun. But a lot of work, too, young brother. Medicine's not an easy program."

"No, it's not," Leon agreed, wholeheartedly. "You talk about me being smart, Connor, but the two doctors I've come to know over these past five years have put me to shame on more than one occasion." He looked at his nephew with quiet contemplation. "Our local doctor even saved Jack's life when the odds were stacked against it. That man continues to amaze me. So, Charlie, if you can be half the doctor that David Gibson is, and Doc Palin was, then you'll have something to be proud of."

"Oh, yeah," Charlie nodded, "Dr. Palin. He was a strange guy, but a good man. Our whole family considered him a friend. He's the main reason I want to go into medicine."

"Really?" Leon asked. "That's good. Doc would have liked that."

Then Evelyn's face appeared at the threshold.

"Supper's ready!"

***

The evening meal was a success. Leon had to admit that Jack's enthusiastic ravings concerning Sarah's pot roast were not an exaggeration. Everyone went back for seconds.

The supper conversation continued from the one in the sitting room. Connor and Charlie were excited about starting their new terms and talked back and forth and over top of each other, until Sarah finally settled them and turned the topic more toward their guests.

"Mr. Nash," she smiled at him. "I realize you haven't been out for long, but do you have any plans for yourself yet? Any thoughts for your future?"

"Oh, ahm," Leon fidgeted, "ah, no, ma'am. Haven't given it much thought really—no."

"Please, call me Sarah," she said as she patted him on his hand. "Jack does."

"Oh. Yes, all right," Leon felt the nervous smile again. "Everyone back home seems to be calling me Napoleon now, or Leon, or just plain Nash. Whichever one you prefer."

He sent a quick, almost embarrassed glance to Kenny, only to find that man watching him intently. Leon frowned, uncomfortable with scrutiny, but Sarah picked up the conversation again and drew his attention back to her.

"I know you don't have much formal education, but Kenny tells me you get along well with children, and you do have a gift for mathematics. Have you considered teaching?"

It was a good thing Jack had already swallowed his mouthful, or he would have choked on it.

Leon sent him a quick, insulted look, then smiled back at Sarah.

"Ah, teaching ... no," he admitted. "I don't think ... ahhmm, I doubt I could get a job as a teacher considering my background. Right now, I'm just doing some light ranch work for my friend and benefactor, Mr. Marsham. He has been good enough to give me and Jack jobs and a place to stay until we get something else going."

"Oh yes. Mr. Marsham," Sarah smiled coyly at Jack. "I understand that one of you at least, is going to be getting more than just a job soon."

Jack looked up from his meal as he realized the conversation had turned in his direction.

He grinned. "Oh! Yes, Penny and me are plannin' on gettin' married next month. So, I suppose that would make Cameron my father-in-law."

"Congratulations," Sarah enthused, and everyone echoed her sentiment.

Everyone except Evelyn. She didn't look happy about this news at all.

Kenny grinned.

"Yes, congratulations, Jack," he put in as soon as he had the chance. "I realized you and Miss Marsham were courting, but I didn't know you were betrothed. This is good news. She impressed me as an intelligent and kind-hearted young lady. You'll make a fine couple."

"Thanks," Jack responded, then perked up. "Say! Why don't you and Sarah come to the weddin'? I mean, ya already know most of the family, so you'd fit right in. I know Jean would love ta meet ya."

"Well, thank you," Kenny answered, "but that day should just be for family and friends, don't you think?"

"You're a friend, Kenny," came the quiet statement from Leon. Everyone stopped and looked at him. He gave a soft smile. "Jeez, I mean, we've been through hell together. Aside from Jack, you know more about me than anybody else. You saved my life, Kenny."

Silence settled on the table.

Then Kenny nodded. "And you saved mine."

"Well, if that doesn't make us all friends . . ."

Kenny and Sarah exchanged smiles across the table.

"Yes, all right," he agreed. "I'll see about arranging some time off at the prison. That takes a little bit more doing, now that I'm the warden, you know."

"But you're the boss," Leon teased him. "You can do whatever you want."

"Ha! Yeah, right."

"Are you gonna move inta the house that's provided for the warden?" Jack asked. "It'd be a lot more convenient to be right there."

Kenny and Sarah exchanged a look as Evelyn glanced back and forth between them.

"No," Kenny stated. "It would be convenient for my work, but Sarah and I decided we didn't want Eve growing up out there."

Leon nodded. "I can understand that."

"And the schoolhouse is right here in town," Sarah added. "So, Evelyn won't have to make that trip every day. With the bridge that was put in across the Laramie River, it's only a couple of miles, but that's a trip easier made by Kenny than by Evelyn." She smiled at her two older boys. "Plus, our two young men here will be going off to college soon, so this house still suits us just fine."

"So, the house at the prison will sit empty?" Leon asked.

"Oh, no," Kenny assured him. "I have arranged for Officer Pearson to move into it. He always stayed in the guards' barracks before, but he's getting married soon, and they'll need a place to live. He's also the senior guard now, and I am confident he can handle anything that comes up."

Leon smiled. "Pearson was a good guy; I was pleased to hear he had made senior guard. And now he's getting married? I hope his young lady doesn't mind living in the shadow of that place."

"Hmm." Kenny nodded. "If she doesn't know what she's getting into by now, she soon will."

"I hope it works out," Leon said. "He deserves it." He flashed one of his rare cheeky grins. "Better watch out, Kenny, he might be after your job soon."

"And by the time I'm ready to retire, he might be experienced enough to do just that. He wouldn't even have to move."

All the adults got a chuckle out of that one.

"Speaking of wardens," Leon began, turning serious again, "what became of Mitchell? I know he retired, but . . ."

"I believe he went back to his home state," Kenny informed them. "He still has family there, so it seemed the logical choice."

"And which state is that?" Leon pushed. "Just so I'll know to avoid it."

Kenny smiled ironically. “I believe he was from Missouri.”

Leon and Jack both stopped chewing and exchanged looks.

“Missouri?” Jack repeated. “He’s from the south?”

Kenny shrugged. “Many of us are,” he pointed out. “I mean, you two are from Kansas. I’m from Kentucky. Why should it surprise you that he would be from the south as well?”

The partners exchanged glances again.

“I don’t know,” Leon admitted. “I suppose it shouldn’t. I just didn’t expect it, that’s all.”

Kenny nodded.

“Well,” he sighed, “I’m full. How about we adjourn to the sitting room for coffee? There are some things I want to discuss.”

This suggestion was agreed to by all the men at the table until Kenny put the brakes on, much to the disappointment of his three sons.

“Just us, fellas,” the father told them, “For now. Perhaps later, our guests can chat with you some more. But for right now, your mother needs help clearing up, and then I’m sure you can find other things to occupy yourselves with.”

“Aww!”

“But Pa!”

“Oh, Father!”

“Nope. Later,” Kenny insisted. “C’mon fellas, give us some time.”

Grumblings were heard all around as Kenny led his guests back to the sitting room and closed the double doors on the complaints. The three men settled in once again, and Leon, for one, breathed a sigh of relief.

“Jack was right,” he said. “You do have a wonderful family, Kenny, and they are enthusiastic.”

Kenny grinned. He knew his brood was hard to take for the uninitiated, and even Jack hadn’t had to deal with all four at one time.

“You handled the situation very well,” he complimented the ex-con. “They were excited about meeting you, especially Connor. You two have a lot in common.”

“So he seemed to think,” Leon said. “I believe he would do better to listen to his professors ... and to his father, than to me.”

“You might surprise yourself,” Kenny countered. “You can offer a different perspective.”

“Ain’t that the truth,” Jack agreed. “You could really liven things up."

Leon sighed. "I suppose."

"You are looking much better," Kenny noted. "Funny, how a head of hair can change a person's appearance so drastically. I could see the resemblance between you and your daughter before, but now—there can be no denying it! She's her father's girl, all right."

Leon grinned with pleasure. "Does that mean I'm narcissistic when I say she's beautiful?"

Jack looked confused, but Kenny laughed out loud.

"No!" he denied the suggestion. "Unless you want to say that every parent is a narcissist. We all think our children are beautiful."

Leon continued to grin. He was relaxing again in the company of this man and knew then, for a fact, that their relationship had grown beyond the bars and the billy clubs. That indeed, it had grown beyond that, even while they had still been bound by the rules and social strata that life inside the prison dictated. Leon knew then that Kenny and his family were indeed his friends, and that nothing would ever change that.

A soft tapping at the door interrupted this observation, and Evelyn opened it to be followed in by her mother, carrying a tray loaded down with coffee cups and three slices of freshly baked pie.

Leon and Jack came to their feet, offering to assist.

"Thank you," Sarah told them, appreciating the manners, but turning them down nonetheless, "but you're our guests, so I'll just set the tray down here and leave you men to it."

She and her daughter made a hasty retreat, while the three men helped themselves to coffee and dessert.

Once they were fixed up, Kenny took another close look at the dark-haired man and decided it was time to dig a little. This was, after all, part of why he had invited them to come for a visit; it wasn't just for the sake of his children's curiosity.

"How are you doing otherwise, Leon? Are you settling in all right?"

Leon shrugged. "Yes. Sure."

Kenny smiled. He and Jack exchanged a look.

"What?" Leon asked, now feeling defensive.

"C'mon, Leon," Jack admonished him, "it's us, remember? You're havin' a hard time of it, and all of us here know it."

"Well, if we all know, then why do we need to talk about it?" was

Leon's sarcastic remark.

"Oh boy," Kenny mumbled as he took a sip of coffee, "still has the stubborn streak, I see."

"Yeah," Jack agreed. "Even prison couldn't beat that out of 'im."

"Oh, you're a fine one to talk," Leon shot back. "I don't know anyone more stubborn than you."

"Leon, why are you getting angry?" Kenny asked him. "We only want to help. It's a tough adjustment to make, and I've seen too many ex-cons not make it and end up right back in prison. As I stated the day of your release, I don't want to see you back there. I want you to be successful."

Leon backed off. Why had he gotten angry?

"Yeah. Yes, you're right," he admitted. "I don't know. I just ... I get feeling so defensive, like I have to protect myself all the time. I know you're both my friends—I know that."

"Well, after five years in that hostile place, it shouldn't come as a surprise that you're still feeling on edge," Kenny acknowledged. "Are you sleeping all right?"

Leon shrugged. "I suppose."

"Leon!" Jack got after him.

"Oh, all right!" Leon gave up the pretense. Trying to sidestep one of these men was hard enough, but both together was a losing proposition.

"Still having the nightmares?" Kenny asked.

"Yes!" Leon threw back at him, finding himself getting angry again. He took a deep breath and a big gulp of coffee. "Yes," he repeated, more reasonably. "Pretty much every night. David has given me some medication to help me sleep, but the dreams still break through."

"The same dreams? The ones about Doc?"

"Yes," Leon nodded, then sat back and ran a hand through his hair. "Over and over again. He's still insisting that it was Carson who killed him."

"Do you think it might just be that you hated Carson so much, you want him to be the guilty party?"

Leon looked up and met those gray eyes.

"Yes," he admitted. "I keep telling myself that's all it is, but the dreams aren't going away. Now Penny is becoming part of them, too."

"You're havin' nightmares about Penny?" Jack asked.

"Yes, ever since her accident."

"Wait, wait," said Kenny, sitting up straighter. "What accident?"

"Ah, Penny got knocked down by a runaway team of horses at the 4th of July celebrations," Jack explained. "Scared all of us."

"Oh, my goodness. Is she all right?"

"Yeah," Jack assured him. "Mild concussion and a couple 'a cracked ribs. But David says she's gonna be fine."

"That's good," Kenny was honestly relieved. "It was just an accident, then?"

This time, it was Leon and Jack who exchanged glances.

Kenny looked from one to the other.

"Was it?" he asked again. "Just an accident?"

"We don't know," Jack admitted. "She said she was pushed, but it was so crowded, with people jostling, trying ta get a good view, we can't say if it was intentional or not. An hour or so before the incident, Penny finally admitted to us that she had been approached by a man she didn't recognize, and though she insists that he hadn't really threatened her, she still felt threatened. If ya know what I mean."

"Oh yes," Kenny nodded emphatically. "That is not to be taken lightly." He sat back and contemplated the situation. "Her father is a wealthy man, isn't he?"

"Well, yeah. But," Jack shrugged, "if someone wanted money, wouldn't they just grab Penny and then start makin' demands?"

"If they wanted money, yes," Kenny agreed. "But perhaps they wanted revenge for some hardship? Does Mr. Marsham have any enemies?"

"Not that I know of," Jack answered. "He's wealthy, yeah. But he got there through hard work and solid investments—and having Penny for his accountant."

Kenny nodded in appreciation of that, but then turned serious again.

"Still," he continued, "a person's mind can become twisted in the way they view things. A small incident, though entirely innocent from a logical standpoint, could grow into a burning injustice, to the point where action is taken to exact revenge for the imagined betrayal. Believe me, it happens. And the person seeking the revenge truly believes that they are justified."

"Is there anything we can do to protect her?" Leon asked, suddenly concerned, along with his nephew.

"At this point, not really," Kenny admitted, "and, perhaps, it was just an accident. But keep an eye on her and caution her to be careful. And she's to let you know if anything else happens that makes her feel 'uncomfortable'. Even if it seems trivial at the time, perhaps ask her father if there is anyone he can think of who might stoop that low. You never know."

"Hmm," Leon nodded.

Another tap on the door.

"More coffee, anyone?" Sarah asked.

"Oh, yes."

"Thank you."

"Thank you, Sarah," Kenny smiled at her. "That was a very nice dinner tonight."

Sarah beamed at her husband, while their two guests backed up Kenny's compliment with ones of their own.

"Thank you, gentlemen. And let me say that you are welcome to join us for dinner, anytime."

"Thank you."

"We just might take ya up on that."

Sarah departed, leaving the men to continue with their discussions.

"Let me know if I can be of any help to you," Kenny offered. "If Penny sees him again and can give a better description, you never know, if he's done time, we might have information on him."

"Oh yeah," Jack perked up. "I never thought 'a that."

"Where's Carson now?" Leon asked, out of the blue. But there was a hard glint to his eye that both men noticed.

"I believe he's still in Arizona," Kenny informed him. "Why?"

"I don't know," Leon admitted in frustration. "Probably just me hoping to find him guilty of something."

"Do you have any reason to feel that he might threaten Penny?"

"No."

"Does he even know Mr. Marsham?"

"No!" Leon insisted again. "Look, just forget I asked. It doesn't matter. I was just thinking out loud."

"Okay," Kenny agreed. "So, everything else is going all right?"

"Yes, aside from what we've already discussed," Leon nodded. "Everybody is being very supportive."

"Good."

"He even has himself a new girlfriend," Jack couldn't help himself, and he grinned like a dog in mud.

The look Leon sent his nephew would have put him right back into prison if it had manifested into action.

Kenny grinned. "A new girlfriend?"

"Yeah ... well, no. I mean ... sort of . . ." Leon sighed in defeat, then slumped his shoulders. "She's David's cousin through marriage, and she's recently widowed, so ... but she's younger than I am ... so she's . . ."

"She's real pretty," Jack filled in the blanks.

"Oh?"

"And rich."

"Ohh!"

Leon tried very hard to stay angry but then couldn't help but return the smiles he got from his friends. He gave it up as a lost cause.

"We're seeing each other," he finally admitted. "But we're taking it slow. We both have a lot of things to work out first."

Kenny sobered and nodded in agreement.

"You're right," he said. "Letting things move ahead too quickly now could ruin what might be a worthwhile thing. This is good news, though. I hope it works out for you."

Leon grinned quietly and nodded.

There came another soft tap at the door, and Sarah opened it to find a shy Evelyn standing there, holding a box.

"It's almost time for Eve to say 'goodnight,'" Sarah explained, "so she was wondering if she could give Mr. Nash his present now."

"Ohh—I forgot all about that." Kenny sat up straighter in his chair. "Of course, Eve, come in."

Leon sent a questioning glance to Jack, who simply shrugged and shook his head. This was news to him.

Sarah gently pushed Evelyn into the room. Looking pleased but nervous, the child came over to the ex-con and placed the little box on his lap.

"This is from Mouse," she said.

Leon felt the box vibrate, and he creased his brow as he glanced at his partner again.

Jack was grinning, but he still didn't know what it was.

Leon looked at Kenny but wasn't getting much more than a smile from him, either.

He looked back down at the intense child gazing hopefully up at him.

"Ahh, well, thank you, Evelyn," Leon found his tongue. "I don't know . . ."

And true to his word, Leon really didn't know what to do next. He sat there, holding the box and feeling the energy emitting from it. He really was at a loss.

"Aren't you going to open it, Mr. Nash?" Evelyn asked, suddenly worried that he didn't want it.

"Oh." Leon came out of his trance. He smiled into those eyes that were so much like her father's. "Yes, of course, I'm going to open it. I was just surprised."

Evelyn smiled with her own excitement, then looked expectantly down at the box.

Leon did another quick look around the room, then, with embarrassingly un-nimble fingers, he pulled open the lid. His throat tightened with emotion as a smile took over his face.

Jack tried to see into the package without being too intrusive.

"Well, what is it?" he asked.

Leon squeezed his hand into the box and lifted out a small, vibrating ball of gray fluff—with legs. The tiny creature let out a tentative "mew", and then the vibrating increased in volume as Leon cuddled the kitten in both his hands, bringing it in against his chest.

She started to knead his hand and rub her whiskers against his thumb.

Then she started to drool.

Leon's face was like a little boy's at Christmas.

Jack could feel his own face grinning like a fool. He glanced at Kenny, who was watching Leon quite intently.

Leon gently patted the tiny head and scratched the upright ears. Her fur was so soft, and her eyes were so green.

"Do you like her?" Evelyn asked, her own eyes shining with hope.

"Oh yes." He swallowed and cleared his throat. "Thank you. This is the best present I've had in a very long time."

Evelyn grinned.

"Mouse had a litter of kittens, and Papa thought that this one was the most like her. The other two were black and white but she would be the one you would like the best."

"I do like her," Leon agreed, "she's beautiful."

He met Kenny's whimsical expression as both men recalled Leon's ongoing conflict with the prison's black and white tomcat.

Evelyn tried to be polite but she could wait no longer. "What are you going to name her?"

"Oh." Leon frowned. "I don't know. I . . ."

"You should name her 'Mouse' after her momma."

"Evelyn," Sarah cut in, "it's up to Mr. Nash what he wants to name her."

Evelyn hung her head. "Yes, Momma. Sorry."

"That's a fine idea," Leon said, and Evelyn looked up with a grin. "But Mouse is her own cat, and she earned that name. So why don't we call this one 'Lil' Mouse', then see if she grows into it?"

Evelyn's grin widened as her suggestion was at least partly accepted.

"Okay, time for bed," Sarah called her over. "Say 'goodnight'."

Evelyn accepted her fate and gave each of their guests a hug and a kiss on the cheek. Then she went to her father and gave him an extra big hug, and he kissed her forehead.

Leon watched this affectionate exchange between father and daughter with just a hint of longing. Then he smiled and continued to stroke the furry ball in his hand.

After the two ladies departed, Kenny and Jack continued to watch Leon, who was himself oblivious to their scrutiny.

He gently stroked the purring kitten while the smile played on his lips like an old favorite song that wouldn't go away.

"You know," Kenny broke the spell, "you don't have to accept it if you don't want to. A house cat can be quite a responsibility."

"Yeah," Jack teased. "What's Jean gonna say?"

But Leon refused to rise to the bait and sat quietly, gently stroking the soft fur.

The other two men exchanged smiles, and then Kenny got up and poured three glasses of brandy. He handed one to Jack, then put the second one on the side table next to Leon before sitting down with his own glass.

"Well, Leon, here's to new friends," Kenny toasted. "It seems you have a few."

"What? Oh, yes. New friends," he agreed and stopped stroking the kitten long enough to pick up the glass. "And to old friends, as well."

Half an hour later, the kitten was sound asleep on Leon's lap, and the three men were relaxed and enjoying idle conversation when another soft rapping was heard on the door.

"Yes?" Kenny called out.

The door opened quietly, and the eldest son poked his head into the study.

"Sorry to disturb you, Father," he lied politely, "but we were hoping that if it isn't too late, and if Mr. Nash isn't too tired, he might show us some of his card tricks."

"Oh ... ah . . ." Kenny looked at Leon enquiringly and was surprised to notice an instant change in his demeanor.

At the first sound of the request, Leon's heart jumped into his throat, and he felt his hands go numb.

Kenny saw his complexion turn pale, and his whole countenance became that of a man who was in distress and trying to hide it.

Leon looked down at the kitten in his lap and began to stroke her again, trying to distract himself from his discomfort.

"Ahh… I don't…" Kenny began to deny the request until Jack caught his eye and sent him a subtle but pointed nod of affirmation. "Sure," Kenny changed in mid-sentence. "I don't think that will be a problem."

Leon drew a sharp breath when he heard Kenny agree, snapping his head up. Then, he and the warden locked eyes.

Connor closed the door with a lot more emphasis than he had used opening it, and they could hear his voice as he headed back towards the kitchen.

"Yes! Father says he will."

"Oh wow! We actually get to see him do it?"

"Quick—where's that deck of cards Papa thinks we don't know about?"

Kenny smiled. "They just think I don't think they know."

Leon shifted in his chair. "Ahh, Kenny, I don't think I should—"

Jack stepped in quickly, clapping a hand on Leon's shoulder.

"Naw, c'mon, Leon," he cajoled with a grin. "I had ta show 'em my fast draw; now it's your turn. It'll be fun!"

Leon felt his palms start to sweat. He was afraid his teeth would start chattering. Suddenly, he was cold.

"No ... I don't really want to."

"Just give 'em half an hour or so." Jack ignored his partner's obvious distress. "That ought'a keep 'em happy. You got that deck 'a cards, Kenny?"

Kenny had been sitting quietly, watching the interplay between the two men. It was clear that Leon was trying to get out of putting on a display, but Jack wasn't letting him get away with it. Jack was pushing him, taking control, and refusing to accept "no" for an answer.

This was odd. Leon had always enjoyed playing with the deck of cards and even showing Kenny some of his ability. So, why was he afraid of it now?

Kenny's scrutiny of Leon was broken by Jack's inquiry, and the older man looked up and met the blue eyes.

Jack smiled, his tone light, but his eyes were deadly serious, and the message he sent was as clear as if he'd spoken it out loud: *Back me up on this. This is important.*

"Yes." Kenny rose to his feet. "I keep moving it around, just to keep the boys guessing. But I know exactly where the deck of cards is."

"Good!" Jack got to his feet and followed Kenny towards the door. "Let's go show those youngsters what a pro can do." Then he noticed that Leon wasn't joining them. He turned in mid-stride and went back to grab the anxious man by the arm. "C'mon, Leon," he said, pulling him to his feet. "You can bring your kitten."

CHAPTER SEVEN
THE TEST

Before Leon had the chance to dig in his heels, Jack hustled him into the kitchen and set him down at the table.

Everyone was either sitting or standing in anticipation of a show.

Everyone except poor Evelyn, who, being the youngest and with an early bedtime, often missed out on much of the fun stuff.

Leon realized he was trapped. He took a couple of deep breaths, trying to calm himself and wondering, yet again, why he was so nervous. He continued stroking the kitten, who let out a purr as she settled on his lap and resumed her nap. Leon smiled at the eager faces around him, then turned and met the gaze of his partner.

Jack smiled and nodded at him quietly, and Leon took another deep breath and settled his nerves.

"Here you go," said Kenny as he plunked the relatively new deck of cards onto the table in front of their guest. “Whatever you want. As long as it doesn’t involve cheating.”

Leon grinned, then wiped his palms against his pant legs.

“Okay,” he said quietly. “Ahh, just let me warm up—it’s been a while.”

“Sure, Mr. Nash,” Connor told him. “I think even watching you warm up will be interesting.”

“Yeah!” Charlie was quick to agree.

Leon smiled again, obviously nervous. But he finally left the kitten to her own devices and picked up the deck of cards. He started easily, cutting the deck, re-stacking it, spreading out the cards, bringing them back together again, and shuffling. All the while, he was flexing his fingers, stretching out the joints as he introduced himself to this particular deck.

The fingers that had been broken felt tight, but as he warmed them up, they, too, loosened and began to do his bidding. His fingers hadn't forgotten what to do. His nervousness was unreasonable. He had no trouble with a deck of cards when he was by himself or playing a casual game with Malachi. There was no reason to stress over simple tricks for a friendly audience.

He relaxed as he became more focused on the cards and less focused on his surroundings, but his surroundings were certainly focused on him. What were simple warming-up exercises to him were amazing examples of nimble dexterity and control to his audience. The three boys watched, mouths open and eyes incredulous, as Napoleon Nash made the cards dance.

The smile on Leon's face transformed from a nervous twitch to an all-out pleasurable grin, as his fingers and his heart warmed up to the challenge. Oh, yes—he was home again. This did feel good. He looked up as he continued to play the cards, and his grin increased when he saw that his audience was entranced. Even Kenny, who knew what to expect, watched in quiet amazement, while Sarah temporarily forgot about the coffee pot she held.

"Okay," Leon said when he decided he had warmed up enough. "Kenny, if you could deal out twenty-five cards from the deck." Kenny, knowing what was coming, was happy to oblige. "Now, the object," Leon explained, "is for me to be able to make five pat hands out of those twenty-five cards that your father is dealing out. It doesn't always work, but it works often enough to be impressive."

And impressed they were. So much so that the boys insisted he keep doing it until he was finally dealt a set that prevented him from completing the play. By the time this happened, Leon was so warmed up to the challenge that he had given the kitten full custody of the chair and was standing up, leaning over the table, like everyone else. He was totally focused on what he was doing.

Once the five-card display had run its course, Leon shuffled the deck and set it upon the table, then looked to the youngest boy.

"Alex, will you please cut the deck twice?"

Alex beamed at being included and did as he was bidden.

"Okay," Leon continued, "now take the top card from all three piles. Good, now look at those cards and memorize them. You got them?"

"Yes."

"You can remember which ones they are?

"Yes, I'll remember."

"Okay. Put one back on each stack."

Alex did so, and Leon collected the deck and began to shuffle it again.

Jack perked up as this was one that he hadn't seen his uncle do before. He had no idea what to expect.

Leon shuffled the deck four times, then held it in his hand.

"Okay, you remember what those cards were?"

"Yes."

"Good," Leon continued, and he took three cards off the top of the deck and laid them face up on the table. "Those are the three cards you had, right?"

Alex frowned.

"No."

Leon frowned too. "No? Those aren't them? Are you sure?"

"Yes. Those aren't them."

"Oh. Okay, well ... ahh, was it these three?"

"No."

"Are you sure? You're positive that you remember them, right?"

"Yes, Mr. Nash. I remember them. I'm sorry. Those aren't them."

Discomfort settled over the room. Leon seemed genuinely concerned about failing to produce the proper cards.

Jack felt some anxiety. This was all his uncle needed right now—to have a trick go wrong. So much for building his self-confidence; this small incident could send them crashing back to the beginning again.

"Hmm," Leon pursed his lips.

Jack thought he could see small beads of sweat coming up on his uncle's upper lip.

"That's odd." Leon frowned. "This is a relatively new trick, but I'm sure I'm doing it correctly." He laid out five more cards. "Are they here?"

"No." Alex looked like he was going to start crying. He wondered if maybe he should lie about it, just to make Mr. Nash feel better. He looked to his father for guidance, but Kenny gave him only quiet support. It was up to him how to deal with it. Alex bit his lip and kept on being honest.

The deck in Leon's hand was quickly running out of cards. Finally, he leaned back with a resigned sigh and looked at the last three cards in his hand.

"Well," he said as he placed them on the table. "I don't suppose it was these three, was it?"

"Oh, wow!"

Everyone laughed with both relief and amusement.

"How did you do that?" Alex asked. "How could you know which three cards to hold back?"

Leon grinned, his dimples dancing.

"That would be giving away a trade secret," he said, as he pulled the cards into a deck.

Jack guffawed as he slapped his uncle on the back.

"Jeez—I should've known!"

"Uh-huh."

Jack smiled. His uncle was finally exploding out of his shell, his confidence building with every maneuver he made, and now, this last trick truly showed that Leon was happily back in his element. They weren't there yet, but step by step, one hurdle after another, his partner was coming back to him.

He flicked his eyes up and found Kenny watching him—sheesh, that man never missed a thing! Kenny hadn't seemed worried or surprised by this last trick, and Jack figured the warden had caught Leon's sleight of hand and had known what was coming. Those boys of his probably never got away with anything.

The half-hour display had quickly turned into two hours, and the boys, especially Alex, were beginning to stifle yawns. Kenny suggested they call it a night but was met by such an uproar of protest that he had to relent and agree to a compromise.

"Okay," he submitted, "another fifteen minutes. And then, you two," he pointed at Charlie and Alexander, "are off to bed. It's late. I'm sure Mr. Nash is getting tired as well."

"Oh, I'm all right, Kenny," Leon assured his friend, "but I wouldn't mind a break to use the convenience."

"Good idea," Kenny agreed. "I'm sure there are others here who could stand to do the same."

"I'm good until we're done," Charlie declared.

"Me too," Alex seconded.

"Well, it's dark out there now," Sarah observed, "so, Connor, if you could take the lantern and show Mr. Nash the way, that would be appreciated."

"Yes, ma'am," Connor agreed, mainly because he was thinking much the same thing as Mr. Nash: it was time for a break.

Connor got the lantern, and then he and Leon made a hasty retreat out the back door.

The rest of the group relaxed. Stretching stiffening muscles, they then settled more comfortably to await the show's continuation.

Sarah stoked up the stove and set about making a fresh pot of coffee. Later, after the two younger boys had gone to bed, the five adults could sit and relax for a bit before their guests made their way back to the hotel. Fortunately, it was not a long walk.

Once the coffee was set on the stove to perk, Sarah returned to the table and sat down.

Jack smiled at everyone there, a mischievous glint in his eyes.

Kenny knew the man was up to something.

"You boys able to keep a secret?" Jack asked Charlie and Alex.

Both boys brightened up.

"Yes!"

"Sure!"

Jack chuckled.

"Good. How about you two?" he asked of the adults. "Can you keep a straight face? Well, I know you can, Kenny. How about you, Sarah?"

Sarah smiled at her husband, then nodded at Jack.

"I've been known to keep a secret or two. What do you have in mind?"

"Well, I just wanna test Leon," Jack admitted. "Actually, I want Leon to test himself, without him knowin' he's testin' himself. If ya know what I mean."

Blank looks were sent back to him.

"Okay," he said. "Just… just play along. The last play he did was pretty good, but I want to see how he handles somethin' he ain't expectin'; somethin' that weren't planned."

He carefully cut the deck of cards, and without moving them from their position on the table, he gently slid out a card from the center of the deck and hid it in his shirt pocket. He then delicately placed the top half of the deck back onto the lower half, then took his hand away, leaving the deck looking much the same as when Leon had left the table.

Kenny and Sarah looked at each other and were understandably dubious.

"You don't mean to tell me that he can—" Kenny began.

"Shh," Jack whispered. "Let's just see what he does. This is more for him than for us. Let's just wait and see."

A few moments later, Leon and Connor returned to the table, and everyone did their best to remain casual.

Leon must have been getting tired because he didn't notice any change in the atmosphere, and, taking possession of his chair, he moved the kitten back onto his lap. They both stretched out their arms or legs, and fingers or claws, before settling in again.

"Okay," Leon announced as he picked up the deck, "one more play, and then we call it a night, all right?"

"Sure, Mr. Nash," Connor agreed.

"Yeah. Thanks for showing us this stuff," Alex seconded, covering a yawn. "It was really interesting."

Charlie didn't want to risk saying anything.

Leon began to shuffle the deck.

"What I'm going to show you now is how to tell when someone is . . ."

He stopped shuffling.

He also stopped talking as a look of consternation flitted across his face.

Jack's heart leaped into his throat; he'd been afraid that Leon wasn't going to notice anything, afraid that maybe he had lost that all-important sensitive touch. But now, Leon was motionless, the deck of cards in his hands.

Silence settled over the table.

"What's the matter, Leon?" Jack asked, innocently. "Somethin' wrong?"

"Well, I..." Leon's brows pinched together for an instant, and then he sat there, staring at the cards, confusion plain as day written across his face.

Then Charlie couldn't hold it together any longer, and he burst out laughing.

Leon looked up, startled.

"What…?"

Then the whole kitchen erupted, and everyone was laughing—except for Connor, who was just as confused as Leon.

Jack reached into his breast pocket and presented Leon with the confiscated card.

Leon's eyes lit upon it, and realization dawned. A grin spread across his face and invaded his dimples.

Jack slapped him on the back again.

"Ho, ho—Leon! Ya did it. You can't tell me now that you ain't ready for a small-town poker game. You ain't lost nothin', partner. You still got it."

Leon continued to grin, feeling embarrassed that he'd been set up so neatly, but pleased that he hadn't failed the test.

Lil' Mouse stretched and yawned, then looked up at her human with love in her eyes, wondering what the commotion was about.

The laughter around the table was infectious, and Leon couldn't help but join in.

Connor still looked confused.

"Boy, oh boy!" Kenny exclaimed, shaking his head. "That was something. If anyone had offered me a bet, I would not have taken it."

"What?" asked Connor, feeling left out. "What did he do?"

"We'll tell you over coffee," Sarah said with a smile. "Meanwhile, you two—off to bed. It's late."

"Yes, ma'am."

"Yes, ma'am. Goodnight, Mr. Kiefer. Nice to meet you, Mr. Nash. Thanks for showing us the cards. You're great."

"Yeah, that sure was something."

The two younger boys then disappeared down the hall to prepare for bed.

Both parents sighed with relief.

"I thought that was going to be harder," Sarah admitted. "It'll still be a while before they settle down."

"Yes, but at least they're headed in the right direction," Kenny pointed out.

"So, what happened?" Connor asked, his curiosity demanding attention.

Sarah filled coffee cups and then sat down as Kenny explained the event that had just taken place.

"Jack removed one of the cards from the deck while you fellas were outside," he told his eldest. "He wanted to see if Mr. Nash could tell, just by the feel of the deck, that a card was missing." Kenny chuckled and looked over at the man himself, "and obviously, he could!"

Connor was suitably impressed.

"Wow," he exclaimed. "I'm really going to enjoy telling Professor McKinley about this." Leon raised an enquiring eyebrow. "Oh, he's the head of the mathematics department, and he holds you in quite high esteem. He wouldn't admit to it at first, but once he realized that my father was a guard at the prison here, well, he grudgingly owned up to it."

"Oh." Leon wasn't sure whether he was pleased. To have a professional man like that acknowledge his abilities was certainly a compliment, but… well, for a man in his position, to openly admit admiration for an outlaw… yeah, it kind of made sense that he'd be cautious about that. "I'm honored," he finally decided.

Kenny had been sitting back, drinking his coffee throughout this exchange. His mind was working on something and finally, he put it into words.

"I'm wondering if there's some way you can use your talents for legal purposes," he commented quietly. "Have you ever considered something like that?" He smiled at the irony. "Start working for the banks or the gambling commission as an adviser or something. Just a thought."

Leon and Jack exchanged a look, and they both smiled.

"Actually," Leon told their friend, "We have done work like that before. Remember at my trial, it did come up that we had done certain jobs for people in high places. Jobs that, on the surface, looked to be illegal, but were sanctioned by the authorities."

"Yes, that's right," Kenny nodded. "What a shame none of them were willing to come forward to back that up."

"Hmm," Leon grumbled. "The higher they are, the farther they'll fall, I suppose. Frank Carlyle would have, but I suspect that Governor Warren made sure he was out of the country at the time of my trial. Last thing he wanted was for Frank to pull up dirt like that—too many high officials would end up looking bad."

"I suppose that's the risk of doing work undercover," Kenny surmised. "If you get caught, you can't expect support from the people who hired you. So, maybe that isn't something you want to get involved in again."

"I don't know what I want yet," Leon admitted, with a heavy sigh. "Right now, I don't feel like I'm up to anything. I still just ... don't know . . ."

"Yes. And that's understandable," Kenny agreed. "It was just a thought. It's good that Mr. Marsham is giving you a haven for now, but I have a feeling that once you get back on your feet, you're going to find ranch work limiting." He laughed. "You're just not a rancher, Leon!"

Leon smiled.

"I know that. But like you say, it's a haven." His smile dropped. "I just wish the nightmares would go away."

Kenny nodded. "You're still healing. It takes the mind longer than the body, sometimes. Dr. Palin's death still haunts you; I know. It does us all. That was a cruel twist of fate. He was a good man who had given a lot to the inmates over the years. He didn't deserve what happened."

"No."

"But the man who killed him is dead himself," Kenny pointed out.

"Is he?" Leon met Kenny's gaze. "More and more, I'm beginning to believe he's not."

Kenny and Jack exchanged looks, and then Kenny sighed.

"Well, as I said before, if you can come up with something tangible, I'll help you with the resources I have available. But, in the meantime, you need to keep going in the direction you are, and get back on your feet."

***

It was well after midnight by the time Leon and Jack made their way back to the hotel. They would swing by again in the morning to pick up the kitten and receive a picnic lunch from Sarah for their train ride home. Both men felt good about the visit and had promised to come back again, as soon as they could. Jack reminded Kenny of his promise to attend the wedding, and they'd all parted company with handshakes and kisses to the appropriate people. It had been a good evening.

***

"What an unusual pair of outlaws," Sarah commented as she and her husband reclined in bed. "Leon is nothing like what I imagined.

All those sleepless nights he caused you, the fighting, and the trouble he got himself into. He seems too quiet and unassuming to have been the cause of so much strife."

Kenny chuckled. "You're seeing him at his best—or his worst. I'm not sure which to call it. Let's just say, you're not seeing him as himself. Napoleon Nash is a brilliant, creative—even gifted—man, but he came into the prison with a huge chip on his shoulder, and the ego to match.

"Mitchel and Carson beat him down; now it's up to him to decide how he'll rebuild himself. I truly believe that the core of the man is solid, and with that group of friends surrounding him, he'll have to work hard not to make good." Kenny sighed as he snuggled in beside his wife. "I think that over the next couple of years, we're going to find out who Napoleon Nash truly is, and then stand by to be amazed.

CHAPTER EIGHT
A GATHERING OF FRIENDS

The Rocking M Ranch

"They're coming!" Penny called to her friends, who were still busy tacking up the numerous horses inside the horse barn.

Jack poked his head out the door and looked down the access lane leading into the ranch yard. Sure enough, Rudy was trotting friskily along, hitched to the buggy, with David at the lines and Tricia and Miranda along for the ride.

"Yeah, they're comin'," Jack seconded to the person still inside the barn. "We about ready?"

"Just about," came Leon's muffled reply from inside.

Jack exited the barn and came up to Penny. He put his arm around her waist and gave her an affectionate squeeze while they awaited the new arrivals.

David directed his little gelding over to them and brought him to a standstill by the happy couple.

Jack took hold of the horse's head.

"Hey, David. Ladies," he greeted his friends. "You're right on time."

"Good," David answered. "No point hanging around."

They disembarked from the buggy, and David moved around to the small storage compartment in the rear where he pulled out a saddle and bridle in preparation for changing his mode of transportation.

The two ladies joined their friend, and Jack couldn't help but notice how fetching they all looked in their riding attire. He smiled a greeting.

"Ladies. I see we're all lookin' ready for our Sunday ride up to the meadow."

“I’ve been looking forward to this all week!” Miranda announced. “Is Napoleon around?”

“Yeah. He’s in the barn, gettin’ the horses ready.”

Miranda smiled, then practically skipped off in that direction, while Tricia and Penny exchanged knowing glances.

Penny then took hold of Rudy’s head, so Jack and David could quickly unharness him and then get the saddle and other riding gear on in its place. With the two of them working at it, it hardly took five minutes for the costume change, and then David threw his saddlebags across the back of the saddle and tied them down. They were ready to go.

Jean came out of the house, bringing small bundles of goodies for their picnic, and, of course, to see them all off on their afternoon ride.

“Hello, David, Tricia. What a lovely day you have for a ride.”

“Hello, Jean,” David returned the greeting with a smile. “You and Cameron doing anything this afternoon?”

“Oh no,” Jean admitted with a contented sigh. “We’re spending this afternoon sitting on the front porch and relaxing. It’ll be nice to have the place to ourselves for a while.”

“Where’s Eli?” Tricia asked her. “Isn’t he going to keep you busy?”

“No!” Jean laughed. “He’s at Sam and Maribelle’s for now, playing with Todd. Sam will bring him home in a couple of hours, but meanwhile, we’ll have some peace and quiet.”

“That’ll be a nice break,” Tricia agreed. She could relate to needing a little time away from the offspring. Nathan was spending the afternoon with his grandma, and this suited everyone just fine.

***

Inside the barn, the horses were saddled and ready to go, and they wondered why they were all still standing around and not getting on with things. They were also looking forward to a fun ride in the backcountry.

Unfortunately, the two humans, who were in charge of things, had tucked themselves into a quiet corner of the barn and were stuck to each other’s lips.

“Napoleon ... we should ... get out there. Everyone’s ... waiting . . .”

“Hmm. Let ‘em ... wait . . .”

Miranda laughed.

"Napoleon, stop that ... Oh! Actually, no ... don't stop that."

"Hello! Anyone in here?"

"Oh crap," Leon mumbled, and the two miscreants straightened themselves up and made an appearance. "Hello, Jean. We were just, ah ... getting the horses ready."

Jean glanced at the saddled horses who were resting on their back hooves, waiting for the adventure to start.

She smiled. "Well, here are your lunches. You may as well get them packed into the saddlebags."

"Oh, yes. Thank you." Leon stepped forward and took the paper-wrapped packages. He handed some to Miranda, and they divvied them up into the various saddlebags.

"You folks have a good time," Jean told them, with the knowing twinkle still glittering in her eye. "We'll see you all back here for supper."

"Yes, indeed," Leon agreed.

"Yes," Miranda seconded. "Thank you so much."

Jean nodded and left the barn.

Leon and Miranda exchanged impish smiles, and then they gathered up numerous sets of reins and led the horses out into the sunlight.

Penny spotted the filly and quickly stepped forward to take the reins of her beloved Daisy, while Jack relieved Leon of Gov's possession. Miranda stood holding the reins of Spike and Monty, not sure who was supposed to get which mount.

"Which of you two ladies is the better rider?" Leon asked.

"Considering Tricia grew up on a ranch, I would expect she is," Miranda reasoned. "I haven't done too much riding."

"Okay," Leon suggested, "then Tricia, you can ride Spike, and Randa, you'll be safe and sound on Monty."

After a bit of shuffling, everyone had their appropriate horse for the day. Neither Penny nor Tricia needed assistance in mounting, so Leon was quick to take hold of Miranda's ankle and give her a leg up into the saddle. She settled in, looking quite comfortable, and gave the little bay pacer a pat on the neck.

"He seems a sweet boy," she commented.

"Yeah," Jack agreed as he swung a leg over Gov's back. "He'll take care of ya."

Leon checked Miranda's stirrup length and took note of her very attractive ankle. He took extra time to double-check the girth, then, satisfied that all was well, he turned to his mare, tugged on the girth and then mounted up.

The group was ready to head out.

Jack turned Gov's head away from the barn and started them off toward the backcountry. Everyone fell in line, and amid much laughing and teasing among the friends, they were underway.

On the front porch, Jean and Cameron settled into chairs on the front porch with their tea and scones and watched the group trot off.

"Listen to them." Jean laughed. "You'd think they were still a group of schoolchildren."

"Sounds nice though, doesn't it?" Cameron said, and he picked up his wife's hand and kissed it.

Jean smiled affectionately at him.

"Yes, it does," she agreed. "It's good to hear him laughing."

***

Half an hour later, after the horses had found their stride, Jack suggested they open them up, and everyone was game for a stretch at a hand gallop. Even Monty, who preferred to pace, got caught up in the infectious excitement and broke out of his usual gait to gallop across the open meadow with everyone else.

Miranda proved to be a better horsewoman than she'd let on and had no trouble keeping up with the group, and Jack let the horses run on for a couple of miles without incident. Once the energy level had dissipated, he brought them all back down to an easy trot, and though still grinning and sparkle-eyed from the exhilaration, they settled in for a fun chat.

Jack led them toward his and Penny's favorite picnic spot on the parcel of land that was the newest addition to the Rocking M holdings. It still held a special meaning to the betrothed couple, and though they weren't about to go into any details, they were looking forward to sharing this place with their friends.

Not surprisingly, as the ride continued, the ladies gradually drifted into their own group to discuss the upcoming wedding. The men were content to sit back and allow the ladies to ride on ahead a few yards.

The ladies didn't notice the disappearance of their male escorts, as they were so deeply engrossed in their conversation.

"Are you getting nervous, Penny?" Miranda asked with a cheeky sparkle.

"I don't know," Penny admitted. "I don't know if I'm nervous or just excited. It's been such a long time coming."

"Yes. You and Jack have certainly been patient," Tricia said. "I don't know if I could have waited that long. David and I were married within three months of meeting one another."

"Three months?" Penny's jaw dropped. "You knew that soon?"

Tricia looked smug. "I knew as soon as I bumped into him. It took David about a minute longer, but I think it's safe to say that we both had the same idea right from the start."

"Yes. I knew very quickly with William, as well." Miranda's smile was wistful. "It took him a while longer. I think he was too accustomed to me as a child for him to consider anything more than that."

"That sounds familiar," Penny laughed. "You can't imagine how long it took to get Jack's attention. But I suppose he did have other things on his mind."

"Yes," Tricia agreed. "Speaking of which, how do you feel about Napoleon, Randa? Do you think it's the real thing?"

"I don't know." Miranda sighed, and Monty cocked an ear back at her. "I mean, there's no doubt about the attraction, but is it the real thing? I don't know. I still miss William so much. I still have vivid dreams about him, where I'm certain that it's the reality, and his death was a bad dream. I even tell myself that this is too real. This can't be a dream. Then I wake up, and the pain stabs through me." She sighed as her memories went back to a happier time.

She looked up and saw the other two ladies watching her with sad eyes. She waved away their concern. "I'm sorry, I didn't mean to be so melodramatic on such a lovely outing. But I wonder if my interest in Napoleon isn't more out of loneliness; I mean, really! He spent five years in prison, and he was a professional gambler." She rolled her eyes. "Among other things. He's everything a respectable lady is expected to stay away from. What will my parents and my friends back East think? And yet . . ." Sigh. "Maybe it's good that we're taking it slowly. Leon can be very affectionate, but I sense him holding back. I don't think he's sure yet, either." She smiled at her companions. "So, we'll take it slowly."

"People will always have an opinion," Tricia said. "You should have heard the tongues wagging when Penny and Jack became a couple. Although I think a lot of that was jealousy."

Penny blushed but was pleased. "Jack is wonderful."

The two older ladies exchanged smiles.

"There you are," Tricia continued. "Jack is wonderful. I expect Napoleon is, too. Once you get past the gambling thing, that is."

"Yes," Miranda lamented. "The gambling thing."

In the second row, all three gentlemen smiled appreciatively as they watched the gentle swaying of the three sets of hindquarters moving in rhythm to their horses' gaits.

"My, that Daisy sure has developed into a fine-looking filly," Leon commented quietly, then sent a sidelong look toward his nephew.

"Yeah, she sure has," Jack agreed, his twinkling eyes taking in the soft, rounded curves.

"Have you taken her out for another ride?" Leon queried.

"Nope. I told ya, Leon, we decided ta wait."

"Wise choice," David said. "Too much riding beforehand can sometimes lead to problems."

The other two men nodded in emphatic agreement.

"Yes," Leon continued, "once you put your foot in the stirrup and throw your leg over a fine filly like that, well ... you're committed. Sometimes the ride can get a bit bumpy."

More emphatic nodding.

"Still," Jack considered his betrothed, "that first ride can often be quite exciting."

"Hmm," Leon nodded, contemplating the truth of this statement.

"No doubt there," David agreed. "But I've found that, over the years, if you take the time and care to develop a good sound relationship with your mount—well, there's nothing else quite as satisfying as that."

Again, the other two men had to concede the probable truth of this statement.

Then all three men were brought up short in their speculations when both Tricia and Miranda pulled up and turned suspicious eyes back at them. Penny brought Daisy around as well, though she hadn't clued into what was going on.

"What are you three talking about back there?" Tricia asked them.

"Nothin'," Jack said.

"Just guy stuff," said David

"We're enjoying the view," Leon added, indicating the rolling pasturelands and distant tree line.

The two older ladies exchanged skeptical looks.

"Uh-huh," Tricia commented. "There's plenty of room for all six of us to ride abreast. Why don't you come up and join us?"

The three men smiled and, pushing their horses to lengthen their strides, they all joined up and became one group.

"I understand you've started to play poker again," Miranda commented to Leon. "How was the game Friday night?"

"Oh. Oh yes. It was fine," Leon smiled. "I had a good time."

"Did you win?" Miranda continued.

"Some. I came out with a little more than I went in with. But ah—no, the big winner of the evening was Frank Upton; he took home the biggest pot."

"And how much was that?" asked David.

Leon smiled at him. "Five dollars."

Jack laughed.

"That must've been a real stressful night!"

Leon nodded, emphasizing the truth of this statement. "It was! Five dollars is a lot of money."

"Yeah, I suppose it is," Jack agreed, but he was still laughing.

"Seriously though," Miranda continued with a nonchalant air, "what was the most money you've ever won—or lost for that matter, in a game?"

Leon sobered and sent an enquiring look to his nephew, but Jack simply shrugged.

"Well," Leon considered the question. "I guess the most I ever won was $35,000.00."

"What?" Miranda was incredulous. "In one game?"

David whistled. "Boy, oh boy. I can see why you'd have an aversion to working for a living when you can make that at the poker table."

Leon chuckled. "Yes, but it's never a sure thing. I've said goodbye to $20,000.00 when I've been just as sure of the winning hand. That's part of the thrill. I'm pretty good at playing the odds, but it's never over until it's over."

"Do you think you'll ever play at that level again?" Tricia asked.

Leon sighed and shrugged. "I don't know. The little games here in town are fun, but to do it professionally again ... I don't know." He sighed, and a smile played about his lips. "But there's that game they put on every year in Denver. It's a closed game—invitation-only, with a $20,000 buy-in. It sure would be nice."

Jack smiled and nodded. "Yup." He remembered how he used to sit by on those games, reading or just snoozing, until the atmosphere in the room would change, and he'd know that a big pot was on the line. It could get exciting for him, too, watching Leon play the hand. "Who knows, Leon? Get yourself back inta top form, and you might get that invite. It ain't like you're still wanted."

"Yeah." Leon frowned as he reflected. "We'll see."

Miranda remained thoughtfully quiet. She was a wealthy woman, and the last thing she needed was to be wooed by a scoundrel.

"I don't know about the rest of you," David said, "but I'm hungry. Is this 'special spot' much further?"

"Nope!" Jack grinned. "Just over that rise there. You'll see an old willow tree and the creek right by it. That'll be the place."

Everyone was pleased with this announcement, and the three ladies kicked their horses into a gallop and headed off in the indicated direction.

The three gentlemen accepted the challenge and went after them, whooping and hollering and laughing their way through it all.

***

Lunch was as pleasant as any of them could have hoped for. Jean's beef pies were almost better cold than they were fresh out of the oven. The lemonade and iced tea were the perfect accompaniment. It seemed all their worries were being washed away by the hot summer afternoon and the gentle breeze that kept the heat from being overwhelming.

Jack and Penny sat, leaning against the trunk of the tree, while the other two couples found equally comfortable resting places, and they carried on with idle conversation.

It was a good day, and Leon felt relaxed, not only in Miranda's company but with his whole situation in general. Things weren't ideal, but they were pretty darn close. He was beginning to feel that life was on the upswing and that things would only get better.

The relaxing picnic finally came to an end, and, amidst heavy sighs of resignation, the three couples arose from their respite. Once they accepted the inevitable, the laughter and good spirits returned, and as the ladies attended to the picnic clutter, the men brought the horses in from the pasture.

As they got the horses ready for the ride back to the ranch house, the optimistic ambiance was shattered by the crack of a single rifle report. All the horses spooked and danced to the side. Heads and tails went up, with eyes and nostrils flaring wide with anxiety.

Both Leon and Jack had their guns drawn in an instant, and they scanned the direction from whence the shot had come until a stricken cry from Tricia brought them both around again.

"Oh no—Penny!"

Jack felt his blood run cold as his six-shooter dropped from his numb fingers. Then he was on the ground, desperately cradling his betrothed.

"Oh no—Penny, Darlin'!" Jack was close to tears, his voice strained and desperate. "David—help!"

Penny lay on her back, her eyes wide and staring with shock and fear. Her mouth gaped as she struggled to breathe. Blood pumped from the gash in her neck, soaking the front of her white blouse and gathering in pools on the ground. Everything turned red.

Jack had a desperate hold on her right hand, while with his other, he tried valiantly to staunch the blood. But the thick, sticky fluid continued to seep through his fingers.

David came to the ground on Penny's other side. He grabbed the picnic cloth and pressed it into the wound.

Penny stared at him, desperately, silently, pleading for help as her free hand grasped David's shirt front, trying to hold on.

She was so scared. What was happening?

"Shh, all right, Penny," David tried to soothe her in a quiet, calm voice. "Try to relax, all right? Try to slow down your breathing. Take deep breaths, deep breaths."

But Penny was beyond reason; she was terrified. She fought to keep breathing, but could only gulp in short, rapid gasps, as she choked on her own blood. The harder she tried to breathe, the more terrified she became, causing her heart rate to increase, and the faster it beat, the quicker it pumped out her life's blood.

"Oh, my God, David," Jack was beside himself. "C'mon. Help her, please—do something. Oh no, this is all my fault; I should've known we were bein' followed—I always know when we're bein' followed! Why didn't I know?"

"Jack, I don't have time for this now," David told him in a terse voice. "Talk to her, try to calm her down. We can worry about whose fault it was later—all right? Can you do that?"

Jack looked at David, his eyes just as terrified as Penny's, but David held him in an intense gaze until Jack finally took a deep breath and nodded.

"Yeah, David. Yeah, all right."

"Good." David turned to the other two women. "Tricia, get my small medical kit out of my saddlebag. Quickly."

"Yes, David—I've already got it. Here."

"Open it." David gently lifted Penny's shoulders and pulled her back against the tree to help slow the bleeding. "Get me a clamp and gauze—anything that will help."

Tricia already had the gauze and a bottle of alcohol on its way to David's blood-covered hands and began searching for a clamp.

David grabbed the items and stuffed the gauze into the wound, both front and back.

"Jack." David took Jack's left hand and pulled it to the back of Penny's head. "Keep the gauze pushed against that exit wound."

Jack could only nod as he did what David instructed.

Penny was choking, sputtering up blood, but at the same time, beginning to weaken and slowly lose consciousness.

David felt desperate, but his professionalism took over his emotions.

"I need a clamp," he said, his voice terse.

"I can't find one!" Tricia was on the ground, dumping items out of the bag, but was unable to produce the required item.

She gave up and then thought of another solution.

"Here, David! Here." She pushed one of her hair clips into his hand. "Will this help?"

"Yes—better than nothing." Though staying focused, his voice showed his strain as he doused the clip with alcohol. "Dammit—did I pack any of that rubber tubing? I bet you I didn't. Goddammit . . ."

"I'll look," Tricia squeezed his arm and then scrambled to her feet and ran to Rudy.

The gelding stood stock still, but his eyes rolled white, and it took every bit of his willpower to stand steady.

Tricia rummaged through the saddlebags but couldn't find anything.

Miranda joined her, trying to help, to be of some use, but feeling so much out of her element.

"What are we looking for?" she asked her cousin.

"Tubing, rubber tubing," Tricia explained. "Anything long and hollow. Oh dear. I don't see it here!"

Miranda felt desperate as she searched the other bag.

"I can't find anything," she whispered as though to herself. In frustration, she untied the saddlebags and pulled them off the horse's rump. "Dump everything out."

The ladies ran to the picnic blanket and upended the bags.

Everything from a sheathed knife and hoof pick to more gauze and bandaging tumbled to the ground.

Tricia and Miranda were on their knees, rummaging through the contents, desperately hoping to find something.

"Here, here!" Miranda triumphantly held up a piece of tubing.

"It has to be longer than that," Tricia told her. "There must be something here."

They continued searching, moving the larger items aside.

Then Miranda grabbed the gauze and rolled it open. The light, flimsy material unraveled, and a longer piece of tubing revealed itself within its folds.

"Here, David." And she shoved the tubing into his hand.

"OH—good! Finally, something's going right." David handed the alcohol to Tricia. "Douce it thoroughly, inside and out."

Tricia moved with a practiced ease born of years of assisting her husband. She seemed one step ahead of him with her duties and had the dripping tube back in his hand before he'd finished the instruction.

Taking the tube, David moved some of the gauze aside. Blood spurted out, but he ignored it and inserted one end of the tube into the wound, pushing it down into Penny's throat as far as he could without losing it.

Penny had passed out, but she was still choking, and David had to work quickly. He requested more hair clips and instantly got a handful. He used these inside the wound to at least slow down the bleeding and then wrapped more gauze around the tube and the back of her neck to staunch the blood even more and secure the area.

They all held their breath and waited while David worked.

Jack still desperately hung onto Penny, even though she was unaware of him. He leaned over her, squeezing her hand and caressing her forehead, as he whispered endearments to her.

"C'mon, Sweetheart," he murmured under his breath. "C'mon, Darlin'. Hang on." He closed his eyes in a silent prayer. *We're gonna get married in two weeks. You can't leave. Jeez—what would your papa say? He'll have my hide if anything happens to you. C'mon, Babe, don't leave me. Don't. Please don't.*

David stopped working and listened, waiting for Penny to let him know whether his makeshift procedure had worked.

Penny's breathing still gurgled, but at least she wasn't choking anymore, and the air was getting in through the tube and past the injury. The hairpins, clamped around the damaged artery, were temporary at best, but for now they were helping. He took a deep breath and put a hand up to his face, rubbing his cheeks, not knowing or caring that he was smearing himself red.

"Okay, ahh . . ." David thought about their next move. "The Marshams' ranch house is closer than town, so Tricia, could you ride back home and get my regular medical bag? Make sure there's quinine and needles and suturing thread and—"

"Yes, David. I know," Tricia assured him as she headed to her horse.

"And get word to Jacobs about what happened," David called after her. "Don't waste time going to him yourself, just send someone, then get back to the Marshams' place. We'll meet you there."

"Yes, David!" Tricia swung up aboard Spike and turned his head toward town.

Then she was gone in a shower of turf and flying hooves.

David turned to Miranda. She stood a short distance off, looking shocked with both hands up to her mouth.

"Miranda!" David got her attention. "Do you remember how to get to the Marshams' house from here?"

"Oh! Ah, yes, I think so," she said, then pointed back the way they had come. "That way, isn't it?"

"Yes, that's right," David concurred. "I want you to ride back there and tell them what has happened. Tell them to get a buckboard out here, as quickly as possible. All right?"

"Yes," she answered, relieved to be able to do something to help. "Yes, of course."

"If you get turned around, just give Monty his head," David suggested. "He's a horse; he knows his way home."

"Yes, all right," Miranda called over her shoulder as she quickly mounted up on the skittish little bay and turned his head toward the barn.

"Okay, Jack," David looked to his assistant. "We need to cover her up with something. We need to keep her warm."

"Oh, yeah. Ahhmm," Jack looked around, his eyes barely focusing, but then the spark in them returned, and his brain started working again. "How about the saddle blankets?"

"Yes. Perfect. Go get them."

Jack went over to the three remaining horses and quickly untacked them. It hardly took him a minute to throw the saddles to the ground, collect the thick blankets, and bring them over to Penny. He knelt again and, draping the blankets over Penny, he tucked her in.

David smiled at the care Jack displayed while he checked Penny's pulse rate and lifted an eyelid to check her pupils. He sighed and sat back on his haunches.

Jack sat back again, as well. Picking up Penny's clammy hand, he raised it to his lips and kissed it gently. Then he sat quietly and gazed down at her, her small hand nestled between both of his.

"Hang in there, Jack," David told him. "Everything that can be done is being done."

Jack simply nodded.

Then David frowned and did a quick scan around their picnic site.

"Where's Napoleon?" he asked, suddenly aware they were one man short.

Jack tensed and looked around, a sudden panic in his eyes.

Sure enough, both Leon and Karma were missing from the group.

"Aww, jeez. Goddammit, Leon," Jack cursed him. "Don't tell me you've gone after the shooter—"

CHAPTER NINE
INTO DANGER

The rifle shot broke through the pleasant summer afternoon, and Leon felt a shivering of terrible déjà vu sweep over him. He swung around, his Remington instantly in his hand, but there was nothing to see; nothing to shoot at. Then, the strangled cry from Tricia brought him and Jack around to face the group again, and Leon felt sick with fear.

Jack ran forward, dropping his gun as he went, and knelt beside his betrothed. He was terrified; Leon could feel it, even from this distance, and he thought he was going to throw up with the rush of memories that came back at him. It was happening again! All the blood—people screaming, pleading with whoever would listen to make things all right.

First, it was Jack, clutching at his shirt, asking forgiveness while his life's blood spread out in pools on the ground. Then Lobo, choking from a punctured lung, pushing Leon away, and dying in his arms, refusing to accept help, refusing to live life as a sickly cripple.

Then Doc Palin, insisting that he would be all right, even as the padding he held against the knife wound became saturated with blood, and Leon was forced to leave him like that. Leave him like that, to die alone.

Now Penny. Oh no, not Penny . . .

Leon could see the blood pumping from the bullet wound in her throat, soaking into her blouse. Jack was clutching at her, pleading with the fates, pleading with David. *Do something! Do something! C'mon, David. Pull off another miracle; you can do it. You've done it before—do it again!*

David had moved in, trying to calm Penny down. Leon coughed back a laugh—how was she supposed to calm down when she was choking to death on her own blood? Leon could see the terror in her eyes. He could feel his nephew's panic. David yelled at Jack to get him to focus, and it worked. Then he was working desperately to slow the bleeding.

Leon stood like a statue, his Remington still in his hand, his body trembling with the shock and the memories, all hitting him at once. Then the anger rose in him. His upper lip tightened, baring his teeth in an animalistic snarl.

Why can't these people leave us alone? Why aren't we allowed to, finally, get on with our lives? Haven't we paid enough for our past crimes?

And Penny. Penny hadn't done anything except be the daughter of a successful man and then fall in love with an ex-outlaw.

Is this the price you had to pay for being happy—is that too much to ask for in this world? Apparently so.

Leon felt his indignant anger grow even more intense, but with it came a cold clarity of mind. His breathing calmed as he watched the desperate scene unfold before him, and he knew what he had to do. He holstered his gun and turned to snatch up Karma's reins.

She snorted and tensed, the whites of her eyes showing wildly, as she sensed the danger in the air and the anger in her human.

With a quick word, Leon brought her to task, and she settled, sort of.

He tightened the girth, then swung aboard, and with barely a touch to her arched neck, she pivoted around and dug deep. They were on a mission, and she knew it. Her hind hooves dug into the grass, and her powerful hindquarters bunched up and pushed off. Within five strides, she had reached her top speed, and they flew across the meadow toward where the shot had come from.

Moments later, they reached higher ground and were into the rocks where the shooter would have had easy cover and access to the group of picnickers.

Leon galloped the mare up the hard trail and swung off her before she came to a halt. He knelt, scrutinizing the area, but saw nothing at first. He moved ahead, searching the ground as he went, then he dove to the ground again, as something shiny caught his eye. He picked it up and, sure enough, it was a spent bullet casing.

He tucked it into his pocket as he looked around some more and found indents in the dirt where the shooter had sat, waiting for a shot to become available. Had the shooter hit his mark, or had he been aiming for Jack and missed? At that moment, Leon didn't care. His friends were being targeted, and that's all that mattered. Then there was a boot mark and a scuff in the dirt; the man was on the move. Leon ran down the slight decline, Karma trotting along unbidden, behind him. He stopped again by some bushes where there was a pile of horse dung and prints made from iron shoes. This was where the horse had been tethered, and for some time, too.

Karma stopped to sniff the dung, but whatever information she gleaned from it, she kept to herself.

Leon moved on another few feet, saw where the horse had turned, and taken off at a gallop. He straightened and, scanning the horizon, got a sense of the land and direction of his quarry. Swinging back aboard Karma, he turned her head along the appropriate trail, and they took off in hot pursuit.

He knew the shooter had a good head start, but Leon also knew he was probably riding the better horse. He pushed Karma hard, asking her for every ounce of speed she could give him, and she gave it willingly.

She didn't know what was going on, but she knew that something bad had happened and that her beloved human was depending upon her now. She was determined to not let him down. She stretched out and dug in, giving everything she could and would keep on giving, until she dropped.

Leon's eyes watered with the wind, but he ignored it and continued to scan the trail ahead of them and watch the horizon for telltale dust clouds. He rarely slowed down, galloping over rough terrain, up and down hills, over rocks and through gullies, risking his own neck, and his horse's legs, in this wild chase to catch up with this ghost that was haunting them all.

He stopped only to double-check the terrain and make sure he was still on the right track. Even at that, he cursed the time that it wasted, knowing that his quarry would not be stopping, knowing that it would only lengthen the lead that the shooter already had.

He pushed Karma even harder, determined to close the gap between himself and the man he pursued. If they were lucky, the shooter wouldn't realize he was being chased, and that could give them an edge. Leon knew he couldn't count on that, though. That man will be high-tailing it for cover, and Leon's desperation grew as the miles stretched out behind them.

***

Half an hour into the chase and Karma was lathered up and blowing hard.

Leon pulled her to a halt and dismounted again, scanning the ground in front of him, looking for signs. He cursed under his breath. The ground was hard here, and the tracks were difficult to pick up. He ran forward, looking, searching for any indication that a horse had been this way. Then he squatted, his finger tracing the partial outline of a hoof print. Yes! He was aboard again, and they were off and running.

They went down an incline, full speed ahead, and Karma lengthened her stride as best she could to cover the open ground ahead of them. But her breathing was labored, and her legs had lost their powerful thrusts. She dug deep and pushed herself; she had to keep going, her human was depending on her. She had to keep going.

There was a loud report ahead and to the right of them.

Leon heard the shot, and in the same instant, felt the shock wave go through his mare's body.

Karma grunted. Throwing her head up, her stride broke, and her legs crumbled beneath her. She went down, hitting the ground hard with her chest. She skidded, scraping the skin and meat off her shoulders, as the ground grabbed her and flipped her over in a shuddering somersault.

Leon saw the ground coming at him as he flew over his mare's head. He had a fleeting image of dark red mane, and the thought flashed through his mind that all he'd succeeded in doing was killing his horse. Then his right shoulder hit hard, and pain shot through his arm and neck. The breath was knocked from his lungs as his head hit the ground, and his brain exploded in fireworks of light. He did a somersault himself then, rolled twice, and ended up lying face down in the dirt a few yards ahead of where his mare had gone down.

Neither of them moved.

***

Jack and David sat by Penny, waiting an eternity for somebody to show up. Jack held Penny's hand, bringing it up to his mouth to kiss and caress, as he encouraged her to hang on.

David kept on monitoring her vital signs, hoping he had stopped the bleeding quickly enough, and that his makeshift tracheotomy would hold until they got her moved to a more stable environment. If she would even survive the move.

Then they heard it; way off in the distance, too far to judge how far, or what direction, but still unmistakable. A single rifle shot and then silence again.

"Oh God, Leon," Jack whispered in dread as he looked in the direction the sound had come from. "Don't you dare die on me, Leon. Not now! I need you—you owe me that much."

David just sighed. What a day this had turned out to be. He, too, hoped that the shot hadn't signaled the end of their friend. Not after they had all come so far.

Then another sound caught their ears, and both men looked in the direction of town and saw a single horse and rider galloping toward them.

"That's not Tricia, is it?" asked David. "I told her to meet us at the Marshams."

"No. It don't look like a woman." Jack squinted. "No; it's a man—see?"

"Ah, yes. Who is that?"

The horseman galloped toward them, then pulled his horse down to a more sedate gait as he approached the two men.

Jack saw the sunlight glint off the tin star and, for once, didn't feel a dread settle over him because of it.

David stepped forward to take the horse's head as the lawman stepped down.

"Ben," David greeted the deputy. "Did you fire that shot just now?"

"It wasn't me," Ben said as he stepped down from his horse. "I heard it, though. Sounds like it came from over that way." He jutted his chin in the direction Leon had gone.

David followed the gesture and nodded. "I hope that's not going to be more trouble. Leon took off that way."

Ben rolled his eyes. "He doesn't let up, does he?" Then he stepped around David, and his eyes fell upon Penny. His complexion paled. "Oh, God. Your wife wasn't exaggerating. Is she gonna make it, Doc?"

"I'm certainly giving it my best shot," David answered, his emotional exhaustion showing through. "We're still waiting for the buckboard to get here. Once we get her back to the ranch, I can do a proper job of treating her. They shouldn't be too much longer. I'm surprised you found us so quickly."

"Your wife gave a good description of where you were," Ben informed the doctor. "She's on her way to the Marshams, but Sheriff Jacobs sent me out here to see what I could find out about what happened."

"Somebody shot her!" Jack couldn't hide his fear.

"Yes, Jack. I can tell that," Ben answered quietly, realizing the man was stressed. "Any idea who did it, or where the shot came from?"

"I think it should be obvious that it's the same man who pushed her in front of the horses, don't you?"

Ben sighed. The ex-outlaw was showing his temper again.

"It might not be, Jack. It could be unrelated. Maybe the shooter was after you or your partner and missed. But," he held up a hand to stop the angry protest, "considering the previous attack, it is beginning to look like someone is trying to harm Miss Marsham. The question is, who and why?"

"Whoever it was, we think he took the shot from over there." David pointed to the distant outcrop of rocks standing stark against the clear sky. "Napoleon went after him about an hour ago. And now that second shot that we all heard. I sure hope Napoleon hasn't run himself into an ambush."

Ben scanned the horizon, then nodded. "I'll ride over that way and see what I can find out. In the meantime, it looks like the buckboard is coming. Do you need a hand?"

"I don't think so, Ben," David assured him. "You go and see what you can find. And please, be careful. I don't need any more patients today."

"Yeah, I will, Doc. I'll see ya later."

With one more glance down at Penny and Jack, the deputy mounted his horse and sent it at a hand gallop in the same direction that Leon had taken.

Five minutes later, Cameron and Sam pulled the buckboard to a halt beside the small group, and Cameron was off the vehicle and down beside his daughter in less time than it took to tell.

"Oh, dear Lord—Penny . . ." Cameron took her other hand and gently cupped her face. He looked at her and trembled, fighting tears, fighting his fear. "What happened? Miranda just said she had been shot. What happened?"

"Yes, Cameron. I'm sorry," David told the anguished father. "It was so sudden. Just—shot her from ambush. The bullet hit her throat and carried on through. Fortunately, it did not hit her spine, but who knows where it ended up. Perhaps in the tree trunk? I managed to stop the bleeding and keep her air passage open, but it was makeshift, at best. I'll do a better job of it once we get her back to your place."

"Yeah. Yeah, all right," Cameron agreed, trying to stay in control. "We brought lots of pillows and blankets. If we can just get her home again . . ."

"Yes," David agreed, quietly. "Let's gently move her into the buckboard and get her home."

Sam stayed up on the driver's seat to hold the team steady while the other three men settled Penny into the back.

Jack was torn. He was scared to death that Penny was going to die on him, and he couldn't bring himself to leave her side. But he knew that Leon could be in trouble, and the pull to go in search of him was tearing him apart. He sat in the bed of the buckboard, holding Penny's hand, but at the same time, sent anguished looks off in the distance— in the direction his uncle had gone.

Cameron was busy tucking blankets around his daughter, making sure she would be well protected from the jostling and bouncing the trip back would cause. He'd never felt so helpless in his life.

David touched Jack's arm and got his attention.

"Don't even think about going after Napoleon," the doctor told him, having seen the conflict he was going through. "Penny is your priority now; you have to stay with her and help Cameron. Ben will find Napoleon. All right?"

Jack looked David in the eye, preparing to argue, but David locked him down and silently challenged him. Jack relented, relieved that someone else had made that tough decision, forcing him to focus on his choices. The problem was that he wanted to do both. But since that was impossible, he let the doctor point him in the appropriate direction. And David was right, too; Ben would find Leon and help him if he needed it."

***

Ben rode on.

He had mimicked Leon's pattern by stopping at the shooter's hiding place, seeing the tracks leading away, and following them along the same route. He moved more slowly than Leon had, being far more cautious than the angry ex-convict had been.

It wasn't that Leon didn't understand caution, nor was he unaware of the dangers, but he had gone off half-cocked and thought only of avenging the cruelty of the act. Ben wasn't caught up in a personal vendetta, and by this time, he was a seasoned lawman, and he knew better. He had no intention of being caught flat-footed out in the open. He took his time.

The distance it had taken Nash forty-five minutes to cover, Ben did in sixty minutes, but at least he was still on the move. He pulled his horse up on the top of the ridge and, squinting against the setting sun, surveyed the flat land before him. He could see something out there—forms on the ground that weren't moving; forms that shouldn't have been there at all. He twisted in his saddle and rummaged around in one of his bags, finally pulling out the spyglass so he could get a better look.

He held the glass up to his eyes, then cursed under his breath. He used the glass to scan the area, checking the surrounding hills for any movement or reflections that might indicate someone waiting in ambush. He saw nothing out of place, but that didn't necessarily mean no one was there. Still, he reasoned, it wouldn't make sense for the shooter to hang around. He'd want to leave the area quickly, so Ben decided to take the chance.

Pulling his rifle out of its boot, he nudged his horse into a quick walk down the hill, then pushed him into a lope, straight toward the two objects laid out on the ground a few hundred yards ahead. He slowed to a trot again as he got closer.

He got to the horse first, and though the animal was conscious, she lay on her belly, her legs folded under her. Her eyes were closed, and her nose pushed into the ground, supporting her head. She did not look well.

Ben sent her a glance, then turned to the prone man as his priority.

Leon was out cold.

Ben dismounted and approached him cautiously, looking around for any sign of an ambush. It wasn't unheard of for a desperate man to use an injured antagonist as bait to draw more of the enemy into the open. Still, nothing happened, and Ben relaxed a little.

He knelt beside the still form of the parolee and carefully rolled him onto his back. There was a large, discolored bump and an obvious swelling on Leon's forehead, with angry red scratches down the right side of his face, where he had skidded into the ground. His right collarbone was pushing up against the shirt, obviously broken.

Ben gently slapped Leon's face, hoping to get a reaction from him. He was not disappointed.

"Nash," he called out. "C'mon, Nash, wake up!"

Leon's eyelids flickered, and then he moaned as the pain in his head grew with his consciousness. He started to move, then groaned again as the pain in his neck and shoulder also made itself known. He found himself wishing that whoever was prodding him would leave him in peace. At least when he was unconscious, he didn't feel any pain.

"C'mon, Nash, wake up. We gotta get ya back to the ranch."

Leon's eyes flickered open, and he gazed up at the deputy, trying to bring him into focus. Then he saw the badge pinned to the man's vest and had a moment of pure panic. He tried to push himself away from the lawman, then instantly regretted the movement when his head exploded with pain. He rolled over and vomited.

"Yeah, well," Ben surmised, "that's what ya get for over-reactin."

Leon settled onto his back again and lay there with his eyes closed.

"Deputy Palin?" His voice was a whisper in the dust.

"Yeah."

"What happened?"

"You tell me."

Leon lay quiet for a moment, keeping his eyes closed as he focused his brain. Suddenly, his eyes opened for a second time and alarm was apparent in them. He tried to sit up, but groaned again and lay back down as his stomach threatened to misbehave.

"Karma. My horse ... is she dead?"

Ben glanced back at the miserable-looking mare.

"No, she's not dead. Probably wishes she was, though."

Leon let loose a sigh of relief.

"Oh, thank goodness. I thought for sure ... Penny! How's Penny?"

"Still alive the last time I saw them," Ben informed him. "Mr. Marsham was just arriving with the buckboard when I left them to come in search of you. They should be almost back at the house by this time."

"Oh ... good."

"Do you think you can ride?" Ben asked. "It's gonna be dark here real soon, and I'd like to get us back to the house before too much longer."

"Yeah, I'll try," Leon offered lamely. "Just help me to my horse."

"No. You ain't gonna be ridin' your horse. You'll double with me. Your mare is no better off than you, right now."

"Karma . . ."

Ben took Leon's arm and helped him to sit up.

Leon sat there, swaying, as his head spun, but at least he didn't throw up again.

Ben took his bandana, and tying his and Leon's together, he made a sling and got Leon's right arm supported until the Doc could do a better job.

Leon sat quietly, letting all this take place. When he could open his eyes, he looked at his mare and saw the pain she was, so obviously, in.

"Help me to stand up," Leon told the deputy. "Get me over to her."

Ben didn't like to take the time for this, but he knew he'd better just do it, or they wouldn't be going anywhere without a fight. He stepped over Leon, took his left arm, and helped pull him to his feet. Leon stood there, swaying, and leaning against the younger man.

"Ya all right?" Ben asked him.

"Yeah, getting there."

He took a step, and with Ben's help, he made his way to his horse.

Karma barely acknowledged him. She continued to sit, her ears flopping to the side, her eyes closed, and her nose resting on the ground. She was breathing in slow, shallow gasps—a sure sign that her head was pounding.

Leon knelt beside her and caressed her face. He felt the stickiness of blood.

"Karma," he whispered to her. Then, rubbing her forehead, he moved his hand up between her ears, and she reacted instantly, jerking her head away. "Whoa, easy girl."

Ben stepped in and took a closer look. "She's got a bullet crease right there, along the top of her pole. She was lucky—that could easily have killed her."

Leon held her face in a hug, being careful to stay away from the injury.

"That's all right, Sweetheart," he murmured to her. "You gave your best, that's for sure. But we have to get you on your feet. We have to get you home."

Leon shakily stood up, and Ben held onto his arm to steady him. He took hold of Karma's reins with his good hand and encouraged her to get up. She barely acknowledged him and made no effort to move.

"C'mon, girl," Leon pleaded with her. "Get on your feet—we have to get you home."

"Nash, we gotta get you home, too," Ben reminded him. "It's already going to be dark before we get there; we have to leave."

"We can't leave Karma here," Leon said. "She'll die if she's left out here like this. Predators will get her."

"I can't help that right now," Ben persisted. "You need medical care—the sooner the better. We have to go."

"But ... I can't leave her . . ."

Ben started to assist Leon over to his patient gelding.

Leon didn't have the strength to resist, but verbally, he kept up a running monologue.

"No. We can't leave her like this. We can wait until she's feeling better and on her feet. She'll die out here if we leave her alone—"

"If she's smart, she'll get on her feet and follow us," Ben reasoned, "but we're not waiting."

"Ycah, but . . ."

Ben maneuvered his horse to a rock, then got Leon up onto it. Leon continued to protest while he leaned against the horse's saddle and allowed Ben to place his foot in the stirrup. Once he was halfway settled, Ben gave him a heave and got him up enough to swing his right leg over and get him astride.

Leon tried to bring his right leg back over the cantle, but Ben pushed it over again.

"Give it up, Nash." Ben mounted up behind him and got the reins organized. "I'm getting you back to the ranch. Now."

Leon leaned forward against the horse's mane, his consciousness threatening to abandon him. "No," he mumbled as he reached out a hand to his mare, "we can't leave her behind."

Ben nudged his horse forward, and they started the slow walk toward the ranch house.

Leon glanced back at his mare, and then he summoned what little strength he had and called to her.

"Karma! Come on, girl. You can do it. Come on!"

Karma's head jerked slightly, and her eyes opened to slits. Her head was pounding so badly, but through the haze of pain, she saw her human riding away. Riding away on ANOTHER HORSE. No, no, no, she would not be left behind! She took a deep breath, and despite the throbbing pain, she finally stretched out her front legs, and with a heave from her hindquarters, she got to her feet. She stood there, swaying for a moment, head down almost to the ground, and a long strip of loose hide hanging from the wound on her chest. She braced herself, planting her legs firmly on her feet and making sure those feet stayed beneath her.

"C'mon, Karma," Leon muttered. "That's a girl. Come on! You can do it. Ben, slow down. She's coming."

"We're already going slow. She's on her feet now, so she'll follow."

"No, slow down. Wait for her . . ." And then he passed out.

Karma took a tentative step, almost losing her balance and falling again, but she caught herself and stayed on her feet, despite the world spinning around her. If she had been physically capable of throwing up, she would have done so, but, being a horse, she didn't have that option. So, she suffered, and the pain attacked her head and her guts, but through it all, she was acutely aware of her human riding away from her, and she wasn't prepared to take that lying down.

She took another step and another, and she followed along in their wake. Her head down, dragging the reins, her ears flopping to the side, her lips drooping, and her eyes closed to slits, she put one foreleg in front of the other, and the hind legs followed.

It was in this manner, four hours later, and in the black of night, that this small procession made its way back to the Marsham ranch house, with Leon slumped, unconscious, and Karma barely aware of who she was.

CHAPTER TEN
COMING TO TERMS

The buckboard arrived at the house just as evening was closing around them. Jean was in a state of nerves, but she still had hot water on the stove, and the bed in the downstairs room ready for her daughter to settle into.

Tricia did her best to keep Eli entertained while Miranda made tea and helped Jean with whatever she needed, just to keep busy.

Finally, with waves of relief and anxiety, the ladies heard the dogs barking and knew that the small group had arrived. The porch lantern had been left burning to light their way, and the team pulled up right to the front steps, while the ladies all came outside with hands to their mouths and hearts in their throats.

"Oh, dear God, Cameron," Jean whispered, beseechingly. "Is she all right? Please tell me she's all right."

Cameron jumped down from the back of the wagon while David and Jack slowly eased Penny out of the bed.

"She's still alive," Cameron assured his wife. "I don't know yet if she's all right."

"Oh, my dear Lord!" Jean was beside herself, and the other women put their arms around her in support.

"Where can we lay her down?" David asked. "I need to do a better job of cleaning up this wound."

"I've prepared the room under the stairs," Jean told him through her fear. "You can put her in there."

David nodded, and then he, Jack, and Cameron carried Penny up the steps and into the house.

Jean gasped in fear when she saw her daughter; she looked so pale in the lamplight, and it contrasted bleakly with the blood that had soaked into her blouse. Jean was close to tears, but she knew she had to hold herself together to be of any use. She gathered up her skirts and followed the men into the small bedroom.

David and Jack gently laid Penny down on the bed, and then Tricia was there with David's complete medical bag, containing all the tools he would need to treat the wound properly.

Jean came forward and took her daughter's hand in both of hers.

"She's so pale," Jean whispered. "David, is she going to be all right?"

"I'll do the best I can, Jean," David assured her. "The fact that we've got her this far says a lot for her chances."

"Yes, of course."

"Momma, what's the matter with Penny?" Eli asked from the door of the room.

Jean looked back at her son, then quickly went to him and leaned down to take him into her arms.

He continued to look over at the bed, his eyes full of worry.

"What's wrong with her?"

"She's had an accident, Eli," his mother explained, "but Dr. David is going to do everything he can to help her."

"Is she going to be all right?" he asked, not putting too much confidence in Dr. David.

"We're certainly going to try," Jean assured him, giving him another hug.

"Jean," David said, pointedly, "I need you to get me some hot water, and lots of towels, okay?"

"Yes. Yes, of course."

Jean went off to tend to this, taking her son with her.

Eli followed along, but his eyes continued to look back at his sister until she was out of his line of sight. He didn't like this situation at all.

David turned to his wife.

"We need to get these soiled clothes off her; get her cleaned up."

Tricia sent him an exasperated look, since she had assisted him in many emergencies and knew exactly what was required. She already had Penny's boots pulled off and was working on the buttons of her riding habit.

Jack was also trying to assist, but David put a hand on his arm to stop him. "Jack, I know you want to help, but I think it's best if the ladies assist me with this, all right?"

"But . . ." He looked stricken; he wanted to stay with her.

"Jack, please," David insisted. "You've done so much already, but now it's best if you and Cameron wait in the living room. Why don't you put on some coffee for everyone?"

"C'mon, Jack," Cameron encouraged him. "Let's let David work. It shouldn't take too long."

"No, not long," David agreed. "Please, just go out and try to relax."

"Yeah, okay." Jack squeezed Penny's hand, then allowed Cameron to lead him out the door, just as Jean came in with the required supplies.

The bedroom door closed on the two men, and they were left standing in the dining room, with Eli impaling them with beseeching eyes.

Cameron motioned the little boy over to sit with them at the table. Once he was settled, Cameron turned his attention to the other man in the room.

"Come on, Jack. Come sit down," Cameron was just as anxious as Jack, but he was older and the father of three, so he was more adept at dealing with emergencies.

Between himself and his uncle, Jack was usually the calmer of the two, but not when the people he cared about were threatened. He never could deal with that kind of stress. He had to do something.

And now, here he was stuck—just sitting. And waiting—while others made the choices. He sat down with a "humph" and ran his hands through his curls.

"I'll go put some coffee on." Cameron gave the other man a pat on the shoulder. "I don't know about you, but I could use some. I'm sure when Napoleon and Ben get here, they'll need something hot as well."

Jack straightened up. "Leon!" Concern and guilt flashed across his face. "I should go look for him. What if he's hurt?"

"Jack, calm down. It's dark out there. I'm sure Ben will find him."

"But what if Ben misses 'im in the dark?"

"What if you miss him in the dark?" Cameron pointed out. "Come on. I know it's hard to just sit and wait, but sometimes there's no other choice. If there's no sign of him by morning, then we can both look for him. All right?"

Jack ran a hand over his forehead and through his hair—again. He gave a deep sigh.

"Yeah. Yeah, you're right. A course."

And so, they waited.

***

Sam came in from the barn and joined them for coffee.

Cameron told him he could go home, but he refused, wanting to wait it out, just in case he needed to run errands. Maribelle knew that if he was delayed past dark, he would stay the night at the ranch. It was safer than trying to ride home, and she had his mother there with her, so she wasn't alone with the children.

It seemed an eternity, but it was only an hour before the bedroom door opened, and David, with the three ladies, came out. All four appeared relieved.

Tricia and Miranda were weary as they sat at the table, but their expressions had softened, showing their relief.

"She's all right?" Jack still felt the need to ask.

"Yes," David confirmed. "She'll need rest, and it will be a while before she gets her voice back. But, yes, I think she'll be all right."

"Oh, thank God!" Jack rubbed his eyes. "Thank you, David. Thank goodness you were with us. Now, if Leon would hurry up and get back, maybe I could relax."

"Where is Napoleon?" Jean asked from within Cameron's embrace.

"He went after the shooter," Jack informed her. "Then, Deputy Palin went after him. If Ben found 'im all right, they'd be back by now."

"There's nothing we can do about it tonight," Cameron reiterated. "Why don't we all just try to get some sleep?"

This suggestion drew skeptical looks from everyone, and no one moved to retire for the night. Jack, for one, had no intention of going to bed until his uncle showed up, and if that meant he was going to be tired when they looked for him the following morning, then so be it.

Jean put more coffee on and heated the leftover meat pie. Everyone was prepared for a long night.

Eli did his best to stay awake with the grown-ups, but now that the crisis involving his sister was on hold, his eyes began to droop, and soon, he was fast asleep in his father's arms.

Cameron decided to put the little man to bed in the master

bedroom, upstairs. That way, he would be in a familiar bed if he should wake up, but far enough away from whatever new activities this night might offer.

When Cameron returned to the table, the conversation was covering the gamut from the price they got for beef to how everyone was looking forward to getting Ned up to stud and what caliber of foals he'd put on the ground.

The group was wearing out, and most of them felt a little shut-eye might not be such a bad idea. But this notion was put on hold when they all jumped at the sound of the dogs barking again. Jack was out of his chair instantly, making a beeline for the front door. Everyone else was close on his heels.

At first, they couldn't see anything beyond the light from the lantern, and all they could hear was the dogs barking.

Then Cassie trotted into sight, still barking, but with her tail wagging and a look of expectation on her face. The two little dogs came into view next, all excited to join in the welcome and announce the new arrivals.

Jack came down the steps and peered into the darkness. First, he could hear the horse coming slowly towards the porch and then he was able to see the horse. Then he saw his partner, and with a curse under his breath, he ran forward, nearly spooking the tired animal.

"Leon!" Jack reached them and grabbed hold of his partner's arm. "Aw, no. Was he shot?"

"No," Ben assured him, "but his horse was, and he took a nasty fall. I expect he has a concussion, and I know he has a broken collarbone."

David was there then, too, exhausted but still on the job.

"Easy, Jack," he cautioned his friend. "Careful with him."

Ben slowly slid off the horse, then all three men carefully eased Leon out of the saddle.

He groaned quietly, but that was all, while he was gently carried into the house.

Sam stood on the porch, watching the procession, when Ben beckoned him over and indicated the horse waiting some distance off, just barely in the lamplight.

Karma stood with her head down and her legs splayed. She was swaying, and when she tried to take a step toward the men, she staggered and very nearly went down.

"Oh, my goodness!" Sam got on the job. "Let me get a lamp and we'll get her to the barn."

He snatched the lantern from the porch and then approached the mare.

"My poor girl," he commiserated. "C'mon, just a little further back to your stall, and then I'll get you fixed up. You'll feel better soon. C'mon. That's a girl."

Karma staggered again, but she gave it one final effort, knowing that her cozy stall was just a moment away—if she could only get there. She struggled, but she did it, with Sam leading the way and encouraging her with every step.

Ben smiled and shook his head as he led his own horse along behind them. He knew he was going to be staying the night himself, even if it meant sleeping in the barn.

***

Inside the second downstairs bedroom, Jack assisted David in getting Leon settled onto the bed. The doctor did a quick examination, checking his pupils and then the darkening bruise on his forehead, while Jack got his uncle undressed. Leon had some bruising on his torso and his arms, along with some painful-looking scraps on the palms of his hands and all down the right side of his face, but other than that, the only injuries were the ones already being addressed.

"He should be all right." David sighed wearily. "A concussion, for sure, so we'll have to keep an eye on him. But no broken ribs or anything else. Just the collarbone. He'll be all right, Jack."

Jack nodded and breathed a sigh of relief.

"Thank goodness. This is all I need, for both to be . . ."

"I know," David sympathized, "but they're good. Now, help me get this collarbone set and clean all the dirt and gravel out of those scraps. Then, we can all get some rest."

"Yeah, okay."

They were finishing up and getting Leon tucked in when someone tapped on the door.

"Yes?" David responded.

The door quietly opened, and Miranda poked her head in. "Is he all right? May I come in?"

"Yes, by all means," David told her. "He's going to be all right.

A little bruised and battered, but he'll be fine."

"Oh, thank goodness." She came to the bed and sat down. She reached over and took Napoleon's left hand in hers and held it close. Then, she smiled at the two men, feeling silly. "I'm sorry. I probably shouldn't be taking such liberties yet."

"That's all right," David assured her. "I doubt Napoleon would mind you holding his hand."

Jack grinned. Leon always found a way to get his fair share of the feminine attention.

"I didn't expect to be so worried about him," Miranda admitted. "Good heavens! It's not like we're courting or anything."

"Better get used to it," Jack cautioned her. "I've spent most a my life worryin' about Leon, and I ain't never been courtin' 'im either."

David ran a hand through his hair. "Well, Jack, I don't know about you, but I could do with some more coffee. And if Jean has any of that pie left ... that woman is too good a cook."

"Yeah!" Jack brightened. "I could probably eat a little more myself, now that Leon is home safe."

The two men quietly left the room, leaving Miranda sitting on the edge of the bed, holding the hand of her friend.

***

The following morning, Leon woke up with a groan and his head pounding. He moaned and tried to open his eyes, but the light coming in through the window was making that almost impossible. He lay there and felt sorry for himself.

Lil' Mouse was curled up at the foot of his bed and started to purr when she felt him stirring. He could feel her stretch and knew she was yawning, but when he made no further move to get up, she settled and contentedly went back to sleep.

A few more moments passed, and he wondered if he should try to get up when there was a light knock on the door.

"Yes," he croaked, then winced with the pain even this caused his head.

Miranda stepped into the room and smiled at him. She held a cup in her hand and padded over to his bed.

He tried to smile at her but had very little success.

"David told me to give you this as soon as you woke up," she said. "I don't know how Jean knew you were awake, but she did."

Leon nodded, then groaned again. He opened his eyes just wide enough to look at the cup.

"What is it?"

"I believe it's some kind of painkiller," Miranda informed him. "David said to make sure you drink it all, then we were to let you sleep."

"Ohh, good."

"Here." Miranda helped him sit up, then brought the cup to his lips.

He took a drink and snorted at the bitterness of it, and this made his head hurt even more.

"C'mon," Miranda encouraged him. "Drink it down, and then we'll leave you alone."

She pressed the cup to his lips again, and he took it all in.

The taste was a challenge, but just like with his Uncle Makua's medicinal concoctions, he knew it would take the pain away once you got it past your taste buds. He drained the cup.

"Here." Miranda presented a small offering from her pocket.

"What's that?"

"A piece of maple candy. It'll help take the taste away."

"Oh." Leon accepted it and placed it in his mouth. His eyes closed as the sweet maple melted and coated his throat. "Mmm, these are good."

He opened his eyes again as he leaned back against the pillow. "How's Karma?" he asked in a whisper.

"Sam's taking good care of her," Miranda assured him. "It seems he has learned a thing or two from Deke. Karma's resting in her stall with Midnight standing by for company."

"Oh ... good . . ."

"Hmm."

He closed his eyes but then jerked himself awake. "How's Penny?"

Miranda smiled at his priorities. "David says she'll be fine. She has a lot of healing to do, though."

"Hmm." He nodded ever so slightly and then, with the candy melted away, he allowed the sedative to encompass him.

Miranda sat with him and held his hand until he fell back to sleep. She smiled and, leaning forward, gave him a gentle kiss on the cheek.

She made sure he was snugly tucked in, gave the cat a scratch on the ear, and then quietly left the room.

***

Sheriff Carl Jacobs sat at the table, sharing a pot of coffee with Cameron and Jack. He was busy taking notes.

"And you never saw anything?" he reiterated. "Never got a look at the shooter?"

"No," Jack told him for the umpteenth time. "We didn't see anybody."

"What about Mr. Nash?" Jacobs asked. "He went after him. Did he see anything?"

"I dunno, Sheriff. You're gonna have ta ask him."

Jacobs looked up as Miranda came out of the bedroom.

"Is he awake, ma'am?"

"No," Miranda answered. "And even when he was, I doubt he would have been up to answering any questions. David said to give him a couple of days."

"Yeah, I know," Jacobs sighed, "but by that time, the suspect is gonna be long gone."

"I don't know about that, Carl," Cameron said. "We thought he was long gone after the July incident. But he stuck around—or came back."

"I suppose we can't call that an accident anymore, can we?" Jacobs said. "It looks like we've got ourselves a real problem here."

Silence settled over the table, nobody wanting to accept the apparent truth of this statement.

Jean came out of the first bedroom. She looked tired and worn, but when Cameron sent her a questioning glance, she smiled at him and put him at ease. "She's fine. David gave her enough medication to knock her out for the day. Sleep is the best thing for her right now."

Both Jean and Miranda went over to the table and sat down.

The coffee carafe made the rounds again.

Eli ate his oatmeal, his large eyes traveling around to the various people sitting at the table—he had no intention of missing out on anything.

"Well, Cameron," Jacobs broke the silence. "I know you've been thinking about it, and now I have to ask ya: do you know of anyone who might have any grudge against you? It could be anything, even something that would appear minor to you and me. Or anyone you're not sure about, who might be capable of going to this extreme to get even for something."

Cameron sighed and shook his head. "I don't know, Carl. I've always tried to treat people fairly, you know that. I can't think of anyone I know who would be willing to do such a thing."

"Kenny said much the same thing when we were visitin' with 'im," Jack commented. "He didn't think for a minute that the incident in July was just an accident. He has offered ta help with information if we manage to get anything to go on."

"That's very good of him," Cameron commented. "I wish I had something to give him, but..." he shook his head. He wasn't coming up with anything.

"Yeah." Jacobs knew that what they had wasn't much. "Well, just keep it in mind. If anything comes to ya, let me know, all right?"

"Of course."

"And, as soon as Mr. Nash can talk, I need to question him. You too, Kiefer. Maybe this isn't about Cameron at all. Maybe it's about you and your partner."

"Yeah, I know," Jack said. "But why not just go after Leon or me? Why go after Penny?"

"Because she matters to you," Jacobs stated. "This whole thing could be about seeing you suffer and lose someone important to you. Killing you might be the final goal, not the beginning. And how do you know this shooter wasn't aiming for you or Nash and missed?"

"Oh, c'mon," Jack snarked. "Penny was the one attacked in July. And now this. Unless you're suggestin' we have two crazy people comin' after us."

Jacobs sighed. "That is unlikely."

"Yeah."

"Well, as I said, if either of ya' can think of anyone capable of this, get in touch. And I still need ta talk with Nash."

"We'll let you know when he's able, Carl."

"All right." Jacobs took one last gulp of coffee, then got to his feet. "I best be getting back to town. You folks take care."

Cameron stood up to see him out. "Okay, Carl. We'll talk soon."

"Yup. Good day to ya."

Cameron returned to the table and sat down with a sigh. "What a day."

"I can't believe this is happening," Jean admitted. "Perhaps when Penny is feeling up to it, we should send her to Denver, to stay with Caroline and Steven for a while."

"Whoever this is would probably just follow her there," Cameron pointed out. "At least here, we can keep an eye on her, make sure there's always somebody with her."

"There were five of us with her yesterday," Jack pointed out, "it didn't stop 'im." Silence again. Jack looked at Jean and Cameron, sorrow and regret on his face. "I guess we'd better postpone the weddin', huh? At least until we get this sorted out."

"Oh dear," Jean slumped. "Penny will be so disappointed. But yes, I suppose that would be for the best."

***

A few days later, Leon was up and about, and the first thing he did was take a slow walk over to the barn to check up on his mare.

He went into the coolness of the structure and breathed in the fresh summer scent of sweet hay and sunshine. He felt better, although he probably wouldn't be if not for the painkillers the good doctor had him on. His right arm was in a sling, and he still sported quite the goose egg on his forehead, along with the angry red scrapes down his face and on his hands. Still, he had to admit that even though he felt a little shaky, he was on the mend.

He walked in through the open barn door and was instantly met with welcoming nickers. He smiled at the two horses looking at him, and hoping for some grain or an apple, something—surely, he wouldn't be coming into the barn empty-handed. His smile grew into a grin as he slid two carrots from inside his sling and offered one to each of the horses.

Midnight happily accepted his and munched it down in no time flat.

Karma was pickier. She sniffed it, then played her upper lip around it. Once she was sure it was a carrot, she nibbled at it, took a tentative bite off the top, and slowly munched it down. She snapped off another bite while Leon held it steady and chuckled at her daintiness.

He waited as his mare finished her carrot, then stepped in closer to give her nose a rub and her neck a pat. She was looking better, but still not quite up to snuff, as her pupils were dilated with the painkiller that Sam gave her in her grain.

The bullet crease on the top of her head was drying up and would soon scab over. Fortunately, any scarring would eventually be completely covered up by her forelock. The same could not be said for the injury on her shoulder, where she had skidded along the ground. It still looked raw and painful, and though Sam kept it clean and had stitched it back together, it would leave quite a scar.

Leon smiled and rubbed her neck while she settled her head against his chest and cuddled.

"Well, join the club," he told her, whimsically. "I suppose we're all sporting battle scars now. But you're still my beautiful girl."

"Oh, really?" came a voice from the barn door. "I didn't realize I had such strong competition."

Leon's eyes lit up as Miranda strolled down the aisle to stand beside the stall. She smiled and stroked the mare. "She is quite beautiful."

Leon just nodded. "So much for guard dogs. I didn't even hear the buggy."

"Oh, no. I rented a horse from town and rode out." Miranda smiled at her audacity. "I'm beginning to enjoy riding. There's so much more freedom on horseback compared to being stuck in a buggy. I'll be glad when you're up and about again, so we can go for more rides together."

"Yes," Leon beamed. "That'll be fun. So, you came out by yourself?"

"Yes."

"Hmm. Well, I believe Jean is in the house with Penny, if you came to see them."

"I didn't come to see them."

"Ohh."

She gave him a stern look. "You had us all quite worried, you know, when you took off like that. Are you always prone to being so impulsive?"

Leon sighed. "No, not normally. That was stupid." He gave Karma a quiet pat as regret passed over his features. "I nearly got both of us killed."

"That would have been a shame," Miranda commented, then

smiled. “As I said, she is quite a beautiful mare.”

“Ohh,” Leon repeated, “so, it’s Karma you came out to see.”

Miranda chuckled. “Don’t be an ass. Of course, I came out to see you.”

Leon couldn’t hold back the smile of pleasure.

“Oh, well,” he teased, “it was kind of hard to tell, you know—I wasn’t sure.”

And then, it happened again: he got trapped inside those dark blue eyes that were laughing at him. His left hand slid around her waist and she moved easily into his embrace, though she was careful to stay away from his right shoulder.

Her arms went around him, and she leaned in, staring into those pools of warm chocolate, and she began to melt.

He came forward and kissed her, gently, at first, then with a little more passion—a little more heat.

Then, he winced in pain as a dark redhead butted into his right shoulder. He sucked his teeth as he pulled away and sent an irritated look toward his mare.

Karma tossed her head and pinned her ears. She stuck out her nose and pushed him again. She was not pleased.

“Karma ... what . . .?”

Miranda laughed. “Oh dear—she’s jealous!”

“What?” Leon was incredulous. “What do you mean, jealous? She’s a horse!”

“Yes, but she’s also a female,” Miranda pointed out, “and you’re a male—her male!” She laughed again at the bewildered look that crossed Leon’s face. “She doesn’t want to share you with anybody—especially another female.”

“Oh, that’s just—”

Before he could finish, Karma gave Leon a slight nip on the arm. With her ears back, she began to toss her head again, even though the movement caused her discomfort.

Miranda couldn’t help it and continued to laugh. “That’s all right.” She put a reassuring hand on Karma’s neck. But the mare was having none of it, and she pinned her ears flatter and took a quick snipe at her rival. “Whoops!” Miranda stepped back and laughed even harder.

“Karma!” Leon reprimanded her, feeling embarrassed over his mare’s behavior.

"No, don't worry about it, Napoleon. I know when I'm beaten. Look, I'll go and visit with Jean while you placate your mare." She continued to laugh. "I'll see you at the house when you're ready."

"I'm sorry," Leon said. "I don't understand what's gotten into her."

Miranda grinned at him, her eyes dancing. "I do. No need to apologize. I'll see you at the house."

"Yes, all right."

Miranda left the barn, and Leon turned a reproving eye to his mare, but he couldn't stay mad at her. As soon as Miranda was gone, Karma's ears came forward, and she nuzzled up, affectionately, to her human.

Leon laughed and stroked her neck.

"You silly old thing," he teased her. "How am I supposed to make any progress with you behaving like that?"

Karma reached over and nibbled on his buttons.

CHAPTER ELEVEN
CAUSE AND EFFECT

The days gradually lengthened as summer waned and life at the Rocking M began to relax into a routine again.

Penny was healing and growing increasingly mobile as the weeks passed. She was frustrated by her lack of energy, though, and still needed an afternoon nap to get through the day.

She was just waking up from such a nap when she heard a soft tapping on the door and Jack's voice coming through.

"Are you awake, Darlin'? Can I come in?"

"Yes." Penny frowned, and she put a hand on her sore throat. She coughed a little to clear it. "Yes, come in, Jack."

Jack softly opened the door and stepped inside. He smiled at her, thinking how beautiful she was with her bedroom eyes and ruffled hair. He came to the bed, sat in the chair beside it, then took her hand.

"How ya' feelin'?"

"Good." She then scratched at the bandage on her neck. "I just wish this would stop itching. I know that's a sign that it's healing, but it's irritating."

"I expect it'll be comin' off soon. You'll be all healed up before ya know it."

"David said I'm going to have a scar there. That's not very attractive. Especially when I start wearing my hair up."

"A scar ain't nothin' ta be ashamed of," Jack said. "Me and Leon have our share, and now, with you havin' one, it'll make ya part of the gang."

Penny smiled at that and then glanced out the window. "What time is it?"

"Almost time for supper. You gonna join us again?"

"Of course," Penny stated as a matter of fact. "I really should get up and help Momma with the preparations."

"Ha! No, you shouldn't, Darlin'. Yur ma wouldn't let ya, anyway."

Penny nodded, and then she dipped her chin as sadness settled into her eyes.

Jack frowned and squeezed her hand. "What is it, Darlin'?"

Penny sighed and sent him a quiet smile. "Our wedding date has come and gone, hasn't it?"

"Oh." Jack slumped. "Yeah, it has. We kinda hoped ya wouldn't notice."

Now it was Penny's turn to laugh. "Of course, I noticed. I had a good cry over it once I realized, but that only hurt my throat more than it already was. I'm sorry, Jack."

"Ain't nuthin' ta be sorry about." He leaned in and caressed her cheek. "We'll have our weddin' day. It's just gonna be a longer engagement than we thought."

"And I'm going to focus on not feeling sorry for myself," Penny squared her shoulders and jutted her chin. "I'm going to focus on getting better as quickly as I can. There is nothing like an incentive to get things done."

"Haw, haw. That's my girl. Now, you best get up or I'll eat your share of supper."

"I'll get up as soon as you leave."

Jack got to his feet and then sent her a cheeky smile. "You sure ya don't need help gettin' up?"

Penny cocked a brow at him. "You rascal! I'm quite sure I can manage on my own. Now get."

Jack leaned over and kissed her on the forehead. "I'll see ya out there."

***

Dinner was a casual affair, and Penny did her best to swallow her food even though it still hurt to do so.

"Just eat the mashed potatoes," Jean suggested when she noticed her daughter's struggles. "I cooked the carrots a little longer, so they'd be softer for you."

Penny glanced at the carrots with a disdain she tried to hide. Carrots had never been her favorite. "I know, Momma. Thank you. I am enjoying the potatoes and gravy. They actually feel good on my throat. I like chicken too, but," she grimaced at the slices of white meat on her plate. "It still hurts to eat it."

"Do the best you can," Jean told her, then cocked a brow at Leon. "Speaking of eating, Napoleon, you can't possibly be done already."

Leon sighed. He had hoped nobody would notice. "I'm sorry. It's a fine dinner, Jean, I'm just not hungry tonight."

"That's what you say every night."

"I got another telegram from Caroline today," Cameron said by way of changing the subject. "She still wants to come visit."

Penny perked up. "Oh, that would be—"

"I told her no."

Penny slumped. "Oh."

"I'm sorry, Sweetheart," Cameron continued. "But it's obvious someone has targeted this family. I don't want Caroline anywhere near this ranch until we get this settled. Especially with Rosie. I expect Steven agrees with me on this."

"I know," Penny said and then smiled at her father. "But it would have been nice to see her. I miss her."

"Speakin' a gettin' this settled," Jack said as he reached for more chicken, "Has Sheriff Jacobs come across any more information?"

"Unfortunately, no," Cameron informed them all. "Both he and Ben have been out to the scene of the crime more than once, looking for any clues to the identity of the shooter, but aside from the spent bullet that had lodged in the trunk of the willow tree, they came up with nothing."

Leon and Jack shared a quick glance.

"Oh, I saw that," Jean laughed. "You two think you're so subtle."

Leon and Jack both shrugged, trying to look innocent.

"What?" Jack asked over a mouthful.

Penny giggled. "Don't you think we've known you long enough now to be able to pick up on your little silent communications?"

"Oh." Leon smiled at having been caught.

"It was pretty obvious," Cameron agreed. "I can't imagine how we missed it before."

"So, out with it," Jean told them. "What are you two thinking?"

"Umm, well . . ." Leon looked at Jack, who shrugged in agreement. "Okay," Leon continued. "We were thinking it might be time to pull in a professional on this."

"What do you mean?" Cameron asked. "Sheriff Jacobs is the best lawman I know."

"Oh, nothing against Jacobs," Leon assured. "But I mean a detective. Someone who is trained to track down leads. It's their job; it's what they're good at."

"Yes, that makes sense. Do you have anyone in mind?"

"Frank Carlyle," Leon said. "He's a bit hard to take, but he knows his job, and he does owe us."

Cameron and Jean shared their own look of communication.

Cameron nodded. "Okay. If you fellas recommend him. When can he get here?"

"That's a bit of a rub," Leon told him.

"Yeah," Jack said. "He ain't always easy ta get hold of. He might even be outta the country. But we'll try."

"I'll be in town tomorrow to see David," Leon said. "I'll send a telegram to Wells Fargo. With any luck, he might even be there."

***

The following day
In town

Leon flinched slightly as David worked the muscles in his upper arm.

"Still sore?" the doctor asked.

"You know it is," Leon griped. "But it is getting better."

"Yes, it is. You've been getting back to your stretches, and it's made a difference. However, . . ."

"I knew it," Leon complained. "There's always a 'however'. What is it?"

David straightened up. "You're losing weight again. What's wrong? You were doing so well during the summer. I thought we had this beat."

Leon sighed in frustration as he pulled his undershirt on over his head.

"I know," he muffled through his shirt, then pulled his arms through and tucked it in. "It's certainly not Jean's cooking; I just can't eat. My stomach turns into a knot every time I try to put food into it."

David sat down and watched him pull on his outer shirt and finish getting dressed. "Have the nightmares started up again?"

Leon sat, then finger-combed his hair back into place.

"Yes," he admitted. "They were easing off until Penny got shot, and now they're back worse than ever."

"Worse?" David frowned. "I find that hard to imagine."

"Me, too. Until they started. Now, they're more about Penny. I see her dying in every sort of horrible, painful fashion that my imagination can come up with. There's no one I can talk to about these. I'm sure not going to mention them to Jean or Jack, either. I'm not comfortable discussing this with Miranda yet, either." Leon shrugged. "So, I'm stuck."

"You're not stuck, Napoleon. You know you can talk to me about these things. In fact, I would prefer that you do. The more you tell me, the better I can treat you. It's a win/win."

"I just wish things would settle down," Leon said. "I used to thrive on challenges and puzzles to work out. Now, I don't even want to face them. I don't want upheaval. Even Jack and Penny's wedding has been postponed. I think that upset me more than it did them. I feel at loose ends, David. I was so looking forward to Jack's wedding . . ."

Leon's voice trailed off, and he sat quietly, hanging his head.

David watched him for a moment, feeling at loose ends himself.

"Don't give up on it," he said. "I've sent some inquiries to friends back East. I'm hoping they've had some experience with nightmares and mental trauma. Perhaps there's even some written material available that could help. This is similar to what Jack went through after his trial, but he was blocking things out—hiding from them. Finally getting him to talk about it all is what got him on the path to healing. But this is not your situation." The doctor was discouraged. Then he smiled and patted Leon on the shoulder again. "Well, let's wait until I hear from back East. Hopefully, they'll have some suggestions. We'll get to the bottom of this, Napoleon. One way or another."

"Hmm," Leon was noncommittal. "In the meantime, I think I'll go get a drink and maybe play a hand or two of poker if there's a game going on. Cameron won't let me work too hard until my collarbone is completely healed. I keep telling him I'm fine, but he won't believe me."

David chuckled. "Cameron is being protective of you, isn't he?"

Leon nodded with emphasis. "It's like he thinks I'm going to break."

"I'll talk to him," David said. "Your shoulder is fine now, and a little physical work would probably be good for you—might just get your appetite happening again."

"Thank you!"

"Mm-hmm. I'll see you later."

***

Leon walked the short distance along the residential road and then turned onto Main Street on his way to the saloon. He was irritated by the sudden apprehension that settled over him. None of them were feeling safe anymore, but everything pointed to the assailant being gone.

In the old Napoleon Nash fashion, Leon was determined not to allow fear of what might happen to rule his days. He wanted to go to the saloon, so he was going to go. That's it. Vendetta be damned.

He quickened his pace and survived the journey unscathed. Then, as long habit dictated, he stopped upon entering and did a quick scan of the room and the patrons there. The main difference now was that, rather than hoping not to see anyone he knew, he would have been happy to see some familiar faces.

Just about every face in town was now familiar to him, and he nodded in greeting to the few who were partaking of the wares. But there was no poker game going on, so Leon continued to the bar.

"Afternoon, Bill."

"Hey there, Nash." Bill didn't even look up from wiping a beer mug. "What'll ya have?"

Leon considered for a moment. Much to his surprise, the home brew that he had voted for during the Fourth of July celebrations had won the day, and since he did like it, he ordered it.

"How about a glass of Mr. Woodcock's Twisted Horseshoe Summer Ale?"

Bill smiled; this brew had been selling well for him. "Sure thing. Comin' right up." Bill poured out the beer and set it, along with a plate of boiled eggs, on the counter. "Here ya go. Eggs are on the house when ya order this brew."

Leon frowned at him. "Since when?"

"Well, since I say so, that's since when." Then he snatched up his rag and busied himself with wiping down the bar.

Leon looked at the eggs and wondered if everyone in town could tell he was losing weight. Then he shrugged, picked up the plate and his glass, and went over to a small table in the corner. He settled in to relax and people-watch before heading back to the ranch to help with evening chores. He had only been sitting there for a few minutes when Ben Palin entered and did his own quick scan of the room.

He spotted Leon and made his way over.

Leon shifted uncomfortably and, much to his annoyance, found himself tensing up and becoming anxious.

"Afternoon, Nash," Ben greeted him. "Mind if I sit down for a minute?"

Leon forced a smile. "By all means, Deputy. Something official come up?"

"No," Ben admitted, then appeared uncomfortable, himself. "Actually ... well, ever since you got released from prison, I've been kind of avoiding you."

"Yes," Leon nodded. "I guess I noticed."

"I didn't know how to respond to you," Ben hesitated, but persevered. "I was real mad at you for a long time."

Leon dropped his eyes and nodded. He knew where this was going.

Ben continued with his explanation. "Warden Mitchell told us you were the one who was responsible for my uncle's death. My uncle befriended you, and you betrayed and then killed him."

Leon felt his throat tighten with old emotions. He nodded again and took a swallow of beer, then nearly choked on it when his throat wouldn't open to let it down. He covered his mouth with his hand until he could swallow, then sent the young deputy an apologetic smile.

"Sorry." He rasped a cough, then took another drink. "I didn't do it, Ben. You know that now, don't you?"

"Yeah," he nodded. "Jack Kiefer made a point of convincing me otherwise. But I still ... I don't know. I suppose seeing you back here brought all that up again, and I started thinking that maybe you actually had done it, and your partner was just covering for ya. So, I decided the best thing for me to do would be to stay away from you to make sure I wouldn't do something I might regret later."

"Hmm. And now? You still think that, maybe, I did it?"

"No." Ben gave a cockeyed smile, then shook his head. "I've had some time to watch you, and I see the way you are with Miss Marsham and Dr. Gibson's cousin. I see the way you interact with the fellas here in the saloon. Jack was tellin' the truth; you're not a killer. I know you didn't do it. So, I want to apologize for some of the things I imagined doing to you."

Leon chuckled. "Yeah, okay." The smile dropped, and he looked Ben in the eye. "I really was fond of your uncle. He took me under his wing and offered friendship when I sorely needed one. He taught me a lot, too. He was a good man, Ben. He didn't deserve the end he got."

"Yeah, I know. I sure do miss him."

Leon tried to brighten things up. "He told me you were thinking about going back East and studying criminology. Make this line of work official and work for Pinkerton's or Wells Fargo. You still planning that?"

Ben sighed with some regret, then shrugged. "I dunno. I was thinking about it, but it's expensive, and my folks need me here. I like it here too, and Sheriff Jacobs is a good man to work for."

"Hmm," Leon nodded. "It's a nice town; you could do worse."

"Yeah." Ben became quiet for a moment, then looked at the ex-convict. "You know, my uncle is buried in the cemetery here. You'd be welcome to go pay respects if you'd like."

"Yeah," Leon mumbled, looking into his beer. "I thought I'd wait until he stopped visiting me before I went to visit him."

Ben frowned. "What?"

Leon straightened up and smiled. "Never mind. Thank you—you're right; I will go see him."

"Good. Well, I suppose I should get back to my rounds."

"Before you leave, Deputy . . ."

"Yes?"

"Has anything new turned up on Penny's case? Were you able to speak with the gals at the Black Rose?"

"Oh yeah, I spoke with them, but you know how they are. The Madam there runs a tight ship. I get along with the girls okay, but they still won't talk about the johns in any detail. I suppose they'd get fired if they did. Bad for business."

"Hmm, yeah, I suppose."

"One of them, Massie, I think. She looked like she'd run into a fist or two, but again, they won't talk."

"All right. Thanks, Deputy. At least you tried."

"Yup." Ben thought about it. "Maybe another woman would have more luck. What about your friend in Denver? What's her name? Isn't she in that line of work?"

Leon nearly choked on his egg.

"If you're speaking of Josephine, don't ever tell her she's a common brothel whore. She's a 'Companion', and she makes sure everybody knows it. Besides, she's anything but subtle. The Madam here would likely view her as competition and clam up even more."

"Oh, yeah. Well, just a thought," Ben said, and then stood and offered Leon his hand. "Good to see ya healed up—and Miss Marsham too. It's a shame we haven't been able to get to the bottom of that."

Leon stood and shook the deputy's hand. "It ain't over yet, Ben. We'll find out who it is."

"Yeah. Well, just remember the conditions of your parole, Nash," Ben reminded him. "I'd hate to see ya get into trouble over this."

Leon cocked an ironic smile. "Oh, don't worry, Deputy; my friends aren't about to let me forget about it."

"Good. Let me know if you need anything."

"I sure will."

Ben turned to leave as Leon sat back down, but then Leon remembered something he wanted to add. "Oh, Ben—"

"Yes?"

"Ahh, thanks for coming after me. That was a stupid thing for me to do. I wasn't thinking straight. So—thank you."

"You're welcome. I'll see ya around."

"Yeah."

***

Autumn 1889

Gradually, the days got shorter and the nights colder. Winter coats were pulled out of chests, and all the horses changed from sleek to shaggy almost overnight.

Jack and Penny sat together on the sofa, relaxing by the warm fire after a good supper.

"It's good ta see ya doin' so much better," Jack told her. "You're almost back to your old self."

"Yes. Except that I expected to be Mrs. Kiefer by now."

"That's still gonna happen. Ya have my word on that."

"Hmm. What about a Christmas wedding?"

"Christmas?" Jack frowned. "I doubt we'll have this situation cleared up by then. Even with Frank on his way, he ain't gonna work that fast."

"Oh, I suppose. Bad weather could make it hard for some people to get here for it, too."

"Yeah. I invited Kenny and his family. They gotta come from Wyoming. Same with Taggard and Martha."

"Yes, yes, all right," Penny laughed and patted Jack's hand. "It was just a thought. But a most impractical one."

Leon walked by the living room on his way to the front door.

"There you are, hiding behind your fiancée."

"Yeah. What of it?"

"C'mon, help me with the evening feeding. It'll get done faster with both of us doing it."

"I dunno, Leon. I kinda like sittin' here by the warm fire with my current companion. You go on ahead, though, and take your time."

"Fine!" Leon snarked as he pulled on his coat and boots. "Then you can get up early and do the morning feeding. How do you like that?"

The next thing they heard was the front door slamming shut.

"Oh dear," Penny chuckled. "He's in a mood. You are going to help him, aren't you?"

"Yeah, of course. I was just teasin'. He'd know that if his brain weren't addled due to lack of food. Besides, he still tires out quick. He won't admit it, but he needs help ta get through this stuff. I'll be right back, Darlin'."

Jack stood, then leaning over, he tucked Penny's long hair behind her ear and placed a series of butterfly kisses along the scar on her neck.

Penny giggled. "That tickles."

"I like your scar," Jack whispered in her ear. "As I said, it makes ya one of the gang now."

***

The temperatures began to drop as the dark of night arrived earlier with each passing day. September and October passed without event, but the overall mood at the Rocking M was undermined by lingering anxiety.

Mucking out the horse barn was a pleasant chore when the weather was decent, but when things changed toward winter, Leon wasn't the only one struggling with his moods.

"Dang, it's cold." Jack pulled off his damp gloves and blew on his hands. "It ain't so bad when the sun's shining, but this rain ain't no fun at all."

"Hmm." Leon plopped a wet forkful of manure into the wheelbarrow. "Even the horses don't want to be out in this. I can feel the pressure from them to hurry up."

To punctuate Leon's words, a pleading whinny came from the pasture gate.

Jack straightened up and leaned on his pitchfork. "I see what ya mean."

"Yeah."

"You okay, Leon? Are ya gettin' tired?"

"Naw, I'm fine. Just wet and cold. Let's hurry up and get this done. I feel the sofa and a warm fire calling to me."

"So, your grouchy mood ain't got nothin' ta do with ya over-exerting yourself?"

"No!" Leon snarked. "It has to do with being cold and wet."

"Ah. And knowin' that Miranda ain't likely ta come out for her visit today? That ain't buggin' ya?"

The moody silence from the other stall told Jack all he needed to know.

"You can hardly blame her."

Heavy sigh from next door. "I don't blame her. It's just . . ."

"What?"

"Well ... I feel better when I'm around her, that's all. I don't like feeling depressed, and she helps to lift me out of it at least for a while."

"I know what ya mean. Penny kinda does the same for me."

"Yeah. Miranda and I aren't ready for that step yet. I don't know if I'll ever be ready to do that again."

"What? Get married?"

"Yeah."

"Kinda early days." Jack dumped another forkful into the wheelbarrow and then stepped to the aisleway. "Has Miranda indicated that she wants ta move forward?"

"No. I think she understands. I have stuff to work out. And she's still in mourning, so neither of us is in a hurry."

"Good."

"Yeah." Leon dumped one last damp forkful into his wheelbarrow, then straightened and stretched his back. "I was just looking forward to seeing her today."

"Uh-huh. I'm done here. How about you?"

"Yup. I'll get hay in the stalls if you wanna sweep the aisle."

"Okay."

Once the final cleaning up was done, Jack pulled open the back door of the barn.

Both men stood there with their full wheelbarrows, watching the sheet of rain come down.

Several shrill whinnies came from the pasture.

The two men looked at each other.

"Well," Jack grumbled. "We might as well get her done."

"Yup."

Then, in tandem, they leaned into their wheelbarrows and made the sloppy dash to the manure pile.

***

That evening, the storm not only continued but intensified its assault.

During this time of year, autumn storms were to be expected, but with everything else going on, the banging and clanging of the blustering winds did not help to calm nerves already on edge. They tried to stay occupied with indoor chores or entertainment during the wilder storms, but it seemed only the cat knew how to appreciate a warm bed by the stove and a roof that didn't leak.

The wind howled around the eaves of the Rocking M, competing for attention with the rain driving into the windowpanes. But the thunderclap, roaring and crashing in the heavens, triumphantly proclaimed superiority over such a piffling cacophony.

Jean frowned as she looked up from her darning.

"What a horrible night," she commented as the lightning flash lit up the room. "Still a few miles before it's right over us."

She smiled at the scene of domesticity lit by the golden light of the oil lamps.

Jack and Leon were playing a game of cards with Cameron at the dining table, while Penny was knitting a Christmas gift for her sister. The cat was curled up on the rag mat in front of the fireplace. It would have been a perfect scene if not for the niggling worm of worry in the background.

Jean sighed and looked down at her work, rubbing the bridge of her nose and blinking away the strain. Perhaps it would be better to do this in daylight; the lamplight was causing too many shadows. She set the sock aside and relaxed into the rocking chair, thinking it was probably time for bed. It had been a long, hard day.

Another boom of thunder distracted Cameron from the game, and, picking up on his wife's thoughts, he made his own prediction.

"I doubt any of us will get much sleep with this storm. I'm surprised Eli is—Oh, never mind."

Eli, all rumpled from a restless bed, appeared at the bottom of the stairs, his fists rubbed tired eyes that fought to hold back childish tears.

Another crack of thunder, accompanied by flashes of light and an increase of pounding rain, won over the boy's bravado.

"Momma!" Bare feet scurried over the carpet, then launched the child into his mother's lap. "I'm scared."

"Oh, Sweetheart." Jean smiled at her husband as she wrapped her arms around her trembling son. "It's just thunder. You've heard that before."

More crashing from outside caused Eli to squiggle in close. "It's too loud."

Leon sat back, no longer able to focus on the game. "It is loud."

"Uh-huh." Jack nodded in agreement, then turned his attention to the child. "But ya know what, Eli? Me and your Uncle Leon used ta spend nights like this sleepin' on the range, just hopin' we could find a cave, or even a rock face, for cover. Seems ta me ya got it pretty good."

Eli pouted. He wasn't interested in hearing how good he had it.

"Since you brought it up," Cameron pinned down the two men at the table. "I can't spare both of you, so have you decided who is taking the buckboard into town tomorrow?"

One look of dread, the other of smug satisfaction, was the response to this query.

"We tossed a coin." Jack's smile widened, "and I won. Leon's goin'."

Cameron switched his gaze. "Your coin let you down this time, did it?"

Leon slumped and then cringed as another thundering boom rattled the rafters. The rain pounded against the shuttered windows.

"I'm sure this storm will pass over soon," he attempted to look on the bright side. "It'll probably be a nice, sunny morning."

***

The rain beat down upon the muddy streets of Arvada as Leon pulled the team of wet horses to a halt under the large loafing shed attached to the backside of the mercantile. Looking over his shoulder, he backed the team up until the rear of the buckboard kissed the edge of the loading bay.

He set the brake, then, organizing his heavily oiled slicker around himself, stiffly climbed down from the seat.

"Howdy."

Leon turned towards the fresh-faced teenager who tended the warehouse. Beads of water dripped through his line of vision, but he still smiled and gave his black hat a tip, splattering more water into the air.

"Good morning." Both men glanced out at the sheet of rain and wondered if this was an appropriate greeting. Leon's smile broadened. "Is Mr. Marsham's order ready?"

"Yup. Got it all stacked and ready to load. Ya bring a tarp with ya?"

"Sure did. It's in the bed along with a rope. It should be enough."

The lad glanced into the back of the buckboard. "I suppose. As long as the wind don't pick up again."

"Hmm." Leon was already bored with this conversation. "Is the team all right to leave here? I want to get a bite to eat and something to take the chill off before I head back."

"Sure. When we're done loadin', I'll park 'em over there under the lean-to. They'll be fine. I'll even give 'em some hay if ya want."

"Yeah, thanks. I shouldn't be too long."

The lad shrugged his indifference and set about his task.

Leon looked out at the wall of rain and hesitated.

Was lunch really that important? He sure could use a cup of

coffee, though. He turned and looked in the direction of the Gibson residence and wondered if he should swing by in the hopes of seeing Miranda.

He sighed and dismissed that thought. It would be rude to show up dripping and expecting coffee when they didn't even know he was in town. And what if Miranda wasn't there? Tricia would probably invite him in anyway, even though she likely had her hands full with a home-bound youngster driving her to distraction.

Checking the boarding house was pointless, since the proprietor, Mrs. Agnes Hardcastle, did not permit men to call on her female tenants. If Miranda did decide to purchase her own home in town, then calling upon her would be easier, though, perhaps, not appropriate. Leon was sure he could be discreet.

Resigning himself to his caffeine addiction, he pulled his slicker snugly around and stepped into the wet.

He sloshed across the street, his black, knee-high boots turning brown with mud, as more water dripped continuously from the brim of his hat. He spied the telegraph office and, since it came before the cafe, decided to check in there first.

He went up the steps just in time to nearly bump into an elderly lady on her way out.

He stepped back and tipped his hat. "Excuse me, ma'am."

She frowned as water from his hat splattered on her face. "Good heavens. Watch what you're doing."

"Oh. Sorry. It is an awfully wet day to be out and about, isn't it?"

"Must needs, young man. Must needs."

"Yes, ma'am."

"Don't just stand there like an oaf. Didn't the good lord endow you with enough manners to assist an old lady down the steps?"

"Yes, ma'am." Leon hid his irritation at the reprimand as he pulled the wet glove off his right hand. "Excuse me, I wasn't thinking."

"I can certainly see that."

But her disappointment with the attitudes of the younger generation did not hinder her expectations, and she clasped Leon's hand as she stepped down onto the boardwalk.

"Have a nice day." Leon almost tipped his hat again, but decided against it.

"Humph." The lady waved him away. "Hard to have a nice day

with weather like this. Be off with you now."

Leon twitched a smile. "Yes, ma'am."

Leon entered the office and dripped all over the interior floor just long enough to be told there wasn't anything for the ranch. With a defeated sigh, he then left to brave the elements again.

***

Leon walked along the boardwalk, careful not to slip upon its wet surface. He glanced over his shoulder to ensure he was alone, which was a safe bet on such a day, and then he tucked in under an awning. He pulled off his left glove and unfolded the note that had migrated effortlessly from the elderly lady's hand into his.

He frowned at the written words, smudged from the wet, but still legible.

I'm at the hotel, room 202. Come at once. G.

He glanced at the mentioned establishment ahead of him, his first instinct suspecting a trap. With all the things going on lately, he didn't think it was unreasonable to be cautious. Then his curiosity got the best of him, and though he would have appreciated Jack's company as backup, he headed for the hotel.

Bypassing the front desk, which was unoccupied anyway, he went up the stairway two steps at a time, then turned down the hallway, keeping his eyes and ears alert.

Everything was quiet and normal. Nothing to be concerned about. At lcast, not yet.

Leon stopped at room 202 and brought his hand up to knock. He hesitated, debating if he wanted to open this can of worms, even though he didn't know what kind of worms they were. He sighed, knowing he couldn't turn away from it now. He had to know.

He raised his knuckle and rapped upon the door.

"Come in."

He instantly recognized the quivering tones of the elderly woman. He hesitated again. This was strange. Then, making his decision, he buckled down, opened the door, and stepped into the room.

No one was there.

"Hello?"

"Yes. Do come in." The voice came from behind the dressing screen. "And lock the door behind you."

A shiver of apprehension went through Leon.

Lock the door behind me? What the hell?

"Hurry up," came the voice again, only this time it didn't carry the hesitant undertones of an older woman, but the strong, vibrant accent of a deeply buried memory.

Leon stood, struck dumb with surprise as she stepped out from behind the screen.

She had discarded her wet clothing, along with the gray-haired wig and the layers of theatrical make-up that had completed her disguise. She stood before him, wrapped in a housecoat as she combed out her thick, red hair.

"Gabriella."

"Don't just stand there. Close the door and lock it. And take off that slicker and—oh, saints preserve us, you're still wearing that same hat! Well, take them off and hang them on the coat tree. You're dripping all over the floor."

Leon blinked and came back to himself enough to close the door, but from there, he stood motionless, gazing upon the woman before him. His senses were in turmoil. His first impulse was to go to her, take her in his arms, and taste those warm, sensuous lips pressing against his.

But his second impulse kept him rooted to the spot. The hurt he thought he'd long buried stabbed through his heart. He couldn't take his eyes off her, as though he were witnessing a horrendous turmoil of events and yet not able to turn away from the inevitable disaster.

A sudden knocking behind him brought him spinning around and going for his gun. The slicker got in his way, and he fumbled, getting angry as he whipped the heavy material aside and finally got the gun in his hand.

Another knock from the other side of the door was followed by an enquiring voice. "You ordered lunch brought up, ma'am?"

The broken, elderly voice responded. "Yes, thank you, young man. Just leave it there. I'll get it."

"Yes, ma'am. Let us know if you need anything else."

"Of course. Thank you." She slipped back into her own

vernacular. "Napoleon, please. Put your gun away. And take off that slicker. It's time for lunch."

Leon slipped his gun back where it belonged but stood where he was.

"What are you doing here?" He finally managed to articulate.

Gabriella threw the gray wig over her auburn locks, then went to retrieve the lunch. She slowly opened the door, peeked out to ensure privacy, then swung it wide and squatted to pick up the heavily laden tray.

"I don't know about you, but I'm having lunch," she said as she walked past him. "Now close the door and join me. I always think better when I've had something to eat."

The aroma of hot coffee got Leon moving more than thoughts of lunch. He finally closed and locked the door, stripped off his outer layer of wet clothing, and hung them to dry.

By then, Gabriella had the lunch tray set on the table and was maneuvering the chairs into position.

Leon joined her and sat down, but his stance was stiff and guarded. He hated how he felt. He used to love this woman; loved her with all his heart, and he wanted so much to feel that way again. But he didn't, and he couldn't. He sat and watched as she fixed his coffee just the way he liked it, then set a sandwich in front of him.

She sat and smiled, hoping to ease his mood. "Eat. I ordered your favorite: roast beef and raw onion with just a pinch of hot mustard."

He glanced at the sandwich but made no move to touch it. "Why are you here, Gabriella?"

She had just taken a bite of the sandwich and stopped chewing to frown at him. She finished her mouthful and then set the sandwich down. "Straight to that? Don't you want to know how your daughter is doing?"

Anger flashed through his dark eyes. "My daughter? Now she's my daughter again? Do you even tell her about me? Does she remember me at all? Would she know me if she walked through the door and saw me sitting here?"

Never one to falter, Gabriella locked eyes with him. "No."

Leon's fist hit the table hard, causing the service to rattle and coffee to splatter.

Gabriella jumped but was determined to stand her ground. "Why do you refuse to see this from my side? For years she had such terrible nightmares about that awful day. Details of you faded away, and that's how I kept it. No—" She raised her hand to stop the protest. "To remain respectable and not have myself and our daughter shunned, I needed to support the presumption that you, my husband, were dead. How can you not understand that?"

Leon sat silently, his jaw clenched and lips drawn tight with anger. His analytical brain could understand it, but his heart was breaking all over again.

"She's my daughter, too—" A sob escaped him before he even knew it was there.

Gabriella was hit with her own hurt, and she reached out a hand to comfort him.

But he would not be comforted. He snatched his hand away from her touch. "You still haven't answered my question. Why are you here? What made you think I wanted to see you?"

Gabriella sighed and sat back. "I wanted to help." She ignored Leon's snort. "You and I both know the pain of losing a child. How could I ignore what is happening here, when I know I can help you and the Marsham family get it sorted?"

Leon cocked a brow. "You know about this?"

"Of course, I do. I get copies of the Rocky Mountain News sent to my home. What little information they give concerning events in Arvada was enough to cause me concern."

"You get the newspapers from Denver?" Leon took the defensive road again. "Are you spying on me?"

"Spying on you?" Gabriella's green eyes flashed with anger. "Of course not! I still care about you, Napoleon. Would I have written to you in prison otherwise? Would I have put pressure on those who could, but wouldn't, help you? I wanted to know how you were doing because I do care about you. Therefore, I care about the people around you.

"The Marshams are important to you and Jack. I was pleased when I read about Jack's engagement to that young lady—"

"Penelope. Her name is Penelope."

Gabriella smiled. "Yes. I had to offer my help, don't you see? None of you deserves this."

"I got in touch with Frank Carlyle. He's looking into it. He may already be in town."

Gabriella snorted. "Carlyle. He has the sensitivity of a weasel. I can do more than he can, and you know it. But first and foremost, we must get Penelope away from here. She needs to be someplace safe, and I can offer that. For her mother and brother, too. We need to get them out of harm's way. Then we can focus on who is doing this and why."

"We don't even know where to start. Cameron doesn't know of anyone who hates him so much that they'd attack his daughter. That's where Frank comes in. He's going to do some digging."

Gabriella shook her head, causing her ginger locks to flutter in an enticing dance. "What makes you think this is about the Marshams?"

Leon sighed. He looked at his coffee cup, then took it and drained it before setting it back down. He knew where Gabriella was going with this.

"It's about us," he finally said. "Whoever was behind my harsh sentencing and my treatment while in prison is now going after Penny because she is engaged to Jack."

"Yes. Once we find out who was controlling Warden Mitchell, then we'll know who is behind these attacks on Penny."

Leon nodded. He didn't want to accept this hypothesis, but he knew it was logical. He and Jack had made enemies, and there were still those who felt they had both gotten off lightly.

He poured himself more coffee and took a bite of his sandwich.

"What's your plan?"

"I can get the Marshams away from here without anyone knowing. You know I can. My elderly lady has let it be known around town that she's looking for her great-nephews, and she believes that you and Jack are them. I can come out to the ranch, in disguise, and help them get organized. You must convince them, Napoleon. They need to understand that they are not safe here."

"Yes. Even with Jack and me on constant guard, things can happen. Things have happened. Where will you take them? To your sister's house?"

"Not the one in San Francisco. Too many people know about that place. They know that you frequented there. Helèna has a townhouse in Topeka where Hannah and I have been living. If they're still at risk there, I have my home in Ontario."

"Is that where Hannah is?"

Gabriella hesitated, then shook her head. "Helèna is looking after her right now. She's in Topeka."

"Oh. When this is over, can I see her?"

Again, Gabriella hesitated. "We'll see."

"Gabriella."

"That's the best I can do for now."

CHAPTER TWELVE
SET IN MOTION

Jack could tell just from the set of Leon's shoulders that all was not well. The sound of the rain battering upon the roof of the carriage barn had hidden the jangle and rattling of the returning buckboard, but Jack had stepped to the open door to dump a pail of dirty water just in time to witness his partner's arrival.

Leon didn't even glance his way but directed the team to the back of the house, where he could unload the household supplies. The gray wall of water hid the details, but Leon's mood shone through, and try as he did, he couldn't undo the knot in his gut or the ache in his heart.

He didn't need to halt the team by the exterior door to the pantry, as they knew the drill and set the buckboard right where it needed to be for easy unloading. Leon set the brake, then forced his cold, aching limbs to lower him to the wet ground.

Water had pooled on his lap and sloshed off the slicker to splatter upon his boots, but he didn't appear to notice. The pantry door opened, and he could just make out Jean through the steady stream off his hat brim.

"Oh, Napoleon, you do look a sight. Once you've unloaded the pantry stores, let Sam take care of the barn supplies and the team. There's beef barley soup on the stove, and warm bread just out of the oven."

Leon nodded as he pulled the tarp away from the sacks of flour. Cold water cascaded off the covering, soaking his boots even more and pouring down his sleeves just to add to the misery of his day. He cursed and tried to shake the water out, then glanced toward the door, ready to make an apology, but Jean had already returned to her kitchen.

***

Leon left the team in Sam's capable hands and was heading for the house when he heard Jack calling him from the carriage barn. He spun and snarled. "What!"

Jack frowned at his partner's sharp retort. "Hey, whatever's eatin' ya, ain't my fault. Ya gettin' soft? We've been out in worse weather than this."

Leon sighed, standing there in the rain with his hat beyond limp, and his slicker losing the battle.

Jack waited for a response, but none came. "C'mon, what's the matter?"

Leon unclenched his jaw. "Gabriella's in town."

"What? Well, why?"

"She thinks she can help sort this issue we are currently dealing with."

"Oh. Didn't ya tell her that Frank is already looking into it?"

Leon sent him a snarl. "Of course, I told her."

Jack waited for some elaboration. "And?"

"You know what she thinks of Frank. She's convinced she'll do a better job."

"I kinda agree with her."

"Well, I don't!" Leon barked.

Both men stepped back from the conversation.

"Yeah, well," Jack mumbled. "Maybe if ya tell me what she's got in mind."

"I'll discuss it with everyone over supper. Right now, I'm soaked through and in no mood."

Jack grumbled under his breath. "Yeah, I can tell." Then he spoke up and nodded. "Sounds good. See ya at supper."

***

When the family gathered around the dining table for supper, Leon's mood had improved. Dry, warm clothes and a bowl full of Jean's soup had lifted his spirits but had not even come close to denting his appetite.

Roast beef, mashed potatoes, and squash, all smothered in rich brown gravy were piled on his plate, and he tucked into it with a zeal that Jack cocked a brow at.

"Ya gonna tell us what happened in town today?"

Leon stopped chewing long enough to look across the table at Jack. He swallowed and straightened as he glanced around to find all eyes on him.

"Something happened in town?" Jean asked, though she knew darn well that something had.

"That explains a lot," Cameron said, as he helped himself to a dinner roll.

"Oh." Leon twitched a smile. "Yeah, I guess I have been kind of snappish since I got back."

Eli's dark eyes widened. "Yeah, I'da been sent to my room if I acted like that."

Jean sent him a stern look. "It's not too late, young man. Mind your manners."

Eli pouted at the unfairness of life.

"Yeah, sorry." Leon truly was contrite. "It was just a shock seeing her again, and I'm still not sure I'm pleased about it."

Penny cocked a brow. "Her?"

"Yes." Leon poked at his roast beef. "Mrs. Gabriella ... well, I guess she's back to using Tanguay, now."

Jean and Cameron shared a glance, but Penny missed it.

"Mrs.?" she asked. "That's disappointing. So, she's not an old flame who got—"

"Penny." Jean stopped her cold. "Perhaps you should let Napoleon explain who she is."

Heavy sigh. "Yes, Momma."

Leon sent her a quiet smile, locked eyes with Jack for an instant, then continued. "She is someone from way back, yes. Ahmm, remember when we first came for that visit, and we talked about women we had known who earned their own way? Caroline had been interested in becoming a detective, and we mentioned Gabriella since she and her husband had worked together in that profession."

Penny frowned. "I vaguely remember something like that. I think Caroline was more interested than I was."

Jean remembered this conversation quite clearly. She also remembered that Leon's reaction to the mention of this woman's name had been one of sadness. Now, she noticed the same lines etched around his eyes and the downward tick of his lip. She had known it then, and she knew it now: there was history between them.

"And she's in town?"

Leon glanced at Jean and brightened his expression. "Yes. She says she has a plan to help with our situation. She's coming out here tomorrow to explain it."

"Do you think she really can help?" Cameron asked. "Isn't your friend, Mr. Carlyle, looking into it?"

Jack snorted at the term "friend", then smiled and focused on his supper.

"Yeah," Leon answered. "They're both good detectives but would come at the problem from different angles. She is recommending that Penny leave here and go into hiding until this is sorted out."

Jean gasped. "What? Just go off on her own to goodness knows where?"

"No, no," Leon assured her. "No, she wants you and Eli to go as well. And she has a safe place for you to stay in Kansas. You'd be out of harm's way there. It's worth considering."

"I don't know," Cameron added more potatoes to his plate. "We don't even know this woman."

"I wanna go," Eli piped in. "It be fun. I never been ta Kansas, b'fore."

The adults smiled at the five-year-old's enthusiasm.

"What do you think, Napoleon?" Penny asked. "Do you trust her?"

Silence followed, and again, Leon and Jack shared a look of a common memory that was not lost on the other family members. Except for Eli, who was too busy sopping up gravy.

"Well," Jack reached for the platter of roast beef, "why don't we just wait 'til she comes out and explains things herself?"

"Fine," Cameron agreed. "We can hear her out, but I don't guarantee we'll follow along with it."

Leon nodded. "Fair enough. Hey Jack, stop hoarding the roast beef. I may want seconds, myself."

"What? You eatin' seconds? You really are rattled."

"Oh, boys, stop teasing each other." Jean chuckled. "You both know darn well there is more in the kitchen."

***

Frank Carlyle rapped his knuckles upon the hotel room door. As he heard the knob turn, it occurred to him to remove his hat. This he did in a quick, unaccustomed motion, sending water droplets cascading toward the door just as Gabriella opened it.

She blinked against the moisture hitting her face, but her old lady make-up and wig took the brunt of the onslaught.

When she saw Carlyle standing there, dripping on the threshold, she sighed and rolled her eyes.

"Mr. Carlyle. Why have you come knocking at my door?"

"I think you know why, Mrs. Tanguay. Or is it Mrs. Nash? No, wait, Mrs. Harden. What name are you going by these days?"

"It's Mrs. Tanguay, if you please."

"Oh, I don't care which one it is, as long as I know what to call you at any given moment. May I come in?"

"No, you may not."

Carlyle smiled. "I knew you'd say that." He pushed against the door.

He came up against some resistance from Gabriella's foot, but he leaned his shoulder into it and got the job done.

Gabriella was pushed back into the room, but she kept her feet and turned on Carlyle with fire in her eyes.

"How dare you force your way in here. This is my room, now get out!"

Carlyle laughed as he closed and locked the door behind him. "My but you are a feisty one. No wonder Nash likes you."

"In case you haven't noticed, he doesn't want anything to do with me."

"A clear sign that he's still in love with you."

Gabriella softened. She didn't want to; she despised this man standing before her. But Napoleon Nash always could soften her heart.

"What do you want?" she finally asked the detective. "Napoleon has already told me that he has asked you to deal with this case. Apparently, my help is unrequested and not required."

"You underestimate yourself, little lady."

Gabriella bristled at the condescension.

Carlyle simply smiled. He walked over to the caddy and poured himself a cup of coffee.

"You see, convincing two women to leave the comfort of their hearth and home is going to take some doing. A man like me isn't likely to have much luck with that. I know I don't exude an aura of comfort and well-being."

Gabriella huffed. "That's an understatement."

Carlyle shrugged. "That's the way it is. Now, if you and I work together on this, you can convince the young lady to go wherever it was you planned on taking her, and I'll convince the father that she'll be safe. Men like to know that men are in charge. As women . . ." Carlyle squinched his face, his hand rocking to suggest indecision, "women aren't known to be that competent."

"You arrogant bastard! I'm far more equipped to get the Marsham women to a safehouse than you are. What were you planning? To shoot your way off the ranch and force them to make a run for it amidst a hail of bullets? That's usually a man's way of getting things done."

Carlyle sipped his coffee, then frowned. "It's cold. We'll have to get another carafe. But you're right, that is the way a man usually does things. I'm the first to admit that subtlety is not my strong point. It takes a woman to be really sneaky."

"Are you going to stand here and insult me all afternoon, or is there a point to this discussion?"

"I already told you. We work together: you give assurance to the women, and I'll provide the competence of a bona fide Wells Fargo agent. I assume you already have a plan to get them off the property undetected, and a place for them to go."

"Of course."

"Fine. We'll go to the ranch together. You can do whatever you do with all this thespian stuff, and I'll focus on doing the job."

Gabriella crossed her arms and fumed. Her lips tightened, and her foot tapped in agitation as her brain considered the options.

She hated to admit it, but Carlyle, as uncouth as he was, had a point.

Men felt more confident in a plan when another man was running it. This was the bane of her times and her life. She knew she was a better undercover agent than most men in that field, yet she couldn't even be hired to do the job professionally.

Mr. Marsham would feel more comfortable with a man in charge. She knew Jack would support her, but Leon was a wild card. He still felt the betrayal of her actions and no matter how good a con man he was, those emotions were bound to come forth and jeopardize the whole plan.

Carlyle stood quietly, watching Gabriella slowly come to terms with the inevitable.

"Fine," she finally conceded. "But only if you agree to my arrangements. I have a safe place for them and a way to get them there. I will brook no interference from you on that matter."

Carlyle shrugged. "Suits me." He smiled, his dark eyes trying to show humor. "Partner."

***

The rain had eased to a cold mist, but the roads and yard were still awash with puddles and mud in the well-traveled areas. It was not a pleasant day for travel, but Leon and Jack knew this would not deter Gabriella.

Before the hidden sun had reached its zenith, the rented horse and buggy squiggled along the lane leading into the ranch yard. The horse's trotting hooves made hollow, plopping sounds as they put tracks in the mud.

Sam ran out to greet them. "Pull in over there by the house. I'll take care of the rig."

Carlyle directed the horse to the hitch rail just off the porch steps, then set the brake. He stepped down, his boots squelching into the mud as he made his way to the steps.

Sam frowned at the gentleman's inattentiveness, then stepped around to the passenger side to assist the elderly lady.

"Thank you, young man," came the quivering voice from behind the black veil. "It's so nice to meet people with manners."

"Yes, ma'am. Here, allow me to help you down."

"That's all right, Sam," Cameron snapped his eyes to Carlyle, then came down the porch steps to take over. "If you would bring the lady's case inside, I would appreciate that. Then you can take care of the horse and buggy."

"Sure."

"And where are Jack and Leon?"

"Still in the barn, finishing chores," Sam said as he lifted the case out of the boot.

"Still? Well, tell them to get up here. We have things to discuss."

"Yes, sir."

Cameron offered his hand to the elderly lady. "Ma'am."

"Mr. Marsham, I presume?"

"Yes. Welcome to the Rocking M."

Gabriella twitched a smile. "Are you sure?"

Cameron didn't skip a beat as Gabriella took a firm grip of his hand and, with her other hand on the door frame of the buggy, she gingerly took the two steps down to ground level.

Cameron put his other hand on her elbow and assisted her up the porch steps to the front door. "Any friend of Jack's and Napoleon's is welcome here."

"I doubt you've met them all, Mr. Marsham. But thank you."

Ignoring her comment, Cameron turned to the detective. "You must be Mr. Carlyle."

"That's right. Good to finally meet you."

"Yes."

The two men shook hands.

Cameron felt a slight unease in this man's presence. He knew Jack didn't trust him, and Leon's acceptance of him was tenuous. He would take his time before coming to his own conclusions.

Stepping into the foyer, Cameron assisted Mrs. Tanguay with her outer attire, then hung them on the coat tree to dry.

Carlyle wiped his muddy boots on the mat, removed his dripping slicker and homburg, and hung them on the same coat tree.

Sam slipped in behind the group, set the case on the floor by the coat tree, then discreetly left to tend the horse and buggy.

Jean emerged from the kitchen carrying a tea service, which she quickly set on the table in the sitting room, then turned to greet their guest.

"Mrs. Tanguay. Welcome." Jean took Gabriella's chilled hand in hers, neatly covering her surprise at the elderly lady standing before her.

"Won't you come in and sit? A cup of tea and a scone will warm you after your journey. I'm sure the roads are atrocious."

"Yes, they are. Thank you." Gabriella agreed as she entered the sitting room. "Oh, your fire feels so lovely."

"Please, sit in the chair closest to it. You must be chilled to the bone." Jean offered and then turned to their second guest. She had to push herself to come forward in greeting.

"This is Mr. Carlyle," Cameron informed her.

"Mr. Carlyle. I've heard so much about you. It's a pleasure to finally meet you in person."

Carlyle tipped his head in lieu of his hat. "Not all of it good, I'm sure."

"Oh." Jean flicked a glance at her husband, then smiled at their guest. "I leave judgment to our Lord."

Carlyle smirked. "Then I'm really in trouble."

"Mr. Carlyle!" The old lady's voice was surprisingly powerful. "You are not putting the Marshams at their ease." Gabriella smiled at Jean. "You must excuse my companion. He's not known for his subtlety."

Penny joined the group and, though feeling apprehensive at first, she wasn't as successful at hiding her surprise as her mother had been. "Oh. Mrs. Tanguay?"

"Yes. You must be Penelope."

"Yes. Oh dear. Oh, I'm sorry, Mrs. Tanguay, I was expecting someone much ... ahmm . . ."

Gabriella cocked a gray brow. "Younger?"

Penny blushed.

Carlyle snorted.

Penny blushed even deeper. "Oh dear. I had my suspicions about your relationship with Napoleon, but now I see I was mistaken."

"That's quite all right, my dear." Gabriella gave Penny's hand a pat. "One should listen to their suspicions."

"Oh." Penny frowned as she noticed the lack of wrinkles on the old lady's hand. "Yes, well . . ."

"Come and sit," Jean motioned to the chair. "I'll pour us some tea."

Cameron headed for the front door. "And I'll go see what is keeping them. They seem to be lagging this morning."

But then the door opened, and the partners entered the foyer.

Leon and Jack pulled off muddy boots and hung damp jackets up to dry. Leon's face was set in a determined frown when he entered the sitting room. His gut was knotted tight, and the anxiety he felt in anticipation of seeing Gabriella again only escalated when he actually set eyes upon her.

But Jack smiled openly and came forward with arms outstretched. "Gabi! It's good ta see ya again, Darlin'. It's been ages."

Gabriella smiled as she embraced her friend. "Jack. You too. You're looking fine. How's Haley?"

"Married," Jack emphasized. "And happily so."

"That's nice. She deserves to be happy. I seem to recall she had quite an interest in you."

Penny smiled and sent a sparkling glance to her fiancé. "Another one? You seem to have a closetful of past lovers."

Jack released Gabriella and slid up beside Penny to slip an arm around her waist.

"Past is the point, Darlin'. And Haley and I weren't really—" Jack stopped as he realized that his interpretation of "lovers" would be different from Penny's. "Ha. Well, we was close, but she wanted things that I didn't. Not then, anyway."

Penny cocked a brow at her betrothed. "And do you want those things now?"

"Yeah, sure. Now. But not with her. You're the only true love in my life, Penny Darlin'."

Penny chuckled and slapped Jack on the chest. "You're teasing me."

Jack raised his hand in all innocence. "I swear ta God. Besides, she kinda took a shinin' ta Leon after she couldn't get nowheres with me."

All eyes turned to the silent partner.

He sighed and rolled his eyes. "It wasn't like that." He walked over to the detective and extended a hand. "Hey, Frank. Glad you could make it."

"Oh, I wouldn't miss this for the world, Nash. Not for the world."

Jack snorted. "Yeah, I bet."

Carlyle smiled at him. "Still not ready to forgive and forget, are ya, Kiefer?"

Jack's response was a set of blue daggers.

"C'mon, Jack," Leon intercepted the glare. "We're all here for a common purpose, remember?"

"Yeah." Jack sat down with a harrumph, and Penny strove to calm the waters.

"I swear, Napoleon, both you and Jack are incorrigible. Who is this Haley person who had both of you smitten?"

Gabriella smiled at the charming young woman, then glanced at Leon.

His mood dampened any chance of joviality within the group. He moved to the dining room and remained standing there, his hands squeezing the back of the chair.

"She offered me a safe place to lay low and . . ." he glanced at Gabriella, ". . . recover."

"Recover from what?" Penny asked, but her teasing manner had quieted.

"Penny," Jean interrupted her, "some things are personal. Leave it be."

"Yes, but as Miranda says, if you want to know something, then ask."

A cocked brow from her mother was enough to quiet Penny's curiosity.

She smiled at Napoleon to ease his mood. "All right. I won't pester you for the details. Another time, perhaps."

Leon was seduced by her charm and returned her smile. "Yes, another time." He settled into the armchair. "For right now, we have other things to discuss." He sent Gabriella a pointed look. "Gabi, don't you think it's time you showed them your true self?"

Gabriella sent a quick wink to her hosts. "Yes, of course. And, truth be known, this wig can sometimes be quite irritating. But I needed this disguise to remain consistent with my story of a little elderly lady searching for her nephews. Anyone watching your house will only have seen that elderly lady and her escort coming to visit."

Then, to amazed expressions, she pulled out the hairpins and lifted the gray wig from her head. She removed more pins and shook her red locks to loosen them from the tight chignon they'd been confined to.

Next, she pulled off the gray eyebrows. Opening her case, she placed the items inside, then drew out a face cloth. She applied some lotion, then covered her face and rubbed vigorously. When she removed the cloth, it was covered in a muddy array of makeup, and she finally revealed her true likeness.

"Wow!" came a little-boy exclamation from the first-floor landing. He arrived upon the scene just in time for the great unveiling. "How did you do that? You rubbed off your wrinkles!" Eli bounded into the room, "Momma, why don't you do that?"

Before Jean could get over her surprise, her little hellion had scooted to a stop beside the intriguing trickster and began examining the cloth and trying to spread it into a face again. "Put it back on. Let me see."

"You must be Eli," Gabriella smiled down at the boy. "I'm sorry, once it's off, it's off."

"Aww . . ." He cocked a brow at her, his little forehead frowning. "You talk funny."

"Elijah!" Jean was mortified. "People have different ways of speaking depending on where they grew up. If we went to another country, they would think you spoke funny. Don't be so rude." She smiled at Gabriella. "I'm sorry. His manners seem to be slipping lately."

"That's quite all right, Mrs. Marsham. Young boys can be so enthusiastic."

Jean sighed. "I suppose that's one word for it.

Gabriella smiled down at Eli. "I grew up in a province in Canada called Quebec. The accent there is quite different from what you would be used to."

Eli cocked his head. None of this made any sense to him.

Jean directed Gabi's attention. "Let's have some tea before it gets cold."

"That would be lovely. Nothing like a cup of tea and a warm fire to chase away the chill."

Tea and finger cakes were passed around, and the group settled in for a discussion.

Gabriella glanced at Carlyle and felt a twinge of irritation when she found his beady, black eyes staring at her. He was waiting for her to break the ice.

She sighed, took a sip of liquid reinforcement, then got down to business.

"Mr. and Mrs. Marsham, someone is trying to kill your daughter. This must be addressed. Mrs. Marsham, you and she must leave here until we can sort this out."

"What good would that do?" Cameron considered this slip of a woman and felt little confidence. "You came here wearing this disguise because you suspected we were being watched. They would simply follow us."

"I assure you, Mr. Marsham, they will not be interested in our departure. I came visiting as Napoleon and Jack's elderly aunt, and it's the elderly aunt they'll see leave. But it will be Penny under that disguise, not me."

"And I've already spoken with the town sheriff," Carlyle said. "I've let it be known that Nash sent for me to protect this family and to investigate the situation. If anyone saw us arrive, they'd think we were here on legitimate business."

Leon frowned. "Was that smart? How are you supposed to discreetly look into this situation if the culprits know you're here?"

Carlyle bristled. "Of course it's smart, Nash. When have you known me to do a dumb thing?"

Jack snorted.

Carlyle ignored him. "If they're watching the ranch, what they will see is an old lady leaving with Jack as the escort and me staying to protect Miss Marsham. It will add more credence to the illusion we are presenting to them."

Leon still wasn't convinced.

Gabriella continued with a more detailed account.

"Jack will accompany his aunt into town so she can catch her train home. Mrs. Marsham and Elijah will join them under the guise of taking advantage of a trip to town to do shopping or run errands. Then, at the last minute, all of you will board the train and head for Topeka, Kansas. Jack will escort you there to make sure no one follows you."

Eli, still sitting next to Gabriella on the sofa, was mesmerized by this strange woman. As soon as she mentioned him coming along, his jaw dropped, and he jumped around on the sofa until his mother settled him.

He stopped his antics, but the excitement was still etched in his youthful face.

"I get to come, too? I've never been so far from home. Where is Kansas? I get to ride on a train! Can I wear a disguise, too? I wanna be an old man."

Gabriella laughed. "I don't think even I could pull that one off."

Eli pouted.

Gabriella gave him a gentle hug. "But how would you like to watch me turn your sister into an old woman?"

Eli giggled with delight and pointed a finger at Penny. "Penny's gonna be an old lady! Penny's gonna be an old lady!"

Penny's lips tightened with the assumption that she was going along with this scheme.

"Stop it, Eli. Nothing has been decided yet." She glanced at her mother, seeking support. "What do you think, Momma?"

"Well . . ." Jean glanced around at the mixed emotions in the room. "Pardon me for saying so, Mrs. Tanguay, but we don't know you. Simply packing up and leaving for another state is not to be taken lightly."

"I agree," Gabriella said. "But neither is your daughter's safety. Her life has been threatened on two separate occasions. You might not be so lucky on the third attempt. I realize it is a difficult decision, but I assure you, getting her out of harm's way is the smart thing to do."

"She's right," Carlyle put in. "Mrs. Tanguay and I have discussed this plan thoroughly, and it will work. It's the best chance you've got."

Leon shook his head. "I can still see a couple of flaws in your logic."

Gabriella hinted at a smile; Napoleon had not lost his touch.

Carlyle growled. "And what's that?"

"What about when Jack, Jean, and Eli don't return here after their little shopping spree? If someone is watching the ranch, they'd be looking for that."

Gabriella and Frank exchanged a quick look.

"I know," Gabriella agreed. "That is a rub. We thought, perhaps, your hired hand could also join the group to help with supplies. He could time his arrival back here for after dark. That way, any observers would hear the wagon return but not be able to see how many returned in it."

"That might work, if they're not paying too close attention," Leon conceded. "But, there's also going to be somebody here who shouldn't be. Disguising yourself as Penny will fool strangers watching the ranch from a distance, but it's not going to fool anyone who comes to visit."

"I did think of that," Gabriella assured him. "Over the next few days, I will disguise myself as Penny, as you say, and go outside occasionally to convince any spies that she is still here. Perhaps you can get the word out that Miss Marsham is feeling unwell to dissuade friends from dropping by."

Leon chuckled. "That would only encourage friends to come around. It's been too long since you've lived in a small town, Gabi."

"Then I will simply retire to the bedroom. I'm sure anyone who is a friend of this family would not be so rude as to barge in on a young lady who is still recovering from two brutal attacks."

Leon shook his head. "Maybe in the city, that would be the case, but not here. Small-town folks care about one another."

Gabriella flashed her green eyes in Leon's direction and was all prepared for a comeback when Cameron raised his hands.

"Enough, Napoleon. Please allow Mrs. Tanguay to explain the rest of the plan. We can hardly make an informed decision with you interrupting her."

Leon's fingers tightened on the chair, but he remained silent.

Cameron sighed in relief and nodded to Gabriella.

Gabriella collected herself, then continued. "We'll give Jack a few days to get them well out of the state, then Carlyle can drive me, as Penny, into town."

"But the people in town will know you are not Penny," Leon quipped again.

"Of course, they will. This is why Carlyle will drive me in, not you or Mrs. Marsham. Seeing a stranger drive into town with a blonde woman at his side will likely go unnoticed.

"Anyone watching from a distance will assume Mr. Carlyle is escorting Penny to a safe hideaway. Once in town, I'll return to my hotel room, discard my disguise, and then sign in at the front desk as myself. Your 'great aunt' paid for her room a week in advance, so once that is used up, I'm sure the clerk will assume that the old woman simply forgot to sign out. I will stay in my new room and begin my investigation.

"The spies will think that Penny is somewhere in town and will be looking for her. They will also be watching Frank. But they won't be watching me, which allows me to don any disguise I wish to start digging."

Leon looked from Carlyle to Gabriella. "I don't know. I'm still getting used to the idea of you two working together."

"You're not the only one." Gabriella sent a reproachful look to the detective. "But Mr. Carlyle is not easy to say no to."

Both Jack and Leon barked out a laugh at this understatement.

"Was this your idea, Frank?" Leon asked him. "Since when do you take a backseat in any partnership?"

"Yeah." Jack narrowed his eyes as he glowered at the detective. "Did ya have ta hit her ta get her to agree?"

"I don't hit women," Frank stated, "unless it's necessary. Mrs. Tanguay agreed with me. A woman can go places and ask questions where a man cannot. And since she already has experience along those lines—"

Leon bristled, but Jack beat him to it.

"Watch it, Frank. Bawdy talk ain't appropriate in a family home."

"Sure, sure, Kid. Relax. Just explainin' the situation."

Jack ignored Frank's defense and returned his attention to his betrothed.

He squeezed Penny's hand, then sent Jean a quiet smile. "If it helps any, Leon and I have known Gabriella a long time, and though we ain't always seen eye ta eye on things, she does have experience when it comes ta disappearing." Sadness ghosted his expression as memories drifted back. "Maybe even better at it than we are."

Leon huffed, and all eyes flicked to him.

It had not been his intention to draw focus his way, but now that he had, he managed to pull himself together.

"Jack's right. When it comes to disappearing under cover, Gabriella is a master. I wouldn't say she is better than I am—" Jack snorted, and Leon sent him a sharp look as he continued, "but she has the means to change your appearance and get you safely out of town. I think it's something you should seriously consider. And Frank is about as tenacious as they come. I have to admit; they'll make a formidable pair."

"But I don't want to leave." Penny sent a beseeching look to her family. "This is my home and ... we're supposed to be getting married!"

Jack squeezed her hand again. "I think them plans have been put on hold, Darlin', no matter what choice we make over this."

Penny hung her head. She knew this herself, but having heard it said out loud, it sent a dagger through her heart.

Gabriella remembered being in love and the dangerous choices she had made to be with him. She swallowed the knot in her throat and glanced at the man she had lost her common sense over.

Leon caught her gaze for an instant, then dropped it.

She let it be. Those memories were painful for both of them.

"I know it's a difficult decision," she said to Penny. "But isn't a postponed wedding better than none at all? Believe me, you don't want to start married life with this danger hanging over you. The consequences could be . . ." Gabriella stopped as her throat constricted. She again looked at Leon.

He returned her gaze, and this time, he held it.

He nodded. "The consequences could be devastating."

Penny looked back and forth between Leon and Gabriella, realizing they were no longer talking about her situation but their own. She could not only see their pain, but even through Jack's simple grasp of her hand, she could tell he shared it. Something terrible had happened between them, and that something had ripped them apart.

Even Carlyle, whom Penny had already decided was a cold snake-in-the-grass, remained respectfully quiet.

Jean suddenly stood up. "I see the tea needs refreshing. I'll make us a new pot. Penny, come help."

"But—"

"Don't argue with me." Her tone was sharper than she intended, and she tried to soften it with a smile. "Come and help me in the kitchen." Then, she picked up the tea service and walked away, expecting her daughter to follow.

"It's okay, Penny," Jack said as he rubbed her back. "Go with your ma. I promise ya, we won't make any decisions without your say."

Penny nodded and, without a glance at anyone, she stood up and followed her mother.

Those remaining in the sitting room now looked to the patriarch, and Cameron considered the dilemma placed before him.

"I agree that Penny would be safer away from here. But I need to discuss this further with my family before putting them into your care," he said to Gabriella. "And, according to you, they won't even be in your care. If they do go to Topeka, who will protect them there?"

"My sister, Helèna, will take even better care of them than I can," Gabriella assured him. "She's a crack shot with a rifle and isn't afraid to use it. I have left my daughter in her care and have no qualms about doing so."

Cameron cocked a brow. "Your sister?"

Gabriella nodded, knowing how much this was for the family to take in all at once. "She's much older than I and wiser than I'll ever be. She worked undercover as an agent in the war and is the most courageous woman I know. But, first and foremost, she is a doctor, and a very good one. She will look after them."

"I think what Cameron is trying to say," Leon pointed out, "is that he doesn't know you, so entrusting his wife and children into your care is a bit difficult. The same holds for Helèna."

"Yes," Cameron continued. "You say your sister is reliable, but since I don't know you, how much weight can your word carry? It would be different if we were already acquainted."

"But Napoleon and Jack know me." Gabriella felt her frustration rise. "Surely, their word counts for something."

Cameron glanced at the two men in question. "What do you say, boys? Would you trust your family to the care of these two women?"

"Yes," Jack answered straight away. "Penny is my family, and I'd sure feel better with her in Helèna's care. I think it's a good plan."

Cameron looked at Leon. "Napoleon? It's obvious you're not comfortable with this situation."

Leon considered the options, then sighed. "I agree with Jack. Jean and Penny would be far safer with Helèna than with anyone else. I wouldn't have agreed to Gabriella coming out here if I didn't think it was feasible."

Gabriella's gaze softened, and she smiled at her ex-lover, but the smile faded when Leon did not return it.

Leon focused instead on Frank Carlyle.

"I admit, Frank, a bit of warning that you and Gabi have joined forces would have been nice."

Carlyle waved it away. "Warnings are for the faint of heart. I don't give warnings, I take action. I thought you'd figured that out by now."

"And I thought we were working together on this."

"Are you getting smart-mouthed with me again, Nash? Do I need to teach you—"

Leon came to his feet, anger darkening his eyes.

"You're not my watchdog anymore, Frank. If you ever lay a hand on me again, I—"

"You're gonna what?" Carlyle stood up slowly, his black eyes boring into the former outlaw. "As long as you're on parole, I am still responsible for your behavior. Whether you like it or not."

Jack tensed at the confrontation, though he remained seated.

"Whatever Leon has in mind, you know I'll back 'im up," he said. "You ain't my watchdog no more, Frank. You're working for us."

Carlyle's response was interrupted by Cameron coming to his feet.

"Gentlemen, I will not tolerate this behavior in my home.

Napoleon and Jack, you both know better. Mr. Carlyle, I would think that a man in your profession would know to show respect in another man's house. And let us not forget there is still a lady and a child present."

All eyes turned to the mentioned pair.

Gabriella sat quietly by the fire, sipping her tea, while Eli stared up at the posturing men. He was wide-eyed with both excitement and fear over the outcome.

Leon glanced at Gabriella and then at Cameron.

"Yes, you're right, Cameron. My apologies. Gabriella, no disrespect intended."

Carlyle cleared his throat. "I also apologize, Mr. Marsham. This is your home, and you are due respect. Sometimes my temper gets the better of me when dealing with these two. I'm sure you can understand. Mrs. Tanguay, my apologies." He looked at Leon as the two men returned to their seats. "We will discuss this later."

Leon gritted his teeth and choked back a retort. Yes, they would discuss this later.

***

Penny removed the kettle from the stove and poured steaming water into the teapot.

Her lips pursed with uncertainty. "I really don't want to go anywhere. This is my home, and I feel safe here. Especially with Jack and Leon, oh, and Papa, too, of course, being so protective. Why should we have to leave?"

Jean put more finger cakes on a platter. "I know. But, Sweetheart, you were surrounded by people who love you when you were shot." Her expression turned reflective. "Perhaps you would be safer someplace else for now. If this woman can get you away, unnoticed, maybe it is something we should consider."

Raised male voices interrupted their discussion.

The two ladies shared a concerned look.

"Oh dear," Jean shook her head. "Mr. Carlyle does seem to get on people's nerves."

Penny nodded. "I'm not sure what to make of that man. Jack doesn't trust him at all, and Napoleon doesn't seem to care much for him either. Yet Napoleon invited him here. Even Mr. Carlyle and that woman barely tolerate each other."

"Yes," her mother agreed. "There is shared history there, between all four of them. It can appear confusing to those of us on the outside."

Penny frowned as her father's voice broke up the argument. "I wonder what happened."

"Perhaps it's none of our business."

Penny laughed. "Oh, Momma, you're no fun. I sense a scandal, and I want to know what's going on there before I deliberately separate myself from my fiancé."

"Perhaps none of them want to discuss it," Jean pointed out. "It really isn't any of our business."

"But aren't you the least bit curious?"

Jean couldn't help the smile. "Of course, I am. But now is not the time. Information like that is best offered freely rather than coerced. Remember, you might learn more with honey than with—"

Penny laughed again. "Yes, Momma, I know. Than with vinegar."

"Yes. Come along. Let's find out what the 'adults' have decided."

***

Mother and daughter returned to the sitting room and offered more tea and finger cakes to the gathering.

Penny looked around at the faces as she sat down again. A decision had not been made.

"Napoleon?"

Leon was startled out of his thoughts. "Hmm, yes?"

"What do you think?"

"Ummm," Leon looked around at those looking at him. "It's a good idea. I think you should go. You're not safe here."

"I don't want to." She took Jack's hand, though her eyes were glued to Leon. "I'd rather stay with people I know and trust."

"You can trust Gabriella and her sister," Leon said. "And Jack will go with you to make sure you arrive safely. I think it's best."

"Then why can't Jack stay with me?" Penny grasped at straws. "Why does he have to come back here?"

"Cause we wanna make it appear that you're still here," Jack reminded her. "If I disappear for weeks, they might get suspicious."

"Plus, Jack and I will protect the ranch," Leon added. "If this assassin thinks you're still here, he may try again."

Penny slumped. "Papa? What do you think?"

Cameron didn't like being put on the spot any more than Leon had, but he also submitted. "You're not safe here, Sweetheart, and both Leon and Jack give good references. We don't even know who is after you or why. It is worth considering. And Napoleon's right; I want Jack here, at least for now."

Penny cocked a brow, feeling the vote going against her wishes. "Jack? How about you?"

"I know you'd be safer with Helèna than you are here. She's trained for this kind'a stuff. She could protect you in ways I ain't even aware of."

Penny's sigh was more dramatic than necessary. She then turned her attention to Gabriella.

"Why are you willing to take such risks?" she asked. "You said your daughter is also staying with your sister. Whoever is after me may not fall for this ruse; they could follow us right to your front door."

"They won't be able to follow a track that I cover, Penny. My first husband worked for the Dominion Police and then the R.C.M.P., and I helped him on many cases. I have also studied law and the many techniques of detection and deception. I know the tricks a nefarious mind can conjure up, and I can head them off in any direction I choose. I assure you, they will not follow us."

Leon interrupted. "When did you study law?"

Gabriella snapped a look at him. "Really? You want to go into this now?"

"Well, I just—"

Again, Penny interrupted. She had a point to make and wasn't about to let Leon steal the stage.

"But still, it's an awful risk. Why are you willing to do this for people you don't know?"

Gabriella turned her frown away from Leon and took a moment to collect her thoughts. A sip of tea made for a good diversion.

"My son from my first marriage was stolen from me shortly after my husband died. Then, my youngest daughter died, murdered in front of my eyes by a selfish fool who thought he had the right. How could I stand by and allow such pain to come into someone else's life? Besides that, I may not know you and your family, but I do know Jack, and he loves you. That matters to me."

"Well," Cameron sighed and leaned back, stretching his tightened shoulders. "This has been an interesting discussion. Obviously, Penny is still not convinced. I also want to discuss this with my wife. In private."

"Of course." Gabriella accepted that the matter was closed for the time being.

"You are naturally welcome to stay until the decision has been made."

"That would make things easier." Gabriella looked at Leon. "As long as it's all right with everyone."

Leon returned her gaze. "It's getting late. I wouldn't send you out on the roads now."

"Of course, you'll stay." Jean stood up. "And you too, Mr. Carlyle. We'll make room. Now, I need to get supper going. Leftovers tonight, I'm afraid."

Carlyle grunted and nodded his thanks.

"Thank you," Gabriella said. "I see my overnight bag is already here, but I will need my trunk from the buggy."

"I'll get it." Leon was on his feet and headed for the front door before anyone else could offer. He pulled on his boots, grabbed his hat and coat on his way out, and closed the door behind him.

"Well," Jean brought everyone's attention back to the matter at hand. "Penny, will you show Mrs. Tanguay to the guest room so she can freshen up? Then come and help with dinner. Mr. Carlyle, we'll fix you a place in Eli's room. Eli can share with us."

Both siblings groaned, but each remembered their manners.

CHAPTER THIRTEEN
A FAMILY TORN APART

Leon strode across the yard toward the carriage barn, barely noticing the cold, damp wind that threatened to snatch the hat from his head.

His mind was in turmoil.

He loved her, and he hated her. He admired her, and he despised her.

Memories, long buried, of having a family: His family, his wife, his daughters. All of them, sitting in the living room of their small home in Gillette and filling it with laughter and love.

Then it had all been taken away from him. Again.

She turned on him and ripped his heart apart. The letters to the prison were one thing. He didn't have to look into those green eyes or listen to her lyrical voice. He didn't have his senses filled with her essence. He could handle her there, at a distance.

But here and now? He was overwhelmed.

How was he supposed to deal with this? How could he sit down to supper with her and act as though all is well, as though all is forgiven?

The door to the horse barn opened, and Sam walked out leading his mare.

"Oh, hey there, Nash. Was there something else Mr. Marsham needed me to do?"

"No, that's okay, Sam. Go on home."

Sam nodded and tightened the cinch on the saddle. "Company staying tonight?"

"Yes, I guess so. The trunk from her buggy; is it in the carriage barn?"

"Yes, sir." Sam mounted his antsy mare. She wanted to get home for supper, too. Then Sam's face dropped. "Oh. Was I supposed to bring it up to the house?"

"No. We weren't sure she was going to stay."

"Oh, good." Sam settled into the saddle. "Well, see you tomorrow."

Leon sent a quick wave after the departing horseman and continued to the carriage barn, his emotions still in turmoil.

He hated feeling like this. Words had always been his weapon: his tool, and he could manipulate them to produce any outcome that he desired. But when words failed him, he felt as vulnerable as Jack must feel when danger threatened and his gun was out of reach.

And, to top it off, there was Frank.

Sometimes it was hard for Leon to accept his presence. Then, when he got proddy like that, Leon wanted to choke him. The only thing holding back his temper was the knowledge that they needed both these people involved.

Gabriella would get Penny away from here, safe and sound, and Frank had the background and knowledge to run these assassins into the ground.

And yet, Leon sighed. He didn't want either of them here. It was a toss-up as to who had hurt him the most. Then he sighed again.

No. Gabriella hurt him the most. The physical pain that Frank had inflicted was nothing compared to the loss caused by Gabi.

Like a festering boil that has suddenly been lanced, the emotions oozed out and choked him with their intensity. That same anger came flooding back from eleven years ago: from that day when she had pushed him away; when she had denied him his paternity.

Muttering under his breath, he unlatched the door to the barn just as a huge gust of wind kicked up and snatched the heavy structure from his hands. It banged against the jam, then bounced back and hit Leon in the face.

"Dammit!" He kicked the door. "Crap!" He limped backward, sucking his teeth. "Don't tell me I broke my toe. God dammit . . ."

His cursing was interrupted by an explosion of electrical light, followed far too quickly by a loud boom of thunder. Dusk turned to night as the storm clouds socked in around the ranch and large raindrops began their descent.

Leon forgot about his throbbing toe and got inside the barn. It was so dark that he headed for the lantern and set the wick. He placed it back on its hook and then turned to search the interior. He spied the trunk over by the wall and grabbed it, hoping to get back to the house before the deluge was upon them.

Fortunately, it wasn't that big a trunk, and he lifted it easily. He turned to the door just as another lightning bolt ripped through the dark clouds, illuminating the ominous landscape, and the barn shuddered from the boom of thunder. The heavens opened, and sheets of water cascaded into the yard.

The wind gusted again, then picked up in a continuous onslaught, sending the rain into a near-horizontal assault.

The lantern on its hook bounced and swayed dangerously, and Leon dropped the trunk to grab it. The last thing he needed was to set the barn on fire. With the moodiness he had displayed, he might be suspected of deliberately starting it.

Realizing the lantern wasn't doing him much good, he blew it out and set it back in its place. He picked up the trunk again, then sighed as he looked at the downpour.

Aw, damn. Well, at least I'm better off than Sam. But he doesn't live that far away. A good hand gallop, and he'll be home in no time.

He stood and stared at the rain. *Maybe I can stay out here for the night. That would suit me better.* He harrumphed. *Naw, that won't work. Jack or Cameron would come out looking for me. Afraid I ran off and broke parole. Oh well. I'll retire early. If Jack wants to stay up and visit, well, on him.*

He lowered his head, hunched his shoulders, and stepped into the dark.

***

Jack rapped softly on the guestroom door. "Gabi, are ya decent?"

Gabriella opened the door and smiled. "What kind of question is that to ask a woman?"

Jack chuckled. "You know what I mean. Can I come in?"

"It's late, Jack. Can't it wait until morning?"

"No, I don't think it should. Everyone has settled for the night, and there won't be an opportunity in the mornin'."

"All right." Gabriella widened the door and invited him in. "How are you, Jack? It's good to see you again."

"You, too, Gabi. We've both missed you."

Gabriella cocked a brow. "Really?"

"You know he has."

Gabriella crossed her arms and turned away. "He has a fine way of showing it."

Jack stepped forward and put a hand on her shoulder. "There are some things you need to know. Ah, can I sit?"

"Is this going to be a long conversation?"

Jack shrugged. "It could be."

"All right. Bring the vanity chair over. You can sit on that, and I'll sit on the bed."

Jack did as she suggested, and they sat, facing each other.

"So," Gabriella sent him a coy smile. "Don't tell me you're beginning to doubt our plans, too."

"No, that ain't it at all. I can't think of anyone I would trust more with this situation."

"Then what is it?"

"Leon."

Gabriella's smile dropped. "Yes. He's certainly made it clear to everyone that he doesn't want me here."

"No, Gabi, that ain't it at all. You got no idea what happened to him in that prison."

Gabriella frowned and puffed up. "Of course, I do. The injustice of that sentence needed to be dealt with. I did everything to help him out of that awful place."

"I know ya did. But you never saw 'im. You never saw how that place wore 'im down. They broke him. His body, his mind, his hopes. He became a skeleton of the man he used ta be. He even tried ta end his life."

"I know." Gabriella placed a hand on Jack's, her gaze softening with sadness. "I couldn't believe it when I heard about that; he was always so brilliant, so full of life. I guess you're right. I can't imagine the atrocities he suffered to push him to that choice."

"Yeah." Jack nodded. "But it's what happened after that that really hit us hard."

"After?"

"Yeah. He was angry, Gabi. Furious that we had stopped 'im. Kenny had to chain him to his bed ta stop 'im from tryin' again. He was lost to us then. No one could reach him. All he knew was anger.

Any other emotions had been beaten out of 'im."

"Oh, my God." Gabi's voice was a whisper. "You were always able to reach him, Jack. Couldn't you . . .?"

Jack shook his head. "No. He shut me out. He told me ta go away and never come back. I knew that if I tried to return, he would have refused to see me. That was the worst thing I'd ever been through, him tellin' me he was gonna kill himself, then refusin' ta let me help 'im. I ain't never been so scared in my life. Why tell me if he didn't want help?"

"But he did want help, Jack. Don't you see? He told you because he knew you would do everything to stop him."

"That's what Cameron said. That don't make no sense."

"No, it doesn't. But what I know about suicides: most of them don't want to die, but they are no longer in control. Their conscious mind has gone somewhere else, but their unconscious mind is screaming for help."

Jack went silent as he recalled that surreal conversation in the processing room. Leon hadn't made any sense, talking about interacting with dead people and seeing things that weren't there.

He sighed. "I felt so helpless. There was nothin' I could do. But Kenny, he—"

"Who is Kenny? This is the second time you've mentioned him."

"Oh yeah, sorry. Kenny Reece was one of the senior guards there. He took Leon under his wing, sort'a speak. Thank goodness he did, too. He was more instrumental in keepin' Leon alive during that time than any of us coulda been." Jack breathed a soft laugh. "And Leon hated 'im for it. But Kenny's the one who gave Leon that cat. Oh, not the one he's got now; she's one of the kittens. But the cat Kenny dumped on him knew how ta bring people out of their slumps. That helped, forcing Leon ta care about something other than himself.

"Cameron even went ta see 'im ta try and drag 'im out of the pit he'd buried himself in. I think that between Cameron's visit and what Kenny did for 'im, Leon was startin' ta think again. But it still weren't enough.

"You wanna know what really dragged him outta that slump, Gabi? The photograph of Hannah you sent to 'im. It gave 'im something ta hang onto; something important enough ta turn away from that destructive path he was on." Jack's chuckle was sardonic. "And then he was mad about that."

Gabriella sniffed, then shook her head at her weakness as she brushed tears away.

"That's one thing about using disguises; there are always plenty of tissues around. Could you hand me some?"

She gestured toward the vanity, and Jack followed her lead.

He snatched up one of the towelettes and handed it to her.

She took it and dabbed at her eyes.

"Is that what this is about?" she asked through her sniffles. "That I allow him to see Hannah?"

"Partly," Jack admitted. "But I figured you'd come to that conclusion yourself anyway. What I really wanted was ta let ya know why Leon has been behavin' so cold towards ya."

"Well, that's obvious. He can't stand the sight of me."

"No, that ain't it, Gabi." He reached over and cupped her oval face in his hands. Bringing her eyes up to meet his, he smiled into them. "He's doin' it 'cause he still loves ya. He just don't know how ta deal with all that hurt. He shuts down, or he lashes out in anger. That's all he knows right now. It's gonna take time."

Gabriella sighed deeply as she brought her tears under control.

"But my being here has thrown him off, hasn't it?"

"Yeah."

"Ohh!" Gabriella growled and, coming to her feet, she paced around the small room. "I should never have come. I thought I could help, but I've just made things worse. Perhaps I should leave all this to Frank."

"No!" Jack was on his feet in an instant. "Don't you dare. I don't trust him, Gabi. Not after what he done ta Leon, and ta . . ." Jack stopped, the sudden knot in his throat preventing him from continuing.

Gabriella placed a hand on his arm. "What happened to Ella was not Frank's fault. He was furious, Jack. He would have killed that man for his stupidity."

"That's what Leon says. I ain't convinced."

"No, Jack. Don't carry that around with you. I know who was responsible, and it wasn't Frank."

Jack looked her in the eye. "And you took care of him, didn't ya, Gabi."

Gabriella cocked a brow and straightened. "I don't know what you're talking about. Dicks committed suicide."

"Uh-huh." Jack sighed and let it go. "Just try ta be patient with

Leon. He wants you here; he knows you can help. He don't know how ta deal with ya, that's all."

Gabriella smiled and then stepped in for a hug. "All right, Jack. I'll put on my tough-girl disguise and try not to let him get to me."

Jack returned the hug. "Atta girl."

***

Leon was in the dark cell. He was scrunched into the corner, clutching his knees to his chest, and shivering with cold and fear.

Why did he keep ending up in this place? He hated it here; he couldn't remember what he had done to deserve it. His teeth chattered as he stared into the blackness, and he flinched in fear at the sound of something scurrying past him.

He pushed himself deeper into the corner and wanted to cry.

"Papa?"

Leon jumped and caught his breath.

"Wha . . .?" He looked around in the darkness and saw nothing. "Who's there?" He could hear the tremor in his voice. "Who's there!?"

"Papa, it's me."

"I can't see you!" Leon called out. "Where are you?"

"I'm right here, Papa. Why aren't you coming?"

Leon fought harder to see through the darkness that hid everything. He grew desperate, then got onto his hands and knees and patted the floor, feeling his way forward, trying to find the source of the voice.

"Where are you?

"I'm right here, Papa. I'm waiting for you."

Leon saw a light shining before him, and slowly, the form of a young girl began to take shape. She stood there, her thick, dark brown hair curling down over her shoulders, and her hands clasped politely in front of her, just like in the photograph. Leon reached for her, trying to touch her, desperately wanting to take her in his arms.

"Hannah? *Huittsuu-a*, my little bird."

The expression on her face tightened, and she suddenly looked confused, then angry.

"Don't call me that! My papa called me that. You're not my papa!"

"Yes, I am, Sweetheart," Leon assured her. "I am your papa."

"No, you're not!" she insisted. "My Momma said that my papa died, so how could you be him?"

"No, no, Hannah—I am your papa! You have to believe me."

"Why should I believe you?" she said, her perky little nose curling up into a sneer. "You're a thief—a criminal! You lie to people all the time. You're not my papa."

"Yes, *Huittsuu-a*, please—"

"How dare you call me that! I told you not to!" she screamed at him. "Only my Momma and my Aunt Helèna call me that. You're nothing, you're nobody! You have no right to call me that!"

Leon sobbed: his heart breaking at her harsh words.

"No, Hannah!" he yelled in desperation, but the girl faded away. The light swirled around her and swallowed her until there was nothing left. "NO—come back! *Huittsuu-a*, please…"

But she was gone, and Leon was left alone in the darkness again.

He desperately patted the floor with trembling hands. He forced himself forward into the black, trying to find her, to bring her back.

The light shone again, and he sat back, overwhelmed with relief. But then he realized that this was not his daughter returning to him. The light grew, and the mist cleared to reveal a Shoshoni woman dressed in a fine deerskin tunic and leggings adorned with colorful feathers, and embroidery enhanced with bone, beads, and fine silver.

Leon gasped. It was his mother. He reached out to her, wanting so much to return to his childhood; to a time when he could run into her arms and be comforted by her embrace.

"*Pia . . .*"

"Ahh, *Netuá*. Look what has become of you," the apparition said. "You are my only child to survive, and you have brought disgrace to our family and our ancestors. You must make this right, *Netuá*. Even your daughter rejects you."

Leon sobbed. Her words stabbed him through his already broken heart.

"I know," he cried. "I know. I am trying so hard. But what can I do, *Pia*? I'm lost!"

"Make peace," she said, and slowly, the mist took over again. The image softened as the light began to shrink, and it slowly dissipated. "Make peace ... make peace ... make peace . . ."

"*Pia!*" Leon sobbed, the anguish pouring from him like hot lava.

Again, he pushed forward, swatting at the air to find her, feeling his way forward with hands groping at the cold dirt, but he was alone in the darkness.

Then the floor gave way, and his hands sank into rolling mud that had once been a solid surface. He panicked, trying to pull back, but the mud had hold of him, and it began to suck him down into its depths. He fought and struggled, desperately trying to get free, but it continued to pull him down, first to his elbows, and then he was up to his shoulders, and he panicked.

He screamed, but strangled terror burst forth instead. The mud kept sucking him down until his chin was sinking into the mire. He felt the sludge roll into his open mouth, and he sputtered and spit, then clamped his teeth shut, pressing his lips tightly together.

Fear froze his heart, but his mind cried out at full volume, as his nose was pulled under and he could no longer breathe. He fought and struggled until his eyes were pulled into the blackness that was blacker than black, and his lungs burned. He fought for air, but all he drew into his lungs was the suffocating mud.

Then he was gasping and scrambling, pushing himself back against the headboard, and clutching the blankets to his chest. There was light in the room; it was coming up on dawn, and he could smell coffee brewing, but his mind swirled, and he couldn't breathe. Fear clutched at his chest, and he shivered from the cold sweat that covered him.

Jean was there—oh no—not Jean again! Why did it always have to be her? Oh, but then, who better? She was the only one, besides Jack, with whom he could truly let down all his defenses, and knew that she wouldn't think any the less of him because of it. He let loose a deep, shuddering sigh, and for the briefest of moments, allowed her a glance into his soul.

She must have heard him in the throes of the nightmare and, knowing that he was still inclined to them, had discreetly peeked in on him. She saw that he was awake, but she could also see the terror in his eyes. She was over to the bed instantly and, sitting down, she laid a gentle hand upon his trembling one. She gave the cold, clammy fingers a reassuring squeeze.

He continued to hug his drawn-up knees, but returned her hold, as he fought to stop the trembling. This was awful, even in front of Jean. He had to stop these nightmares; he had to stop being so weak.

He desperately held her hand, as though it were his only hold on sanity. His jaws tightened stubbornly as he refused his emotions full rein.

He wasn't fooling Jean, and her other hand came up and joined the first to hold onto him.

"Ohh, Napoleon. No. It's all right."

"When are they going to stop?" His voice was a whisper, a tight, pleading whisper punctuated by his ragged breath. "I'm losing my mind—I don't know who I am anymore."

"Shh," she continued to soothe him. "You're not losing your mind, Napoleon. You know David said this is your mind trying to heal. You're all right. You're safe here."

"I'm scared to go to sleep."

She continued to sit with him, offering him support in her presence and the touch of her hand until, finally, his breathing settled, and she felt the trembling ease.

He sighed deeply, looked up to meet her eyes, and smiled, though it was a weak smile.

She rubbed his drawn-up knee, still covered by the blankets.

"You feel better now?" she asked him.

"Yes. I'm sorry.'

"Stop apologizing, it's not your fault," she told him. "You're not losing your mind. There's just so many things you need to work out, and I have a feeling that Gabriella showing up here has dredged up some old memories—opened some old wounds."

He gave a sardonic laugh. "Yes!"

He sniffed and wiped his face on the long sleeve of his undershirt. He then uncurled his legs and maneuvered to sit on the bed beside Jean, but he modestly kept the blanket pulled up so it covered his long johns. Leaning forward, he rubbed his face and gave another deep sigh. He still felt worn out, like he'd just been put through the corn grinder.

Then the front door opened, and Jack's familiar footsteps came in and headed towards the kitchen. He passed by the open door to Leon's room, then stopped when he saw the people in there, and he backstepped. It didn't take him long to know what was going on.

"Aww, jeez, Leon. Did you have another nightmare?"

"Yes, he did," Jean answered for him. "Quite a bad one too, by the sounds of it." She smiled a reassurance at Jack, knowing he would be concerned. “Has Mrs. Tanguay stirred yet?”

“I don’t know. I heard her up and pacin’ during the night, so I don’t think she slept much.” He looked at Leon. “I’m thinkin’ she’s got too much on her mind.”

Leon sighed but didn’t respond.

Jack hated to see these two people, whom he cared about, in such misery. Too much water under the bridge, he supposed.

“I expect she’ll be down soon,” Jack continued. “She’ll wanna know what you and Cameron decided. Have you decided?”

Jean nodded as she stood up. “We’ll discuss it over breakfast.”

Jack smiled. “Okay.” His nose twitched, and a twinkle hit his eyes. “Ahh, I smell coffee. Ya want some?”

“Yes, Jack. Thank you. Are you ready for some coffee, Napoleon?”

“Yeah.” Leon sighed, then glanced up and locked eyes with his nephew.

Jack looked worried, and Leon smiled at him, hoping that would be enough to let his partner know that he was all right. “Yes, coffee sounds good. Just let me get dressed.”

“We’ll see you in the kitchen,” Jean said. “The rest of the household should be up soon, and maybe we can make some hotcakes this morning.”

“Sounds good,” Leon agreed, though he didn’t come across as convincing.

Jean gave his knee another pat, then she walked out of the room and closed the door behind her.

Leon sat on the edge of his bed for a few more minutes, trying to settle his thoughts. He was still jittery but knew from experience that a cup of coffee and a conversation with friends, in the light of day, would soon chase the night's fears away.

A slight movement caught his eyes, and he smiled as the half-grown fluff ball came out from hiding under the dresser.

“Scared you, did I?” he asked the kitten.

Murr came the feline response as she trotted to the bed and jumped up.

Leon began to stroke her, and his smile broadened as loud purring took over the room.

***

The breakfast table was set, and the family settled in for bacon and hotcakes when Gabriella hurried down the stairs, still setting her auburn locks up into a bun.

"I'm so sorry. I intended to come down and help with breakfast, but I'm afraid I overslept."

"It's quite all right," Jean indicated the empty chair. "You had a busy day yesterday, and a lot on your mind. Would you like some coffee?"

"Oh, please."

Jean stood to retrieve the coffee pot, and Gabriella hesitated to sit.

"I can get it, Mrs. Marsham. No need for you to bother yourself."

"It's no bother. I see other empty cups here anyway. I'll bring the pot in. Please, sit down and have some breakfast."

The four men and the small boy rose when Gabriella joined them, and Cameron pulled out a chair, inviting their guest to sit and eat.

"Thank you." Gabriella sat and smiled at the others. "Good morning."

Jean returned with the coffee just as pancakes and bacon made their way around the table.

"This is wonderful bacon," Gabriella commented after her first taste. Do you purchase it in town?"

"Oh no," Jean poured more coffee for herself. "The mercantile is wonderful for dry goods and such, but we grow most of our food or trade with our neighbors. Beef for pork, eggs for jams, or canned preserves. Things like that."

Gabriella nodded. "That does make sense. I wish we had that option living in the city."

"I'm sure life in the city offers other advantages."

"Yes."

An awkward silence settled over the group. The desired topic waited in the background until the casual formalities were done with.

Cameron opened the conversation.

"I know you're all wondering what our decision is."

All eyes turned to the patriarch.

"After much discussion," Cameron continued, "Jean and I have decided that it would be best for Penny to leave here."

Penny groaned. "But I don't want to."

"It would be for the best," Jean concurred with her husband. "None of us wants to leave, Penny. But I think Mrs. Tanguay has a good point. You've been attacked twice now, and both times you had friends and family around you. It's not safe for you here."

"But—"

"I agree," Leon said.

Penny looked at him with betrayal in her eyes. "Napoleon! I thought you, at least, would be on my side."

"I am on your side, Sweetheart. But I agree that you would be safer away from here. Helèna is very resourceful. She'll look after you."

"But for how long?"

Frank joined the conversation. "As long as it takes, little lady. But with Mrs. Tanguay assisting me at this end, I'm sure we'll find those responsible in short order."

Gabriella sent Frank a flashing glare, which she quickly smothered. "We'll get to the bottom of this, I assure you. But I won't give false promises. I have a feeling this runs deep, and it could take some time to dig up who is responsible."

"But, what about Thanksgiving?" Penny frowned. "And Christmas! Surely, we'll have this all cleared up by Christmas."

Silent looks went around the table.

Penny put down her fork, no longer interested in eating. "First my wedding and now the winter festivities."

Jack, sitting next to her, gave her hand a gentle squeeze. "I know, Darlin', but it's for the best. I don't know what I'd do if anything happened . . ."

"I wanna go!" Eli declared over a mouthful of hotcakes. "I wanna see Penny turned into an old lady, and I wanna go on a train ride, and I wanna see Top'ka!"

"Topeka," Gabriella corrected him, then smiled. "At least someone is enthusiastic."

"It appears the master of the house has spoken," Cameron said with a chuckle.

"Yes," Jean sent her son a stern look, "even if it was over a mouthful of food."

Eli grinned at his mother, pleased the adults were finally listening to him.

***

Leon and Jack sloshed through the mud at the back of the horse barn. With the creek running through the property no more than a few yards away, this section turned to soup during the wetter months.

Jack focused on staying on his feet when a curse from his partner caused him to stop and look back. What he saw caused him to smirk.

Leon stood on one leg, his other stockinged foot hanging above the opening of his boot. He leaned on his shovel to avoid falling over.

"Dammit. The mud has sucked my boot right off."

"Toes up, Leon."

Leon frowned. "What do you mean?"

"When walkin' through mud like this, ya gotta keep your toes up. That way, your boot won't come off."

Leon pushed his foot back into the boot, then, with toes up, he struggled to pull himself free of the mud.

"It's not coming."

Using his shovel to steady himself, Jack pulled his boot out of the sucking mud and made slow progress back to where Leon still tugged and cursed.

"Take it easy. If ya pull too hard, you're just gonna—"

Too late.

"Dammit!" Leon lost his balance and went over. Landing on his rump in the mud, he felt the cold dampness as it invaded his dungarees and then his long johns. "Oh, yuck. And you spent five years dealing with this?"

Jack chuckled. "You get the feel of it, eventually."

"I already got the feel of it. Give me a hand, will ya?"

Jack set his shovel down, then grabbed Leon's free hand with both of his. "Ya ready?"

"Just a minute."

Leon positioned his shovel handle to give him more leverage, then nodded. "Okay, pull."

Jack leaned back and pulled, putting his weight into getting his partner back on his feet.

Leon managed to struggle up, then overbalanced. In a desperate effort to save himself, his foot came out of the boot once again and, this time, came down hard into the mucky mire.

Jack tried to hold him up, but Leon's balance was gone. His other foot came out of the boot and plunged into the wet muck. The next thing he knew, he was full-length and elbow-deep in the mud again.

Then it started to rain.

"Dammit!"

In his frustration, Leon punched the mud with his fist, which caused the thick, brown fluid to splatter up and slap him in the face.

He glared at his partner. "What are you laughing at?"

"You!" Jack guffawed, then struggled to put on a straight face. "Jeez, Leon, we used ta deal with this kinda mud all the time when we were kids. What happened?"

"A strong aversion to living off the land. C'mon, help me outta this crap."

A feminine chuckle brought both pairs of eyes to the back door of the barn.

Leon slumped and groaned.

Jack grinned. "Penny, Darlin'. Is it lunchtime already?"

"It is, but I'm sure it can wait. My goodness, Napoleon, you are a sight. What are you doing?"

Leon's response was a moody snark.

Jack smirked. "We was about ta dig a trench along here so's ta run this standin' water into the creek. Your pa had some of the fellas bring half a wagon load of gravel from the riverbed. He figures it's time ta put more down here ta dry this area up."

Penny sighed and nodded. "Yes. This section always gets so muddy. The gravel helps, but it does need to be replaced every few years." She frowned and glanced up into the dull gray heavens. "It's really starting to come down now." She looked at the lump of mud-covered humanity still figuring out how to get to its feet. "I'll bring some water from the well so you can get washed up. Momma would have a fit if you walked into her clean house looking like that."

Penny pivoted on her heel and disappeared through the barn.

Jack returned his attention to his partner.

Leon had positioned himself on his hands and knees, and managed to straighten up onto his feet. Now that he was no longer concerned about losing his boots, he didn't have any problem staying upright.

The two men locked gazes.

Jack tried hard to keep a straight face, but finally, he snorted and then laughed out loud.

Leon slumped, but then, he too cracked a smile, and before he knew it, he was laughing along with his friend.

"C'mon, Leon. Let's get ya cleaned up before ya freeze ta death."

***

Stripping down to bare skin and Jack dumping two buckets of cold well water over his head wasn't the worst thing that happened to Leon that day.

Sam, walking in on them with a towel and some clean clothes while Leon still stood, naked and shivering in the barn alcove, caused Sam more embarrassment than it did the ex-con. Prison life had beaten that out of him.

No, the worst thing that happened was Leon entering the warm ranch house and coming face-to-face with Gabriella's smirk.

"Don't start," Leon said, as he wagged a finger under her nose. "This was not my fault."

"Of course, it wasn't. I simply marvel that a grown man would still find pleasure rolling around in the mud."

Leon's jaw tightened, and an explosion would have been imminent if Jean hadn't stepped in.

"Come, sit down, Napoleon. I've kept the stew hot for you, and there's fresh bread. I have water heating on the stove so you can have a real bath after you've eaten."

Leon came off his snit, and his gaze softened to a smile as he accepted Jean's invitation.

"Thank you, Jean."

"Jack, you too. Come and have some lunch.

***

An hour later, Leon emerged from the washroom, still drying his tousled hair, but finally feeling warm and clean again.

He came up short when he nearly bumped into Penny, blocking his way.

"Napoleon, may I speak with you?"

Leon's brows arched. "Sure. Ahh, just me? Don't you want Jack here, too?"

"No, just you. Jack and Papa are out digging that trench. Eli is there too, thinking he's helping them."

"Ha! Yeah, okay."

He still hesitated while he scanned the living area.

Penny read his thoughts. "Don't worry. Mrs. Tanguay is upstairs, and Momma is in the kitchen."

Leon smiled with relief that Gabriella was not hovering around to ridicule him.

"All right. Let's sit."

They entered the sitting room, where the fire was still crackling, sending heat into the cozy space.

They sat down on the sofa together.

Leon shifted to face her. "What would you like to talk about?"

Penny sighed and produced a gesture that seemed to encompass the whole world.

"This," she said. "All these things are going on. All these decisions are being made without any regard for what I want."

"Hmm." Leon nodded. "You feel like events are running out of control and you're just along for the ride."

"Yes! Everyone is saying I should go along with all this, that I should trust her, but ... you don't trust her, Napoleon. Why should I?"

Leon sat back on the sofa, a heavy sigh being his only response.

Penny took this as a sign she was on the right track.

"It's obvious that you two have history, but it's not a good history, is it? You and Detective Carlyle have history, too. You get along with him all right for the most part, but I still feel some resentment there. But it's worse with Mrs. Tanguay. You're trying to cover it, you're trying to be civil, but ... she was a detective of sorts, too. Did she have a hand in turning you in? Did she help send you to prison?"

"No, no, Penny. Just the opposite. She did all she could to hasten my release."

"Then why have we not heard of her? We know everyone who was helping you. Why did she not come forward?"

Leon sat up straight and took Penny's hand in his. "I expect Jack mentioned her; you just haven't connected it. But I'm sure you realize by now that Gabriella works behind the scenes. That's what she does best. She wrote to me in prison, and to Jack more than once, letting us know she was doing all she could to help. And she did. She's on our side. You have to believe that."

Penny frowned and chewed her lip. "I don't know. There's

something you're leaving out. I'm getting strong images of betrayal. But not from Jack, he only feels sadness. Whatever wounds she inflicted, he has forgiven her. But you haven't. Jack has not forgiven Detective Carlyle for whatever transgressions he perpetrated against you two, but you have. Why is it that you can forgive him, but not her?"

Leon flicked a smile, then squeezed Penny's hand.

"I'd forgotten how intuitive you can be sometimes. I haven't fooled you at all, have I?"

"Intuition has nothing to do with it," Penny insisted. "All one has to do is watch and listen. I need to know why you don't trust her before I place my life in her hands."

"I do trust her, Penny. I told you that."

"And yet, you haven't forgiven her."

"I'm not going to get out of this one, am I?"

"No."

Leon took a deep breath and braced himself.

"Okay. Gabriella is my wife."

Penny's eyes widened with shock as her shoulders bolted straight with disbelief.

"What! But you and Miranda . . ."

"I know, I know. I suppose it's more appropriate to say that Gabriella was my wife. Oh, it seems like a lifetime ago now. I was still running Elk Mountain, and Gabriella and I were very much in love. My uncle was a Shoshone Holy Man and married us in that tradition. I honored the marriage. I wanted her as my wife and planned on spending my life with her.

"But she knew our marriage would not stand up in court, and that gave her a way out if things turned bad. We had some wonderful times together, but eventually, and not surprisingly, considering my profession, things did turn bad. Very bad.

"She left, and at a time when I very much needed ... oh well, that doesn't matter. She disappeared from my life, annulling our marriage, and I didn't hear from her again until her letter arrived at the prison. When I ran into her in town last week, that was the first time I'd seen her in over ten years."

Penny sat quietly, holding her friend's hand. Tears pricked at her eyes with the onslaught of pain that attacked her sensitive soul.

"I'm sorry, Napoleon. I'm so sorry. Momma was right. I

shouldn't have pushed."

"No, Sweetheart," Leon stroked her cheek and smiled. "It's alright. We're expecting you to trust your life to a woman you barely know. You have every right to ask questions."

"Okay."

"Do you feel better now? Will you do as she suggests and trust that she knows what she's doing?"

"I'm not sure."

Leon frowned, wondering what more he could say to reassure.

Penny sent him a cheeky smile. "She had your love, and she walked away. How is that sensible?"

"Ha!" Leon grinned and hugged her even closer. "Thank you."

Penny smiled into his shoulder. "For what?"

"For making me laugh again." He kissed her forehead. "I love you, ya know. You're a dear, dear friend. You and Jack are going to be great together."

***

The following morning, Eli sat at the dining room table, transfixed as he watched his favorite sister gradually transform into an old lady.

"Wow," he said for the umpteenth time. "Do I get to wear a costume too?"

"How about a wig?" Gabriella asked him. "I have one in my case that should fit you."

"Yeah." Eli jumped down from the chair and rummaged through the open makeup case. He found a wig that was far too big for him, but he thought it was perfect. He returned to his chair, balancing the wig upon his straight, blond hair.

Gabriella put the finishing touches on Penny's gray-haired wig, gently tucking the last of her yellow locks into place and out of sight.

"There we are. Stand up and see how it all feels."

Penny rose to her feet, then put a hand on her expanded midriff. "It feels so awkward. How does someone who is truly fat get around with this? Especially in the summer. I'm getting warm already."

Gabriella chuckled. "Naturally heavy people adjust to the weight as it comes on. I'm afraid a body suit is not quite as comfortable as your own skin. But it does serve its purpose."

Penny took some steps, feeling bloated and ugly.

Eli poking his finger into her artificial layers did nothing to lift her mood.

"Eli, stop it!"

"You're all squishy." He giggled and poked at her again.

Gabriella crouched down to Eli's eye level and took his attention away from teasing his sister.

"We're all playing a game, remember? In this game, your sister is an old lady."

Eli looked up at Penny and snorkeled. "Yeah, she is an old lady."

"So, you're not going to give the game away, are you? You must play the game with us all the way into town."

"What do I get to play?"

"You're going to be the Watcher, and it's a very important role. We usually pick men to be the Watcher. Do you think you're old enough to handle it?"

Eli puffed up. His youthful face turned serious, and he nodded vigorously, causing the wig to wobble sideways, making him look like a drunken judge. "What do I do?"

"You need to look at people's eyes. If you see anyone looking at your sister or mother for more than ten seconds, you must tell Jack. Maybe you can squeeze his finger or wink at him. The trick is to keep anyone from knowing the Watcher has spotted them. Can you do that?"

"Sure." Then the lad frowned again. "How long is ten seconds?"

"Can you count to ten?"

"I can count to five!"

"That's perfect. Count to five twice, and that's ten. Can you do that?"

Eli scrunched up his mouth as he digested this information. Then he smiled and nodded, causing his wig to fall to the floor. He ignored it now that he was entrusted with something far more important.

"Yeah, I can do that. Easy!"

"Good. Now, let's go speak with your parents."

***

"Oh my." Jean couldn't help the exclamation when she saw her daughter waddle into the sitting room. "I wouldn't have recognized you."

"Do I have to wear this all the way into town? This wig itches, and the makeup on my face feels like it'll crack if I smile."

Jack came in behind them and put an arm around Penny's shoulders. "It's ta keep ya safe, Darlin'. Once you're on the train, you can take it off."

"At least try to wait until you're out of the county," Gabriella suggested. "Out of the territory would be better."

Penny groaned as she fought the impulse to scratch her scalp. "Oh no."

"So," Gabi sent a compassionate look to the Marshams, "who's going?"

Cameron put an arm around his wife.

"Penny, Jean, and Elijah." The couple shared an emotional look. "I need to stay to make sure the place still runs." He nodded towards Jack, "And I've got the feeling that you and Napoleon will be busy elsewhere. Sam is a good hand, but he can't do it all, and the other hands are out on the range, getting things ready for winter. At least I'll know my family is safe."

"Cameron, I'm real sorry about this," Jack said. "You folks deserve better."

Cameron nodded. "We all deserve better, but sometimes we have to work extra hard to get it. Keep them safe for me, Jack. Get them there."

"I will."

"Aren't we all going?" Eli squeaked. "I thought we were all playing the game."

"Your father has to stay here," Jean told him.

"But why?"

"Someone needs to look after the ranch."

"Anything you want to take with you, you'll need to fit into that one carpet bag," Gabriella reminded them. "Keep it to necessities. Helèna will help you with the rest once you arrive. You can write and send telegrams, but not directly. They will go via the Wells Fargo office in Denver. We can't run the risk of someone picking up the address from your mail."

Eli frowned. This conversation proved to be most confusing to him.

"Why can't we take our own clothes?"

"You never mind," Jean told him. "We'll get you new clothes in Topeka. That's all you need to worry about."

Eli sighed dramatically and shuffled his feet. He hated being treated like a child.

"It's all right, little man," Jack assured him. "Don't forget the important job you have to do."

Eli grinned, forgetting his irritation. "Yeah! I'm the Watcher."

Jean sighed. She smiled at Jack for averting a minor tantrum, then looked at Gabriella. "You seem to have thought of everything."

"I hope so." Gabriella paused, her lips straightening. "There is one more thing. My daughter will be there. She's fourteen."

"Oh my. That's a handful. But don't worry. I've brought up two daughters myself. I'm sure we'll all get along famously."

"You don't understand. She doesn't know about the life I led with my first husband."

"Ah." Jean nodded. "And you want us to keep it that way? Keep your secrets, secret?"

Gabriella heaved a sigh of relief, sensing the understanding in the other woman's gaze.

"Please. It's the only place I could think of to send you."

"You're youngest daughter." Jean reached out and gently touched Gabriella's hand. "I understand why you're here. Thank you."

"Secrets?" Penny narrowed her eyes. "She doesn't know you worked for Wells Fargo?"

"I was never officially with them, but no, she doesn't. I gave up that life years ago."

"Oh. Yes, I suppose that kind of work would be risky when you're raising a child."

"It is." Gabriella glanced at Penny, but it was long enough for her to pick up a sense of who this young woman was. Then she smiled. No wonder Jack loves her. "Sometimes you have to give up things you love to keep your children safe."

Penny was fortunate that the makeup hid her features, as confusion over this woman was written on them. She was willing to go along with the plan only because of Leon's assurance, but she found it difficult to imagine them as a married couple.

Working to get her mind around that concept blocked any enlightenment about the child and her parentage. Penny presumed the girl was a product of Gabriella's first marriage. If she hadn't had so many other concerns, she would have realized that the numbers didn't add up to support this assumption.

***

Penny made her way out to the horse barn. Pushing open the doors, she stepped quietly inside and looked around the musky interior.

"Napoleon?"

"Yes?" came the familiar baritone from the direction of Karma's stall.

Penny smiled and made her way down the aisle. Sure enough, her friend was in the stall with his beloved mare, grooming her with a soft brush even though her thick coat was already shining.

Karma's eyes morphed into white-rimmed saucers when the strange apparition came into view. The creature sounded like a human she knew, and even the scent was similar, but the apparition approaching her told a different story. With her head held high, the sensitive mare snorted and backed into the far corner of her stall.

"Oh, I'm sorry." Penny clucked softly to her. "I didn't mean to scare you."

Leon chuckled. "Don't worry about it. But you are quite the sight."

Penny slumped and slipped a hand under the wig to scratch. "Argh, you have no idea how uncomfortable this is. I don't know how Mrs. Tanguay puts up with it."

"Hmm. You look like you're ready to go. Did you come in to say goodbye?"

"Yes."

Leon gave Karma a soft pat and joined Penny in the aisle. "I suppose I should keep up appearances in case we are being watched. After all, it is my great-aunt who is leaving." Leon offered his arm to her. "Lean on me a little. Think of yourself as an elderly lady whose joints are worn out."

Penny focused on these instructions, and by the time they reached the barn doors, she had the deception down pat.

"Oh dear," she stressed. "I should have been doing this on my way in. I never thought about it."

"It takes practice."

CHAPTER FOURTEEN
THE GREAT DECEPTION

"Oh my!" Penny almost faltered in her persona at the sight that met their eyes. "I have to admit, she is good."

Even Napoleon was taken aback.

Gabriella was more than good. If Leon hadn't known that Penny was on his arm, he would have sworn that the blonde woman standing by the carriage was her.

The carriage was all set to go, with as much luggage as seemed appropriate for an elderly lady heading for home.

Sam stood at the head of Berry and Spike, who had been assigned harness duty to take the family into town.

Eli was jumping up and down in his excitement to be off on a real adventure. It was all Jean could do to keep him contained.

"Elijah, settle down. Remember, this is part of the game. All we're doing is going into town to do some shopping."

Eli stopped in mid-jump, his expression dropping to disappointment.

"But I thought we were goin' on a train ride."

Jean sighed. She hated lying to her children, but under these circumstances, she decided it was the best thing to do.

"Not today. Today, we are going to do some shopping. We can get some penny candy at the mercantile. You like those."

Eli slouched. "I suppose."

He clambered into the carriage with his mother right behind him.

Leon stepped up with Penny in hand. He smiled briefly at Gabriella, then returned his attention to Penny.

He leaned over and whispered in her ear. "Now, give me a hug like you're saying goodbye to your favorite nephew."

"I thought I was her favorite nephew," Jack piped in.

Penny almost giggled, but she controlled herself. She looked up into Napoleon's eyes and smiled at him.

"That will be easy." And to prove the point, she gave him a big hug, though she was careful to avoid rubbing her face against his shirt. "Goodbye, Napoleon. At least for now. I'm going to miss you. Don't let these two detectives push you around."

Leon chuckled and kissed her on the forehead to avoid smudging her disguise. "I won't. Take care of yourself, Darlin'. I'm sure I'll see you again soon."

Then everyone settled, and they made ready to depart.

Leon turned to Jack. "Take care of them and be careful."

"Of course. You be careful too. If this little ruse is workin', they'll still think Penny is here. They may try again. Keep your eyes focused outside of your head."

"I will."

Jack climbed into the driver's seat and Sam came up beside him just as Cameron finished his goodbyes to his wife and children.

The two men shared a quick look of understanding, and then Jack clucked to the team, and they headed out of the yard.

"I didn't think this would be so hard," Cameron mumbled as he watched his family depart.

"It's for the best," Gabriella said. "They'll be safe with Helèna."

Cameron sent her a sad smile and nodded.

Leon turned away and went up the steps to the front porch.

Frank sat at his leisure watching the little family rituals.

Leon hesitated and looked down at him. "Not much for goodbyes, are you?"

Frank snorted. "What goodbyes? We'll see them again. Besides, your wife and I have plans to make."

"She's not my wife anymore, Frank. You can let that one go."

"You sure about that?"

Leon's focus shifted briefly as Gabriella came up the steps. His eyes flickered toward her, but before making contact, he looked back at Frank. "Yes."

Then he walked into the house.

Gabriella stopped and watched him leave. His cold behavior hurt more than she thought possible. Tears burned in her eyes, but she fought them into submission.

"What has gotten into that man?" Cameron commented as he joined the group on the porch. "He's the one who recommended you come here to help, then he treats you like an impostor."

Gabriella sent Cameron a sad smile. "As far as he is concerned, I am an impostor. I hoped we could come together again as friends, but it seems I am only here to help with this situation and nothing more. I suppose I can't blame him for that."

She turned away before any platitudes would attempt to deny what she already knew. She returned to Penny's room to nurse her hurt feelings in private.

***

Leon was in a sour mood. The longer he was in Gabriella's company, the more difficult it was to remain civil to her. He had joined the family to bid farewell because he knew it mattered to Penny, and it was necessary to keep up the appearance of seeing his "great-aunt" off. That was important, and if anyone knew how to play the "long game" in a con, it was Napoleon Nash.

But now, with most of the family gone, the large ranch house was quiet and devoid of distractions. He could feel Gabriella's presence oppressing him, as though her very existence insulted his deeply buried wounds.

His one consolation was that she and Frank would be heading to town in a couple of days, and he would gain some respite from her company.

The only reason he was willing to accept her was the hope of seeing his daughter again. But even to this, Gabriella was not willing to commit, so, as far as he was concerned, she could do what she came here to do, then leave.

He decided now was a good time for a ride. Karma was the one lady in his life who could lift his dreary moods and draw him into a more sociable frame of mind.

He exited his downstairs bedroom just in time to come face-to-face with Cameron's stern look.

"Napoleon, it's time we talked."

The brief lifting of Leon's sour mood disappeared. The last thing he wanted to do was discuss this with anyone, even Cameron. He set his jaw and stood with hands on his hips, challenging the other man, daring him to push this dictate.

Cameron was not intimidated. He'd had to give Jack a sock on the jaw to get him to buck up and start behaving himself, and he wasn't beyond doing the same thing to Napoleon.

The rancher returned Leon's glare, his jaw tightening, and his hands closing into fists.

"Sit down." Cameron's tone was low but menacing. He knew from Napoleon's current animosity that the ex-con would eventually challenge his authority. This issue was as good as any other to re-establish the ground rules.

Leon continued to glare at him, stubbornly not moving.

Cameron pushed, daring the other man to make good on his challenge. It seemed an eternity: the two men were locked in a battle for dominance, but, as before, at Leon's arrest, it was the younger man who backed down.

This wasn't Elk Mountain, and he wasn't the great outlaw leader anymore. He wasn't anything anymore. He blinked a couple of times, his stance softening, then he looked away. He was still angry; he was still defensive, but Cameron had him beaten, and they both knew it.

"Have a seat, Napoleon," Cameron repeated, but without quite the same menace to it.

Leon sighed. He pulled a chair out from the dining table. His movements were filled with resentment, and the chair banged against the table legs, nearly tipping over. Leon grabbed the chair, picked it up, slammed it into place, and then sat down. He folded his arms and glared at the tabletop. He prepared himself for a chewing out, knowing he deserved it, but not willing to own it.

Cameron sighed, quietly pulled out a chair, and joined him. He was then hit by a sudden déjà vu: over five years ago, the two of them had sat together at a table much like this one, and Cameron had assured his friend that he would not be forgotten.

So much water under the bridge since that day. So many changes.

"What is this all about?" he finally asked. "You recommended this woman to help us, but now you treat her like she's the devil incarnate. What's gotten into you?"

Leon sat looking at the table. His emotions jumped between anger and hurt, his jaw tightening with protective stubbornness. The man he was now wanted to tell Cameron what had happened, but the previous Napoleon Nash, the hardened outlaw who kept things close to his chest, found it hard to break old habits.

Cameron sat quietly and waited. He could see the struggle, just as

David had seen it that night in the Gibsons' kitchen. David had known then that all he had to do was wait, and Napoleon would find his way. Cameron knew the same.

Finally, Leon gave a little cough. His shoulders relaxed a little, and he shifted forward as his finger traced a small circle on the top of the table.

"Jack was right about what he said last night," he finally admitted. "Gabriella and I have history." Leon frowned as he felt his pain rising to choke him. He pursed his lips as he fought for control. "I don't want to talk about it."

"Too bad." Cameron was prepared to be ruthless. "The tension between you and Gabriella has affected everyone. She did a great deal to help you with your previous predicament and has come here, willing to put herself and her family at risk to help us. The least you can do is meet her halfway. The fact that you have history is all the more reason for you to show her respect."

"Respect."

It was a whisper that Cameron barely caught.

Leon sighed and straightened up. He looked Cameron in the eye. "Fine. All right. But I tell you this out of respect for you, not her. I loved her once upon a time. I'd never loved anyone like I loved her, and she stabbed me through the heart. She took our daughter and pushed me away. She denied me access to any contact at all. I have a fourteen-year-old daughter who doesn't even know I exist."

Silence settled over the table.

Cameron's edge softened as he realized Leon's cold dispassion was a defense, resulting from a deep-seated pain.

He nodded. "I can understand why you would be angry about that. Am I correct in assuming that her youngest daughter, the one who died, was also yours?"

"Yes." Leon's resentment sank into hurt. He swallowed against the tightness and gazed at the table, his thoughts miles and years away.

Cameron sighed and gave a minuscule shake of his head.

"I'm sorry, Napoleon. I didn't know. That's a hard thing to get over. But don't you think Gabriella has suffered too? Don't you think she only did what she did in the best interests of your remaining daughter? You were an outlaw, running a gang of outlaws. Can't you see what a detrimental lifestyle that would be for a family?"

"I did," Leon admitted. "Time and distance convinced me that it was all for the best; that Gabriella was right. I thought I had forgiven her. I thought ... but then she shows up here, out of the blue. No warning. Just, 'Hi, I'm back. I'm here to help.' Like the past eleven years just disappeared." He tensed again as his lip curled slightly in a snarl. "Like she can simply walk back into my life as though nothing had happened."

"That would have been a shock, yes," Cameron agreed. "No wonder you were in such a mood that day. But you agreed to her coming here to the ranch. You could have turned her away in town, and we would never have been the wiser. Why didn't you do that, if you couldn't handle her being here?"

"I thought I could handle it," Leon protested. "And I knew she could help. I was grasping at straws. For Penny's sake, I thought I could bury what we had been through and do what needed to be done."

"Then you'd better do that. For Penny's sake. And for the sake of those of us who have to live with both of you in the same house. She is the mother of your children, Napoleon. Nothing that has happened can change that fact. She deserves your respect. As long as she is in my home, you will be civil."

Leon sat solemnly. He knew Cameron was right, but knowing it only made him more resentful.

Cameron could see that he wasn't getting through. There was more to this than Leon was letting out, but he had to let it out before he could move on from it.

Cameron waited for the right moment, then pushed again. "And what about Detective Carlyle?" he asked. "It's not just you and Mrs. Tanguay who have history, is it? You all know one another, but Jack can hardly hide his disdain for the man. How does he play into this drama?"

"Ohh, Frank." Leon sighed and rubbed a hand over his eyes. "I've known Frank just as long as I've known Gabriella. He's a right bastard, that's for sure. I was arrested and handed over to Frank and his partner. They took turns questioning me, though 'interrogating' is more like it. For three days and nights, they pounded on me and would not let up. No food, no water . . ." Leon's eyes glazed over as he went back to the time when Frank Carlyle had put the fear of death into him. "Thank goodness Jack and the gang got me away from them."

Cameron was not surprised. Leon and Jack had lived dangerous lives outside the law. Frank Carlyle had had a job to do, and he knew how to do it.

"Is that why Jack feels so much animosity towards him? Because of his treatment of you at that time?"

Leon looked at Cameron with eyes filled with sorrow.

"No. That was the beginning of it, but there was more. Much more. Frank knew I was infatuated with Gabriella, and I later learned he had paid her to spy on us. She caused some damage, for sure, but even that wasn't the worst of it. Not for me, anyway."

Leon struggled. Before he could stop it, a tear rolled down his cheek. He scowled and quickly brushed it away, but not before Cameron saw it

"Napoleon, was Frank responsible for the death of your daughter?"

Again, Leon sat and gazed into the distant past. Another tear rolled down his cheek, but this time he did not attempt to brush it away.

"When Gabriella sent me a telegram informing me that we had a daughter, I was scared. I was so young. Living wild and free. I didn't want the responsibility of a family. Gabriella had betrayed us, and I was trying to forget her. But I still loved her so much.

"She made it clear she didn't want me around. She was simply informing me about the child and wasn't seeking help. But my curiosity got the better of me. I had to see my daughter."

A smile escaped him. "It was love at first sight. I held her in my arms and gazed into her beautiful brown eyes. I can still feel her tiny hand grasping my finger."

The smile disappeared, leaving only sadness. "Hannah. Gabriella named her after my mother. I was lost then. No going back. Suddenly, I wanted to be a father; I wanted her in my life."

He sighed and glanced at Cameron, to find that man smiling. It was a sad smile, but full of understanding.

"It's amazing how that happens," Cameron said. "Many young men don't want the responsibility of a family until one is thrust upon them. Then it becomes everything that matters."

"Yes," Leon agreed. Now that he had begun, he couldn't stop. It was painful to dredge up these memories, but it felt like the right thing to do. It felt good to finally let it all out.

"Gabriella insisted on staying with her sister, Helèna, in San Francisco. But when she became in the family way again, she agreed to marry me and take a house in Gillette, so my family could be closer."

"You were married?" Cameron asked. This development surprised him more than anything else he was hearing.

Leon flashed a smile. "Yes. We were married by my uncle in the traditional Shoshone Blanket Ceremony. It would not stand up in the white man's court, but it was good enough for me. It was an honor. Mukua was a good man. I miss him. He was another whom Morrison butchered . . ." Leon shook his head, waving that memory away. "No, never mind. That's not a part of this.

"Anyway, Ella was a sweetheart. So much more like her mother in coloring than Hannah. Green eyes and auburn hair. And very opposite to Hannah in her character as well." Leon smiled again, looking back at his younger daughter. "Where Hannah was boisterous and outgoing, Ella was gentle. She was quiet in nature and always smiling."

Leon sat for a moment in silence as memories of Ella flooded his mind.

Cameron waited. He needed time to digest all this, and yet, he knew that there was more to come. Much more.

When he was ready, Leon continued. "I spent more and more time with my family in Gillette. I was so happy there. I should have realized it couldn't last. I was lying to myself because I wanted it so much. But I wasn't willing to give up my profession yet. I was stupid and selfish. I should have . . ." He sighed again, the regret over his past choices weighing heavily on his heart.

"I was there for Christmas that year," he continued. "We were walking through town to take the girls on a sleigh ride.

"Frank was smart. Well, that's not a surprise. He hadn't forgotten about me, not by a long shot. But he waited and bided his time. He waited until I had my family around me so that I wouldn't resist. And he was right, it worked. Before we knew what was happening, we were surrounded.

"Ella had been fussing, so I was holding her in my arms. There's no way I was going to resist. But one of the junior detectives decided that my surrender wasn't good enough, and he fired a shot at me. The bullet scraped across my ribs." Leon's hand rubbed the area of the old wound. "But it hit Ella full on."

Cameron closed his eyes, his jaw clenched tightly against this tragic event. "Oh no."

Leon's breath was ragged, his eyes glistening with threatening tears.

"My baby girl died in my arms. I saw the life drain from her beautiful eyes as her blood soaked into me."

"Oh, good lord, Napoleon. I had no idea you went through this. I thought I knew you. I thought I knew what your life had been, but you've never given any hint of this."

Cameron took a deep breath and then let it out slowly. "And you blame Frank for it."

"No," Leon admitted. "No. But Jack does, and he won't let it go. Frank was furious. He's not normally a passionate man, but he would have wrung the life out of that officer if the others hadn't pulled him off. Gabriella doesn't blame Frank either. We both knew who was responsible. But not Jack. We all have a hard time tolerating Frank; it's just his manner, but Jack loathes him. He tolerates him only because we've had to.

"Anyway, the next day, Gabriella came to the jailhouse where I was being held. She told me she was leaving and taking Hannah with her. I was not to follow. I begged her to let me at least say goodbye to my remaining daughter, but she refused. She left me during my worst agony. When I needed her the most, she turned her back and walked away, taking everything that mattered to me with her."

Leon sighed and shook his head at the memory of betrayal.

"Gabriella had been married before and had a son, Theo. Her in-laws did not approve of her, and when her husband died, his folks legally stole Theo and disappeared.

"Gabriella was devastated. She did everything she could to find him, but she never did."

Leon's sympathy for Gabriella's plight was short-lived, and anger surfaced again. "Then she turned around and did the same thing to me!

"She denied me my daughter, and that was the last I heard from her until she wrote to me in prison. It was the last I saw of her until she showed up here in town, offering to help."

Again, silence settled over the two men.

Cameron was at a loss. The usual platitudes seemed like mockeries compared to this tragic stream of events.

"Do you understand now?" Leon whispered. "I can't even look at her without the pain stabbing me in the heart again. I wish I didn't feel this way. I remember the joy of loving her and would welcome it again. But it's too late. Rather than hold her in my arms, I want to push her away. I want to hurt her the way she hurt me."

"I know. You're afraid she is going to hurt you again, so you lash out to protect yourself. I understand that."

Leon looked at him, the pain still hard in his eyes. "I don't."

Cameron flashed a quick smile, still sad but filled with encouragement.

"I think that you wanting to forgive her is a good sign. You've already been there once. You had come to realize her reasons for doing that, and you forgave her. It's only the shock of seeing her like this that has brought all those angry emotions to the surface again.

"Give it time, Napoleon. But in the meantime, I insist on a truce. And I'll say the same to Jack if his resentment of Frank becomes intolerable. Perhaps it is a good thing that Jack is away for a while."

"Maybe that's what I should do, too," Leon mumbled.

"Run away?" Cameron huffed. "Don't you dare. With Jack gone, I need you here. We just have to find a way to work together."

Leon's jaw tightened as his resentment struggled to return. With Jack gone, he felt like no one was on his side. Not even Cameron.

"Fine," he snarked as he roughly pushed his chair back. "I'm going for a ride. I need some time to clear my head."

Cameron nodded. "Just don't forget to come back."

***

Gabriella's eyes flickered open, then gazed around Penny's bedroom. She sat up and dropped her tired head into her hands. She had hoped she would feel more positive after a nap.

She hadn't shown it, but the events of the last couple of days had been extremely stressful. Once the Marsham family had finally been underway with a ruse she hoped would be successful, her tiredness blanketed her shoulders. The continued resentment and cold responses from Napoleon had sapped what little energy she'd had left.

She vaguely recalled hearing Napoleon and Cameron talking in the dining room, but she had drifted off to sleep before getting the gist of their conversation. Now that she was awake, the household was eerily silent.

She rolled onto her back and stared at the ceiling, her thoughts returning to the conversation she'd had with Jack the previous evening. It had been heartbreaking.

Leon needed care, patience, and routine, and it was clear her presence upset his sensibilities. The burning anger thrown at her as she had walked out of the jailhouse in Gillette had hardened into a cold hatred that assaulted her every time he condescended to glance at her—which was rare.

Once he had said his goodbyes to the Marshams, he avoided her eyes and strode off towards the house. His message was clear; letters of support and forgiveness were one thing, but dealing with her in the flesh, after everything else he'd been through, was more than he could handle.

Watching him from under her eyelids, he broke her heart all over again. He was so thin, gaunt, and lost. All she wanted to do was take him in her arms and rock him gently back to safety. But the light had gone out in those wonderful eyes, replaced by ghosts and shades of horror. They no longer danced with mischievous promise—they slashed like a razor as they dashed by her because just about anything else was more interesting.

It did not occur to Gabriella that his cold shoulder was due to the opposite reasons from her rationale. From her side, she could only conclude that he hated her, and believing this broke her heart.

The sound of a horse and buggy coming into the yard distracted her. She was tempted to look out the window to see who it was, but she was not in her disguise as Penny, and they needed to keep that illusion as long as possible.

She resigned herself simply to listening.

***

Cameron sat at the dining table, attempting to catch up on the neglected business end of running a ranch. He sighed as he glanced over the separate piles of paperwork placed strategically over the entire surface of the table. This part of ranch life was tedious on a good day, but now he found it almost impossible to concentrate.

Penny had taken on much of the accounting, but once she was married, she would live in her own home, and those duties would fall to him. He had resigned himself to this fact, but thought he would have plenty of time to deal with it.

It occurred to him that once their current situation had been rectified, it might be time to convert one of the spare bedrooms into an office. He had even considered hiring an accountant to come out once a week to handle it. That would be much easier than gathering all the papers together and taking them to an office in town.

The more he thought about this, the more he liked it. The ranch was doing well, and he could afford to pay someone else to take it over. He frowned as another thought occurred to him. With Penny moving out, Jean would lose her assistant, and Eli could run any mother into the ground. Even an experienced mother like Jean.

Penny did a lot more around the house than either parent realized until they were faced with her absence. Although he wondered if Jean would accept help. She could be headstrong, wanting things done her way.

Then the sounds of a horse and buggy coming into the yard distracted him from the mundane but also caused him a pang of anxiety over how to deal with visitors. Hopefully, both Frank and Gabriella would stay hidden.

He arose from the table, hoping to cut the visitors off, but as he opened the front door, Miranda and Tricia were already ascending the steps. He decided it would be rude to block them from entering; besides, they appeared to be carrying food.

"Good afternoon, ladies."

"Cameron, how are you?" Miranda greeted him.

"We heard that Jean is away for a few days," Tricia said. "We brought you some soup and casseroles to tide you over. I know Penny is here, but I'm sure she could use some help."

"Yes, thank you." Cameron welcomed them in. "I'm afraid I can't be much of a host. Penny is not feeling well, so she's not up to a visit."

"Oh dear," Tricia was concerned. "Is it serious? Would you like me to send David out?"

"Oh, no," Cameron assured them as he helped with the baskets. "Just an upset stomach and a headache. She's sleeping now."

"How unfortunate," Miranda said, as she and Tricia headed for the kitchen. "I hope she is recovered in time for the Thanksgiving Dance. If Jack and Penny don't go, then Napoleon may not want to go either."

"We'll see," Cameron was non-committal. "Penny has been through a lot lately. She may decide to stay home."

"I can understand that," Miranda said. "We came out hoping to cheer her up, but I suppose sleep is best for her. We have chicken soup!"

Cameron chuckled as he followed them through.

"Chicken soup is always welcome. Thank you."

The baskets were set on the counter, and Cameron helped to unpack them. Two loaves of bread, a block of cheese, a sealed pot of soup, three casseroles, and two pies were soon spread out and ready to be enjoyed.

"This is very thoughtful of you, ladies," Cameron said. "I'll put them away in the pantry for later."

"We can put them away," Tricia insisted as she picked up a casserole with that intent.

"No, no," Cameron stopped with a touch to her arm. "You've done enough already. And if I put them away, I'll know where they are when we need them."

"Yes, of course." Tricia tweaked a brow as suspicion tugged at her, but she let it go.

Miranda glanced around with a twinkle of hope in her eyes. "Is Napoleon here?"

"No, he's not. He went out for a ride."

"Oh." Miranda's expression faded. "On such a cold day?"

"He needed the fresh air."

"And Jack?"

"He drove Jean and his aunt into town to catch the train."

"Really?" Tricia's suspicions returned in full. "I'm surprised we didn't run into him on the way out here."

"He said he was going to stay in town and pick up some supplies." Cameron lied. He averted his eyes, feeling uncomfortable with the lie and knowing that Tricia already suspected. "You may run into him on your way back."

The ladies took the subtle hint.

"Yes, perhaps we will," Tricia said. "It is getting late, and we wouldn't have been able to stay long anyway. Give Penny our best. I hope she feels better soon."

"I'm sure she will," Cameron said. "Thank you."

***

Sam had discreetly arrived back at the ranch after dropping off the family at the train station. He now held the bridle of the harness horse as the ladies stepped back into the buggy.

"Thank you, Sam," Tricia said as she gathered up the lines. "Give our regards to Maribelle. Perhaps we can all get together for tea once Penny is feeling better."

Sam smiled, but, like Cameron, he could not meet the ladies' eyes. "Yes, Ma'am. Careful driving home. The road is rough and getting icy. It'll be dark soon."

"Don't worry about us," Miranda assured him. "Percy knows his way back to the barn."

Sam tipped his hat. "Yes, ma'am."

Tricia clucked to the gray gelding, and the buggy started on its way.

"That was odd," Miranda said once they were clear of the barnyard.

"Yes," Tricia concurred. "I can understand Jack running errands while he's in town, but why would Napoleon leave the ranch, just for a ride, when it's getting close to feeding time?"

"My thoughts, exactly." Miranda frowned. "Did you get the feeling that Cameron was hiding something?"

Tricia sent her a coy smile. "Yes."

The two ladies locked eyes and began to laugh.

"I think we're going to have to keep a closer eye on the Rocking M."

***

Gabriella continued to lie on the bed, staring at the ceiling, even though she was now wide awake.

Their ruse might be more difficult to pull off than she had thought. People here do take more of an interest in their neighbors than most city-dwellers. Even though the two visitors had sounded concerned, Gabriella had picked up a note of suspicion in their voices. Things were not as they should be on a working ranch, and both ladies had known it.

Well, let them flutter about with their nosiness. We'll keep them at bay.

She sighed, and her thoughts returned to the man who had drawn her here.

She needed time to think and to re-group. This could not go on. Operating under this kind of emotional stress was likely to lead to mistakes, and she couldn't afford those, not when lives were at stake.

Suddenly, and most unexpectedly, tears pricked at her eyes.

So much energy had gone into being brave, getting on with life when the majority of her family had disowned her after the birth of her second bastard child. She had dared to hope that, maybe, with Napoleon's outlaw life behind him, they could make a go of it as a legitimate family. But now she could see how deluded she was and how desperate she had been for her child's father to be a part of her life again. A part of their lives.

The burning tears persisted. She was the one who had pushed him away, after all.

Pain gnawed into new, sensitive areas. She had lost her family, her career, and her reputation through her involvement with this man, but she had clung to the memories and a stupid hope that something might be possible in the future. Or at the very least, that their love had mattered.

During their conversation in town, his only interest had been his daughter. His desire to see her and to know her again was all that mattered. Never once did he hint of them starting over, of being able to forgive and come together as a family again. The only person he wanted a relationship with was Hannah. His anger at her refusal to give a definite answer spoke volumes.

When he had agreed to her coming out to the ranch, she had hoped it was an indicator that he was ready to forgive her. But no. His only concern was for the safety of his friends, and she had offered that safety. That was all. That was it.

The tears ran freely now, forcing her to sit up and seek a handkerchief from the vanity. She wiped her eyes and blew her nose, then looked at her puffy features in the mirror.

She groaned.

How can I face them looking like this? I have no intention of letting Napoleon know that I've been crying over him.

She sniffed into the hanky again as she scanned the top of the vanity for anything that might cover the redness. The face powder was there, but that wasn't going to do it. She went over to her make-up case and brought out the heavy-duty pancake.

She dabbed it under her eyes and around her nose so the redness was covered. Then she blended it into her natural skin tone using a lighter foundation. Once satisfied with that, she patted on some face powder, then stood back and scrutinized her work.

Well, it'll have to do.

***

The smell of cooking wafted from the kitchen, and her stomach growled with anticipation. She would eventually have to face Napoleon, and dinner seemed the most logical time.

She was just turning away from the vanity mirror when a soft knocking came at the door.

"Mrs. Tanguay? It's Cameron."

"Come in."

Cameron fixed her with kind eyes as he stepped into the room.

"Supper will be ready soon, but if you're up to it, there is something we should discuss before going down to eat."

"Certainly. Please sit. And call me Gabriella. Or just Gabi; it's not as much of a mouthful. I think we are beyond formal terms now."

Cameron nodded as he sat on the bed.

"Penny's room," he stated, as he looked around. "I've had some heavy conversations in here."

Gabriella gave a weak smile.

"I'll bet. I'm starting those myself."

"Yes. Daughters, huh?"

"Yes. They grow up so fast."

"Gabi, I had a long talk with Napoleon about how he's been treating you. I've told him it's not acceptable."

"So, as long as he's under your roof, he lives by your rules?" She gave a rueful chuckle. "I thought he'd welcome me after the things he wrote while in prison. I was deluding myself."

"No, you weren't. You bring up a lot of emotions in him, and he can't deal with that right now. I expect his rudeness comes from avoiding those other emotions. Dismissing you is easier."

"And it certainly worked. I'm well and truly dismissed." She sent Cameron a soft smile. "I intend to leave in the morning if you'll give me a ride into town."

Cameron frowned. "Are you sure? Why don't you give him some

time?"

"He does not want me here," she shrugged with frustration. "There is no point to my staying longer. The important things have been done. Your family is well on their way to safety. Jack will see to that. I can't begin my investigation while I'm stuck at the ranch. The town is where I'll find my leads."

"I don't think you should go yet. We still need to give the illusion that Penny is here. On top of that, it feels like snow is on the way. It's not that far to town, but it's easy to get lost in blizzard conditions if you're not familiar with the road. He'll be much better behaved now. I promise."

"Yes. That's what every woman wants in the father of her child—a man who must be told off to make him tolerable company." She shook her head. "No. I'm sure word will get out that Penny is not well, and that will explain her absence from the daily routine. You have Frank here. Frank is who Napoleon wanted in the first place. I'm, shall we say, superfluous?"

Cameron laughed. "You are never that." He arched a brow at her. "Why don't you stay a little longer anyway? Give him a chance, but set some boundaries. Prison changed him, and he's still working out who he is."

"I can't sit back and allow anyone to treat me like that. I'm being told to be patient with him, so I can't tell him off. The only sensible thing is to leave."

Cameron put a fatherly arm around her shoulder.

She gave an involuntary shudder of emotion as she realized it had been well over a decade since she had experienced this kind of male contact.

Cameron gave her a gentle squeeze.

"Gabi, you don't need to bite your tongue and take it. And he's not avoiding you."

Gabriella snorted. "He could have fooled me."

"Yes, he has," Cameron pointed out. "Rather than avoid you, he's doing the opposite; he's provoking you." Cameron stopped and frowned. "I've told him to show you more respect, and you to give him patience and understanding, but maybe that's not what he needs. I haven't seen him act like this with anyone else. He wants a fight. He's pushing for it. Perhaps you should give it to him. I have a feeling you can handle anything he throws at you."

Gabriella sighed deeply. "Oh yes. We've had some humdingers, but we've always come through them and things are better afterwards."

"There you go." Cameron patted her arm. "Maybe we have been going about this all wrong. Don't change how you treat him. Do what you have always done. If he comes at you, let him have it."

"Hmm," Gabriella considered this. "You're right. I've been treating him with kid gloves because of what he's been through. But that's not us. Normally, I would never let him get away with this."

"Come down to dinner. Hopefully, we can get through it before the battle begins. You need to taste the chicken pie Jean left. She's a very good cook. We also had some visitors this afternoon who dropped off an enticing dessert, among other things." He stood and looked down at her. "If he comes at you again, I'll back you up." Cameron hesitated, then continued. "He told me about, well, what happened in Gillette."

Gabi felt her face crumble and hoped her make-up wouldn't crack along with her resolve.

Cameron pretended not to notice. "You bore that man two children—it's time he was reminded to treat you with respect."

"Thank you," Gabriella told him. "Most people would regard me with contempt for having one child out of wedlock, and the second within the structure of a heathen marriage. My own family, other than my sister, won't even speak to me anymore."

Cameron sighed and nodded his understanding.

"Things happen," he said. "I'm not saying I condone it, but I also know how controlling Napoleon can be, especially when you knew him. He was a man used to getting what he wanted, a man not willing to accept no for an answer. I can see how he could be persuasive in all matters—love included."

Gabriella sighed, then smiled, ironically.

"You have no idea how correct you are," she admitted, then nodded. "All right. I will stay and give him a chance."

***

Gabriella took a few more moments to make herself presentable. She huffed as she scrutinized herself in the mirror.

Why should it matter? He won't look at me, anyway.

And yet, she still gently set a wayward curl back in place, made sure her makeup was still intact, and stood up. She ran her hands over her blouse and skirt to soften any creases, then turned and headed downstairs. She felt more anxious than hungry over the prospect of seeing Napoleon at dinner, until the enticing aroma of baked chicken pie wafted from the kitchen. She frowned and rubbed her hand over the gurgling, hoping that her hunger wouldn't embarrass her. Napoleon, especially, would love an excuse to ridicule.

She entered the dining room, and the three men stood as she approached the table.

Cameron came around and pulled the chair out for her.

"I'm glad you decided to join us. A lady at the table always adds a touch of class to a meal."

Gabriella smiled at him as she sat. "Thank you."

She couldn't help but glance at Napoleon. He was like a magnet to her eyes. A thrill stirred her heart when he showed some grace by meeting her gaze and nodding a slight acknowledgment.

Servings of chicken pie were already set on the diners' plates, but as soon as all were settled, Cameron sent the dishes of mashed potatoes, carrots, and a gravy boat around the table for all to help themselves.

"Dig in, folks."

"Thank you." Gabriella smiled as she poured gravy over her potatoes, then passed the boat along to Frank. "This smells delicious."

"Jean's a wonderful cook," Leon said, then looked surprised at himself for actually making conversation.

Gabriella was surprised at the warmth that washed over her at the casual comment. "Yes, I can see that."

Frank shook his head as he dug into his pie. "If you two lovebirds are planning to make up, how about waiting until after dinner? I'm hungry."

Leon rolled his eyes. "Subtle as ever, eh Frank?"

"I'm tellin' it like it is. You two have had eleven years ta kiss and make up. I'd appreciate it if you don't get all hot and bothered at the supper table."

"So," Cameron intervened, "when do you intend to leave for town?"

"Two days." Frank waved a fork at Gabriella. "We wanna give them rascals a good eyeful of 'Penny' before we head out. The longer they sit around watchin' us, the better chance the real Penny will make it to safety."

"I'm still not comfortable with Mrs. Tanguay setting herself up as a target." Cameron leaned back in his chair as he contemplated the three other people at the table. "They don't have to see Penny to assume she is still here. Why don't you simply stay out of sight until you and Frank head into town?"

Both Frank and Gabriella shook their heads.

"No," Gabriella said, beating Frank to the punch. "If I'm going to stay and carry through with this, we're going to do it right. If they don't see Penny outside and walking around, they will become suspicious. Who knows? There might be some imagination attached to whoever is doing this, and they could realize that we snuck Penny out from under their noses."

Leon zeroed in on the one thing that mattered to him. "What do you mean, 'if' you're going to stay? Wasn't that the whole idea?"

"Yes, it is," Gabriella answered. "I had thought it might be better for all concerned if I left sooner rather than later. But I realize now that this is not the case. We must give your family enough time to leave the state. Don't worry about me. I'm quite capable of looking after myself."

Leon almost choked on his potatoes. "She's got that right. You don't need to worry about Gabriella, Cameron; looking after herself is always her first concern."

Gabriella pursed her lips. The warm thrill of his initial acceptance faded, and her green eyes flashed with anger.

"My actions were not to protect myself but our daughter. You know that."

"But you took it to extremes. You disappeared without a trace. You stole my daughter."

"Stole her?" Gabriella glared at him across the table. "I had to get Hannah away from you and your life. You were poison back then. You had a chance to change your path, but you didn't take it. Look what happened because of your arrogance!"

The fact that Leon had recently turned this same accusation upon himself only made her statement more painful.

"I'm well aware that what happened was my fault. You don't need to rub it in."

"I never blamed you for Ella's death. I blamed your choices. The 'profession' you refused to give up!"

Frank glanced back and forth between Leon and Gabriella, a twinkle peeking out from his beady eyes.

"Ahh, married bliss, eh? The main reason I never tied the nuptial knot. I have no time for such nonsense."

Gabriella sent Frank a sharp glance, then dropped her fork with a clatter.

"I'm sorry that my appetite does not do your wife's cooking justice," she said to Cameron. "This can't be any more comfortable for you than it is for me. I must apologize for bringing this to your door."

"It's not you who brought this here," Cameron told her. "But I do hope you'll stay to help sort it out. Despite certain inconveniences." He sent a warning to both Leon and Frank. "I'm sure we can all work together if we try."

Gabriella nodded. "I have no intention of walking out on you."

Leon snorted.

Cameron sent him a reproving frown. It appeared their earlier talk hadn't had the desired effect. He had said all he was going to, though, and decided to trust Gabriella to handle this, no matter how uncomfortable it became.

Gabriella continued, ignoring Leon's rudeness. "A man was hanging around town. Five foot eight, light brown hair, and a dagger tattoo on his right forearm. He had a favorite at the Black Rose. Her name is Molly. He asked questions about the Rocking M." She glanced at Frank. "I suggest we start there, but if you go in to speak with the madam, don't be clumsy. The last thing we need is for this man to know you're on his trail."

Frank scowled. "I know my job, little lady. And I'm never clumsy."

"Just socially inept," Leon mumbled over a mouthful of chicken pie.

Frank darted a glare at him. "What?"

"Nothing, Frank. You were saying, Gabriella?"

Cameron sighed and rolled his eyes. This power play going around the table was giving him a headache.

Gabriella conceded and continued with her findings. "I was in town for a few days before I came here." She sent Frank a pointed look. "Women talk; you know how we are."

"Women-talk is just that," Frank grumbled. "Gossip, and nothing more."

"Gossip often holds an abundance of truth," Gabriella said as she stirred her mashed potatoes. "Common sense should tell you that."

"I use tried and trusted methods, honed to perfection over the years." Frank's smirk was superior. "I don't rely on common sense."

Silence hit the table. Leon did not react, but Gabriella and Cameron looked at Frank with incredulity. He snorted at their obtuseness.

Cameron coughed, then brought their attention back to the matter at hand.

"Does Gabi's description sound familiar at all, Napoleon?" Cameron asked.

Leon shook his head. "Five foot eight, light brown hair. It's about half the men in the state."

"What about the tattoo?" Gabriella pressed. "Is that familiar? Do you know anyone like that from your past? Or prison: what about prison?"

Leon slumped as he set his fork down beside his plate with a little more intention than required. His lips tightened as he struggled with the knot of angst as memories flooded over him.

"Will you just leave me alone?" he asked her. "Do you really think I want to reminisce about THAT place?"

Gabriella gave him a soft smile. "I'm sorry. No, I'm sure you don't."

His dark eyes burned into her, and she felt the heat of his frustration.

"Why did you come here?" he asked in a strangled whisper.

"I came to help," Gabriella answered truthfully. "I didn't realize how uncomfortable that would make you, so I will be leaving soon."

Leon pushed himself away from his plate, suddenly off his food.

"Good. I don't need this," he snarked. "I need to get on with my life."

"Napoleon," Cameron pressed, "Gabi has some good information. She can help."

"That's no substitute for a professional detective," Frank interjected, trying to re-establish his foothold.

Cameron held Leon's gaze captive.

"Frank makes a good point, as well," he said. "We need someone who can disappear and go places we can't go, and we both know who that is."

Leon sent Cameron a look. He knew Frank often presented himself unfavorably, coming across as a fool. But he also knew Frank was more than capable; he was a brilliant detective and knew his business. What he didn't know was how to convey it. Social niceties were not his strong suit.

"It's not all about you, Napoleon," Gabriella pushed, fixing him with an intense stare. "There could be other lives at stake. Nobody's trying to make life hard for you, but it would help if you'd just try to remember about the tattoo."

Leon smashed his fist into the table with a shattering crash.

"Will you leave me alone!" Leon could feel his emotions taking control again, but he wasn't able to stop them. "I can't do it! My God, what right do you have to come around here demanding I put my mind back in that hellhole! I'm just starting to put it behind me."

Gabriella poked at her food. She could feel her frustration growing. "Just think about it," she suggested. "Sleep on it."

"Sleep? What kind of sleep do you think I get?" Leon snarled. "The sooner you get the hell out of here, the better. There's nothing on this earth worth that kind of torment."

Gabriella's eyes widened, her maternal ire flashing like oil tossed on a fire.

"Nothing? How dare you!" She pointed at Cameron. "This man's daughter is worth it, and so is mine!"

"What is that supposed to mean?"

"You ass! You're so busy wallowing in self-pity, you can't see beyond your own hard-luck story. These people who have targeted Penny are doing it to get back at you and Jack. That much is obvious. Can you even think beyond that and realize your daughter could also be in danger? Are you that egotistical?"

Leon laughed. "Now who's being egotistical? You're going to turn this whole thing into being about you! Nobody even knows that Hannah is my daughter. Not even her!"

"For her safety and mine! Oh my God! I can't believe what a bastard you've become." She came to her feet and grabbed the serving spoon from the bowl of potatoes. She plunged the partially filled spoon into the gravy boat and then catapulted the spoonful of potatoes and thick liquid into Leon's face.

Leon jerked back in surprise as the chunks of potatoes and steaming gravy hit him between the eyes and began to ooze down his nose.

"What the hell!" he yelled at her as he came to his feet. "Have you gone crazy?"

"I've tried to be understanding and go easy on you, but that's over." She slammed the empty spoon onto the table. "I've seen too many graves, Mister Nash, and I won't stand over another to save you from fighting a few ghosts." She stomped away from the table, throwing a final remark over her shoulder. "You need to step up and start helping the people who helped you."

Cameron and Frank now came to their feet, exchanging a look as Gabriella disappeared up the stairs.

"Never a dull moment with her around," Frank smirked.

"I did tell her she should try to be a little more assertive." Cameron folded his arms. "So, I bet you're glad she resolved to go easy on you, eh, Napoleon?"

Leon stood, his face red with anger.

"Does she think I'll let her get away with that?" he snarled, as he wiped gravy away from his eyes. "Where is she?" He threw the soiled napkin onto the floor and headed for the stairs.

Frank moved fast, heading him off before he had passed the table.

"What do you think you're doing?" he demanded. "Remember, you're on parole and, like it or not, you are still accountable to me."

Leon glared at him as he tried to push through. "You expect me to let her get away with that?"

Frank's answer was instantaneous. He grabbed Leon by the collar, placed his leg behind Leon's heel, and pushed him backward.

Leon lost balance and ended up sprawled out on the floor. He growled his anger, but before he could scramble to his feet, Frank was on him with a knee on his chest and hands around his throat.

"You settle down," Frank growled, "or, I swear, I'll squeeze until you pass out."

Leon grabbed Frank's hand as he gasped and swatted at the detective, desperately trying to get him off.

Cameron rushed over to the pair. "Mr. Carlyle, let him up!"

Frank ignored him and pinned a struggling Leon to the floor.

Cameron grabbed Frank and pulled him away, then gave the detective a push back and stepped between the two men. "That was uncalled for!"

Leon, his face blotched with both anger and lack of oxygen, coughed and gasped for air as he rolled onto his hands and knees.

Frank was furious. "What do you think you're doing?" He glared at the solid rancher. "I'm in charge of that man, whether he likes it or not. His behavior has already put him on a fine line. If I were to report this to the governor, he could lose his parole and be sent back to prison." He switched his glare to the man still gasping on the floor. "How would you like that, eh, Nash? Right back into that hell-hole you don't even want to think about?"

Leon gasped for air. "Damn you, Frank."

Cameron still stood between the two men. "There was no need for violence, Mr. Carlyle. There are other ways."

Frank snorted. "Don't you be telling me my business. I've been dealing with Nash for over fifteen years. The only thing he respects is a strong hand."

"Napoleon respects me, Mr. Carlyle, and I have never raised a hand to him."

"But you're not the one charged with keeping him in line. I am. And I'll use whatever methods I need to keep him and Kiefer honest."

"You will refrain from violence in my home, Mr. Carlyle. Is that clear?"

Frank pushed his anger down. His inner code of ethics acknowledged Cameron's demands for respect while under his roof.

"Fine, Mr. Marsham. Besides, I think this little refresher on the rules ought to hold him in line for a while. Ain't that right, Nash? You know who's boss again?"

"Go to hell."

Frank chuckled. "Right after you." He glanced at his plate, still covered with pie and potatoes. "If it's all the same to you, I'll take my supper and retire to my room. I think this social gathering is at an end."

Without waiting for a response, Frank picked up his plate and utensils, poured himself a cup of coffee, and disappeared.

By this time, Leon was up and sitting on his chair, holding his throat.

Cameron also returned to the table and, sitting down, rubbed both hands over his face. "Oh, my goodness. And you call that man a friend?"

Leon swallowed; his eyes closed against a throbbing headache.

"It depends on the circumstances."

CHAPTER FIFTEEN
BUCK UP

Gabriella retreated to Penny's room and paced a track on the floor. Her fists and jaw were clenched in anger as she fumed at the man she'd once loved. The man she still loved.

She knew she had to calm down; she had to resolve this issue, even though Napoleon was making it almost impossible. Or maybe because he was making it difficult. He was struggling, she knew that, but she was at a loss as to how to help him.

Other than to simply leave.

***

Beads of sweat glistened on Leon's brow as he tossed and turned, muttering and murmuring incoherently. The same scene kept playing, over and over again, in a hellish loop.

They were back in the infirmary. Harris had come up behind the Doc and pinned his arms to his side—the start of the end for Doc Palin. Boeman had taken the knife, which had supposedly been protruding from his gut, and plunged it into the helpless man. The scene never changed; it played repeatedly, relentlessly, and maddeningly worming into his brain. Every time the knife drove into Doc's flesh, he cried out, but nothing changed. Doc was dying, and there was nothing he could do to stop it.

Then Leon was running through the prison proper. Harris was ahead of him, just out of reach. Both seemed to be fighting an invisible force that slowed their legs and made them fight for every step.

Harris made it to the staircase and, grabbing the hand railing, he pulled himself up to the second level, fighting against gravity at every turn.

Leon reached him and, in slow motion, grabbed him by the throat and pushed him against the railing.

You bastard!

He drew his hand back and landed a solid punch on Harris's face.

There was a light touch to his hair, and he was back in the prison cell again, dreaming of Gabi—of the feel of her curves in his arms, the smell of her musk, and the taste of the salt on her naked, sweating skin. He dragged her into bed and swung himself on top of her. He needed a release and taking her was one way of stopping the horrors.

Napoleon, stop fighting. Rest. You need to rest.

He clamped his hand over her mouth.

Quiet, Gabi. I don't want to talk ... not now. I don't have much time. They'll be back in a minute. You know what I want.

He felt her ruffle his hair again before pulling his hand away.

Who? Who will be back?

Harris and Boeman. They'll do it again; they'll kill Doc.

It's a dream, Napoleon. It's all a dream." He felt her arms cradle him. *Let it go, mon amour, let it go.*

I can't. Doc keeps coming back.

He felt her kiss the top of his head. Then her voice again, sounding close to his ear and yet coming from a great distance.

Is he coming back, or are you bringing him back?

Blackness closed in, the smothering, soul-sucking shadows of the dark cell.

It's gone dark, Gabi! I can't see! Where are you? Where have you gone?

Now her voice echoed from the center of his soul.

I'm still here. Take control of these dreams. Ask him what he wants.

A pinpoint of swirling light grew until it filled the dark cell—he was back in the infirmary again, and Harris had grabbed Doc.

Good God, NO! Not again. What do you want? Just tell me what you want!

The scene changed tempo, playing at the slowest possible speed. And then he saw it—the tattoo of a dagger on Harris's right forearm where his sleeve dragged back against the Doc's struggles.

Oh, Doc! I see it! I know what you're showing me.

His eyes opened with a start, the low, autumn sun streaming in through the gap in the curtains. He glanced around the room; he was alone. He rubbed his face and shook himself awake, and then sat up and pushed the blankets aside. Of course, he was alone.

He felt rather than heard Mouse join him on the bed. Then she came over to where he sat and, with a drooling purr, rubbed her head against his elbow. Then she stood on the crook of his arm and attempted to rub her cheek against his.

He smiled and settled her onto his lap.

"Good morning to you, too." He scratched her behind the ears, and she leaned against his chest, her purr at full strength. "You always seem to know when I've had a bad night. I'm surprised I didn't wake Jean again." He frowned. "Oh, no. Jean isn't here. Odd, I would forget that."

Mouse acked again and continued to purr.

Leon sat quietly, contemplating the dream. Was it simply Gabi's suggestion of the tattoo that brought it into his dreamscape, or had it triggered a buried memory? Either way, a talk with David about this seemed inevitable.

The anger he had felt over the potato/gravy incident lingered with him well into the evening. The time he spent in the bathroom, washing his hair and cleaning the mess off his shirt, was spent cursing and damning the day he'd met that demon woman.

He had managed a civil goodnight to Cameron and then retired to his room, where the cursing and damning continued. But then, an odd thing happened: the cursing abated, and his mind filled with the image of her sparkling green eyes and lovely oval face. The sound of her laughter and lyrical French accent brought a smile to his lips.

Then he surprised himself when a humorous snort escaped him. He chuckled and shook his head in amusement. The incident from the previous evening had now become a fond memory of the woman he used to know, used to love. That was the Gabriella he remembered; the fireball who could stand up for herself and wasn't afraid to put the great outlaw leader in his place if he dared step over the line.

He groaned as feelings of both guilt and desire settled onto him. The passion he had felt for Gabi in the dream had not been a fantasy. As much as he wanted to deny it, she still had a strong hold over him.

The very thought of her in his arms, in his bed, almost brought him to arousal.

He frowned and, lifting Mouse off his lap, he looked down at his crotch.

Nothing was happening.

He sighed and resettled the kitten.

Oh well.

***

After Leon got dressed, he creaked open his bedroom door and peeked into the living area. All was quiet. This was good; the last thing he wanted was another confrontation with Gabi or Frank.

The aroma of coffee from the kitchen caught his attention, and he tried to fight the temptation of that first cup. Sam must have put the coffee on to brew before heading to the barn for morning chores. This was a clear indication that Leon had slept late. He thought about skipping his coffee for now but lost the battle for caffeine when Mouse scooted past his legs and, with a triumphant *ack*, trotted toward the "food room" for her breakfast.

Leon sighed. So much for sneaking out to the barn unnoticed.

Still, if I'm quick about it, I might get out of here unscathed.

He padded after his cat as she made her way to the kitchen. He poured himself a cup of coffee, then rummaged through the cold box until he came across the remnants of the chicken they'd had the previous night. He set out a dish of it for the cat, then leaned against the counter to watch her eat while he sipped his morning brew.

He was already late to the barn, so a few more minutes weren't going to hurt.

Thank goodness neither Frank nor Gabriella appeared to harass him.

He knew his resentment toward the detective would dissipate as the day progressed. Leon still had problems with authority, and when pushed hard enough, he fell back into his old pattern of fighting it.

Gradually, just as he had done in prison, he'd realized how his behavior created the abuses. Especially when Leon knew the people he tried to push and the consequences of ignoring their warnings.

Kenny hadn't put up with his tantrums, and neither did Frank. By the time Leon calmed down, he'd realize he'd asked for it and let the matter go.

He almost laughed again at Gabriella's treatment of him. He knew he had to keep that contained when he saw her. Nothing would get her fired up again like him finding humor in the incident. He sobered and sighed. The anger tried to regain its hold, but he contained it. Maybe that was the best he could hope for between them.

He realized their squabble the previous evening had gotten out of hand, and though he was trying, he still found it hard to forgive. He thought he could; he wanted to but seeing her and hearing her voice in the present, rather than in memory, caused more pain than pleasure.

He loved her still. That was obvious after the dream he'd just had. He wanted her near him and to feel her body next to his in that loving embrace. But apparently, that only happened in the dream. In reality, her closeness only unsettled him.

Perhaps it was better that she planned to leave soon. Distance might help him sort things out.

He thought of Miranda then, and the feelings of warmth and pleasure of her company washed over him.

He smiled. He did like Miranda.

***

The horses had finished their breakfast and were out frolicking in the fresh snow by the time Leon got to the barn to help with chores. Fortunately, the blizzard that Cameron had predicted had been short-lived, and the day had dawned brilliantly white and clear blue.

"Sorry, Sam. I had a bad night."

Sam tossed a forkful of manure-laden straw into the wheelbarrow. "That's okay. I'm almost done anyway. If you could throw some hay down from the loft, that would be good."

"Sure."

Leon headed for the ladder up to the loft when he did a double take as Penny walked into the barn. A split second later, he realized it wasn't Penny, but Gabriella disguised as her. He marveled again at how well Gabi could pull these things off.

"We need to talk," Gabi said. "I don't want bad feelings between us. It's a beautiful morning for a ride. Let's get out for a while."

Leon leaned against the ladder. "Yes, we do need to talk. But I am already late getting out to help Sam with the chores. The least I can do is stay to help finish. Maybe this afternoon."

"That's fine," Sam said as he pushed the wheelbarrow towards the back door. "As I said, I'm almost done anyway. And she's right, it is a nice day for a ride. Take advantage while you can."

Leon hesitated. He already felt bad about being late, but he and

Gabriella did need to talk.

He sighed, relenting to the pressure of others.

"Yeah, okay. I'll have to change, though, and bring the horses in from the pasture."

"I'll go get them," Sam offered as he pushed the wheelbarrow out the door. "Just let me dump this last load."

"Fine, it's settled," Gabriella smiled sweetly, causing Leon to feel that there was a trap in the making. "I'll help Sam tack them up while you get changed. It's a lovely day, but it is chilly."

Leon took note of Gabriella's attire. She was bulked up with layers under her riding habit, and a robust, knitted bonnet, obviously designed for colder weather, was snuggly tied down over her blonde wig. A layer of make-up to change her natural skin tone to match Penny's covered her face.

"Are you sure this is a good idea?" Leon had second thoughts. "I doubt Penny would go for a ride under the current circumstances. It could be dangerous."

"It will encourage them to believe that Penny is still here. In case you haven't noticed, Penny is a vivacious young woman, so it would be difficult to keep her cooped up for months on end. I believe it's right in line with her character to go for a ride. Especially with you as an escort."

Leon's jaw tightened in that oh so familiar expression of stubbornness. "She's supposed to be sick."

Gabriella shrugged. "She got better. If people ask after her, you can tell them that she went to join her mother and brother to visit friends."

"It's still dangerous. I'm worried about you."

"I can look after myself, as you have so aptly pointed out on several occasions."

Leon's stubbornness persisted. "We can go talk in the house if you're so insistent on having that conversation right now."

"Oh, Napoleon. I'm all dressed and ready for a ride. If you don't want to come, I'll go by myself."

"What's the point of that?" Leon countered. "We both agree we need to talk."

"Then go get changed!" Gabriella's frustration pushed through. She came very close to stamping her foot.

Footfalls of another kind interrupted this debate. The clomping of horses' hooves on the wooden floor announced the arrival of Karma and Berry.

Karma's ears pricked when she saw Leon, and she nickered at him. Her eyes were bright with excitement at the promise of a ride with her human.

Leon surrendered. "All right, you win. But only because Karma wants to go, too."

Gabriella rolled her eyes but took what she could get. "Fine. Now go get changed. I'll wait for you."

Leon's irritation rose again at her ordering him around, but he let it go and headed for the house.

***

Karma chose to ignore her human's bad mood. The sun shone with a cold intensity that caused the packed snow on the road to sparkle and crunch under her hooves. Her nostrils flared with the sharp, crisp air that caused crystals to form on her whiskers. She danced under her rider, hoping he would let her open up and go for a gallop.

Leon's dark moods usually lifted whenever he rode his mare, and today was no exception. He stroked her arched neck and felt the irritation lift from his shoulders. He glanced at Berry and noted that he, too, was fresh and wanted to move. Perhaps a gallop now would help with conversation later.

He knew Gabriella was an excellent horsewoman.

Of course, she is. She's excellent at everything she does.

"Let's let them run off some energy," he suggested. "The snow is just the right texture for good footing."

"Good idea." Gabriella's eyes sparkled in anticipation. "I'll race you to the Jefferies' turn-off."

With that, Gabriella leaned forward and touched Berry with her heel.

The gelding's eyes sparked, and with a grunt, he dug in and took off.

Karma, caught by surprise, reared in her excitement, then, before her front feet hit the ground again, she lunged forward in her determination not to be left behind.

Leon grinned; his bad mood was left behind. The thrill of

Karma's powerful gallop always awakened his spirits, and before he knew it, he was laughing into the wind.

Karma caught Berry within a few strides, and Leon let her breeze on by him as though he were standing still. At the speed they were going, it didn't take long to cover the three miles to the corner, and the horses were ready for a more casual gait.

Both people were flush with excitement as they brought the horses down to a walk.

"Oh, my goodness!" Gabriella's eyes sparkled with laughter. "She's so fast."

Leon stroked his mare's neck. "She is. And that wasn't even her top speed. She's given Cameron two very nice foals. I'll introduce you to them later."

"I would like that." Gabriella's heart warmed at the sight of Leon's eyes bright with pride and delight. "It's so nice to hear you laugh again. I've missed your laugh."

Leon's mood softened. Suddenly, though only for an instant, he saw Gabriella as she used to be: the love of his life, and the mother of his children.

He sent her a warm but quick smile, then directed Karma to continue along the road toward town.

"What did you want to discuss?"

Gabriella pushed Berry up to walk parallel with Karma.

"I know you're still angry with me," she said. "I know that you're trying now, not to be. But you still are. We need to sort this out. It's not healthy: not for me, for you, or for Hannah. It's been over ten years, Napoleon. Do you still hate me so much?"

"I don't hate you," he mumbled. "I hate what you did. I love you." Leon paused. He heard the words come out of his mouth, but he had no recollection of saying them.

Gabriella's brows arched in surprise, and she leaned toward him. "What was that?"

Leon sighed. He'd said the words now, so he could no longer hide them away. He focused his eyes up to meet hers. "I love you. I always have and always will. That's why what you did hurt so much, and why I doubt we could ever go back to how things were. You knew what you were doing to me. You know what it's like to have your child taken from you, never to see them again, and you still did it to me." Leon bit his lip as he shook his head. "How could you?"

"I had to. I hoped that one day, you would understand. It was hard for me, too, you know."

"But telling our daughter that I'm dead? You gave up on me. You shut me off from Hannah forever with that lie."

Gabriella gently pulled on Berry's mane to give herself something to focus on.

"You don't know what it was like for me. You have no idea. Even staying with Helèna, her neighbors knew me. As far as they were concerned, my husband was dead. How could I tell Hannah something different?"

"Then why go back there? You had money to start over and a way to support yourself. Why not move somewhere no one knows you? You could have said you were divorced."

Gabriella laughed, but it held a bitter edge. "Divorced. That's almost as bad as having a child out of wedlock. It's the woman who is held responsible for a marriage ending, you know that. It doesn't matter if her husband was a womanizer or an abusive alcoholic ... or an outlaw. It's always the woman's fault. I would have been shunned, and Hannah would have been teased shamelessly.

"At least, if my husband were deceased, we would be met with pity and support. There is no shame in being a widow, especially a widow with a young child to raise."

Gabriella paused as her mind's eye went back in time.

"Besides," she said quietly, "I couldn't live alone. Oh, thank goodness for Helèna. It was a terrible time for me, too, Napoleon. You act like you're the only one who was devastated by Ella's death. I couldn't eat; I couldn't sleep. I sank into a very dark place. Even worse than when my son was stolen. At least with Theo, I had hope. I still do. I have someone working on it, and he's just tenacious enough to get the job done."

Her green eyes danced as she spoke of her son and hope still sparkled within their depth.

"Theo is a young man now, of course, so if, no, when we find him, nothing will prevent us from knowing one another again." She stopped talking for a moment as sadness washed over her. Then she sent her companion a soft smile. "It may still be a vain hope, but it is still hope.

"There was no hope with Ella. She was gone, taken from us by that one cowardly deed. Even the death of her murderer did not relieve the anguish of it. Every day, I wondered if I would have the strength to face the next day.

"The only thing that kept me going was Hannah. Her love and her need for her mother were my lifeline. She kept me facing each day until, finally, I could stand on my own feet and face them myself.

"Now, Jack tells me our beautiful daughter did the same thing for you. That in your darkest moments, it was she who drew you back from that abyss."

Leon remained silent. The turmoil of emotions swirling around his heart kept thoughts from forming and words from expressing.

Gabriella reached over and touched his arm. "I'm so sorry I hurt you, Napoleon. But I had no other choice, don't you see that? Our daughter is more important than either of us, and I would do it again if I had to."

Leon nodded, though he couldn't show his pain by looking at her. "I didn't know you went through that. You could have gotten in touch, you know. Jack and I would have helped you in any way we could. I would have respected your wishes that I stay away if you'd only kept in touch. I lost so much that day. It wasn't just Ella, but you and Hannah, too. The life we had together, unrealistic as it was, was heaven to me. It all fell apart after you left. I lost everything that mattered."

"You still had Jack and Mukua. Mukua was your teacher, but Jack has always been your anchor. He always will be."

"And you had Helèna. So, I suppose, we both had people around us, we just felt alone without each other." He hesitated, using Gabriella's tactic to buy time by pulling on Karma's mane. "I want to apologize again for the way I have been behaving. You, as well as Cameron and Frank, have a way of letting me know I need to smarten up."

Gabriella snorted. "Frank. I would despise that man if he weren't so good at what he does."

"Ha, yeah. He's an original, all right."

Another moment of silence settled between them before Leon could muster up the courage to ask again.

"Can I see Hannah? She's old enough now, isn't she?"

"I told you, you could once all this is behind us."

"No, you said maybe. I need to know."

"Yes. I owe you that much."

Leon grinned. "Thank you."

"But not as her father," Gabriella insisted. "A long-lost uncle or cousin, but not her father. Not yet, anyway."

"Then when?"

She sighed. "I don't know, Napoleon. We'll see how it goes."

"Well, that's better than nothing. Thank you."

Gabriella nodded. "What was it you wanted to talk about?"

"Oh!" Leon perked up, having forgotten about his intention. "I had one of those bad dreams again last night."

"Oh dear."

"No, but this one was different."

"Oh?" Gabriella frowned. "In what way?"

"It was the scene in the infirmary again," Leon explained. "The one when Doc was killed. But this time I saw that tattoo on Harris's arm. But I don't know if it was there all along, and I'm remembering it, or if it's just because you suggested it, and that stayed in my mind. I don't know, Gabriella. I feel like I'm walking in a mist and my brain can't clear it away."

Gabriella averted her eyes at the mention of the recent nightmare, but she gathered her courage and carried on.

"The prison system is designed to break a man down. Let your friends support you as you heal. And don't fool yourself. Jack knows you're struggling. You can't fool him. Cameron and Jean do, too. You're lucky, Napoleon; you have good friends here. They'll help you through it. You can come out of this a better man than you ever were."

The snow muffled the rifle shot so that it, in itself, did not cause alarm. But Leon saw the hole suddenly appear in Gabriella's hat, and the look of shock that burst from her eyes sent a chill over his entire body. He grabbed her and pulled her toward him and off Berry, then allowed the momentum to take them both to the ground.

CHAPTER SIXTEEN
A LOST LOVE

The soft snow on the side of the road cushioned their landing, but Leon did not stop there. He wrapped his arms around Gabriella and rolled until he felt the ground decline beneath him. They tumbled into the small ditch that had been washed out by Spring runoff, and then Leon dragged Gabi behind a row of prickly snow-covered shrubbery. It wouldn't stop a bullet, but it did hide the couple from view.

He poked his head around their cover and then peeked up over the top of the natural ditch to search the area for an assailant, but all was quiet. The one good thing about those who attacked from ambush was that the perpetrator was usually a coward. A face-to-face encounter, especially with Napoleon Nash, was the last thing he wanted.

Leon was satisfied that the assailant was gone and, not about to make the same mistake twice, he did not go chasing, hell-bent, after him.

Leon turned to Gabriella. He knelt beside her in the snow, and fear clutched his heart. She wasn't moving. He cupped her pale face in his hands, praying her eyes would open, but all he got was silence.

"Gabi, please." His plea was a desperate whisper. "Please wake up. Gabi . . ."

He placed an ear to her chest but couldn't hear any reassuring heartbeat. He was fleetingly aware that her body felt hard under her layers of clothing, but his mind was too full of fear to register this oddity. Pulling off his glove, he pressed a finger to her throat, but his hands were too numb with cold to feel anything.

"I knew we shouldn't have come out." His voice was terse as his trembling hands fumbled with the ribbon that held the hat on her head. "Why did you make me? Why did you have to insist? You always have to push." He set the hat aside and began his inspection. Still grumbling with frustration, he fumbled with the pins holding the askew blonde wig in place.

He almost began swearing because his fingers couldn't do the job. He was both in a panic to examine the wound on her head and dreading what ghastly injury he might find there.

His fingers warmed up with the exertion they were being forced into, and Leon ran his hands through her hair, not quite believing his sense of touch or sight.

He had expected to find a gaping wound with dark blood saturating her auburn locks, but he found neither. Though relieved, the lack of an injury made no sense. He searched deeper and found a large bump on the side of her head, but his fingers came away clean.

Picking up her bonnet, he checked it for bullet holes and found the torn material where the projectile had struck. But it had not penetrated. Though incredible, the bullet had ricocheted off into the white expanse.

He frowned, still not quite ready to believe it. But then he noticed the hat felt hard and heavier than it should. He tapped his knuckles against it and was met with a soft thunk that did not fit the material. A helmet? Trust Gabi to have a bulletproof bonnet.

A quiet groan from the woman lying in the snow brought pangs of guilt that the mystery of the hat had pulled his attention away from her well-being.

"Gabi." Leon gently stroked her face as her eyelids fluttered and then slowly opened. "Gabi. Oh, thank God."

He pulled her into a hug, which caused her to groan again.

"My head." She moaned as her skin turned a sickening shade of gray through the makeup. She brought her hand to her throbbing skull and closed her eyes again.

Leon shook her. "Gabi. Wake up!"

"No, I'm all right." She moaned, but her eyes did open again. "My head is pounding."

Leon sighed, releasing the tension he hadn't been aware of.

"Thank goodness. You scared me half to death." He pulled her into another hug, but gentler than the first. "I thought I had lost you for good this time."

He released her and gazed upon her face. He frowned. Her make-up had smudged with his handling, and now, he could see bruising on her cheek that was not theatrical.

"What's this? I protected your fall. How did you get a black eye?" He wiped more grease away. "And a bruised lip. Gabi?"

She flinched, then brushed his hand away.

"It's nothing. I walked into the closet door of my room. It was dark, and I'm not familiar with the layout. Don't worry about it."

His eyes met hers. "How can I not worry about it? This looks like more than just walking into a door. You look like you were pushed or... hit." He frowned. "What's going on?"

"Nothing." Gabriella's forehead creased with irritation, then instantly relaxed when the pounding in her head increased. She put her hand to her brow again. "I tripped on the carpet and hit the edge of the door. I'm fine."

Leon sighed, then he chuckled and shook his head. "You're still the same, after all these years. Still stubborn, irritating, infuriating. And lovely. I have missed you, Gabi."

"And I you."

Leon leaned forward, and their cold lips met in a soft, tentative kiss.

***

Karma nickered.

She was used to gunfire, so the muted report of the rifle had not startled her, but her human tumbling off her back and dragging the other human along with him had caused her some distress.

But being a well-seasoned "outlaw horse", she had not panicked. She jumped forward a couple of strides, then stopped and turned only to find that her passenger had disappeared. She pricked her ears and flared her nostrils, searching for his location. She soon found it.

The odd behavior of humans often confused her, but knowing they were close at hand, and all was quiet around them, she relaxed and settled down on her back hoof to wait.

Berry, still young and inexperienced, would have lit out for home under these circumstances, but the calming presence of the mare steadied him. He stood quietly beside her and waited for whatever was going to happen.

Leon, encouraged by the presence of Karma, conducted another quick survey of the surrounding landscape. As the mare indicated, all was quiet. Either the assailant was secure in the belief of his success, or he simply did not want to hang around in case of pursuit.

Leon dropped back down beside his companion.

"Come on, Gabi. We need to get to town."

Gabriella frowned as she struggled to sit up. "To town? I can't go into town yet. I'm not ready."

"You need to see the doctor." Leon was adamant as he helped her to her feet. "You were unconscious. You need to be checked over."

"I'm fine. I promise I will rest when we get back to the ranch."

"No. You're coming into town to see David. The town is closer now anyway. Just a quick check, and then we'll return to the ranch. Likely, no one will even notice you."

Gabriella cocked a brow at him. "You, riding into town with a stranger? And a female stranger at that. Don't be so naïve, Napoleon. Or do you think I am?"

"No, I don't," Leon said. "But I think a doctor should check you out. David will be discreet. This could work to your advantage, you know. That assailant thinks he killed Penny, so you, riding into town tomorrow disguised as Penny, would only confuse the issue. Your clothing is the usual riding apparel for women, so if you don't wear the blonde wig, no one will think you're Penny. I doubt he will head back to town now, anyway. If he does show up later, you'll already be there as yourself, and not Penny. It could work."

Gabriella sent him a skeptical look as she attempted to stand. "I expect he'll keep going and not return to town. If he does, and there's no word of Penny being killed, he'll know he missed his mark again. But my showing up in town with you is not a good idea, and you know it. I think, as usual, you are simply trying to manipulate the situation to get your way. I wish to ... oh, my goodness. . ."

Gabriella swayed as her head spun.

Leon grabbed her as she plunked down to her knees.

"I'm not trying to manipulate you, Gabi. You need to see a doctor. We'll plan our next move after David has checked you out. We can ride double on Karma."

Gabriella held her head, feeling nauseous. "For once, you may be right."

***

Leon knocked on the door, hoping that David would be at home.

Tricia answered. "Oh, Napoleon." Her eyes flickered to the pale woman leaning on his arm. "Oh dear. You look like you're about to faint. Please, come in. What's happened?"

Napoleon helped Gabriella into the kitchen and pulled out a chair for her.

"My friend here took a fall from a horse," he explained. "She was knocked out. Is David here?"

"Yes, he is," Tricia told him, as she poured water into the kettle for tea. "He's just returned from his morning rounds and is freshening up. He'll be able to see you in a moment, ma'am."

"Oh, sorry." Leon had forgotten his manners. "This is Mrs. Tanguay. She's visiting from California. Gabi, this is Mrs. Gibson, the doctor's wife."

Tricia smiled, having noted the title. "Nice to meet you, Mrs. Tanguay. Would you like a cup of tea while we wait? It might help settle your nerves."

"No, thank you. And please, call me Gabi. Mrs. Tanguay makes me sound so old."

Tricia offered her hand. "A pleasure to meet you, Gabi. I'm Tricia." Once the pleasantries were done, Tricia cocked a brow at Leon. "Miranda will be here soon for lunch if you would like to stay. She's wondering why you haven't been around to call on her lately."

"We've been busy. You know what it's like on a ranch this time of year."

Tricia laughed. "Why do you think I married a doctor?"

"Good plan," Leon said. "Ranching's not really for me, either."

"Really?" Tricia chuckled. "I never would have guessed."

Footsteps sounded along the hallway, and then David joined the group in the kitchen.

"Good morning, Napoleon. I thought I heard your voice."

"David, hi. This is Mrs. Tanguay. She took a nasty fall off a horse, and I thought she should come in to see you. Just to be sure, you know."

"Yes, of course. Mrs. Tanguay. Nice to meet you. You had a fall?"

"Yes," Gabriella rolled her eyes as she rubbed the back of her head. "I consider myself an excellent rider, but the silly beast spooked at nothing and reared. The next thing I knew, Napoleon was holding me and looking very concerned."

"Oh." David's frown mimicked Leon's. "You were knocked out?"

"Yes," Leon interjected before Gabi could downplay the event. "She was out for about a minute. It seemed a lot longer at the time, though."

"I'm sure you're exaggerating," Gabriella said, but no one listened to her.

"Ah." David's brow went up as he nodded. "Yes. Napoleon was right to bring you in to see me. Come along. It won't take long."

Gabriella sighed but accepted the inevitable. She pushed herself up from the table and allowed David to escort her to his office.

Leon found himself locked down by Tricia. She pursed her lips, obviously expecting more of an explanation of Gabriella's sudden appearance than the one already offered.

***

David passed the candle back and forth in front of Gabriella's eyes. She followed the flickering flame as instructed until David was satisfied.

"Your left eye is a little slow." David blew out the candle and opened the blind, allowing sunlight to flood the room once again.

Gabriella frowned and brought her fingers up to press against the middle of her forehead.

David stepped up to her and tilted her chin.

"Try to relax," he said as he peered into her eyes again. "Hmm. Yes."

He drew the blind back down halfway to dim the light. "Sorry," he said. "I expect you still have quite a headache. But I needed the brighter light to be sure."

"Yes," Gabi sighed as she rubbed her temples. "Sometimes the exam is worse than the condition."

"I know." David came back to stand before his patient. He wasn't done with his examination yet. "I apologize for that as well, but it's the best way to check for a concussion. Which you do have, by the way. It's mild, but you need to rest."

Gabi sighed. "Yes, I suspected as much."

David's gentle fingers checked the bump on Gabriella's head.

"Did you? Then why did you resist coming to see me?"

"Because I have some medical knowledge myself. I know how to treat a concussion."

"Really?" David showed interest. "Do you have training as a nurse?"

Gabriella chuckled, then groaned as the throbbing in her head worsened. "If you call field experience training." She hesitated, unsure how much of her personal life she should share with David, but he had a calming way about him that encouraged trust. "My sister is a doctor."

David stepped back, his brows raised in surprise. "Your sister?"

"Yes." Gabriella's trust turned to irritation at what she considered a typical response to this information. "Does that upset your established view of how things should be?"

David smiled to put his patient at ease. "Not at all. I know several women who have earned their doctorate." He frowned and shook his head. "I find it frustrating how many of my learned colleagues still hold the notion that women are incapable of grasping complexities. Napoleon's friend, Dr. Soames, is well-learned in several of the sciences and was very helpful to the prison doctor during times of crisis."

Gabriella harrumphed. "And yet, she was not the senior doctor there. Women are still forced into a secondary position even when they are better educated than their male counterparts."

"That was not the case at all, Mrs. Tanguay. Dr. Soames is well-accomplished and holds two or three degrees in the sciences, but not medicine." David hesitated as he reflected upon this fact. "She wouldn't need to have a medical degree to practice if she chose to."

"Perhaps her male counterparts felt threatened by her and wouldn't allow it."

David felt a tingle of irritation at this instant assumption of male dominance. He pushed the feeling down, though, and realized that she probably did have a point.

"Dr. Soames did not appear to be a woman who would allow such obstacles to deter her. It may simply be one field of education she never got around to."

Gabriella relaxed. "You are a breath of fresh air, Doctor. No wonder Napoleon speaks highly of you."

"Hmm." David smiled as he reached for a towel and gave it to her. "I would appreciate it if you would clean off that makeup so I can do a more thorough exam."

Gabriella pursed her lips. Her mood was swinging between irritation and ease, and back again. She attributed this to her headache.

"A more thorough exam? You wanted to check for a concussion, which you did. I have other things to get done today."

"No, you don't," David countered. "If you have even an inkling of medical science, then you know that a concussion requires rest. I also want you to be close by. I assume you already have a room in town."

"No, I do not." Gabriella chose to be stubborn. "I'm staying out at the ranch."

"Not anymore. Get a room in town. I insist. The night clerk can check on you every few hours to make sure you're all right. Goodness knows he has little else to do. Or you can stay here in our guest room. But you are to stay quiet for the next 24 hours at least."

Gabriella bristled. Even though she had already planned to stay in town, she didn't like the doctor ordering her around.

"I'm fine, Doctor. As far as I'm concerned, this examination is over."

"Mrs. Tanguay, please. I can tell from the makeup that has already been smudged off that you have other injuries. I would be no kind of doctor at all if I didn't investigate." He frowned as another thought occurred to him. "Why are you wearing make-up?"

"Do you think only loose women wear make-up?"

David's exasperation with this argumentative woman was beginning to show.

"No," he answered pointedly. "But it appears that you applied the make-up to deliberately cover your bruising, but if you received the bruising due to the fall from a horse, you would not know . . ." His voice trailed off as he realized there was more to this injury than he'd been informed of. "Mrs. Tanguay, how did you receive these bruises?"

Gabriella sighed. "If you must meddle, I tripped over the bedroom carpet in the dark and slammed into the closet door."

David barely heard her as his focus shifted when he noticed redness through the smudged face paint on her neck. Without waiting for permission, he used his thumb to wipe clean that section of her throat. He frowned. "This bruising was not caused by a fall from a horse." He used the towel to wipe away more of the pancake. "Mrs. Tanguay, have you been attacked?"

Gabriella snatched the towel away from him. She was accustomed to male doctors treating their female patients with a condescension generally reserved for children. They came to their diagnosis without listening to the woman's concerns and ignored any evidence that contradicted their conclusions. She had not expected Dr. Gibson to be any different, so his perception and persistence caught her unprepared.

She didn't like being caught unprepared.

"Everything is fine, Doctor. You need not concern yourself."

David's jaw set in a firm line. Without a word, he turned and opened the office door.

"Napoleon! Will you come in here, please?"

Gabriella groaned.

***

As David and Gabriella disappeared down the hallway, Leon turned to face a curious Tricia.

The kettle on the stove broke the stalemate.

"Oh!" Tricia grabbed a towel and moved the whistling appliance off the stove. She prepared the tea ball with leaves, set it in the pot, and poured the steaming water over it to steep.

She then turned to Leon and smiled. "How is Penny?"

"What?" Leon had expected an interrogation concerning the mystery woman. "Oh. She's much better now. Thanks."

"Good." Tricia sighed and smiled as she sat down at the table. "That's good to hear. Perhaps Miranda and I will try another visit."

"Ah, no." Leon thought fast. "She had originally planned to join her mother and Eli on their visit to California. Then, of course, she fell ill. As soon as she was feeling better, she couldn't wait to get on the train and join their friends. We all thought some time away would be good for her."

"Yes, of course," Tricia agreed. "She has been through so much lately. There's nothing like a little holiday to clear the cobwebs. But still, that means Gabi is staying at the ranch with just you, Jack, and Cameron present."

"Yes," Leon concurred. He didn't think it prudent to mention

Frank.

Tricia smiled, a twinkle coming to her eye. “Don’t you think that’s highly improper? It was one thing while Penny was there, but for a woman on her own, to stay in a home with three men, even if she is married—”

“She’s widowed.” Leon cringed. He regretted his comment as soon as he’d said it. He really was off his game.

“Widowed?” Tricia’s brows reached for her hairline. “Oh, come, Napoleon! Do you want her reputation to be ruined? She mustn’t stay there on her own with three men, even if it is you three. I’m surprised Cameron permitted it.”

Leon held up his hand to stop the reprimand.

“Don’t worry. She’s getting a hotel room for tonight. That’s why we were riding to town.”

“Oh.” Tricia came down off her rant. Then she frowned. “On horseback? With her luggage?”

“Cameron is going to bring her luggage in later. It was a nice day, so we decided to ride in ahead of him.”

“Oh.” Tricia was not convinced. There was more going on here than Leon was divulging.

The front door opened, and Nathan bounced in, all rosy-cheeked and bright-eyed. He was about to dash into the kitchen when Tricia stopped him with a hand and a sharp look.

“No, you don’t, young man,” she told him. “You take off your boots and wet clothing before you come a step closer.”

“I don’t wanna come in,” Nathan insisted. “Bobbie wants me to come over to his house so we can build a snowman. His backyard has more snow than our backyard.”

“It’s almost lunchtime. You should come in and eat first.”

Nathan let a frown settle on his youthful face. “I don’t wanna come in for lunch. I wanna play! I knew I shouldn’ta come in ta ask permission.” He stamped his foot, causing snow to plunk onto the floor.”

“You always ask permission before you leave the yard, young man!” Tricia reprimanded him.

Nathan crossed his bulky arms and sulked.

“And because you did ask, as a good boy should,” Tricia continued. “You may go to Bobbie’s house.”

Nathan’s scowl disappeared, and he jumped up and down,

sending more snow to the floor.

"Yeaaa!" He turned and pulled open the front door. "Momma says I can!"

"But don't expect another offering of food before suppertime!"

The front door slammed upon Tricia's words, and the exasperated mother sighed and rolled her eyes.

"No one can say I don't try."

Leon chuckled. "He's more and more like his father with every passing day."

"Ohh, you have no idea."

Then the front door opened again, and Miranda stepped into the front hall.

"Oh my." She glanced down at the pile of snow at her feet. "I passed Master Nathanial on the run. I take it he was here first. Hello, Napoleon. I saw Karma and Berry parked outside. Who else is with you? Oh dear, is it Penny? Is she still not well?"

"Oh no, Penny is much better," Leon answered. "She's actually on her way to join her mother and Eli."

"I'm glad to hear she is feeling better." Miranda removed her coat and hat, wiped her boots, and joined the others at the table. "What a shame we missed her, though. A visit would have been nice."

Tricia stood up and poured tea for three.

"That was good timing, Miranda," she said as she joined them at the table and set the cups down. "I'm sure you could use a warm cup of tea right now."

"Definitely!"

Leon smiled at the sparkle in her eyes. She was still flushed from the cold and full of her usual high energy. He felt a niggling of excitement wash over him at her proximity.

"It's good to see you, Miranda. I'm sorry I haven't been more attentive. It's been crazy at the ranch these last few days."

"They have a widow-woman staying with them," Tricia nipped in with a mischievous glint in her eye. "A young, attractive, widow-woman."

"Ohh?" Miranda turned questioning eyes to Leon.

"It's not like that," Leon insisted. Damn, now he had both of them on his case. "She's a friend who came to visit. Now that the ladies of the house are away, she's going to take a room at the hotel."

"Ah, I see." Miranda deflated with the lack of juicy gossip. Then another thought occurred to her. "But why would they leave to visit friends when a friend had come to visit them?"

"Well, she's actually . . ." Leon hesitated. He'd put his foot in it again. He took a sip of tea to give himself a moment to decide his next move. Both ladies waited for him to continue. "Ah, she's a friend of mine and Jack's. From way back." Both sets of eyes gazed at him, wanting to know more. "Umm. Oh. She did a lot to persuade the governor to get me my parole. Now that I'm out, she thought she would come by for a visit. To see both of us."

Tricia and Miranda exchanged looks.

Miranda sipped her tea, then smiled at Leon. "She sounds like quite the lady. I look forward to meeting her."

"You won't have to wait long," Tricia informed her. "She had a fall off a horse on their way to town. She's seeing David now."

"Well, good. We can all have lunch together."

The office door opened, and David's voice interrupted the conversation.

"Napoleon! Will you come in here, please?"

***

Leon stepped into the office, and his eyes sent Gabriella a question. She looked away, her lips set in a tight line.

David closed the door and then came around to sit at his desk. He indicated a third chair.

"Sit down, Napoleon. Please."

Leon shrugged and, pulling the chair over beside Gabi, he settled in.

"What's this about, David? Are Mrs. Tanguay's injuries more serious than I thought?"

"Yes, you could put it that way."

Leon frowned. "What is it?"

David sighed as he steepled his fingers under his chin and sat back in his chair.

"There is more going on here than either of you is willing to say. I don't wish to intrude on private matters that aren't relevant to health concerns, but . . ."

Leon sat back, then sent David a pointed look.

"But you will, anyway. Come on, David, out with it."

"Okay." David sat forward again, folding his hands on his desk. "There is more than simple friendship between you two; that much is obvious. What is it? A love affair? Partners in crime? What?"

"I met Gabriella when I was in my twenties," Leon said. "I was running Elk Mountain at that time. Frank Carlyle hired her to infiltrate the gang and gather information."

"Napoleon!" Gabriella was incensed. "What are you doing?"

Leon raised his hands in surrender. "I forgot to mention how tenacious David can be. Once he's on the scent, he won't give it up, so we might as well tell him now and save ourselves the stress."

Gabriella glared at him. "But we have to . . ." She glanced at the doctor and lowered her voice. "... we have to keep this quiet."

"Nothing said here will leave this room," David assured her. "You may speak freely."

Gabriella turned away, her eyes filled with irritation. Her hands and jaw were clenched, letting it be known that she had no intention of speaking at all, freely or otherwise.

David turned to Napoleon, expecting him to continue.

"Carlyle's plan backfired. Gabriella and I fell in love. We had two children together, and we married."

"My goodness." It took a lot to surprise David, but Leon had succeeded. "Just when I think I know you, you reveal a whole new level. You're married, and you have two children? Why did we not know about this? It certainly didn't come up in your trial."

"I made sure of that," Gabriella stated. "I know how to cover my tracks when I need to." Then she scowled when she realized she had been pulled into the conversation.

"Yes, I'm sure you do," David said. "Where are your children now?" He sent Leon a stern look as another thought occurred to him. "And why have you been courting Miranda while married to another woman?"

"We haven't seen one another in over ten years," Gabi informed him. "It wasn't a real marriage anyway."

David's brows jumped up. "What!"

"Gabriella," Leon tried to smooth the waters. "Let me tell it. You're becoming argumentative."

"Fine. I'll let you know when you get it wrong."

"Oh, for crying out loud." David rubbed his eyes and sighed. "Somebody, please tell me what is going on here."

"All right, here it is," Leon said. "You know my heritage, David."

David nodded. "French Huguenot, I believe. And ... Cheyenne?"

"Shoshone."

"Right."

"My uncle was a holy man, and he married us in the Shoshone tradition. No Christian church would ever sanction it, so in that respect, we were never married. But it was real to me."

He glanced at Gabriella, but she avoided his gaze.

David felt the slight tension rise between the couple before him and realized how the rift between them had begun.

"Gabi and our two daughters lived in Gillette so I could visit with them when my profession allowed."

David cocked a brow at Leon's description of his criminal activities, but remained silent.

"Carlyle set a trap that resulted in the death of our youngest daughter."

Gabriella tensed but remained silent.

Napoleon glanced at her, knowing that this was painful for both of them.

"I was arrested," he continued. "Gabriella left, fearing for the safety of our older daughter. She wrote to me in prison and, I know, had a lot to do with pressing for my parole, but her showing up here in town last week is the first time I've seen her since ... since Ella died."

Silence settled over the room.

A distant tinkling of Miranda's laughter drifted to them from the kitchen.

David glanced from one patient to the other, noting their seated positions.

Napoleon had his arms and legs crossed. He had shifted so he was turned away from Gabriella, and his dark eyes stared into the lower corner of the room.

Gabriella also had her arms crossed. Her legs were drawn tightly together, her feet tucked beneath the chair. She had also shifted away from Napoleon as she stared out of the partially covered window.

"I am so sorry," David broke the strained silence. "I had no idea." He gave the grieving parents another moment to recover, then returned to his professional mode. "Mrs. Tanguay, Napoleon said that you left because you feared for the safety of your child. Were you afraid of Napoleon? Has he ever hit you?"

"Hey!" Leon came out of his trance. "Jeez, David. That's going too far, even for you."

David held up a hand to silence him but remained focused on Gabriella.

The question had also pulled her out of her silent musings.

"No, I wasn't afraid of him." Her tone was matter-of-fact. "I was afraid of his lifestyle. I was foolish to think we could make it work, and poor Ella paid the price. I had to raise Hannah where it was safe."

"Yes, I can understand that."

Leon snorted but held his tongue.

David sent him a glance, then turned back to Gabriella. "So, Napoleon, himself, has never hit you?"

Gabriella hesitated, then shook her head. "I assure you, Doctor, during those years we were together, Napoleon never hit me, nor threatened our children. He was a good father."

Leon glanced at Gabriella, surprised by the compliment.

David nodded his understanding. "The reason I ask is that Napoleon developed a reputation in prison as being violent and unpredictable. He was known to attack other prisoners and even the guards if provoked. I realize the prison environment could well be what caused these outbursts, but, considering his previous lifestyle, I need to be sure that this kind of extreme violence is not the norm for him."

Gabriella looked him straight in the eye. "No, Doctor, it was not the norm."

"Then how did you come to attain those bruises?"

Gabriella prepared to answer, but nothing feasible came to mind.

"She got them when she walked into a door," Leon put in, but saying it out loud made it sound even less feasible than when Gabriella had offered it. Something more was coming, and he knew he wasn't going to like it.

"No." David shook his head. "The black eye, possibly, but not the bruising on her neck."

"On her neck? What bruising on her neck?"

With some reluctance, Gabriella pulled down the collar of her blouse, revealing the angry, red compression bruising around her throat.

"What the ... how did you get those?" Leon came to his feet to peer more closely at the marks. "I didn't do that. Tell him, Gabriella. I would never do that."

"Napoleon, sit down."

"But, David, I —"

"Sit down!"

Leon scowled, his hands on his hips, but he did return to his chair. He looked to Gabriella again and, more softly, implored her. "Tell him I didn't do that, Gabriella."

Gabriella met his worried gaze, her eyes glistening.

"I'm sorry, Napoleon, but you did."

"What? But —" Leon became acutely aware of the irritation on his own neck from Frank's disciplinary action and was glad that his bandana covered it up. "I wouldn't do that. Honestly, David. I wouldn't."

"Not intentionally," Gabi told him. "And it was my fault. I knew better than to touch someone while they were in the throes of a nightmare. But you were trying so hard. You were in so much pain; I had to help you."

Leon frowned; his brain was swirling. "You mean that dream I had last night? You were there? You were talking to me? That wasn't part of the dream?"

"It was part of the dream," Gabriella told him, "I was part of your dream, too. I was trying to help you control it."

"You had another nightmare last night?" David interjected.

The other two people turned to look at him.

"Ah, yes," Leon said. "It was the usual one, where I'm reliving the attack in the infirmary. But this time, I saw Harris clearly and, at Gabriella's prompting, Harris's sleeve fell back and revealed a tattoo. Gabriella found a lead here in town for the man who shot Penny. He had a tattoo on his upper arm. If we could prove that this tattoo was the same one Harris had, it would tie many things together. But I couldn't remember Harris's tattoo, or even if he had one.

"I heard Gabi's voice telling me to slow the dream down, and that's when I saw the tattoo on Harris's arm. I was so angry, I attacked him. But it was in the dream. I didn't attack Gabriella."

David leaned back with a sigh. He had wanted information, but he hadn't counted on this much.

"Dreams are tricky things," he said. "There isn't much information out there about them, but I think there's more to them than most doctors believe. They can appear very real, like yours have done. And the waking world can intrude upon them, especially if the awake person touches and speaks to the sleeping person. You heard her voice in your dream and recognized it as such. But when she touched you, she became Harris. To you, in your dream, you were attacking Harris, but in reality . . ."

Leon stared at David with his mouth agape.

Then he sat back and stared into nothing as his brain tried to comprehend this atrocity.

Gabriella leaned over and touched his knee. "You didn't mean to, Napoleon. It was my fault."

"Oh, God." Leon's complexion paled, but his eyes were bright with moisture. He blinked, and a tear slid down his cheek. He brushed it away with some anger, then sat, dejected, and shaking his head.

"I'm so sorry, Gabriella. I'm so sorry. First, Jack and now you."

"Jack?" Gabriella frowned and looked at David.

"Jack did the same thing," David informed her. "He tried to wake Napoleon from a nightmare and ... well, let's just say he will never do that again. Anyway, at least I know now how you got those bruises, and that it wasn't intentional. I, for one, am relieved. I still don't know you very well, Napoleon, and I would hate to discover that you are a naturally violent man. Indeed, a wife-beater.

"I realize this is difficult for you to take in but know that this was not your fault. And it sounds like some good things may have come from it. But, from now on, Mrs. Tanguay, I suggest you refrain from entering his bedroom while he is sleeping."

Gabriella frowned with irritation. "I was only in his room because I heard him crying out. Besides, I will not be staying at the ranch from now on. Both of you are insisting I take a room at the hotel."

"Fine," David accepted that. "But why are you here in the first place? I don't accept this coincidence. You arrive amidst all this upheaval, and then Penny falls ill. And I don't accept the claim that Jean would leave her daughter at a time like this, especially if she were unwell."

Gabriella slumped and sent Leon an exasperated look.

Leon was recovered enough to roll his eyes.

"I told you he was tenacious."

Gabriella frowned at David. "You are far too astute for your own good."

David smiled. "I need to be astute to do my job. I doubt your sister is a slouch."

Gabriella laughed despite the strain. "You are certainly right there, Doctor."

"So," David sat back and steepled his fingers again. "What's going on?"

Leon and Gabi exchanged a look, and Leon shrugged.

"Well," he began, "Gabriella showed up in town about a week ago . . ."

***

"So, it's all a ruse," David said once the story was out. "You came to town disguised as their elderly aunt. Penny, disguised as you, left when Jean and Eli did. And Jack went along to ensure safe passage. In the meantime, you, disguised as Penny, have been staying at the ranch to confuse the assailant if he, or they, are still around.

"Apparently, they were because you were shot from an ambush while riding into town this morning. But you were wearing a protective helmet?"

"Yes," Gabi concurred. "And an armored vest."

"Interesting. I would like to see those."

"Perhaps."

Leon rolled his eyes at Gabi's typical evasive comment when asked to do something she didn't want to.

"And you think the assailant is the same man who's been hanging around town?" David continued.

"That's right. There's a woman at the brothel whom he favored. I need to go and speak with her. If this man has a tattoo, then it might very well be the escaped convict, Carl Harris."

"And Detective Carlyle is also in town. And you're all working together?"

"Ah, yeah." Leon could understand David's skepticism. "Frank Carlyle wasn't responsible for our daughter's death. That man has paid for his crime. We're all just trying to get this whole thing figured out."

"So, Dr. Gibson," Gabriella said. "I'm sure you can understand the need for secrecy in this matter."

"Of course." He smiled at Gabriella. "You are an extremely

complex woman. I can see why Napoleon was drawn to you. I can also see why you are often at odds with one another. Two strong personalities cannot come together without conflict. Ah, this brings up another matter, Napoleon."

"It does?"

"You and my wife's cousin. Are you a single man, or . . .?"

Leon and Gabi exchanged a look.

Gabriella nodded. "You can rest assured, Doctor, what Napoleon and I had is over. We share a daughter, that is all."

"Okay. Napoleon, do you feel the same way?"

"Yes. I love Gabriella and always will, but we do better as friends than spouses. I hope to know my daughter again, one day, but that's it."

"Good." David appeared satisfied. "Miranda has been through a lot this past year. I would hate to see her get hurt again."

***

Miranda was instantly drawn to the woman who came into the kitchen with Napoleon and David. She covered up her curiosity in the guise of concern.

"Oh my, that eye does look painful. Tricia says you had a fall from a horse."

"Yes, that's right. Such a nuisance. But it looks worse than it is."

Miranda stood up and extended a hand.

"I'm Miranda Thornton. I hear you're a friend of Napoleon's from way back."

"Yes." Gabriella smiled and returned the greeting. "We've known each other for some time."

"How wonderful!" Miranda's eyes sparkled. "We'll have to get together over tea and compare notes."

"Yes. Perhaps."

"Oh, stop it, Miranda," Tricia cut in as she set a sandwich on the table for her husband. "You're making Napoleon nervous. There are still some sandwiches left. Sit, and have something to eat."

"Thank you, but I couldn't," Gabriella said. "I'm quite tired and would prefer to simply return to my hotel room and rest."

"That would be a good idea," David's voice came from behind them. "I would prefer you stay in tonight and come see me again first thing in the morning."

"Napoleon, how about you?"

"No, thank you, Tricia. I should escort Gabriella to the hotel, then get back to the ranch."

"Really?" Miranda's cheerful mood dropped a notch. "I haven't seen you for ages, and when I finally do, you have to rush off."

"Oh. I'm sorry, Miranda, but . . ."

"No, you stay and visit with your friends," Gabriella said. "I'm sure I can find my way to the hotel."

"Don't be silly, Gabriella. I can take you over and make sure you get settled."

"Well, I need to get going," David said over a mouthful of meat and bread. "I have a couple of calls to make this afternoon. Tricia, would you wrap up a couple of sandwiches for me to take?"

"Yes, all right. Do you expect to be late getting back?"

"No, no, I don't think so. They're just routine check-ups. Napoleon, come in to see me on your own sometime soon, all right. We need to work on your shoulders."

Leon slumped. He hoped David had forgotten about that, what with everything else going on. "Yeah, okay. I'll try to get in tomorrow."

"Good." David took the paper package that his wife handed him and headed out the door. "I'll see you later. And remember, Mrs. Tanguay, rest."

Gabriella smiled sweetly at him, and Napoleon knew she had no intention of following his advice.

"We should go, too," Leon said. He smiled at Miranda, but the look that met him made him feel guilty. "I'll see you tomorrow when I come in to see David."

"Yes, all right. I'll see you tomorrow. It was lovely to meet you, Gabriella."

"You as well." Gabi said. "And you, Tricia. Thank you for your hospitality."

"Of course. You're welcome anytime."

***

"I'm sure it's nothing," Tricia poured more tea and set out finger cakes. "As he said, she's just a friend."

Miranda sighed. "Yes, I know you're probably right. But there was something about her, like she was sizing me up. You know, the way women do when they're both interested in the same man. And Napoleon seemed ... uncomfortable."

"Probably because he knew you were thinking exactly what you're thinking."

Miranda chuckled, the spark returning to her eyes.

"Yes, of course. I'm being silly. I'm sure he'll remember to ask me to the Thanksgiving Dance when we talk tomorrow."

CHAPTER SEVENTEEN
CONFLICTS

The following morning, Leon returned to town with the buckboard. If he had to come in anyway, he might as well deal with the never-ending need for supplies. This way, Gabriella could relax on the return ride to the ranch and not have to ride a horse.

He'd had some trepidation about leaving her alone in town with a concussion. He didn't trust the night clerk to check in on her periodically. She would have been better staying with the Gibsons, even just for that one night, but it didn't surprise him that Gabriella had refused that offer. And, if David had been okay with it, then perhaps he knew the night clerk better than Leon did.

The previous evening, she had checked in under her real name, leaving the elderly great-aunt's room unoccupied. Leon had escorted her to her new room, much to the raised eyebrows of the hotel clerk, and had made sure she got settled in.

So, it was with some surprise, overpowered by irritation, that the knock on her room door, the following morning, resulted in silence.

He returned to the front desk and got the clerk's attention.

"Mrs. Tanguay, is she not in her room?" He looked over the clerk's shoulder at the keyboard on the back wall. "Did she drop off her key?"

"Do you know the number?"

"Eight."

The clerk turned to the large board where all the keys were hung. Even Leon could see that the number eight hook held its key.

The clerk sent him a plastered-on smile.

"I'm afraid she has stepped out, sir. May I tell her you called?"

"No, that's okay. Do you know when she went out?"

"I just came on duty an hour ago, so no, I don't."

Leon sighed. "All right. Thank you."

***

Leon watched the veiled woman make her way onto the street from the back of the Black Rose. He let her cross the road and walk a few hundred yards before falling in behind her and catching up once she turned the corner.

"David told you to rest," he murmured. "Have you been out all night?"

Gabriella kept walking as Leon came up beside her.

"Of course not," she assured him in hushed tones. They didn't need passers-by to overhear them. "I spent a very restful night. I knew that if I wanted to speak with one of the prostitutes, mid-morning is the best time. It seems Molly may have been his favorite, but the feelings were not reciprocated. I told her I was his wife and showed her my face. For ten dollars, she sang like a bird. She would have told me his birth weight if she had known it."

"Was it Harris?"

"He called himself 'Mitch'. He had a thing for knives and talked about having gotten away with murder, as though that would endear him to the poor woman. He frightened her."

Leon let his frustration shine through. "So, there was nothing to prove he was Harris?"

"The tattoo might, and he talked about his childhood in Sheridan. The man's parents came from Yorkshire, England, and moved West around 1870. He had two brothers and one surviving sister, having lost the youngest to scarlet fever at the age of eight. His father was a miner seeking a better life, but they were dirt-poor. It would appear they did not find what they were looking for."

She turned her head to him, her dark eyes burning through the veil.

"Whoever he is, he's a suspect, and criminals are often stupid—they will change their name, but give intimate details about their personal life, which destroys the alias," she explained. "Some things are clear, though: he was passing through town, he was violent with Molly, and talked about criminal connections. He had money to flash around, with no obvious means of support, and he was heading for

Missouri to see a man about some business. If there had been any other itinerant in town, the girls there would have known about it. There was no one else like him. The other visitors to the brothel all worked and had a reason to be here. Harris's past should be easy enough to find out, but we need to keep an open mind, in case it's not him."

"It could have been someone working in town. We don't know it was this 'Mitch'," Leon pointed out. "And why would Harris be after Penny? It doesn't make any sense."

"True. But if the real suspect is still around, he will probably try again. He does not know Penny is gone. We must stay alert." She shrugged. "Sometimes you have to go on instinct. Mitch was an aggressive drifter with money to burn, who hot-footed it after a second failed attempt on Penny."

Leon smiled in admiration. "You haven't lost it, Gabi."

"It is not difficult. Those women have had hard lives and been treated like lepers. If somebody treats them like an equal, they are grateful. I am just glad I got there before Frank muddied the waters. What does the idiot mean when he says he doesn't rely on common sense?"

"Many of the criminals Frank has gone after have been mentally deranged and dangerous. What common sense is to the average citizen doesn't even come into that type of person's realm of perception. You, of all people, should realize that. Frank has a way of clearing his mind of everything but the facts and then getting into the head of the person he's after. He doesn't have time to consider 'common sense'. People do tend to think he's stupid because his mind is rarely in the here and now. He often says things that are inappropriate or illogical, so it's easy to underestimate him."

"Ahh!" Gabi conceded. "When you put it that way . . .. Still, I would prefer to follow this lead myself. This 'Mitch' is worth a look, and I have a direction to go in."

"You?" Leon stopped her with a hand on her arm. "You're not ready for that kind of travel, Gabi. Let Frank go after him."

Gabi puffed. Even through the veil, Leon could see the gleam in her one eye. "I have no intention of letting Frank—"

"Gabi, you're still not well. Let Frank do it."

They walked on in silence for a few minutes.

Gabi had no intention of arguing since she had already made up her mind. She felt fine, aside from a swollen eye that she couldn't see out of.

She pushed aside her irritation, then picked up a more casual line of discussion. "Are you going in to see the doctor?"

Leon sighed with inevitability. "Yes. He won't let up until I do."

"It appears that I'm in the same situation," Gabriella sighed. "Is he always such a mother hen?"

"Yes!" Leon laughed. "But he's the best doctor I've ever known. He saved both mine and Jack's lives. Even at a time when I didn't want to be saved."

"Oh." Gabriella was enlightened. "He's the doctor who came to the prison."

"Yes."

"I guess that means I will have to go see him. I owe him."

Leon frowned. "What do you mean?"

She stopped and turned to face him. "He brought you back to us. And Jack, too. That's a debt I may never be able to repay."

"Do you mean that?"

"Of course." She looked up into those dark, brown eyes that nearly took her breath away. She quickly turned and headed back toward Main Street. "I'm afraid this concussion is taking its toll. I need to rest and freshen up. I think you and I are both getting too old for this.

"You're not old," Leon said, seriously. "You look exactly the same as you did when we first met. That's one of the things that shocked me; it was like all those years never happened."

A gentle chuckle came from behind the veil. "Of course, I've changed."

Leon shook his head. "Nope. You're still a beauty, Gabi. I was completely smitten that day you walked into the mercantile store in Denver. Jack was sure I had lost my mind, trying to spark you when we had a big job on the line."

"Oh yes. The job that put you and Jack on the Most Wanted List. It also brought Frank Carlyle and Hezekiah Hoag into our lives. Congratulations."

"Yeah, well. Not everything is foreseeable. I wonder what happened to Detective Hoag. Frank never mentions him anymore."

"Hmm. Probably best. You don't need both of them on your back."

Leon barked a laugh. "That's for sure." He softened his stance and became serious. "I did love you, Gabriella. You do know that, don't you? I still love you, but . . ."

"Yes, but . . ." She sighed. "Life got in the way."

"But that doesn't mean we can't work with what we have. We could try again."

Suddenly, the breath was gone from Leon's lungs. He couldn't believe he had just said that.

"Again?" Gabriella cocked a brow at him. "With you on parole? I doubt it would work. Besides, I've made a good life for myself. Hannah is doing very well and is happy. And, now that she's older, I'm going back to school to further my forensic studies."

"You mentioned that when you first arrived," Leon recalled. "It sounds like you're very busy. And happy."

"Yes, we are." A sadness settled over her then. "I'm still looking for Theo, but..." She shrugged it off, regretting that she had mentioned it at all.

Leon took her hand in his and gently squeezed it. "Still no leads?"

"Some. One of the reasons I went back to Canada after we parted was that there was a lead. It did get us closer, but it fizzled, just like all the others."

"You're still able to pay someone to look for him?"

"Yes, from my own earnings. And Helèna has helped, too. She's very supportive. And the detective I hired has done a lot on his own time." She frowned as she considered this aspect. "I think he feels that he owes me something. He's just as passionate about finding Theo as I am."

"Owes you something?" Leon's brows knitted. "Why?"

Gabriella's lip twitched, and she wished she hadn't brought that up. Maybe that bump on the head was still affecting her brain. "It doesn't matter." Then she smiled, and an impish glint came into her eyes. "Perhaps he is smitten with me, and he's trying to win my affections."

Leon laughed. "I certainly can't blame him for that."

"Perhaps." Gabriella became reflective again. "He's very good with Hannah. Always has been. And she certainly considers him a friend."

"Just a friend?" Leon's tone suggested a hint of jealousy. "Not a father?"

"Hannah knows he's not her father," Gabriella assured him as she patted his arm. "But she does trust him. She feels safe with him. Always has, even when I didn't . . ." She laughed then. "Oh, it doesn't matter. Despite my first impressions, he is a good man. He's doing everything he can to find Theo. Other than that, he's simply a friend."

"Hmm," Leon nodded. "Still, I assume he also believes that Hannah's father is dead and is hoping to step into that role?"

"No. He knows you're not dead. But he does understand the secrecy around it all."

"I wish I did," Leon mumbled, then changed the subject. "Now that your son is older, perhaps he will come looking for you."

"That is certainly a hope. I fear, though, that his grandparents have filled his head full of lies about me. He may not want to find me."

"If he's anything like his mother, he'll want to find out for himself.

Gabriella smiled. "Thank you."

Leon took her hand and brought it up to his lips for a soft kiss.

He suddenly caught a movement behind her, and guilt hit his gut. Again.

"Oh no. I thought she was visiting with Tricia."

Gabriella turned to see Miranda coming towards them.

"Oh dear." Gabi slipped her hand out of Leon's. "She clearly wants to speak with you." She smiled and turned to face the approaching woman. "Miranda. How are you?"

"Hello." Leon piped in.

Miranda darted quizzical eyes from one to the other. "Gabi? That's you? Why are you hiding behind that thing? You have such a pretty face." She stopped and frowned with trepidation. "Oh dear. Have I done it again? Are you in mourning, Gabi? Is that why you traveled here on your own to visit with friends?"

Gabriella shook her head. "I'm not a recent widow. He died many years ago, while I was in my confinement, and my daughter is fourteen now. I'm wearing black because it is practical for traveling, and I'm wearing a veil because of this." She lifted the fabric to expose her black eye, then quickly dropped it again. "It looks even worse than it did yesterday, and I can't bear to have people gawking."

"I certainly understand that. It looks dreadful, but it appears to be closing up. You are going to see David today, aren't you?"

"Yes, I will. Napoleon has told me there is no point in trying to avoid him."

Miranda laughed. "Yes, he's right about that. David is relentless. And you, Napoleon? David said he wanted to see you as well."

"Yes, we're both heading there now. Why don't you join us? It would be nice to visit while I'm in town."

Miranda smiled, trying to hide her relief. "Yes, it would. Tricia expects me for tea, so we can take turns visiting."

"Sounds lovely," Gabriella said. "But I think I need a rest first. I guess that concussion is wearing on me. I also need to get my things together for the trip out to the ranch when we're done here." She glanced up at Napoleon. "We'll have to leave right after my session with the doctor, or we'll be caught by darkness."

"Yes, I know," Leon assured her.

Miranda tried to hide her concern. "Oh. You're not staying at the hotel tonight?"

Leon piped in. "David wanted her to stay close for the first night, but there's plenty of room at the ranch. She'll still have her privacy."

Miranda frowned. Just when she'd think there was nothing but friendship between Leon and this woman, one of them made a comment that made her instincts tingle. She didn't want to start a scene right there in the middle of the street though, so she kept her thoughts to herself.

"That will certainly make things easier," Miranda commented and hoped her ruse worked. "And Cameron is an excellent host. I hope you feel better soon. If you're going to be around for a few more days, perhaps we can get together for tea with Tricia."

"Yes, perhaps."

"Come along, ladies," Napoleon gallantly offered an arm to both women and hoped that he pulled it off with natural grace. "Since we will pass the hotel on the way to David's home, we can all go together."

Miranda laughed at his antics and happily took his arm.

Gabriella smiled under her veil, but when she took Napoleon's other arm, he felt the tension in her touch.

He secretly gave her hand a gentle squeeze.

***

Gabi hung her coat and hat, with the veil, on the hooks by the door, then sat in the small wooden armchair to unlace and remove her damp boots.

Before she had the first boot off, her throat tightened on her, and tears burned her eyes.

She was angry at herself for feeling such emotion. Why should it matter? She should be happy for Napoleon that he had found someone else, and Miranda is a lovely woman.

Gabi wiped away a tear, but she couldn't stop the first sob from escaping. This was silly. She and Napoleon had just agreed; it could never work between them now. Too many hurts, too many lies. Too much history there.

So why had she just pulled out a hanky and was now sobbing into it?

***

"Napoleon, come in. Have a seat."

Without a word, Leon sat in the chair and unbuttoned his shirt. He knew the routine.

David cocked a brow. It had taken some doing, but finally, Napoleon accepted the massages and no longer complained about them. He had probably come to realize that they helped.

"You can keep your Henley on," David told him. "I know it's chilly, and I can do my work through it."

"Oh. Okay."

Leon had been about to pull the undershirt over his head and was pleased at the reprieve.

David began working Leon's shoulder muscles, but then he stopped and peered more closely at the skin on the back of his neck. "What are these bruises here?"

Leon slumped. His throat had stopped hurting ages ago, so he had forgotten all about the possible bruising still healing.

"Do we need to go into it, David?" he asked. "It's nothing. Just a disagreement between Detective Carlyle and me."

David frowned. "He laid hands on you?"

"It's nothing," Leon repeated. "I deserved it anyway. I got angry and stepped over the line. Just leave it be, will you?"

"All right," David agreed, much to Leon's surprise. "Have you seen Mrs. Tanguay today?"

"Yes. I was just speaking with her. She's returned to her hotel room to freshen up before coming over here."

"She went out?" David frowned. "I told her to rest."

Leon snorted. "You want a list of all the things I've told her to do, and how many of them she actually did?"

David smiled. "No, I don't think that will be necessary. Ohh, there's a good knot."

Leon gasped.

"Just relax." David continued to work the offending muscle. "I guess it's not surprising you would be all bound up. It's been a stressful time for everyone. Especially you."

"Me?" Leon released a breath and tried to relax. "I would think Penny and Jack have had it worse."

"They are having a difficult time right now, I agree. But I expect that Mrs. Tanguay's unannounced arrival was quite a shock to you. Especially with what you're already going through."

Leon released another breath. "I suppose."

"Are you sure it's over between you?" David moved to the other shoulder. "She is the mother of your children; by all that is proper, you should have married her."

"I did marry her."

"In a pagan ritual that a proper church would never condone."

"Ha!" Leon shook his head. "A proper church, David? What is a proper church?"

"Well, I suppose, one sanctioned by God."

"By whose definition?" Leon relaxed as his brain had something to work on. "There are so many different versions of faith, and everyone, from the Pope in Rome to a Shoshone in a buffalo robe, insists that theirs is the only true faith. It seems that what a person believes depends more on where they were born and what their parents taught them, rather than what the actual truth is. And yet, most of them share similar themes. Are they all true according to the individual, or are none of them true, and we grab onto a falsehood to make the passing into nothingness less terrifying?"

David sighed. "I have no idea. And to be quite honest, I've never taken the time to study theology. Trust you to come up with a question that no one can answer."

"Hmm. It's something I've been thinking about a lot lately."

"Perhaps you should read some books on the subject. The library in Denver might have something."

"I had some books on theology in my own library," Leon mumbled with some regret. "I lost them all when Jack and I decided to go for our pardons."

"That's a shame. Perhaps when things settle, you'll be able to rebuild it."

"I intend to." Leon became reflective then. "I could always ask Dr. Mariam. She's a theologian. I should have spent more time talking with her when I had the chance."

"She is an amazing woman," David agreed. "You do surround yourself with interesting people. You can put your shirt back on now. Do you still have any liniment?"

"Yes." Leon pulled on his shirt and rolled his shoulders back and down a few times. "That does feel better. This whole session seemed easier." He frowned as a thought came to him. "You're not usually one to preach on Godliness. You did that on purpose, didn't you?"

David sat down facing Leon. "Yes."

"You sneaky bastard."

David grinned. "I know you, Napoleon. All I needed to do was get your mind busy on something, and you'd forget about everything else."

Leon sighed and rolled his eyes. "Jack always said I spend too much time inside my head."

"You do," David agreed. "But at least the conversations you have there are not a waste. It also works well as a diversion. Your muscles are getting better, though. You were tighter than I'd hoped, but that's to be expected when you have more stress than usual."

"Yeah. Speaking of which."

David cocked a brow. "Yes?"

"These nightmares. David, they're getting worse."

"Really?" David frowned. "I was under the impression that they were easing off."

"Easing off?" Leon cringed at the volume of his tone. He sighed and quieted himself. "I've just had one of the worst nightmares since I was released. I even attacked Gabi. How can they be getting better?"

David sat back and considered the situation.

"They are getting better. Circumstances brought on this more vivid nightmare, and your reactions to it. Even Mrs. Tanguay understands that. You need to let them run their course."

Leon sighed, and his shoulders slumped.

"Can't you just give me more laudanum?"

"No."

"Why not?" He cringed again at his tone.

David ignored it, understanding his frustration.

"The nightmares are the natural healing process. It's your mind's way of working things out. The more sedative I give you, the harder your mind will fight against it, and, ultimately, we will lose the battle. I'll keep you on the same dosage, but I'm afraid we must let these nightmares run their course. I believe I have a book or two about dreams, if you would like to borrow them."

Leon was disappointed but not surprised.

"No, that's okay, David. Doc Palin let me borrow his copies. I'm not sure I agree with all of it, but I'll settle for your word on it."

"Good. Thank you. So, back to our original question. Are you sure it's over between you and Mrs. Tanguay?"

Leon hesitated as he buttoned up his shirt.

"Napoleon?"

Heavy sigh. "I dunno. As you said, she is the mother of my children, and we were married, once upon a time. But she has told my daughter that I'm dead. So, there is that."

"Hmm. That could be a problem. But not an insurmountable one if staying with your family is what you choose to do."

"But Miranda is wonderful. She is beautiful and reassuring... I feel so at ease in her company. When I'm with her, I want to be a better man."

"But . . .?"

Leon's dark eyes were filled with confusion and sadness.

"But. I had a family with Gabriella, and she is very lovely as well. She's exciting, unpredictable, and as clever as they come. She keeps me on my toes. She's constantly challenging me to do better."

"Hmm." David tapped his pen against the desktop. "That is not the way most men describe the mother of their children. It sounds exhausting."

"And exhilarating," Leon added.

David laughed. "Yes. Well, it's obvious to me that you have unfinished business there. You need to get this sorted before you can move on. If you decide not to move on, you must let Miranda know."

Leon rolled his eyes. "If only it were that simple."

"Just be honest. Tell her how you feel. Miranda is an intelligent woman in her own right. But she does need to know where you stand."

"Yeah."

"Now," David sat forward and, putting the pen down, he folded his hands upon the desktop. "You seem to be having more than your share of feminine attention lately. Does this mean that your other problem has resolved itself?"

Leon swallowed, his nerves tingling. "What other problem?"

David cocked a brow. "Are we going to start playing games now? You know exactly what I'm talking about."

Leon shifted. This subject still made him uncomfortable.

"No," he finally admitted. "I still can't ... well ... with a woman. I thought, with Gabriella, since we ... well ... I know her. I thought, maybe. But ... well, I don't really feel like humiliating myself any more than I already have."

"Have you tried?" David asked.

"What? Humiliating myself?"

"No!" David frowned at him. "Have you tried a visit to the Black Rose? I hear the ladies there can be very helpful."

"No." Leon played with one of his buttons. "As I said, I don't want to humiliate myself even more."

David nodded his understanding. "How about when you're alone? Are you able to become aroused and take it through to completion?"

"Well ... when I'm alone ... yes. But what good is that? It's not real. It's just a necessity."

"Yes, but it reaffirms that your problem is not physical," David explained. "It's emotional. You need to relax and give yourself some time. The more you worry about it, the more stressed you will become, and then the less likely you will have success." He smiled to ease Leon's ego. "Considering everything that is going on in your life right now, the best course of action, on all levels, would be to take things slowly. Once you sort out what you really want, the rest will come together."

"You sure?"

David smiled again. "Reasonably sure, yes."

Leon allowed a throaty chuckle. "Yeah, okay, David."

***

Leon knocked on the hotel room door.

"Gabi?"

All was quiet inside the room.

"Gabi, are you awake?"

Still no answer. Leon glanced around to ensure privacy, then, slipping his lock picks out of the sheath in his boot, he crouched down to work his magic on the lock.

Within seconds, he heard the light lock click open and, straightening, a small smile tugging at his lips, he turned the doorknob and slipped inside the room.

His smile turned to a frown when he saw Gabriella sprawled out upon the bed, apparently sound asleep.

"No, Gabi . . ." He was by her side in two strides and began shaking her. "Gabriella, wake up!"

Gabi groaned and, rolling onto her back, she blinked awake. She rubbed her eyes and struggled to sit up.

"What is it, Napoleon? Has something happened?"

"No, thank goodness." The relief in his voice was obvious. "You said you were going to just rest. It could be dangerous to sleep on your own when you have a concussion, even a mild one. If I'd known you were going to do that, I would have come and stayed with you."

"From the state of my attire, it should be obvious I hadn't intended to drift off." Gabriella stood up and gazed at herself in the vanity. "Oh dear, I am a mess." She picked up the hairbrush and did her best to straighten things out. "I haven't even gotten my things together. That's going to make us late." She frowned and looked at Napoleon's reflection in the mirror. "What are you doing here? Aren't you supposed to be spending time with your lady?"

"I'm meeting with Miranda at the Gibson's when I escort you over there."

Gabriella slumped. "Really? Escort me? Do you think I'm going to just disappear?"

"Yes!"

Gabi turned away from the mirror and sent him a stern look. "I assured Dr. Gibson that I would go in for a check-up today, and I will. I don't need you to escort me."

"I'm going to anyway. So get ready, David's waiting."

"Aarg!" Gabriella tossed the hairbrush back onto the vanity.

"You are the most stubborn man I have ever met."

"Ha! You should talk. Miranda's a walk in the park on a warm summer's day compared to you."

Leon instantly regretted his remark when he saw Gabi slump. He was on his feet and to her side in a flash.

"I'm sorry. I shouldn't have said that."

"But you're right. Miranda seems very nice."

"She is. But she's not you."

Gabriella turned and gazed up into his dark eyes. "We already discussed this. There's too much history between us for it to work now. It was a wild, exhilarating ride, but it's over. I will never be a walk in the park on a summer's day. I will always be thunder and dark, rolling clouds constantly beating on you to be better than you are. You don't need someone like me in your life anymore."

"Maybe you should let me be the judge of that." Leon cupped her chin and leaned in for a soft, warm kiss.

Then his arms were around her, and he pulled her body in close to his.

She responded in kind, holding him tightly, as her lips opened to accept his advances.

Leon felt arousal swarm through his body only to be followed by a crippling fear. His breathing became irregular, and he pushed away from her, embarrassment and shame smothering his passion.

Gabriella stepped back.

Now that the emotions had eased off, she was irritated at herself for allowing this man to rob her of her common sense again. In her own agitation, she didn't notice Leon's discomfort.

She pursed her lips and straightened her skirt. "That wasn't very smart."

"No," Leon agreed as he brushed his hair back. "I'm sorry. Even David said not to . . ."

Gabriella huffed. "Not to what?"

"No, never mind. It doesn't matter."

"Fine."

They stood for a moment, an awkward silence expanding around them.

"We should go," Leon finally stated. "David is waiting for you."

"And Miranda is waiting for you."

Leon dropped his eyes. "Yes.

***

David smiled, reassuringly, at the woman as he ushered her to a chair.

"How are you feeling today?"

"The headache is gone, but..." Gabriella lifted the veil, revealing a purple eye. The congestion was forcing the eyelid closed, beneath pinching, tight flesh, relieved only by the gaping gash being forced open by the swelling.

"Hmm. Yes." David leaned over to examine the cut. "I didn't think this cut was going to need stitches, but I see the swelling has split it open. It'll need stitches now, I'm afraid."

"Are you sure?"

David gave a wry smile. "Do I strike you as the kind of man who is uncertain?" He strode over and lit a lamp before pulling the drapes closed. "It's likely to be a bad scar now, unless we close the wound." He placed a hand under her chin, moving the oil lamp in front of her face, staring into her eyes. "The pupil reaction seems fine. Let me see that neck." He ran gentle fingers over her throat, scrutinizing the bruises. "Do you hurt anywhere else?"

"No."

He walked over, pulled the curtains back open, and then approached the cabinet, removing a kidney bowl and some supplies. "How squeamish are you, Mrs. Tanguay?"

"About the same as you are, I suppose."

David returned and set the bowl on the table beside his patient. He opened the small bottle of disinfectant and soaked a cotton ball with some. "I'll be as quick as I can."

Gabriella flinched at the sting caused by the liquid as it absorbed into the tender flesh.

"What is that?"

"It's alcohol," David told her. "It'll clean the wound and help reduce the chances of infection. I would have done this the other day, but the cut seemed to be closing all on its own."

"So you said." Gabriella sighed. "I'm well aware of what alcohol can do for a wound, I simply didn't expect you to know."

David cocked a brow at her as he inserted the suturing thread into the curved needle. "Really? You seem to hold most doctors in low regard, Mrs. Tanguay. I hope I don't live down to them."

"On the contrary, Dr. Gibson, you appear to be very proficient." She flinched again at the needle piercing the already delicate flesh. "I want to reassure you that I am not here to disrupt Napoleon's life. We have both agreed to move on. He will sort his head out soon, especially when I am gone."

David tied off the first stitch. "He told you this?"

"More or less."

He started on the second stitch. "How do you feel about it?"

Gabriella smiled as her one good eye reflected upon the past.

"You must realize that when Napoleon and I first got together, we were both so young." She sucked her breath as the second stitch tightened. "But my life had forced me to grow up quickly. My first husband was murdered, and my son was taken from me before I was twenty-two. I'm also five years older than Napoleon, and they do say girls mature faster." She chuckled as she thought back. "Oh, but he was glorious. So fancy-free and cock-sure of himself. And yet, he had a way about him, a true confidence not often seen in such a young man.

"I tried to stay away from him; I knew he was trouble." She shrugged, and a soft smile came to her lips. "But what's a lady to do? He persisted. We were both moths drawn to the opposing flame; we couldn't help but self-destruct."

She flinched slightly as David started the next stitch.

"It's over, and we both acknowledge this," she continued, using it more as a distraction than an offering. "Does it hurt when I see him with Miranda? Yes, of course it does. But am I willing to risk everything I have built for myself and my daughter to try again? No."

"She is his daughter, too," David pointed out as he tied off the third stitch. "Doesn't he have the right to know her?"

"Yes, he does. I have already told him so. But not as her father."

"Do you really expect to keep that hidden? Considering her parentage, I expect that Hannah is an intelligent and perceptive young lady."

"Oh, Doctor, you have no idea!"

"Well, then . . .?"

"We'll manage something."

"Are you sure that's—"

"Doctor." Gabriella had had enough of this conversation. "This is hardly your business. I have assured you that Napoleon and I will not pick up our relationship where it left off. That is all you need to be concerned about."

David set the needle and suturing thread into the kidney basin, then scrutinized the woman sitting before him.

"Napoleon is not only my patient, but my friend. Miranda is my cousin through marriage. There is plenty here I need to be concerned about. My cousin has been through a difficult time, Mrs. Tanguay. Her husband has recently passed, and she came here to find some peace and to heal.

"She met Napoleon on his first night back in town after his release. Neither of them was ready for a new romance. But we don't usually have much say in that. They were smitten, right away, even though it took them a while to admit it.

"They're both fragile right now. Can you blame me for being a bit protective?"

"No, of course not." She stood up, getting ready to leave. "I'm sorry, Doctor, I didn't realize your relationships with Napoleon or Miranda. Of course, you would have your concerns. I also didn't realize how fragile Napoleon is until I arrived here. I'll be gone soon. I will stay at the ranch tonight, but I have a direction of travel for the suspect and I'm following that."

David's eyebrows shot up. "I would prefer that you don't. You need at least another two days of rest."

She nodded. "Of course, Dr. Gibson. I suppose you're right, again. Napoleon said much the same thing."

"Good." Though David doubted her sincerity. "I would like to check on you again in a couple of days, anyway."

"I'm sure someone can drive me into town. Then, after that, I must head for home. As Napoleon pointed out, we have someone else who can follow up on the lead."

"I'm glad to hear that. Those stitches must come out in ten to fourteen days. Any doctor can remove them. Make sure it gets done. I'll see you again in a couple of days."

"Yes. Until then."

Gabriella stood up, sent him a nod by way of farewell, and left the office.

CHAPTER EIGHTEEN
CONFESSIONS

Once Gabriella had disappeared into David's office, Napoleon returned to the kitchen to join Tricia and Miranda. He was ill at ease, knowing they were hoping for some gossip. He was determined not to give them any. Or at least, not Tricia.

"Would you like some tea, Napoleon?" Tricia asked him. "It'll be a chilly ride out to the ranch later on."

He nodded, thinking that a cup of tea might settle him, when a loud bang from down the hall jangled his nerves. Then Nathan charged down the hallway from behind, on his way from his bedroom to the kitchen. He held a toy wooden horse in his hand, galloping it through the air, making quite a bit of noise.

"Giddy up, giddy up!" came the childish, high-pitched exclamation. "I'm the sheriff, and I'm running down those outlaws! Watch out Nap'olin—there's outlaws!"

Once Leon had brought himself down off the figurative ceiling, he chuckled ironically. "There you go, Sheriff Nathan! You go get them!"

The energetic child charged into the kitchen. He banged into the table, causing the dishes to shake and clatter, as a chair scraped along the hardwood floor. It didn't faze the would-be sheriff, though, and he galloped around the table with righteous enthusiasm.

"Oh, Nathan!" Tricia reprimanded him. "Be careful—watch what you're doing. You know you're not supposed to run in the house."

"But I'm after outlaws, Momma!"

Leon quickly stepped aside as the little hurricane left the kitchen and charged down the hallway again, and with the slamming of a door, the child disappeared back into his bedroom. Leon chuckled at the boy's antics. A chilly autumn day—the child had to entertain himself somehow.

"My goodness!" Miranda laughed. "I don't know how you handle that boy, Tricia. You're a wonder-mother."

"He is a handful," Tricia agreed, as she swiped a loose hair from her forehead. "Come sit down, Napoleon. Have some tea."

Leon sat down just as a cup of tea with some biscuits was set in front of him. Tricia replenished the snacks for herself and Miranda, then joined them.

Leon sipped his tea and avoided eye contact.

Tricia and Miranda exchanged glances, then looked over to the unfortunate male.

Both women were curious about Mrs. Tanguay. The story that Leon and Gabriella had spun about her being an old friend just stopping by for a visit didn't ring true. It was too much of a coincidence for her to arrive so soon after the recent attack upon Penny. And now, the ladies of the ranch had left. It wasn't adding up.

Leon remained silent and, for some reason, felt exposed.

"Napoleon," Miranda began, "I'll be heading home soon. Would you care to walk with me?"

"Oh." Leon swallowed. "You don't want to visit here?"

"Tricia and I have been visiting all afternoon. I'd like to visit with you before you head back to the ranch."

"Yes, of course." Leon glanced down the hall towards the office. "I should escort Gabriella back to her hotel room first. She fell asleep and didn't have a chance to get her things together."

Miranda and Tricia exchanged a glance.

"You know I don't live far away. You'll have plenty of time to walk me home and get back here. I expect she is going to be a while with David anyway." She placed a hand on his arm. "We do need to talk. All right? You can walk Gabriella back to the hotel after that."

Leon felt a warm tingle from her gentle touch, and he smiled as he covered her hand with his. "I'm sorry. I guess I have been neglecting you lately. I don't mean to. Gabriella showing up here unexpectedly has thrown me off balance."

"Yes, I could tell."

"Next time I'm in town, we can plan on lunch together. Just the two of us," Leon suggested, trying to save the day.

"Let's talk first," Miranda said. She took one last sip of tea and stood up. "Thanks for the tea, Tricia. I'll see you later."

"Yes," Tricia agreed, pointedly. "I'm looking forward to it."

Leon smiled at Tricia as he joined Miranda and helped her with her coat and hat. The hidden meaning behind her words was not lost on him.

He donned his own coat, hat, and gun belt, nodded a farewell to Tricia, and then opened the door for Miranda and him to leave.

The day was chilly, with gray and heavy skies, but not raining—not yet. Or maybe it would snow again; it felt cold enough. There had been snow overnight, and some of it was starting to pile up in the more shaded areas against the buildings and down back alleys.

It felt comfortable having Miranda here beside him as they walked down the steps and out to the boardwalk. It also felt awkward. Leon wasn't accustomed to feeling confused around women. This was all so new for him, and he didn't like it much.

But David was right; he didn't know what he wanted, and it wasn't fair to lead Miranda on like this. He had just resolved to open the conversation along these lines when Miranda beat him to it.

"William was the love of my life," she stated bluntly, and Leon felt his heart skip a beat. Confusion again. "I still miss him so terribly much."

The couple walked, arm in arm, and Leon brought her hand over and cupped it in both of his.

"Yes, I know," he admitted.

Miranda sighed. "I'm not ready for this, Napoleon," she told him quietly. "I like you very much, and I want us to be friends, but I don't think I'm ready for anything more. Not yet."

Leon felt his heart constrict. He wondered why. Isn't this the outcome he was aiming for himself?

"Oh," was all he could manage.

She smiled and looked up at him. "And I strongly suspect that you have been feeling much the same way."

"Oh. Well . . ."

"You and Gabriella," Miranda continued bravely, "she did a very good job of covering for you, but I saw that look of guilt flash across your face. The two of you have history, don't you? Unfinished business?" She smiled for real. "Even though she insists that you are 'just friends'!"

"Yes," Leon admitted quietly.

Miranda couldn't help the knife that went through her heart. She wondered why. If she wasn't ready, why would this hurt?

"Are you in love with her?"

"I don't know," Leon felt this was a lie, but he wasn't willing to admit to anyone else that, just maybe, those feelings were still there. "I was, once, but that was long ago now. And she ended it. She sent me letters while I was in prison and said things that caused me to wonder if we could start up again, but ... since she's been in town, she has made it clear that she's not interested. She came here to help figure out what, or who, is behind these attacks on Penny."

Miranda nodded, trying to fight the tightness in her throat. "I knew there was more to it than what you were saying."

"We had to keep it quiet," Leon insisted. "I'm sorry for the subterfuge, but it was essential no one know."

Miranda walked along quietly for a moment, taking this in.

"So, Penny never was sick?"

"No," Leon admitted. "Penny left the same day with Jean and Eli. And Jack. Gabriella was pretending to be Penny so that whoever was after her would not realize she had already left. But now Gabi has a lead, and I suspect she will be leaving town tomorrow."

"I see." Miranda had thought this would be easy; that she didn't really love this man. But now ... or was this just loneliness—just ego?

"Perhaps she did come here, thinking of starting things up again. But you do seem to be keeping her at arm's length. Are you sure she isn't simply reacting to you pushing her away?"

"No, Miranda, she's not. She would be leaving now either way."

Miranda sighed and hesitated a moment, then resolved herself to ask the hard question. "If she wanted you to go back, would you?"

Leon stopped their slow progression. He turned the lady towards him and cupped her face in his hand. Her cheeks were cold, and she looked up at him with eyes that were sad and bright with emotion. Leon felt torn—again! He was used to being in control, even with women, but now, he had two women on his hands who were not afraid to step up and take that control away from him. Gabriella and Miranda were alike in so many ways, and yet, so different!

"I don't know," he admitted, again. "I love Gabi; I always will, but I don't know if I still love her in that way. I'm so confused, Miranda. I don't even know who I am anymore. These nightmares are driving me crazy, and now, all this stuff is going on with Penny." He shook his head, his torment showing plainly in his dark eyes. "I just don't know."

She smiled up at him, feeling her heart breaking again, only this time, it was for him. He looked so lost. Her hand mimicked his by coming up and caressing his cold face in her warm palm. "Then I think it's best that we both back off until we do know."

Leon dropped his eyes from hers. He didn't answer her; he didn't like it. Everybody was making decisions for him, and he was being left out in the cold. Even if they were the right decisions, he wasn't the one making them.

Miranda brought his chin up to look her in the eye again, and she smiled. "If William were still alive today, I would not leave him for you. I would look upon you and think, my what a handsome man he is . . ." Leon grinned, but his eyes remained sad, "but that's as far as it would have gone. I don't want to make the mistake of committing myself to another man simply out of loneliness, and I certainly wouldn't want you to do the same.

"And I certainly wouldn't want you to commit to me only to realize later that there's someone else you'd rather be with if only you had given it one more try." The sadness in his eyes nearly choked her, and she brought her hand down from his face and gently shook his arm. "C'mon, Napoleon, don't look like that. You know this is the right thing to do. I'm not going anywhere. We can still be friends, and if we both want to take things to the next step later, well..."

Leon smiled at her, then nodded. "Yes, all right." Then they went arm in arm again and continued to walk to Miranda's new home. "Does this mean you'd rather not go to the Thanksgiving Dance with me?"

Miranda laughed. "No!" she teased. "I still want to go. Just no expectations. And if your friend, Gabriella, is in town, and you want to dance with her, well, now you can feel free to do so."

Leon nodded again, and the couple continued their walk in silence.

They reached Miranda's little house, and Leon walked her up the porch steps. She turned the knob of the front door and was just about to enter when Leon put a hand on her arm.

She looked at him, and their eyes met and held.

"I do love you, you know," Leon told her quietly.

"I know," she whispered, "but this is something you need to work out. This is important."

Leon kissed her gently.

She returned it, then pulled away. She smiled at him, then turned and walked into her home, closing the door.

Leon stood on the front porch for a few moments, feeling wretched. He was in love with two different women at the same time, and both had pushed him away, giving him permission to begin courting the other. How was this fair? How come he didn't get any say? He shook his head in resentful futility, then turned and clomped down the steps to return to David's place.

Now he had to face Gabi—oh God—could this day get any worse?

***

Miranda quietly removed her coat and hat and went over to the stove. She struck a match and lit the tinder inside the belly of it, then prepared to make herself a pot of tea. Yes, some tea would go down nicely, right now—something to take the chill off.

She picked up the kettle, walked to the sink, pumped some water into the pot, then set it back on the stove. She could already feel the warmth rising; it wouldn't take long for the water to heat.

She took the tin of biscuits down from the shelf, the ones that Jean had given her last week, and they were good, too. Jean was such a kind woman, and now all this turmoil is sweeping through their family. That wasn't right. She took down a saucer and a teacup, the little plate for the biscuits, and set everything on the table. She could feel the warmth from the stove now, and soon, the kettle began to whistle. She got her teapot down, poured some hot water into it, swished it around to warm the pot, and then dumped the water into the sink.

She opened the tin of tea leaves, put some into the ball, then set the ball in the teapot and poured hot water over it. She stood there, staring into space, waiting for the tea to steep. She wasn't thinking about anything; she couldn't focus her mind on anything. She just stared.

After a few moments, she picked up a potholder, then the teapot, and moved over to the table to pour herself a cup. She set the pot down and pulled the tea cozy over it to keep it warm, then settled into the chair and stared into space again. She held the warm cup in both hands, but she didn't drink. She didn't even look at it; she just stared into space.

Then she started to cry.

***

Halfway back to David's house, Leon decided to run a quick errand while he had the time, so he headed up to the main street to send a telegram.

They finally had a little more to go on in describing the assailant, and he wanted to run it past Kenny to see if it matched up. Why get Frank to do it when Leon was already in town? He didn't know why Harris would cause all this trouble—it didn't make any sense to him, and maybe his mind was playing tricks on him. Perhaps it was as Kenny said. Leon wanted to make those people guilty; he wanted to make them responsible, so he could have a reason to go on hating them, a reason to seek retaliation.

But, on the other hand, maybe it was something. Maybe his subconscious mind was trying to tell him, letting him know that he knew something he didn't realize he knew. Or, maybe Doc Palin was really haunting him, pushing him to seek justice, but then, that could mean that all of this was interconnected, and that didn't make sense either.

Leon groaned. This was crazy. And Doc Palin had said that life wasn't about seeking revenge, it was about learning and growing and moving on, but was that really Doc talking to him, or just the delusional rantings of a brain on the edge of death?

Leon sighed, shaking his head as he mumbled to himself.

No wonder I'm having nightmares!

All these questions, swirling around him, and then, just as he was beginning to feel halfway normal again, Gabi showed up out of the blue. She had always upset his equilibrium, but now her presence was sending him spiraling into the hurtful memories and old wounds he had thought healed, only to have them lie in wait.

And then, there was Miranda. She took his breath away whenever he looked at her. She was exciting and fun, and he was comfortable around her. He didn't have to be on guard with her all the time, wondering when the next confrontation was going to hit him square in the face. He and Gabi were always in a battle to see who would end up on top. He could relax with Miranda.

But Gabriella! Oh, Gabriella. Not only was she the mother of his children, but she was beautiful, brilliant, and challenging. But always, constantly pushing him. He used to thrive on that; he even enjoyed it. But now? Now, he just felt worn out by it, yet drawn to it at the same time. Like a moth to flame.

Both had pushed him away. He knew they were right; that he needed time to sort things out, but he still resented it.

He let out a deep sigh and focused his mind on the matter at hand.

The suspected assailant had a dagger tattoo, and his dream featured Harris with one. Ask Kenny whether that fits Harris's description, then go from there. One step at a time. Hopefully, the rest of it would eventually sort itself out.

CHAPTER NINETEEN
TOPEKA

Topeka, Kansas

The dusk gathered around the travel-weary group as they pulled themselves up the steps of the red brick house in Topeka.

Jack took up the rear, and though just as tired as his companions, he was still on the job. He looked cautiously around the shadowy street and waited on the lower step until Jean and Penny had reached the porch stoop.

Jean shifted Eli in her arms, then reached up and rapped on the door with the bright, brass knocker. As she waited, she noticed the plaque that sat to the right of the knocker, "Doctor Helèna Dion", and for some reason thought it odd. She put it down to simply being tired. Why couldn't a woman be a doctor?

Then the door opened, and a woman with slightly graying hair and little sparkling spectacles scanned the group before her gaze settled on Jack, who had just arrived on the stoop.

"Mr. Kiefer, how good to see you again." She ushered them inside, darting a look up and down the street. "Nobody followed you?"

"Nope." Jack stepped towards her, his smile spreading. "I can't thank you enough for this, Helèna." He wrapped his arms around her and dropped a kiss on her cheek.

"Mr. Kiefer!" Helèna chuckled. "I think that's the first time a man has kissed me in nearly twenty years." Her smile brought out the ruddy apple cheeks in her round face. She turned to her new guests. "I'm Helèna Dion, Gabriella's sister."

"They're here?" A dark-haired girl appeared at the top of the staircase. She smiled at the group by the door, then trotted down the steps to greet their guests. "How lovely." Her gaze settled on Penny.

“Finally, someone my own age to talk to.” She placed a hand on Penny’s arm. “You have no idea how boring it’s been, stuck in this house with just my aunt for company.”

Helèna fixed her niece with a stern look that concealed a twinkle. “Hannah, that is not how young ladies introduce themselves to visitors.”

Hannah widened her eyes in faux innocence, but the bedevilment dancing in the chocolate depths was all too familiar. “Sorry, Aunt Helèna.”

“Say hello properly.”

Hannah stood up straight and tossed back her dark brown locks. “Good evening. My name is Hannah. It’s good to have you here.” The façade dissipated before their eyes as her face spread into a dimpled smile.

Penny blinked in disbelief, the “secret” suddenly hitting her between the eyes.

“Oh! She’s—”

Jack stretched out an arm and hugged Penny to him.

His voice was a whisper in her ear. “Yup. And she looks so much like him.”

The shape of her face was the main difference between Hannah and her father. Being more oval like her mother’s. Her lustrous hair was lighter than his, and the sultry, deep brown held hints of her mother’s auburn, which could be seen around the edges and in its luxuriant shine. The light from the hallway seeped down into each strand, barely settling, but gleaming from her dancing, cat-like brown eyes.

Jack’s heart skipped a beat. Suddenly, he was back in Gillette, and he was sitting on the floor playing with the exuberant child. Looking into that child’s eyes now, he could see the same sparkle, the same love for life. He knew then, beyond a doubt, that Leon needed to meet her. She was too much like him for them not to know one another.

As for Hannah, she was far too interested in Penny as a potential escape from tedium to take note of anyone else. When introduced to Jack, her gaze politely met his, but there was no recognition.

“She’s irrepressible,” Helèna shook her head and flicked a smile at Jack. “I can’t think where she gets that from.”

“A double dose, I reckon.” Jack grinned, his focus drawn back to the teenager. "I knew you when you were no taller than that banister. You were a little beauty then, too."

She gave a gasp. Suddenly, this stranger held her interest. "Did you know my father? What was he like?"

Again, Jack felt sadness and regret. It wasn't fair that he should meet Hannah, and Leon could not. His resolution to make that happen hardened in his soul.

"Yes," Jack told her. "A wonderful man, clever, loyal, and brave. He would be so proud of you; I can tell you that."

It was then a small memory pricked at Hannah. She looked into that open, friendly face and felt a warm tug.

"You do look familiar, somehow," Her brow creased. "But I don't remember anything specific." Then her face lit up with a smile that melted Jack's heart. "Perhaps we can talk later, and you can tell me more about those times. I've forgotten so much. I'm afraid Momma doesn't talk about them anymore."

Helèna saw trouble coming. "Enough of this." She ushered them down the hallway towards the kitchen. "You must be tired after that journey. I have a little supper prepared, and then you can bathe and retire if you wish. Penny, I assumed you would not mind sharing a room with your mother?"

"That's fine." Penny hugged her mother's arm. "She's good company."

***

Later that evening, while Penny and her mother were in their room getting ready for bed, Jean noticed the quiet look of consternation on her daughter's face. All through the simple but satisfying dinner, Penny couldn't take her eyes off Hannah. She was very much like her mother, but with every movement, every gesture, Penny saw so much of her friend coming through in the teenager. Even her mannerisms were just so ... Napoleon!

Penny sensed that Hannah had no idea who her father was, and she kept her mouth shut on the topic, but inside, the resentment grew. No wonder Napoleon had been upset at Gabriella's unannounced arrival. No wonder he was so hurt! To have a child and not even know her; to not even be acknowledged as the father, not even to the child herself. And what kind of woman was this Gabriella Tanguay, that she would allow herself to be put in such a position to have a child out of wedlock in the first place? She'd had two! Hadn't she learned from her first mistake?

By the time dinner had been cleared away and the three members of the Marsham family had settled into their room, Penny was seething with self-righteous indignation.

Jean had just gotten Eli settled into the cot and was turning down the blankets on the double bed when she decided that Penny had stewed in silence for long enough.

"Hannah is quite a precocious young lady, isn't she?" Jean finally broached the topic.

"Hmm," was Penny's only comment.

"What are you thinking about?" Jean asked, knowing a lot was going on behind those brown eyes.

"She's obviously Napoleon's daughter," Penny finally quipped. "It's so obvious even in her manner."

Jean smiled. "Yes. No denying the paternal line there."

"And yet, Gabriella seems to think she has the right to deny him!"

Jean sighed and sat down on the edge of the bed. "You must remember that Napoleon was an active criminal at the time of Hannah's birth. Hardly an ideal situation for raising a family. Gabriella did what she thought was best for the safety and welfare of her daughter."

"If the situation wasn't ideal, then what was she doing with Napoleon in the first place?" Penny fumed. "If she didn't want to marry a criminal, then what business did she have doing ... that ... with him!" Then she mumbled under her breath. "We all know what kind of women have children out of wedlock."

Jean's brows went up at her daughter's self-righteous comment. "Well now, aren't you a fine one to talk!"

Penny puffed herself up and sent her mother an indignant stare. "What's that supposed to mean? I didn't—" She stopped in mid-denial and turned red with embarrassment. "Well, we didn't ... it was only once!"

"And once is often all it takes, young lady," Jean pointed out. "The only difference between you and Gabriella is that you were very lucky!" Jean softened her tone when she saw her daughter's obvious distress. "Come," she said, patting the spot on the bed beside her, "sit down with me."

Penny slumped in defeat, then did as her mother suggested.

Jean put her arms around her daughter's shoulders and hugged her close.

"Try not to be too judgmental of others, Penny," was Jean's quiet suggestion. "It is that very attitude you've just displayed that has forced Gabriella to deny Hannah's true paternity. She had to lie to people, to say that Hannah was the legitimate child of her marriage and that the father had passed away. She's even had to lie to the child herself, to protect her from the cruel remarks of self-righteous busybodies!"

Penny gave an ironic laugh. "You mean, like me."

"Well, I wasn't going to actually say that . . ." Jean smiled and hugged her daughter even closer. "Oh, Penny. You of all people should understand how a woman can get lost in a man's eyes," she gave a quiet laugh, "and Napoleon has such beautiful eyes, does he not?"

Penny snorted. "Yes, all right, Momma—you've made your point." Then she turned serious again. "It has been hard, waiting. There were times when we came close again, and it was always Jack who put the brakes on before we went too far. I never could. I knew Jack wanted to, just as much as I did, but somehow, he was able to say no."

"Hmm," Jean thought about that for a moment. "Jack pays close attention to what Napoleon does. He was aware of the consequences and, perhaps, after seeing what Napoleon went through and realizing he made that same mistake with you, well, maybe that gave him the resolve he needed to wait. Oh! But that was a terrible thing to say!"

Penny frowned. "What?"

"It's like saying that beautiful young lady downstairs was a mistake," Jean explained. "That, by rights, she should never have been born—and that is a terrible thing to say of any child. Oh my! Here we are again, in one of those gray areas. By our teachings, having a child out of wedlock is wrong, and we shouldn't do it, and yet, once that baby is born and full of life and joy, then how can she not be one of God's children, and made welcome!"

"Oh, Momma!" Penny teased, "You always did see things from both sides. It must make life very confusing sometimes."

Jean laughed. "Yes! I have caused your father many a sleepless night, I can assure you."

Penny became serious again and sighed a deep sigh. "Do you think that Napoleon and Hannah will ever know one another? It doesn't seem fair that she can't know who her father is—especially when her father is ... well—Napoleon Nash! And that Napoleon knows he has a daughter, but isn't even allowed to visit her? That's cruel."

"Yes. This has been hard on him," Jean agreed. "And, of course, seeing Gabi again has brought up all those old wounds on top of everything else he's struggling with. But I can see Gabriella's point of view—"

"There you go again, seeing both sides!"

"Yes, I know," Jean laughed, "but Gabi has said that perhaps, in time, when Hannah is a little older and able to understand, then she'll tell her who her father is. Then, perhaps, Napoleon can meet her. But, in the meantime, we must not say anything. Do you understand? This is how Gabi wishes it to be, and we must respect that."

"Well," Penny huffed, "It seems to me that Hannah is old enough now. She's not much younger than I am."

"Children mature at different rates. Her mother will know best when the time is right."

"Hmm." Penny was not convinced.

"And be careful where you cast stones," the mother sternly reminded the daughter. "There, but for the grace of God. You could have easily ended up in the same situation as Gabi, but with the added support of family. Gabriella had no one, at first. Thank goodness, her sister, at least, did not abandon her. But she's a strong woman to have held it together until that happened. She deserves our respect, not our disdain."

"Yes, Momma."

***

**The Rocking M Ranch,
Arvada, Colorado**

Leon stretched and yawned, slowly waking to the dawn. He took a deep breath and stared up at the ceiling, or, more appropriately, he stared in the direction of the ceiling, as he wasn't focused on anything. He'd had the nightmares again, but it had been one of those nights that come along occasionally that didn't run him through the wringer and leave him shaking and terrified at the other end of it.

He felt, rather than heard, Mouse stretch and yawn, and Leon smiled. For an animal that was supposed to be nocturnal, she sure liked to spend the nights sleeping at the foot of his bed. Of course, the chilly autumn temperatures could have something to do with that; come springtime, he'd likely never see her.

Finally, Leon flipped the covers off and sat up. He shivered a little in the dawn chill and quickly grabbed for his clothes that were hanging on the nearby chair, then frowned as the mixed aroma of dirt and body odor assaulted his nostrils. It flitted through his mind that he had been wearing this set for a while now, and he should exchange it for something cleaner.

He tossed them aside and berated himself for not having set out clean clothes for this morning. He shivered as he tugged open the dresser drawer and pulled out his other set of clothing for the day.

He quickly pulled on his trousers over the long johns. His socks and shirt followed, and then one of the sweaters Jean had knitted for him while he'd been in prison. He had been afraid that these items would bring back too many bad memories to be useful to him now, but the fact that Jean had knitted them for him had overshadowed the bad vibes. He pulled the sweater on over his shirt and smiled with appreciation.

Mouse was already on the move, and with a good morning *ack*, she jumped off the bed and trotted over to the closed door, purring and weaving back and forth, waiting for him to catch up.

"Yes, I know," Leon mumbled as he headed in that direction, "you want your breakfast. Why don't you prove to us all that you're your mother's daughter and go catch it yourself?"

"*Ack!*"

"Hmm."

Leon opened the door and headed toward the kitchen, with the little gray tabby cat trotting along beside, ahead, and around him. He went to the pantry, grabbed a piece of chicken, cut off a slice, then chopped it into bite-sized pieces and set it on the floor for his pet.

Mouse trotted forward, and with loud, appreciative purring, began to devour her breakfast.

"You're spoiling that cat, Nash," he heard Frank's voice from the kitchen door. "How is it ever going to learn to catch mice, if you keep feeding it?"

Leon simply shrugged. "She'll get around to it when she's ready. She's still just a baby."

"Hmm," Frank grumbled. "Can't understand why you have a cat in the house in the first place. They belong in the barn."

Leon smiled as he leaned down to stroke his furry friend. Her purring increased, but she continued to eat. "She's not a barn cat, Frank. She's special. I don't care if she never catches a mouse in her life. She has a more important job than that."

Frank snorted. "Can't imagine what that would be."

"No, I don't suppose you can," Leon mumbled as he straightened up and started making coffee.

Cameron came into the kitchen then, yawning and looking disheveled. "You fellas are up early," he commented. "The only one to beat you was Gabi."

Leon looked around, suddenly concerned. "Gabi? She's up already?"

"Up and gone," Cameron said. "She sure is a firecracker. I tried to get her to wait and have breakfast first, but she was determined. Said that her saddlebags were packed and ready to go, and if I could loan her a horse, she would be on her way."

"Cameron, you didn't loan her a horse, did you?" Leon was almost pleading with him.

Cameron sighed, looking defeated. "Napoleon, when was the last time you were able to talk that woman out of doing anything?"

"Hmm, yeah. Good point," Leon slumped "I'd better get after her. Which way did she go?"

"What do you mean by 'you better get after her'?" Cameron asked him. "You can't just go riding off into the hills. Who knows how long it would take you to catch up with her; she has a good couple of hours' head start."

"Then the sooner I get started, the better, isn't it?"

"Leon, you're not going," Cameron was adamant. "I can already see it; you'd catch up with her, then decide to join the manhunt. You'd end up violating the conditions of your parole, and then you'd really be in trouble, wouldn't you?"

Leon's body language spoke of defeat, but his brain wasn't ready to give up. "I don't like the idea of her going off to track down this 'Mitch' fellow all on her own. I know she's capable, but if he's who I think he is, then he won't hesitate to kill a woman, and I can't sit here and do nothing!"

"Then send Frank," Cameron suggested. "You brought him in on this case so he could do the things you can't do. He'll find her."

"That's sound thinking, Mr. Marsham." Frank puffed up with finally being recognized. "I was just about to suggest the same thing. I'll have no trouble tracking her, and I'll bring her back here even if I have to tie her to her saddle."

Leon's jaw tightened. He knew Gabi wouldn't put up with Frank telling her what to do, and good luck tying her to a saddle. Frank was capable enough, but he always made the mistake of underestimating women, especially this particular woman.

Cameron's voice broke in upon Leon's musings.

"You have no other choice, Napoleon," Cameron said. "You don't have the time to ride into town to get permission, and you are not leaving this ranch without it."

***

Half an hour later, Frank was mounted on one of Cameron's fine horses and all ready to go. He looked like he was just heading out for an afternoon ride; he was so confident this little excursion would be short-lived.

Leon stood beside the horse's head; his brow furrowed with concern.

"Don't worry, Nash," Frank assured him. "I'll find her. Tracking down people is what I'm good at."

"Yes, I know, Frank." Still, Leon was not confident. "Well, take care of yourself. I'll see you later."

"Look for us around lunchtime," Frank boasted, then he booted his horse forward and took off in the direction Gabi had gone.

Leon stood, watching him go, with hands on his hips and a sinking feeling in his heart. Sometimes being on parole was hard to take. He couldn't believe he was standing here, letting Frank Carlyle ride off and attempt to do a job that he should be doing himself. Gabi wasn't going to listen to Frank; Leon already knew that. Hell, Gabi probably wouldn't even listen to Leon. And then, yes, Cameron was right, Leon would have carried on with her, rather than let her carry on alone. Then he really would have been in trouble.

Knowing that, however, did not make standing here and watching Frank ride off to do what he himself should be doing any easier.

It was going to be a long day.

CHAPTER TWENTY
WORKING FOR A LIVING

Frank Carlyle froze at the metallic sound of a rifle being cocked behind him. He smiled, knowing he had guessed right.

"Hands up, where I can see them," warned the lyrical female voice behind him.

"Gabi, is that you?"

"Thank your lucky stars it is. Put your hands down, Frank. What are you doing, creeping around behind me?"

He dropped his arms and swiveled around on his horse. "Nash sent me. He wanted to come himself, but he couldn't just set off across the country. And I wasn't creeping."

Gabriella lowered her weapon and strolled out from behind the trees. "Too right, you weren't. Who taught you how to follow people? I spotted you an hour and a half ago."

"Of course, you did. I wasn't trying to hide. Sometimes, the best way to find someone is to let them find you." He raised his eyebrows at her male attire, topped off by the long, brown, waxed coat. "I thought I was following a lady."

Gabriella narrowed her eyes. "At least I'm dressed sensibly for the job. You're wearing a suit—and a fedora? Are you kidding me?"

Frank gave a harrumph of irritation. "I came to take you back, not head off across country. This is no job for a woman. I'll go after this 'Mitch' character once I have you back at the Rocking M."

Gabi walked over to the trees and led her horse out of concealment. "I'm not returning to the Rocking M. Either come with me or go back. We've lost enough time." She fixed him with a hard stare as she mounted up, "And I'll decide whether I'm capable of doing something or not, not a man who thinks all women should just stay home and have babies."

Frank snorted. “Seems ta me, that’s exactly what you were doing.”

Gabi’s anger flared. “Are you kidding me? I’ve accomplished more in the last ten years than you have in a lifetime. I don’t need your condescension.”

“I don’t have time to be nursemaidin’ you,” Frank insisted. “This is going to be dangerous enough without feminine distractions.”

“Sure is,” Gabi agreed. “I had a rifle pointed at your head five minutes ago. You like living on the edge, Frank?”

“I knew you wouldn’t shoot me,” Frank told her. “It takes a woman a lot more insane than you to shoot a man from ambush. You’re not Jesse James, you know.”

She gave him a smile of amusement. “Or Hezekiah Hoag?”

“What?” Frank faced one of those rare occasions when he was caught flat-footed. “What do you know about Detective Hoag?”

“For one thing, he’s not a detective anymore, Frank. I thought you would have known that.”

“Of course, I knew it,” Frank sneered. “But why would you?” His dark eyes narrowed with suspicion. “Have you been keeping track of him to exact your own special form of revenge?”

“Oh, please. If I wanted revenge on either of you, it would have happened years ago, and you wouldn’t have seen it coming.” She pushed Berry into action and slipped past Frank. “Tell Napoleon I will be in touch.”

Frank urged his mount forward and grabbed her reins. “If you think I’m going to let you take off after a violent drifter, you’ve got another thing coming.”

“Remove your hand, or I’ll do it for you.”

Frank laughed in her face. “C’mon, Gabi. I hate to admit it, but you and I make a great team. Always have.”

Gabriella’s lips pressed into a white line. She hated it when Frank threw that one indiscretion in her face.

“You tricked me into betraying the Elk Mountain Gang, and you know it.”

Frank shrugged, and what might be considered a humorous glint sparked his beady eyes. “You didn’t have to give us that information, but you did. Two can play that game, Gabi.”

“I was angry at Napoleon then, but ... oh, never mind. Your plan backfired anyway, didn’t it?”

Frank barked a laugh. “Not completely. We might not have

gotten the two main fish, but we got a few outlaws off the range. Not to mention the go-between they used. Wells Fargo had been after him for years, but we could never quite pin him down. The information you gave us was real helpful, Gabriella. I'm surprised Nash forgave you for that. Just goes to show, there's not much honor among thieves after all."

Frank was deliberately pushing her buttons, and Gabriella's features hardened as she fought the impulse to draw her gun and cold-cock this irritating man.

Frank saw her struggle, and his thin smile broadened.

"And I definitely recall you saying you had no romantic interest in Napoleon Nash." He laughed and shook his head. "It's no wonder Pinkerton's stopped using women for detective work. You're too easily manipulated by dimples and a pair of brown eyes."

"It occurs to me that you also have brown eyes, Frank, and something that might aspire to be a dimple, but I have no problem resisting you."

Frank laughed again. He was enjoying this tit-for-tat. "Thank God for that. But just because you've done a bit of undercover work with your first husband, and for me, doesn't make you a trained professional."

"I have a lot more experience and knowledge than most detectives I've encountered, and I can use a gun just as well as you can. I came here to help, and you can either join me in this, or go back to the ranch without me."

Frank shrugged. "I already admitted that we make a good team. I told Nash I would bring you back, but plans are always subject to change. I'll need to buy supplies at the next town, though. I didn't pack for a long journey."

"Fine," Gabriella begrudged the renewed partnership, but it appeared to be the only way to move ahead. "Just keep in mind, I'll treat you the way you treat me. If you want respect, you'd better give it."

Frank smiled, scratching his cheek. "I've known you a long time, Gabriella Tanguay, or is it Harden? No, wait, it's Nash. Oh, no, we're back to Tanguay again. It's kinda hard to respect a woman who can't keep straight who she is."

"Shut up, Frank!"

Gabriella jerked her horse's head around and set off towards the next town.

Frank's irritating laughter already made her regret this decision.

***

Leon sat by the wood stove in the living room, casually stroking the sleeping kitten on his lap and staring off into space. He was worried. He and Cameron had kept themselves busy all that afternoon with chores around the barnyard; there was never a lack of things to do here. Sam had been out and helped with mucking stalls and doing some repairs, but he had long since headed for home and supper.

It was dark now, except for the reflective light caused by the six more inches of freshly fallen snow. Oh, yes—it had started to snow by early afternoon, and by evening there was a solid covering on the ground. Of course, this was a personal insult to Leon; the fates giving him one more reason to worry.

Cameron slipped up behind his friend unnoticed and tapped the younger man on the shoulder.

Leon started slightly and came back to the present.

"Hmm? What?"

"Here," Cameron said, handing him a glass of brandy. "Help chase away the chill."

"Oh. Yes. Thank you."

Cameron sat down opposite his friend and studied him for a moment.

"You're worried about them, aren't you?"

"Hmm? Oh. Yes," Leon admitted. "Though I don't know why I bother. I can hear Gabi already complaining. *Don't insult me with such nonsense, Napoleon! I'm quite capable of looking after myself.*"

Cameron chuckled. He was already well enough acquainted with Mrs. Tanguay to be able to hear her tone in Leon's words. Then he sighed and turned serious again.

"It's hard not to worry about the people we love."

Leon sent him a strange look. Was he still in love with Gabi? He still cared about her, but did he still love her? He didn't know.

The two men continued to sit in companionable silence, both off in their own thoughts as they sipped their brandy.

Mouse purred through her slumber.

Cameron missed his wife and children, hoping, but not too

optimistically, that they would be home for Christmas. It seemed that this could be another year of somebody being absent and missed during the holidays. It was supposed to have been a special holiday this time around. Now, the family was splintered more than ever, and worry of another kind had settled over the Marsham family.

"Five years ago," Leon mumbled quietly, almost to the point that Cameron wasn't sure he'd heard him.

"What was that?"

"What? Oh, I was just thinking," Leon spoke up a little louder. "It was five years ago that I was sentenced to that—place."

Cameron sighed but didn't respond. What could one say to that? It had been five years of hell, and Cameron knew it. It had been hard on everyone, but not as hard as it had been on Leon. Now, others were gone and being missed.

"I'm sorry," Leon quickly spoke again.

"It's not your fault," Cameron assured him, "and, at least, they are safe now."

"No, I meant ... oh well, yes, that too. But I meant about my behavior while Gabi was here," Leon clarified. "I don't mean to be such an ass, and I certainly don't mean to challenge you. Goodness knows, you and Jean have done more for us than . . ." Leon took another sip of brandy, feeling awkward, but feeling the need to apologize, nonetheless. "I don't seem to be able to control myself very well, these days—especially where Gabi is concerned."

"She does bring the 'outlaw' out in you, all right," Cameron observed, with a smile.

"Ha!" Leon grinned and nodded. "Yeah, she does. I do care about her, though—it's just bad timing. That seems to have been the problem right from the start, between her and me; bad timing."

"Relationships don't often go the way we think they should," Cameron observed. "I guess that's why when you do meet someone special, and the timing is right, then it's quite a wonderful thing."

Leon nodded and looked into his half-empty glass, his other hand resting quietly on the sleeping kitten. "It seems it's not right for Miranda and me, either. I had hoped, but ... too much baggage there, I suppose."

Cameron smiled. "Don't write it off that quickly, Napoleon. Give it time to sort itself out. Goodness knows you've got enough to deal with already. The timing with Miranda may not be right for now, not for either one of you, but six months from now . . .? Just give it time."

Leon nodded again. "David said, quite bluntly, that I should sleep alone until these nightmares ease off. I certainly don't want to go killing someone in my sleep. Wouldn't that be a fitting end to a life of crime? To be hanged for killing someone in my sleep! Still, if I did that to someone I cared about, life wouldn't be worth living anyway."

"You're awfully melancholy tonight," Cameron commented. "Is there more on your mind than the events of today?"

Leon looked at his friend, then back into his glass. "Five years," he repeated. "Five years—wasted."

"No, they weren't wasted," Cameron contradicted him. "They were hard years, I know. But not wasted."

"How do you figure that? What did I accomplish?"

"You survived," Cameron stated, bluntly.

Leon snorted.

"No," Cameron remained firm. "Sometimes just surviving is accomplishing a lot. You've been through hell, but you've come out the other end, damaged, but still fighting. You're going to be all right, Napoleon. I know you doubt it sometimes, but I've told you before, you have strength in you that you're not even aware of, and when all is said and done, you are going to be a better man because of all this.

"On top of that, you've reconnected, although distantly, with your daughter, and now, with her mother as well. Whether you end up spending your lives together or not, at least you have the opportunity to mend some fences."

"Yes," Leon was skeptical, "if Gabi will let me."

"Again, give it time," Cameron advised him. "You may come to know your daughter yet. And that might not have come about if you hadn't gone to prison."

"I suppose."

"I think it is also safe to say that you have a good friend in Mr. Reece," Cameron continued. "You don't know where that could lead."

Leon let loose a heavy sigh. "Yes, all right!" he finally conceded. "I'm sure never going to forget Doc Palin either." Then, he laughed. "He and I had some good times together. I remember I hadn't even been there six months, and we both got knee-walking drunk. Oh ho! Kenny was mad. Oh, he let me have it, too—big-time. Never did that again." Leon released yet another sigh and smiled over at his companion. "Yes, you're right. I suppose it wasn't a total waste of time. Sure is a hard way to make friends, though."

"Often those are the best friends to have," Cameron mused.

"Yup."

"Jack tells me you also developed an appreciation for classical music," Cameron continued. "I have to admit; I was surprised by that one. And David says you learned quite a bit about medicine while working in the infirmary. All very positive things."

Leon gave a snort. "Oh, I had no real talent as a medical man," he admitted with disappointment. "I was just cocky enough to think that all I had to do was read the books and learn the terms, and then I could heal people. Ha! No—medicine is a gift. Doc Palin had it, even though he'd never had any formal training. And David, ha—yeah, David; now there's a truly gifted man. I could never do what he does."

Cameron smiled. "You think that because you can't be the best at something, then that means what you can do with it isn't valuable?"

Leon shrugged. "I don't know."

"You have a brilliant mind, Napoleon; I envy you that," Cameron told him. "But you can't expect to be the best at everything. You have to give the rest of us a chance, you know."

Leon grinned, then nodded concession. "I guess, I did just get used to things coming easily. I suppose humility was something else I learned in prison." His expression became reflective. "Yeah, I learned that one really well."

"A bit of humility is good for all of us," Cameron pointed out. "You'll find your balance again. You're already on the road towards it."

Leon smiled and stroked the kitten, who stretched out a front leg as her purring increased. "Yeah, I suppose. I hope so, anyway."

"You will." Cameron finished off the last of his brandy. "Well, I'm off to bed. Are you going to wait up for them a while longer?"

"No," Leon conceded. "They're not coming back—at least, not for some time. I knew that as soon as Frank went after her. Once Gabi's on the scent, she doesn't turn aside; she'll stay on Mitch's trail until she runs him to ground. It could get dangerous." He sighed again and finished his brandy. "Oh well. Those two seem to make a formidable team, if they don't kill each other in the meantime."

***

Leon yawned and stretched before closing the curtains against the swirling snow outside. It was really coming down now. He glanced at the dresser and decided it was time for a heavier sweater for the next day.

He pulled the drawer open, his heart skipping a beat at the sight of a note lying on top of his neatly balled-up socks. The familiar copperplate handwriting bore the word "Napoleon." How the hell had she gotten this in here without waking him? He shook his head ruefully; was he losing all his skills?

He reached out tentatively, unfolded the sheet, and ambled over to the bed, where he sat down.

My dear Napoleon:

Please accept my sincere apologies for any upset I have caused you. I had to keep my investigation into who might be trying to hurt Penny a secret because I had no idea who was behind it. I could find absolutely no motive locally. She is a popular and respected young woman, and I'm sure she and Jack will make a lovely match.

You and Miranda were happy together before I showed up. It was not my intention to interfere with that. She is a lovely woman, and I believe the two of you will be good for each other.

Leon sighed. He knew where this was going, and his heart started to ache.

I know you'll be angry with me for leaving without telling you, but we both know you would have tried to stop me. Then there would have been a horrendous fight, and we would have ended things on a bad note.

He snorted softly and nodded. She was right about that. But when was she ever wrong about anything?

When you think of me, I want you to smile, not scowl.

Please contact me through Helèna once this is all over, and I will honor my promise to arrange a meeting with Hannah.

Let Cameron know that I will return his fine horse via rail freight.

In closing, I wish you all the best for the future. I am sure you and Miranda will have a happy life ahead. I urge you to move forward with confidence that I will do everything possible to provide you with the fresh start you want and need.

My deepest love to you always,

Gabriella.

He sat there in stunned silence as her words soaked in. She'd already said she was going to do this; she was going to back off and let him and Miranda continue their relationship. But seeing it in writing made it so final. So over.

He sighed when he realized he might have given that impression. With his inconsistency and lack of conviction, he had sent Gabriella the clear message that he wasn't ready to rekindle their relationship. Even though he had said the words, she had seen the doubt.

But if that were true, then why was his throat burning, and why was his heart so heavy?

He would have been angry at her for making this choice for him if her words hadn't hurt him so deeply. He stared aimlessly into the far corner, already missing her.

***

The following morning, Leon and Sam took the buckboard into town. The break in the snowfall gave them the perfect opportunity for a special trip to restock supplies before everyone got snowed in.

Sam pulled the draft horses up at the mercantile, and both men jumped down into the snow.

"I'll be back in a minute," Leon told the younger man. "I just want to check the telegraph office."

"Sure thing, Mr. Nash. I'll get started here."

Leon made his way down the boardwalk toward the office, knocking the snow off his boots as he went. He silently wished—and not for the first time—that Jack would hurry up and get back. He must be close by now, unless he decided to stay on a few days. Oh, but he would have sent word, so he must be on his way back. Leon wondered if he had met Hannah, and if so, what he had thought of her? He felt jealousy and curiosity fighting for control.

Leon entered the telegraph office, breathing warm air onto his cold hands.

"Hey, Clayt," Leon greeted the telegrapher. "Anything for us?"

"Yeah, actually," Clayt went to his files and brought out some pieces of folder paper. "Two for you and one for Marsham."

"Oh!" Leon was surprised. "Two, huh? Sounds promising. Thanks."

Leon stepped outside and began to read while he walked, almost bumping into a bundled-up woman coming the opposite direction.

"Good afternoon, Napoleon," came a familiar voice.

Leon glanced up and felt a twinge of irritation. He didn't have time for this.

"Good afternoon, Isabelle," he returned her greeting, then quickly went back to his telegram, totally oblivious to the look of daggers being shot back at him.

"Napoleon!"

Leon groaned and snarled to himself, but then, he forced a smile as he stopped and looked back at the young woman. "Yes?"

"Are you planning on attending the Thanksgiving Day dance?"

Oh crap! "Ahh, I'm not sure. Maybe."

Isabelle smiled. "Well, since you and Miranda aren't courting anymore, perhaps—"

Leon frowned and fell into her trap. "How did you know that?"

She smiled at her success. "So, it is true. Small town, you know. Rumors spread. But I thank you for confirming it."

"And you're going to do your best to spread it around even more, aren't you?"

"No need for that. All the single ladies know it now. Such a nuisance for you if you arrive without a date. Perhaps—"

"Yes! Perhaps I'll see you there," Leon quickly interjected. "Must be off. Good afternoon, Isabelle."

He turned on his heels and quickly made a beeline back to the safety of Sam's company. He could almost feel the frustrated glare directed at him, but he ignored it and went back to his telegrams. He unfolded the first one and smiled. It was from Jack.

N.N. All's well. Heading home. J. K.

Oh good. Leon missed him. With all this going on, he needed his friend back home with him. It was also nice to know that everyone had arrived safely in Topeka, and hopefully, they would remain that way. He turned his attention to the second telegram. This one was from Kenny, and Leon's heart skipped a beat.

N. Yes. Complete description sent by train. Should arrive tomorrow a.m. K.R.

Yes! Leon nearly laughed out loud. Yes! Harris did have a dagger tattoo on his arm. Yes! Oh—damn! He had to let Gabi know, but he had no idea how to reach her. Dammit. There was no point in contacting Helèna; she certainly wouldn't be there. With all their arguing, back and forth, they had never set up a way for them to stay in touch. And now, more than ever, he wondered if she would even want to.

Leon clenched his jaw in anger; he hated this—he hated waiting! He felt almost as impotent as he had in prison. Everybody else was making decisions for him, and all he could do was sit there and take it—and wait.

***

Denver, Colorado

Frank swirled the amber fluid in his glass and sat back to puff on his cigar. He leaned forward, opening his mouth to greet the tall, slim madam of the house, when a movement caught the corner of his eye. He groaned. Gabriella was in the hallway, talking with a small, mousey woman by the front door. What the hell was she doing here? Couldn't a man even frequent a brothel without her turning up? Well, at least she was wearing a dress this time. A woman in trousers was too scandalous for Frank, even if it did make horseback travel more comfortable.

He narrowed his eyes and strode over to the door.

"She ain't on the payroll," the madam drawled behind him. The woman shrugged, looking Gabriella up and down. "Not yet, anyway."

Frank turned and had this woman assessed in an instant.

Her coal-black hair stood out starkly against waxy skin, and the scarlet lipstick was bleeding into the wrinkles around her unsavory gash of a mouth. If she had been beautiful once, the hard life she lived had sucked it out of her, but she was no one's fool, and Frank didn't intend to play her for one.

"If you like 'em beat up, Massie had a tough 'un three days ago," the madam informed the gentleman. "She might fit the bill."

"Why would I like anyone who had been beaten up?" Frank demanded. "What kind of a man do you think I am?"

The madam scrutinized him with sooty eyes. "A detective," she declared, coolly, "or a salesman, or maybe even a quack." She folded her arms, causing her cleavage to wrinkle like crepe. "Somethin' dodgy, anyways. I can spot 'em, and I've got enough experience to do it before I'm stupid enough to marry 'em."

"You can spot 'em, eh?"

"In a snap. What brand of snake oil are you peddlin'?"

Frank sighed. "I'm not selling, I'm buying." He pulled the woman aside, into the corner of the hall. "Information on a man I believe to have passed this way."

"The law? I knew it," the woman sneered. "I could smell it, even without you all got up in new duds, like some kind of shiny cowpoke. Straight out of the box, are we, Sonny?"

"Well, you pegged that right," Frank told her. "You can spot new clothes from a mile away. Good for you. I was wearing a suit when the lead came in; hardly fitting attire for a manhunt, wouldn't you agree? Yeah, I'm a detective, workin' for Wells Fargo. This man, who passed through here, the one who beat up Massie, might just be the guy I'm looking for. He beat his wife half to death if that means anything to you."

The woman shrugged a bony shoulder. "So? Men like that keep me staffed. Why should I care?"

"Her father's rich, and very, very angry. He's offered to pay a thousand-dollar reward to anybody who gives information leading to his arrest."

The smutty eyes smoldered with doubt and greed. "You ain't wanderin' around these parts, carryin' that sort of money."

"Of course not. I can offer ten now, and the full thousand when we catch him. Five foot eight, light brown hair, dagger tattoo on his right arm. Goes by the name of Mitch. Ring any bells?"

"I tell you what, honey, come back here with a thousand dollars, and I'll ring your bell till the clapper drops off. Now, pick yourself a woman, or leave."

Frank simmered; he really did have a hard time reading women. "Twenty," he offered.

"Bud!" the madam bellowed. "We got another one. Get him outta here!"

An ape of a man, wearing a suit that was too small for him, appeared out of the side room. Frank felt himself grabbed by the collar and hustled on tiptoe towards the front door, passing Gabriella and the mousey woman on the way. The woman spoke to Gabi in a language he didn't understand. They laughed, watching while he was tossed, unceremoniously, out onto the boardwalk.

***

Frank heard a gentle tap at his door. He groaned as he tossed back the bedclothes. "Who's there?"

"Gabriella. Let me in."

He sighed and scowled as he grabbed the quilt off the bed and wrapped it around himself. He then ambled reluctantly to the door and opened it. "It's about time. We were supposed to meet three hours ago."

"I got busy," Gabriella told him. "Let me in, will you? Before someone sees me."

Frank stepped aside and let her enter the room. "Don't get any ideas now. I'm a respectable man."

Gabriella cocked a brow at him. "Hardly. You played the oily detective type well. I expect you've had experience with that."

"It got you and that mouse on good terms, didn't it? There ain't nothin' like two ladies thinking they're sharing a joke at a fella's expense to create a bond. You want a drink?"

Frank went over to the side table and lifted the decanter. Without waiting for an answer, he poured some golden liquid into two small shot glasses and offered one to his visitor.

Gabriella frowned, then shrugged. "Oh, why not? We can celebrate our first successful con together."

Frank indicated the armchair for her, then sat on the edge of the bed.

"That wasn't our first con, Gabriella. Weren't we recently discussing your infiltration of the Elk Mountain Gang?"

"You're never going to let that one go, are you, Frank?" Gabriella asked as she sat down. "Careful, your quilt is slipping."

Frank smiled and took a sip of his brandy. "Hmm. Far from top shelf, but not bad for a hotel. Try some, it might calm your nerves."

"My nerves are just fine." But she did take a sip, then frowned. "Well, I've had better."

Frank took another sip and set the glass aside. "Enough foreplay. What did you find out?"

"I got lucky. That woman you saw me with came from Montreal, so she was dead keen to talk to somebody in her own language. I enjoyed it, too." Her eyes took on a wistful air. "I so rarely get to use it anymore." She shook herself back to reality. "Mitch was here three days ago. He beat up a girl, accusing her of asking too many questions."

"Yeah," Frank mumbled, "the woman who ran the place told me about that."

"Great. We seem to be working together, at last," Gabriella commented. "Did she say which way he went?"

"No," Frank admitted with a sneer. "She's a sly one. You'd think she'd want to get back at a guy who beat up one of her girls."

"Bad for business; it might chase all the other johns away." Gabriella took another sip. "I didn't get any more information from her, either. I'll try the stables in the morning; maybe they saw where he headed after he picked up his horse." She paused. "Or, do you want to do it? I don't want to cramp your style; we're both here to investigate."

"No, you do it," Frank told her. "They're more likely to feel sorry for a woman. Maybe you can spruce up that black eye makeup and really get their sympathy. I'll go see the sheriff. Once I've identified myself as a Wells Fargo man, he might tell us something we can use."

Gabi's countenance softened. "That sounds like a plan. I'll be honest with you; I wasn't sure we would work well together, but we're doing just fine, aren't we?"

"I suppose so," Frank concurred. "I wasn't sure about this situation either. Working with women doesn't come naturally to me. They think differently than a man does."

"I'll choose to take that as a compliment."

"Take it any way you like," Frank told her. "Now, get out of here; I need my beauty sleep." He cocked an eyebrow at her, and his lip twitched into a crooked smile. "Or do you intend to spend the night?"

Gabriella laughed as she walked toward the door. "Don't be a horse's ass. I'll see you at breakfast."

"Fine by me, Sweetheart," Frank said as he saw her out. "The last thing we need is complications."

And the door closed upon her retreating back.

CHAPTER TWENTY-ONE
THE LONG CHASE

Autumn, 1889.
Waterville, Kansas

Two friends who used to be outlaws rode side by side in companionable silence. One of them was no longer an outlaw, having paid his dues to the Territory of Wyoming and become a free man.

The other was, for all intents and purposes, dead.

It was cold, and every day grew colder, but it was a different kind of cold from what these men were accustomed to. Though both of them had been born in the South, neither had stayed long, and they were reminded of why they never came back. The temperatures didn't drop as low as they did in Wyoming, but it was damp, with a chill that seeped right down to the bone.

The dead man coughed a couple of times and pulled the collar of his winter coat tighter around his throat.

The free man cast a worried glance at his friend but hesitated to say anything, not wanting to suggest that the other man was weak or hindering them in any way. Another spasm of dry coughing changed his mind.

"You doin' okay, Gus?" Malachi asked, trying to hide the worry in his tone.

"Yeah," Gus grumbled from behind his turned-up collar. "Stop naggin' at me."

"Wull, it's jest that, yur cough is soundin' worse, an'. . ."

"I'm fine, Ky!" Gus insisted, then coughed again. "It's only another five miles to that next town. I'll get warmed up there."

"How much money we got left?" Malachi asked, again trying not to sound worried.

"Enough for tonight," Gus assured him. "Might even be able to order up a bath, if we take it easy on the drinkin'."

Malachi smiled in anticipation. "Yeah! Bath'd be nice. That'd warm ya up, eh Gus?"

Gus coughed a couple of more times and shivered inside his coat. "I sure hope that lawyer friend of the Kid's forwarded the money like he said he would," the presumed dead man grumbled. "If he didn't, it'll be the last warm meal and soft bed for some time ta come."

Malachi's usual happy expression dropped to a frown. They had been on the trail of Harris for some time now, and they had hoped to catch up with him before the colder weather set in. So much for hopes. If it hadn't been for the retainers that Steven Granger had been wiring to them over the last few months, they would have had to give up the chase—or go back to robbin' banks to support themselves. Both Kiefer and Granger were adamant that they refrain from doing that.

Their trek had been challenging. Harris did not stay in any one place for long, and he managed to keep just far enough ahead of his pursuers to be elusive and to remain a free man. It wasn't clear to the two ex-outlaws whether Harris knew he was being tracked, or if he was just being cautious, knowing he was a fugitive and that the law might still be looking for him.

Truth be known, the law had given up on Carl Harris. Though flyers and warnings had gone out right after his escape from the prison, after a week, law officials had grown tired of the chase and given up on it for more pressing matters. The $500 reward posted on him was enough for an easy catch, but not enough for the long haul over several territories. The only ones actively seeking him now were the two bedraggled ex-outlaws.

The initial supposition that Harris might have headed north to Canada was quickly dismissed, as a quick jaunt in that direction yielded no clues or evidence to support it. The boys then turned east, into the Dakotas, and finally picked up a hint or two from various towns that a mean-spirited transient had been through. Checking out the local brothels with the convenient excuse of seeking information, not only provided some much-appreciated entertainment but also confirmed many of those hints and rumors. It was clear that the fellas were on the right track.

Much to their relief, Harris avoided Wyoming; apparently, none of them wanted to let their existence be known in that Territory. He kept up a southerly route headed into Nebraska and then—disappeared.

Gus sent Kiefer an inquiry about whether he wanted them to continue the manhunt. Since Nash was out of prison now, was finding Harris all that important? Kiefer's response was a definite "yes!". There were other reasons now for them wanting to have words with Harris. Clearing Nash of the accusation of murder had been the main one, but finding out who had killed the Doc was still a priority. Gus and Malachi were to stay on it.

Quite a bit of grumbling resulted from this response, but since it also included more money from the lawyer, they decided that sniffing around to find Harris's trail again wouldn't be too much of an inconvenience. As summer approached, Gus found the fresh air and warm temperatures healing for his spirit and battered body.

Both men felt good, and with the steady income they were receiving without risking their necks, they found the incentive to continue the quest. They circled Nebraska for most of the summer, not too concerned that they weren't accomplishing anything.

Mid-August rolled around, and Gus and Malachi were beginning to feel right at home in Nebraska. They would sit around the campfire and talk about settling down in these parts, perhaps even starting up a new gang and getting things rolling again. Maybe they could both come up with their own aliases, and that way, Gus could remain dead, and Malachi could still be considered a free man in Wyoming. They could wear disguises—yeah—that could be fun. Gus could shave off his mustache!

Gus scowled—that was going too far.

Malachi thought it was a good idea.

***

Superior, Nebraska

By the end of August, their dreams of starting a new life were put on hold when they rode into a small town with the presumptuous name of Superior, near the Nebraska/Kansas border, and found it in a somber state of mind. Riding down the main street, towards the livery stable, it didn't take much, even for two strangers, to realize that something was amiss. The partners exchanged concerned glances as they carried on about their business and dismounted outside the stables.

"Howdy gents," the liveryman greeted them as he took hold of the bridles. He referred to all potential customers as "gents", regardless of their attire. "Needin' ta board these animals, are ya?"

"Yeah. Just overnight," Gus told him. "How much?"

"Two bits, per horse, per night."

"Two bits!?" Malachi squeaked. "That's downright robbery!"

The liveryman shrugged. "Includes hay, grain, water, and a rubbin' down. You don't think it's worth it, then you can leave 'em tied up outside the saloon all night. Might not be there in the mornin' though—if ya knows what I mean."

Gus snorted. "Yeah, yeah," he grumbled as he dug into a pocket. "Two bits per horse, per night. Sounds fair enough."

"But, Gus . . .!"

"Shuddup, Ky!" Gus told him. "Rather pay the man four bits than have to come back here in the mornin' and pay $50.00 for new horses and tack. Granger is payin' us enough ta live on, sort'a, but not enough for them kind of expenses."

"That's sound thinkin'," the liveryman praised the deceased outlaw. "I can see you have a fine head for money matters."

"Hmm." Gus handed over the money. "Just make sure they get hay and water and grain—and a rub down. And they better be here in the mornin'!"

"Of course—I'm no thief!"

The honest businessman received a derisive snort from both his customers.

The two travel-weary men untied their bedrolls and saddlebags, grabbed their rifles, then turned and headed to the hotel.

That welcoming establishment was only half a block away, but even then, the two partners couldn't help but notice the solemn expressions and lowered eyes on many of the people who passed them by.

They trotted up the stairs and into the lobby, then headed straight to the counter to check in and get settled before making their way over to the saloon.

"Afternoon, gents." It seemed everyone was a gent in this town. "What can I do for you?"

"One room with two beds," Gus ordered. "You got that?"

"Yessir," the clerk smiled graciously, then added with a thinly veiled hope: "We offer a convenient bath house right next door, if you gentlemen are interested."

"Wull, yeah ... that'd be nice," Malachi admitted. "Dang, Gus—we been on the trail fer about a week. A bath'd be a good idee!"

"Fine," Gus mumbled as he took the key to their door. "Say—what's with the somber mood in town? Somebody die, or somethin'?"

"Oh, well—yes, actually," the clerk looked remorseful. "One of the gals who works at the saloon got beat up pretty bad the other night. I mean, that's no big deal—just a saloon gal, if ya know what I mean. But that fool deputy we had here, well, he was kinda sweet on that little trollop, and he decided to confront the fella that beat her up. Now, everybody with any sense would see that this fella was trouble, and best to just leave him alone. But that young idiot went into the saloon, all puffed up and challenging him, and ended up gettin' a knife between his ribs. Died right there on the floor of the saloon."

Gus and Malachi exchanged a look.

"This fella locked up now?" Gus asked the clerk.

"Ha! No, sir," the clerk informed them. "The sheriff weren't around. I suppose there were enough fellas in that saloon ta take him down, but ya know, that man was mean, through and through. And him, standin' there holding the knife with blood all over 'im, and that killin' lust in his eyes, well, that just kinda took the 'hero' outta most folks."

"Yeah, I suppose it might, at that," Gus agreed. "He still in town?"

"Oh no—thank goodness! No, he done took off right after that. The sheriff went out after 'im but didn't have no luck. Just plum disappeared."

"Hmm. Okay, thanks."

***

Once in their room, behind closed doors, Malachi let his concerns be known.

"Wull, what are we gonna do, Gus? Don't that sound like Harris ta you?"

"Yup."

"Wull, don't 'cha think we should git after 'im?"

"No, I don't."

"Wull, why not?"

"'Cause the sheriff has gone and run him off scared," Gus explained. "Plus, our horses are done in, and I, for one, want a bath and a decent meal. Plus, we go spend some time down in that saloon, we just might pick up a bit more information that could give us a better idea of which way to go."

"Yeah. I suppose yer right."

"We get a decent meal, a good night's sleep, and we'll head out after 'im in the morning—if it's actually Harris who done this."

Malachi gave a resigned sigh, though, truth be known, he was looking forward to food, a bath, and a bed, too. "If you say so, Gus. I just don't wanna be losin' 'im again."

***

A couple of hours later, the two friends looked and smelled more like civilized gentlemen. A bath and shave, laundered clothes, and a decent meal, all combined to change mean and nasty to clean and contented. Sidling up to the bar at the local saloon, they ordered beers, then turned around to survey their environment.

It looked just like any of the other numerous saloons they had frequented over the months of travel, and they both glanced across the sea of faces, hoping that something would stand out as significant.

Gus grunted; nothing was obvious.

They each took a swig of their beers and checked out the one poker game that was in progress, but other than that, there wasn't much going on.

Malachi gave a toothy grin to a young, perky, little upstairs gal who sashayed by them. He was getting serious about a proposition when Gus suddenly elbowed him in the ribs.

"Hey! What ya do that fer?"

"Keepin' yer mind on the job, is what fer!" Gus reminded him. "Take a look over there." He pointed his chin towards the far corner of the saloon.

Malachi followed the gesture and saw what had gotten his partner's attention. A young gal had walked out from behind a group of patrons and was heading toward the bar to fill an order. Both men, leaning up against the bar, watched her coming.

She wasn't spectacular in any way, other than the black eye and a discolored, swollen lip. Then, as she got closer, it also became apparent that both her wrists were red and bruised, along with her upper arm. Apparently, Harris had secured her to the bed while he beat her.

She came up to the bar, ordered a round of drinks, and waited for the bartender to get them ready. Gus sidled down to stand beside her and took another swig from his beer.

"That's some black eye yer sportin' there, missy," he commented. "How about I buy ya a drink, and you tell us how ya got it?"

She sent him a battle-weary glance. "I'm busy. I already got customers. Maybe another time."

"No, listen," Gus wasn't ready to give up, "my partner and me are trailin' a fella that kinda fits in with what happened to you. Once you've finished with your other customers, come join us at that table over there. Just wanna ask ya some questions."

"The sheriff already asked me questions." She picked up the tray of newly filled beer glasses and turned to leave. "Why don't ya go buy him a drink?"

"'Cause I don't think the sheriff can give us the up close and personal details that you can," Gus continued to push. "We'll be sittin' right over there—with a bottle. You come on over when ya can."

She smirked and walked off with the tray.

Gus nudged Malachi toward an empty table, then turned to the barkeep.

"What she like ta drink?" Gus asked him.

"Who? Annie?"

Gus nodded.

"Well, she does find it hard to say 'no' to a glass of bourbon."

"Okay," Gus agreed. "So, why don't you just bring us a bottle of bourbon and three glasses to that table over there?"

"Sure."

Gus deposited more coinage onto the countertop, then followed Malachi over to settle in at the table and await their appointment.

The two men finished their beers and were dipping into the bourbon when Annie finally appeared. She wasn't pleased about being there, but the sight of the bottle had caught her attention, and she gradually talked herself into making the trip over.

Malachi stood up and pulled out a chair for her. She sent him a gesture that might have been interpreted as a smile as she sat down and waited for her drink.

Gus did not disappoint, and he poured them all a round.

Annie took her glass and downed it in one swallow. She flinched as the alcohol invaded her split lip but it didn't discourage her from placing the glass on the table in anticipation of another shot. Malachi sent a lopsided grin to his partner, and Gus again did not disappoint. She downed the second one, then seemed content with that—for now.

"So, what d 'ya wanna know?" she asked. "Some bastard paid for sex and figured that beating me up was part of the deal—nothin' new there. Why you so interested in him?"

"We got business of our own with that particular gent." Gus refilled her glass in anticipation. "If he's the same man we're lookin' for."

"Yeah? Well, he already killed the deputy." A look of sadness drifted over her face, which she tried to hide by taking another drink. "You want my advice, you stay away from that asshole; whatever your reason for tryin' ta find 'im, it ain't good enough."

"Well, he done killed a friend'a ours, over in Wyoming—if it's the same fella," Gus informed her. "I'd say that's good enough."

Annie snorted and looked over into Malachi's admiring blue eyes. "Look at you," she sneered, but with a hint of sympathy in her tone. "You don't look like you got more'n ten brain cells ta rub together, and you think you're gonna run down that bastard and live to tell of it?"

Malachi's smile dropped to a frown, thinking for sure that he had been insulted, but her kind tone made it difficult for him to figure it out. "Wull, we come real close a lotta times!" he insisted. "Ain't that right, Gus? Come real close."

"Yeah?" she asked. "Well, any closer and you'd both probably be dead by now."

"That ain't new ta me," Gus mumbled. "You just let us worry about that part of it—all we want from you is a little bit of information."

Annie shrugged, as if it was nothing to her, and indicated her desire for another drink.

Gus accommodated.

"What can I tell ya that ya don't already know?" she asked him. "You're the one's been trailin' 'im."

"We just want confirmation that we're still trailin' the right man," Gus explained. "So, if you can give us a description . . ."

Annie shrugged, looking uninterested. "He was average," she said. "Average height, average lookin'. I suppose his hair was brown, but not too dark. Straight and long, almost down to his shoulders. His eyes—I dunno. Green, or blue, maybe. He was too busy beaten on me for me ta get the color. All I saw was mean."

"That's it?" Gus asked.

She shrugged again and sighed as she thought about it some more. "I think he had a tattoo or somethin' on his arm. Can't tell ya what it was, though. So—that sound like the man you're lookin' for?"

"Yeah, could be," Gus nodded, then poured her another drink. "Do ya know which way he was headed when he left town?"

"South," she stated adamantly. "I know, 'cause I watched him leave, just ta be sure he kept on goin'."

***

Early the next morning, the partners were on the trail once again, heading south. They followed Harris's progress easily at first because once he stopped running scared from the sheriff, he went right back to his favorite pastime of indulging in brutal sex. Even Gus and Malachi, who had seen all types of personalities during their years of outlawin', were disgusted with the living carnage they encountered in the wake of this man.

It was no wonder that Harris and Nash hadn't gotten along, and that Kiefer was so adamant that they find him. Harris was in real trouble, and the partners didn't find it hard to believe that this bastard had been doing hard time in the Laramie Prison. The fact that he had helped with a prison escape and hadn't seemed to mind assisting with the assaults on various people fit in well with the characteristics he was displaying now. The sooner this killer is sent back to prison, the better off the average citizen will be.

A few days into the hunt, they crossed into Kansas, but then they lost his trail again. The string of beaten saloon gals dried up, and all they received from their inquiries of Harris was just a lot of shrugged shoulders and wagging heads. The partners didn't think it was wise to split up, even though doing that would cut their search time in half. But the other problems this might cause did not make the separation worth the risks.

So, they stayed together and started riding in circles again, seeing if they could pick up any hint of a brutal womanizer making the rounds.

Late Autumn
1889

The weather had turned cold, and Gus's cough reclaimed its hold on his lungs. He tried to keep warm, but the rains came, and he felt the chill go right through him and wrap itself around his bones until he was convinced that he would never warm up again.

Malachi was worried, hoping Gus was right that more money would come their way soon. Then, maybe, they could hold up for a few days and give his friend a chance to recoup.

Those five miles to the next town were about the longest Malachi could remember ever having ridden. He could feel the dampness that came with the wind that never seemed to let up, and he was just as healthy as he ever was. But Gus? No, Gus couldn't say the same, though he'd challenge anyone to say differently.

Gus never did quite recover from that encounter with Marshal Morrison, and with every bout of the racking, dry cough that came his way, he silently cursed that man who had stolen away his home, his health, and the majority of his friends. His only comfort was that Gus had done the same thing to him—maybe even more so. Yeah. Gus took some comfort from that.

Finally, they reached the town of Waterville, and the first place they stopped at was the telegraph office. They needed to send another telegram to Kiefer. Hopefully, he would receive it quickly, and they'd have an answer back by morning.

But dismounting in front of that business proved challenging. Both men were cold to the point that nothing wanted to move. Their hands and feet were so numb that the simple act of holding the saddle horn and stepping down to the ground caused pain to shoot through their extremities.

Once down, they stood beside their horses, gritting their teeth, rubbing their hands, and shifting their feet to bring circulation back into them. When the pins and needles subsided enough for them to move, they carefully stepped onto the boardwalk and then shuffled into the office.

The heat from the stove in the back corner was both welcome and oppressive, and the abrupt change in temperature made them woozy. Gloves came off, and scarves loosened as their bodies adjusted.

The telegrapher stepped up to the counter with an overly friendly smile.

"Good afternoon, gentlemen. How can I help you on this balmy day?"

Malachi looked confused as he blew on his hands to assist in warming them, but Gus sneered at the man's inappropriate good spirits.

"Sending a telegram." His tone indicated that this should be obvious.

"Certainly." The telegrapher's mood would not be smothered, and he snatched up a pencil and pad from under the counter and set them in front of his customer. "Write it out and I'll send it. After you pay the fee, of course."

Gus grumbled, then his expression turned dubious as he peered at the pencil. He set his gloves on the counter, then blew on his hands and rubbed them together to get them working again.

He attempted to pick up the pencil, but it was to no avail. His fingers refused to cooperate. He growled in frustration and turned to Malachi. The innocent blue eyes that gazed back at him was a reminder that expecting Ky to write anything was pointless. Unless he was forging it.

He turned back to the expectant telegrapher.

"You'll have ta write it out. I'll tell ya what ta say."

"Certainly, sir." He retrieved the pencil and pad and prepared to write. "And might I say, there is no need to feel embarrassed. Many fine folks never learned ta read and write."

"I ain't illiterate," Gus scowled. "I know my letters, my hands are just too cold ta work."

"Of course."

Gus was ready to explode at the man's ingratiating smile when Malachi nudged his arm.

"It don't matter none, Gus. I get called that all the time, and I don't even know what it means."

"Yeah, well . . .."

The telegrapher looked at Gus as the pencil hovered expectantly over the pad.

"What is your message?"

"Fine. It's goin' to J. K., Arvada, Colorado. Continue with search? Send money. Waterville, Kansas. G. S."

The telegrapher nodded as he finished writing down the message.

"Very good, sir. That will be ten cents."

Gus rummaged through an inner pocket and forced his tingling fingers to secure some coinage. He pulled it out, opened his fist and pushed the appropriate amount onto the counter.

"There. Send it right away."

"Yes, sir. Right away."

"And let us know when there's a response."

"Of course. You and your friend have a good evening."

"Hmm. C'mon, Ky. I gotta warm up for real."

"Yeah." Malachi smiled at the telegrapher, then followed Gus out to the waiting horses.

They headed to the livery, where their horses were taken care of, and then followed the old routine of getting a room and finding the bathhouse. Gus's cough was getting worse, so Malachi ordered a bottle of whiskey in the hopes it might help take off the chill. After a hot bath, a couple of shots of whiskey, and some dry clothes, both men did feel better, and though Gus's cough stubbornly continued to linger, he felt rejuvenated enough to head down to the café for some dinner.

After dinner, they headed to the saloon, not so much for another drink, but for information. Harris liked his drink and his women, and the best place to get both cheap was the saloon. So, that was the best place to sniff out any tracks he left behind, if there were any to be found at all. Unfortunately, they struck out again; nobody had seen anyone of that description, and all the saloon gals appeared to be intact. The boys called it an early night and headed back to the hotel, hoping that the morning might bring better news.

***

The following morning, they received a response to their inquiry but were surprised to hear it from Nash rather than Kiefer. On top of that, it was addressed to Malachi, since Nash wasn't permitted contact with any known criminals—even dead ones, so Gus was left out of the loop.

The mustachioed apparition snarled over the apparent insult, but Malachi thought it was quite fine, and he beamed with his new sense of importance. Then, without any sense of irony, he handed it over to his partner.

"Ah, what's it say, Gus?" Malachi asked.

Gus snarled again and snatched the paper away from him. "Well, says here ta keep after 'im, no matter what." Gus snorted, thinking this was an easy thing for Nash to say since he wasn't the one traipsing around out here in the damp, bone-numbing cold, looking for a brutal murderer. Then he took a page from Nash's book and laughed sardonically as he read the next bit. "'Be careful—could be dangerous.' Yeah, no shit, Nash . . ." He turned serious again and nodded in approval. "Says here they're gonna wire us some more money. Should be at the bank tomorrow afternoon."

"That's good news," Malachi chirped in. "I'm runnin' outta chewin' tobacca!"

"Hmm." Gus didn't care about Ky's chewin' tobacca. "I guess we're stuck here for a couple 'a days. Probably for the better—looks like it's gonna rain. Again."

Unfortunately, Gus's weather forecast was wrong. It didn't rain—it snowed. Gus could usually tell by the smell in the air when snow was on the way, but this climate was so different from Wyoming that even the snow down here was too wet to smell like snow. Hell! No wonder Nash and Kiefer left this miserable state—or was it a territory? Whatever! Gus didn't like it much, and his damaged body liked it even less.

By that afternoon, Gus's head was pounding, and by the time evening came upon them, he skipped dinner altogether and went straight to his bed. By the next morning, he was sick as a dog, and though he was conscious and aware, he was miserable. The coughing spells that attacked him, racked his lungs, and ripped apart his throat, not to mention bringing such a pounding to his already aching head, that he was sure his skull must explode from the pressure.

Malachi waited impatiently for the much-needed funds to arrive, so he could get the town doctor to look at the sick man. Hopefully, a doctor would be able to give him something to help calm the coughing down.

Gus merely grumbled. They didn't need to be wasting money on no damn sawbones. He was fine. He just needed a day or two in bed to get the chill out of his bones; that was all. Didn't need no damn doctor.

Fortunately, by the time the money arrived that afternoon, Gus was feeling so retched that having the doc examine him no longer seemed like such a bad idea. He still kept up the pretense of being irritated about it, but that was true to his nature, and his snarling was ignored.

Malachi stood awkwardly at the foot of the bed while the learned gentleman completed his examination. He listened extensively to his patient's lungs while at the same time taking note of the numerous scars pockmarking the man's chest. But being a discreet medical man, he chose not to pass judgment.

Gus grumbled and coughed throughout the session but didn't have the energy to protest further.

Finally, the doctor sighed and put his stethoscope away. "Has this man had pneumonia before?" he asked the anxious friend.

"Wull, yeah," Malachi answered nervously. "Ain't we all?"

The Doctor sent him a scrutinizing look from under his bushy white eyebrows. "Not everyone. And this man's lungs have been very badly damaged." He sent another glance over the numerous scars. "And not just from illness."

Malachi shuffled his feet, not wanting to get into those particular details. "Wull—he's gonna be fine, ain't he?"

"We've caught it in time," the doctor assured the friend, "as long as he stays warm and in bed. The pneumonia hasn't taken a strong hold yet, but the previous damage to his lungs is exacerbating the cough."

The doctor extracted a brown bottle from his satchel and assisted the sick man to sit up and take some of the medicine.

Gus grimaced at the taste. "What are ya doin'? I don't need no damn—" Then his coughing took over again, contradicting his protest.

"You need to take this," the doctor insisted. "It will ease your cough and help you sleep. If the congestion in your lungs worsens, I'll need to apply mustard compresses to clear them. It's a nasty business, and I expect you would rather not go through that."

Gus puffed and then lay back on his piled-up pillows. He made no further comment as his eyelids began to droop.

The doctor nodded, then handed the bottle to Malachi.

You get a dose of this into him every four hours or so, even if you have to wake him up. Think you can do that?"

Malachi grinned with relief as he took the offered bottle. "Yeah, sure, Doc. I can do that."

"Good." The doctor stood up with another sigh and, this time, sent the patient his scrutinizing look. "He's not a healthy man at the best of times. He's done serious damage to those lungs, and he can't afford to get hit with a bad bout of pneumonia—it would kill him, sure as shootin'." He inwardly cringed at his poor choice of words but quickly recovered. "This climate is not doing him any favors. You might suggest that he move someplace warmer and drier—California or Arizona would be better for him, I'm sure."

Malachi grinned. "Yeah, Doc. Thanks. I'll be sure ta mention that to 'im."

"Good!" The doctor seemed satisfied with that and headed for the door. "You just make sure he stays warm and dry—and in bed. I'll come back tomorrow afternoon to check up on him."

"Yeah, Doc. I'll be sure ta do that."

Malachi closed the door behind the doctor, then went to the dresser and got himself a fresh chaw of tobacco and popped it into his mouth. He turned and smiled at his sleeping friend. He moved over to the one chair in the room and settled into it with a contented sigh. Then, still chewing on his habit, he again looked at Gus, and the smile slowly dropped from his face.

What the hell was he supposed to do now? For a man who couldn't read, nurse-maidin' a sick friend didn't offer much in the way of entertainment.

His smile returned when he remembered his usual occupation when there was nothing else to do. He snatched his saddle bag from the dresser and took out his sheathed knife and his widdling stick.

He settled back and proceeded to create a mess of wood peelings and tobacco juice around the vicinity of his chair.

CHAPTER TWENTY-TWO
HOME AGAIN

Arvada, Colorado.
Late Autumn, 1889

Leon was bored, restless, snarky, frustrated, angry, irritated, then back to bored again, then frustrated, but in the end, irritated seemed to be winning the day. He was going after the piles of semi-frozen manure with a vengeance that many people, including Harris, would have recognized.

How had Jack put up with this? Five bloody, boring years of mucking stalls and mending fences—my God! How had he done it?

Even inside the lined gloves, Leon's fingers were feeling numb, especially after having to take an axe to the water troughs to break up the ice that had formed overnight. Then he took the pitchfork and fished out the larger chunks. As for the rest, he'd had to remove his gloves and grab the pieces of floating ice with his bare hands to free up the water so the livestock could drink. He had done this job as quickly as he could, but even after drying his red and freezing hands on some burlap and quickly nestling them inside his gloves again, it hadn't done much to warm them up.

Dammit. He hated this. He wanted out. He needed to move—needed to be going, somewhere—anywhere! How was he supposed to keep his nimble fingers soft and sensitive to the subtleties of a card deck, or the seductions of the tumblers, if he was abusing them with this harsh work? The conditions of his parole were starting to drive him loony bins. Kenny was right; Leon was no rancher, and he wondered how much longer he could stand living like this.

The Thanksgiving dance had been a dismal failure. At least, as far as Leon was concerned. Gabi was gone and had basically given him the boot. Though truth be known, Leon had asked for it, and he knew it. Of course, knowing it only made him angrier, resentful, and frustrated. He wanted to be with her so badly. Why had he behaved like such a jackass?

Then, there was Miranda at the dance, wearing that very fine green satin dress. Oh my. What right did she have to look so beautiful? She had caught his eye from across the room, and his heart melted. Then she smiled at him, and his heart broke. He wanted to be with her so badly. Why had he let her push him away? Why couldn't he take control and sweep her off her feet and make her love him, make her want him?

And then, there was Gabi . . .

Leon laid into the straw with the pitchfork, throwing it in heaps down from the loft and into the various stalls. He attacked the coarse stocks, cursing and grinding his teeth in his impotent anger. Before he knew it, his hands had warmed up, and he was sweating under his heavy winter clothing. Still, he kept on attacking the barn chores and cursing his life, until, by chance, he heard the jingling of horses' harnesses and the barking of the ranch dogs. Someone was here. Leon grinned; he knew who it was—finally! And in that knowing, his foul mood disappeared, and he dashed to the barn door.

"Napoleon!" Cameron yelled, needlessly. "Jack's back."

Leon was already out of the barn and up to the wagon, practically pulling Jack from the seat and giving him a quick bear hug, then a slap on the back.

"Hey, hey, partner!" Leon was practically jumping up and down in his excitement. "Finally! It's great to see you."

"Yeah, I can tell, Leon," Jack responded, but he was grinning also, and just as pleased. "I kinda missed you, too."

"Yeah, yeah!" Leon was laughing, still holding onto his partner's arm. "I've been going crazy here, Jack. Oh man—it is so good to see you!" He forced himself to calm down then, and his eyes turned serious. "Did everything go as planned? Is everyone all right?"

"Yeah," Jack assured him. "You got my telegram, didn't ya?"

"Well, yes ... it's just . . ." He looked his nephew straight in the eye, and Jack saw a mixture of emotions. "Did you see her?"

Jack dropped his smile and put a hand on Leon's shoulder. "Yeah, I met her." His blue eyes sparkled again as he looked over at Cameron. "Let's get inside first, okay? It's freezin' out here." He gave his uncle's shoulder a reassuring pat. "Everything went fine, Leon."

Leon nodded and accepted this for the time being.

"It's good to have you home, Jack," Cameron told him. "Napoleon and I were getting on each other's nerves—just the two of us, and a cat—rattling around in a big, empty ranch house. Come on inside and warm up. There's a pretty good stew still simmering on the stove if you're hungry at all."

Leon laughed, still excited to have his nephew home. "Jack's always hungry."

"Yeah, well, this time, I gotta agree with ya, Leon," Jack acknowledged. "I am feelin' a might peckish."

Sam got down from the driver's seat and moved up to the horses' heads, bringing Jack's carpet bag with him. Cameron took the one piece of luggage from him and then smiled at the young man.

"Do you fancy some coffee and some stew before you head back to town?"

Sam shrugged, looking around at the snowy landscape. "Sure, why not?" He untied the lead shank from the near horse and led the team over to the hitching rail by the barn. It was cold out, but not wet, so they would be fine tethered there for half an hour or so.

Cameron nodded toward the house with his head. "Come into the kitchen; that'll give this pair a chance to catch up."

Once inside the house, everyone helped themselves to a bowl of stew and some bread that Leon had made the day before. It was nothing like Jean's delicious offerings, but in times of hardship, one must make do. Everyone poured out a coffee for themselves, then, true to his word, Cameron and Sam stayed to enjoy their lunch in the kitchen, allowing Leon and Jack to settle at the dining table and talk in some privacy.

Leon fixed Jack with intense, dark eyes. "So, everyone is safe?"

Jack sat down with a weary sigh. "Yeah. I'm sure glad to be back though; that was a long haul, doin' it round trip like that."

Leon took a seat opposite and bit his lip. "Well, come on, Jack. You said you saw her, right? Is she ... well, I mean, is she . . .?" Leon got stuck for words, envy and jealousy struggling for dominance.

Jack's eyes softened. "Aw, Leon, she's a heartbreaker. Just the most beautiful gal I ever laid eyes on." He leaned forward. "I gave her a hug for ya. I had a moment with her just before I left and told her that she was named after your ma. She knows her pa would love her and be the proudest man on Earth. I made sure I told her that." He sat back, "It pleased her."

Leon's curiosity now battled for the top rung, and it finally won out over envy. "What's she like?" he asked in an intense whisper. "Is she still as clever and precocious as she was as a child?"

"I'll say. That same spark, and sharp as a razor," Jack grinned. "I think I fell in love, which is a bit worryin', 'cause she's so like you, it's scary."

Leon sat back, feeling pensive. "She looked like Gabi in the photograph, except for the dimples."

Jack nodded. "Yeah, but her hair's kind'a a mix between yours and hers, but wavy, just like her ma. Her eyes are the same shape as Gabi's, but brown. And she's got your complexion and those dimples. The same nose and mouth, just like she did as a young'un, but that ain't the half of it. Every movement and gesture is you. There's no denyin', the apple didn't fall far from that tree."

Leon frowned. "She's got my nose?"

Jack grinned. "Yeah, Leon, but don't worry about it; on her, it's cute—perky."

Leon's brows went up. "Perky?"

Jack's grin expanded. "Yeah!" Then he laughed. "Who'd a thought your ugly mug would make such a pretty girl? I suppose that face had to work somewhere." The smile dropped from his expression; his tone suddenly earnest. "I'm gonna speak to Gabi, Leon. I'm gonna make sure you meet Hannah real soon. It's only right."

Leon sat back. "She did promise me that once this is all over with, I could meet her, as long as I didn't tell her who I was. Hannah thinks I'm dead, and Gabriella wants it to stay that way."

"That ain't fair," Jack groused. "There ain't no good reason why you can't be her pa. She's old enough now and definitely smart enough to keep a secret."

Leon shrugged. "I dunno. If she's that bright, she's going to figure it out on her own eventually. Maybe I should just be patient and let things play out the way they will."

"Well, it won't do no harm for me ta talk ta Gabi about this. Maybe I can get her ta see reason. Where is she, anyway?"

"She's gone."

Jack's brow furrowed, and his eyes asked the question.

Leon sighed. "She dug up information on a 'Mitch' character we think is Harris. She got a direction of travel, and she took it. She left, Jack, without even letting me know she was going. Just up and left."

"Yeah, but would you a let her go, if she'd told ya?"

"No, of course not. All on her own, going after that madman! There's no way I would have let her . . ."

He stopped talking when he noticed Jack smiling at him.

Jack shook his head. "And you're wonderin' why she didn't tell ya."

"Yeah, well ... at least she's not alone. Frank went after her."

"Frank?" Jack scoffed. "I'd like to be a fly on the horse for that one. Who do ya think will win?"

Leon couldn't help the snort. "Damn, that's anyone's guess. Maybe they'll take turns."

Jack chuckled, but he sobered when he saw Leon's expression drop. "What is it?"

"Things changed. It went bad."

Jack's eyes narrowed, guessing that he was not going to be surprised by anything he was about to hear. "Bad?" he asked, suspiciously. "How bad?"

Leon sighed and played with his stew.

Jack waited patiently. He knew it was coming.

"Well," Leon began, "I know I was treating her badly when she first got here, giving her the cold shoulder and all that."

"Yeah. I tell ya, Leon, if you'd treated me that way, I'd a socked ya one."

Leon cringed. "Cameron let me know I was out of line, too. I should have listened to him. I always say that in hindsight, I should have listened to him. But I didn't, and then it got worse. We started shouting at each other over the supper table. I knew she was just trying to help, but my temper got the better of me, and everything escalated. Frank didn't help. She walked off in a huff, and when I tried to go after her, Frank . . ."

Jack's tone hardened. "What?"

"Well, he . . ." Leon shrugged. "He tripped me."

"He tripped ya?"

"Yeah. But once I calmed down, I realized I deserved it. "

Jack's brows shot up. "You actually realized you was bein' unreasonable?"

"What? Is that so hard to believe?"

Jack laughed. "Yeah!"

Leon puffed. "Is it my fault she can infuriate me like that?"

Jack really laughed then. "Dammit, Leon. Ha! You two ain't changed one little bit."

At first, Leon was set for a rebuke, then changed his mind and chuckled instead. "I suppose. The following morning, she got all dressed up like Penny and insisted that we go for a ride. She wanted to talk."

"Eww. Was that smart? I mean, it's one thing for her ta trapse around the ranch in a wig, but ta leave the property. I'm surprised nobody took a shot at ya."

"Hmm. Somebody did. And we're pretty sure it was Harris."

Jack almost came to his feet. "Somebody did!"

"Yeah," Leon was emphatic. "He hit her, too. But she was wearing some kind of head protection under her hat. She was knocked out for a few minutes and had a concussion. But otherwise, she was fine. However, that's not the worst of it."

"It's not?"

"She had some bruising on her face and neck. She insisted it was from the fall off the horse, but David wasn't accepting that. It turns out she came into my bedroom the previous night, while I was having one of my nightmares." Leon stopped for a minute, shaking his head with regret. "Apparently, I hit her. She touched me while I was asleep, and I thought she was Harris."

Jack nodded; this, he could relate to. "Gabi's not unreasonable, Leon. She'll understand once I tell her about your nightmares. I'll go and talk to her."

Leon pushed his bowl away from him, sending it skidding towards his nephew.

Jack put out a hand and stopped it from crashing to the floor, then he looked back at his uncle.

Leon's jaw was tight, along with his throat; anger and regret smoldered in his dark eyes. "She already does know—she was great about it, but that doesn't stop me feeling like a worm. And, of course, David knows about it. He'll be discreet, but just knowing that he knows . . . anyway, that's not all."

Jack sat back, folding his arms. "Yeah?" he asked, cautiously. "What else happened?"

"While we were in town, we ran into Miranda. I had already told Gabi that I was seeing someone else, but that it wasn't serious. Still, it was awkward."

"Yeah, I suppose. But what's the big deal? You were seein' a woman. That ain't a crime. You haven't seen Gabi in over ten years."

"Yup, that's what she said," Leon handed Jack the letter Gabi had left for him. "Actually, both ladies were very understanding."

"Then what's the problem?"

"Read the letter."

Leon sat in silence, watching his partner digest the contents of Gabriella's letter. He fidgeted until a pair of contemplative eyes looked into his.

"She's given ya permission to get on with your life. I'd say this was written by a woman tryin' ta give you the easy way out." Jack tapped his fingers absently on the arm of the chair. "She didn't mean ta hurt ya, Leon. She dropped in, unexpectedly, on a man who'd been writin' to her for years. I really don't think she 'da come, if she'd known how you'd react. She's smart enough ta find another way."

"I know that," Leon ran his hand through his dark locks.

Jack was confused. "So, she left the way clear for Miranda. What's the problem?"

Cameron and Sam returned from the kitchen and made their way toward the front door.

"I'm heading into town with Sam," Cameron informed them. "Can you fellas tend to the evening chores?"

"Sure, Cameron. No problem," came the unified response.

"Good. See you in a few hours."

Jack and Leon locked eyes. They both knew Cameron was only heading into town to give them more time to talk.

They both smiled.

Jack went into the kitchen, returning momentarily with the coffee pot. He replenished both their cups, took the pot back to simmer on the stovetop, then returned to sit down again.

Leon avoided his eyes, tracing his finger along an invisible figure eight on the table.

"So," Jack continued, bringing his uncle's attention back to him. "What's the problem? You like Miranda, don't ya?"

"Miranda has decided to put things on hold. She could see there was unfinished business with Gabi."

Jack arched his brows. "Hmm. So, basically, both have backed off. One has told you to make up your mind, and the other thinks you already have and has headed for the hills."

"That's about the size of it."

Jack laughed, even though he knew this was hard for Leon.

"Nothin' comes easy for you, does it?" He shook his head and, sobering up, sat quietly to contemplate the man sitting across from him. "So, what about you?" he finally asked. "What do you want? If it's Miranda, the way's clear. Go tell her." Jack watched his uncle nervously pick away at a scratch on the table. "What's stoppin' ya?"

"I don't know. I just don't know. Why does everything have to be so hard? Why can't everybody just let me get on with my life?"

Jack watched his friend struggle, then he gently reached out and placed a hand on top of Leon's fidgeting one, calming him down.

"Leon, let's just try ta make this a bit simpler, okay? It seems ta me that if you wanted Miranda, you'd simply ride into town and tell her. Something is obviously stopping you."

"Yes."

"So, what is it? You're jugglin' a lot a questions all at once. You used ta be real good at that, and you will be again. But, right now, you've got ta think in straight lines, just until you're yourself again. Think of the answer to that one question; what's stoppin' ya from goin' to Miranda and takin' her in your arms?"

Leon sat back, looking into the distance.

"It feels like a lifetime ago since we lost Ella, but at the same time, it's as though it only happened last week. Maybe I don't want to go down that road again. I asked Gabi if we could give it one more try, but she didn't think it was a good idea. Maybe she's right, and I should just leave it be."

"Okay. So, you want to try again with her, but you're afraid of gettin' hurt. And she said no, anyway."

"Yes."

Jack snorted. "Since when did her sayin' no, stop ya?"

"We have history now," Leon argued. "And it's not all nice history."

"No foolin'," Jack agreed. "Did it ever occur to ya that she said no for the same reason that you're not gonna push it?"

Leon blinked, then he looked at Jack with an open expression of bewilderment, followed by sudden enlightenment.

"She pushed me away for the same reason I treated her so badly when she first got here. She's afraid of getting hurt again."

"Well, yeah!" Jack rolled his eyes. "For a couple a smart people, you ain't too bright."

Leon threw up his hands. "And maybe she's right. This is the second time she has walked out on me without giving me any say in the matter. I'm not gonna chase after her, Jack. I told her I would like to try again, and she's run out on me. Again."

"It seems ta me they're both just givin' ya room. They're leaving it up to you ta make up your mind."

"Then fine. Leave it be. I sometimes wonder if reconnecting with Hannah is the only reason I want to try again with Gabi. Let's face it, Gabi and I drive each other crazy. Even David said that sounded exhausting."

"You two always did set off the fireworks."

"I need to take a step back and see how this all plays out. Even Cameron said as much. And, you know, when Cameron says something, it's worth listening to."

"Yeah, you got that right."

"I am worried about Gabi, though. But you know what she's like once she gets an idea in her head. Frank said he was going to bring her back."

"Ha! Yeah. And you're surprised that didn't happen?"

"No. I was just hoping, that's all. I expect they've gone after 'Mitch' together. And if Mitch really is Harris, like Gabi suspects, then they could be heading into more danger than they know."

"But why?" Jack was just as confused as everyone else. "Why would Harris wanna harm Penny?"

"I have no idea. But he'd kill a woman as quick as look at her. I'm worried sick, but I have no way of getting in touch."

Jack wandered over to the window, staring out aimlessly at the snow.

"I wouldn't worry too much about that," he finally said. "Steven and I hired Malachi and Gus to track Harris down shortly after he escaped from the prison."

"You did? Why?"

Jack turned to face him. "It started because we wanted evidence that you didn't kill Dr. Palin. Harris was the only one who could clear ya."

"Oh." Leon nodded.

"Then, when ya got your parole, well, there was still some question as to who murdered the doctor, so I told Gus and Malachi to stay on him. They had him at Robert's Rendezvous through that winter, but then he disappeared. His comin' here would fit that." Jack sighed and, folding his arms, considered the situation. "Now, if you're right, and Mitch and Harris are one and the same, then ... oh sheesh! We really do have ta find 'im. That man is dangerous."

"You got that right." Leon was emphatic. "And you sent Gus and Malachi after him?"

"Well . . ." Jack shrugged in his defense as he sat back down at the table. "Just ta track 'im. Not try and capture 'im."

"Oh, good." Leon was relieved. "Do you know where they are?"

"The last I heard, they'd tracked 'im into Nebraska, then were headin' for Kansas."

Leon nodded. "That makes sense. Gabi received information that Mitch was heading for Missouri, so that's where she and Frank are likely headed. Dammit!" He slapped the table in frustration. "Why couldn't she leave me a way to get in touch with her?"

Jack shook his head, waving Leon's concerns away. "Frank'll be in touch, and the next time Gus contacts me, I'll let 'em know ta be on the lookout for 'im. I know now where Helèna's Topeka home is. If Gabi's in that area, she's bound ta go there eventually. I expect she'll get in touch then." Jack hesitated, almost scared to ask the next question, but knowing he had to. "Do you think the bullet that hit Gabi was meant for you? I mean, if that was Harris, he might be holdin' a grudge."

"I had thought of that," Leon answered. "It would certainly make things easier to deal with. I want you and Penny to have a happy life. I owe you that. I don't know how I would have survived without you."

"They're safe now, and we'll get to the bottom of this," Jack assured him. "Think hard on what you want, Leon. If you wanna give it another try with Gabi, she needs ta know it, and I'll be happy ta help. She's a good detective, but even she could be forgiven for not pickin' up on the clues you were givin' her."

"No," Leon was adamant. "Like I said, she's the one who keeps running out on me, and I am not going to chase after her. I'll probably see her when I meet Hannah, and maybe we'll have had enough time by then for things to calm down." Leon absently played with a crumb on the table. "Maybe I'll see things clearer by then."

"Yeah. Or maybe you will have missed your chance. When Frank gets in touch, I'll go see her and explain things to her."

Leon rolled his eyes. "You're not going to let this go, are you?"

Jack sent him a cheeky grin. "Nope."

Leon sighed. "I can't stop you from talking with her if you're this determined to do it. Maybe just suggest that when this is all over, and I come to meet Hannah, we can discuss things further then."

"Uh-huh."

"I mean it, Jack."

"Sure thing, Leon."

Leon was not convinced of Jack's sincerity, and he knew how bull-headed his nephew could be. There was no point in continuing with that discussion, so Leon brought up another topic that had been niggling at him.

"Jack," Leon asked, "how did you do it?"

"Do what?"

"Almost five years. You were living a prison term just as surely as I was, but you did it voluntarily. How'd you do it?"

"I had a mission, Leon. Besides that, it weren't all that hard for me to stay put. Bein' on the run after we left Elk Mountain got me thinkin' about settlin' down on some land and bein' part of a family again—you know that. It was just bad timing between me and Haley."

Leon nodded.

Jack sighed and thought about his situation. "I love Penny, I really do." He smiled with reminiscence. "Who woulda thought that scrawny little tomboy would end up takin' holda my heart like this?" He turned serious again, then looked solemnly into his uncle's eyes. "I wanna settle down with her, have some land, and build on that. I wanna have young'uns with her while I'm still young enough to enjoy them. Is that such a bad thing ta want?"

"No!" Leon was quick to assure. "I envy you that. Here I am, pushing forty, and I'm still not sure I could do it. I'm in love with two different women, and I don't even know if I'm capable of settling down with either one of them. I just know I want to! But the last six or seven months I've been trapped here—I'm starting to go nuts. Now, that scares me."

Jack frowned. "It scares ya? Why?"

"It's like I'm not able to settle anywhere," Leon explained softly.

"Even in Gillette, when I had my family, and I was happy being with them, I couldn't give up Elk Mountain. Just one more thing that drove Gabi away from me. I always have to be going somewhere—I always have to be challenging something. I don't think that's normal. Do you think that's normal?"

Jack laughed, but quickly stifled it, knowing that his uncle was being serious and that he was indeed concerned about this.

"It's normal for you, Leon," he stated. "You know, I think one of the reasons you're feelin' restless is 'cause you ain't been able ta find anything that matters enough to ya, ta make ya wanna settle down."

Leon sat, looking into space, and Jack realized he needed to elaborate.

"Leon, you got so many things goin' on inside of ya right now. Why do ya feel ya have ta solve all of 'em this instant? One thing at a time, ya know? Even your brain can't handle all these things at once. You're not trapped here on the ranch."

Leon snorted. "Yeah, I may as well be. I can't go anywhere without permission. I may as well be back in prison!"

Jack sat back and sent his uncle a reproving look. "There is no way you are gonna convince me that livin' here is the same as bein' in prison! C'mon, Leon!" Jack was suddenly on his feet again and pacing, but he still had Leon locked down in a gaze that wouldn't waver. "Stop bein' so cynical, will ya? Sure, ya got some restrictions on ya, but they're livable. And nobody's whippin' on ya! You got people here who care about ya—and you know it!"

"Yeah, yeah. All right!" Leon quickly figured out that he wasn't going to get away with that self-pitying drivel with his nephew. "I guess I just don't know what I want. I envy you, Jack, that's all. You know what you want in your life now, and you know who you want to spend it with. I just feel lost, and so ... indecisive."

"One thing at a time, Uncle. I've had five years ta figure all this stuff out. You've just begun. Let me talk ta Gabi; let me explain some of this to her." He picked up on Leon's instant pessimism and pushed his case. "She might just decide ta come back anyway. Once she knows."

Leon hesitated, but his tightened jaw softened as he considered Jack's words, and then he finally relaxed his stance. He looked up at his nephew, meeting his eyes, and then he shook his head.

"No. I don't want to see her. Not yet. She hinted at some interest in the private detective she hired to find her son. That's the kind of man she married the first time around. Maybe she'd be better off with him."

"Ain't that up ta her? Weren't you just sayin' how you resented her pushin' ya onto Miranda? Now you're doin' the same thing, pushin' her onta some suit."

"Maybe, maybe not. But I'm not chasing after her, Jack.

CHAPTER TWENTY-THREE
A TRAIL OF BLOOD

Missouri
Winter 1889

The hunched figures rode into the wind, snow mingling with hard hail pellets that stung the skin, forcing them to pull down their hats and cover their faces with bandanas.

The taller rider pointed, yelling against the swirling blizzard.

"There's a homestead over there! We've got to take cover. We can't go on like this!"

The smaller of the pair nodded, directing the horse toward the obscure structures.

The storm intensified, greying out the visibility until they became mere shadows in the frozen, pallid landscape.

The two horses willingly stopped by the door of the cabin and stood on shaky legs as the snow-encased forms on their backs dismounted.

The larger form took the two horses and pushed through the swirling snow toward the barn.

The smaller form came onto the porch of the cabin and stamped its feet, then pushed the heavy coat collar and bandana away from its face to reveal the feminine oval of Gabriella's features. She hammered at the door, her brows gathering in consternation at the lack of response. She paused, listening hard against the barrier, then yelled above the wailing of the blizzard.

"Is there anybody there!"

No response.

She shuffled over to the window and, glancing in, gasped at what she saw. Darting a look toward the barn where Frank had taken the horses, she made a snap decision. This situation couldn't wait. She pushed aside her coat, drew her gun, and strode over to the door, standing to the side as she released the latch. She pushed on it, but the door didn't budge. She considered breaking the window, but noting the snow piled up against the threshold, she gave the barrier another try. Putting her shoulder up against the wood, she shoved, and the door broke free from the ice and swung open. She waited with strained caution before stepping into the little cabin and then quickly scanned the one-room interior before going further.

The place was in complete disarray. Chairs were overturned, and pots and dishes were scattered on the floor. There was a pile of wood by the cook stove, but the stove itself was untended and cold. They would have to remedy that, but for now, Gabi's eyes were drawn to the body on the carpet.

Congealed blood pooled around the man's head from the gash across his throat. His gaping mouth was still open in his last strangled scream, but the opaque, sunken eyes spoke volumes about how long he had lain there. About two days, Gabriella's educated guess told her.

She holstered her gun as she noted a second body lying on the bed by the far wall. She approached, scanning the woman and feeling her heart sink at the sight of the large spreading of blood on her dress that had caused the clothing to stiffen in the cold. She lifted the skirt, revealing the nature of her intimate attack, then gently rearranged the soiled clothing. The least she deserved was some dignity after this horror. She looked down upon her pale, waxen face, taking note of the hands that were bound to the bed frame and acknowledging the brutality that this woman had suffered. She looked very young, no more than twenty.

Gabriella guessed the murdered man was her husband, killed first to allow whoever did this to take his time with her. She cursed her worst Quebecois oath and, reaching out a hand, she stroked the woman's cheek. Then she stopped, stock-still. The skin wasn't cold! For sure, she wasn't warm, but she didn't have that marble-cold chill of a cadaver. Gabriella leaned over, testing for the weak breath, then stood up in shock.

This woman must have been lying here for at least as long as the dead man. Gabi scanned her for injury and quickly identified the stab wound to her upper abdomen. Some bastard had left her to die a slow, agonizing death.

Gabi sliced through the ropes and bustled over to the range. She had to get the stove stoked to bring heat to the cabin and perhaps some comfort to the stricken woman. Water; the woman needed water—and painkillers. Was there any? An abdominal injury? No, she couldn't give her water. Perhaps she could just moisten her mouth.

She spied the bucket of water beside the stove and noted the thin layer of ice on the surface. She opened the stove door, set in two logs and some kindling, then stood up and scanned the shelves for a match. She spied the box of faggots, grabbed one, and struck it against the stove top to light the fuel.

"What the hell?" Frank stood in the doorway.

"Sorry." Gabriella tossed the match into the crackling kindling and stood up. "I didn't have time to fetch you. I saw the blood and came in. She's still alive—just."

"You came in? What if he'd still been in here?"

"Then he'd be dead, Frank. I've done this before, remember?" Gabriella used the dipper hanging on the wall to break the ice on the water, then scooped some water into a small cooking pot and set it on the stove to heat. She turned to face Frank and motioned to the cadaver on the floor. "Can you find a blanket to cover the body with? It wouldn't be wise to disturb it before the authorities can get out here."

Frank glanced at the bloody mess on the floor.

"You don't mind being in the same room as a dead body?"

Gabriella rolled her eyes. "Is it your intention to rile me, or are you really that obtuse?"

Frank snorted. "Just checking."

He spied the large wardrobe and walked across the room, figuring that was the best place to find a blanket. He was right.

Gabi took a knife from the counter and returned to the woman. She gently began to cut away the stiff, blood-covered clothing. She kept her own body between Frank and the woman to give her as much privacy as possible.

"She's been raped and left to die, poor dear."

"Hmm," Frank mumbled as he draped the blanket over the husband's body. "I'll search the barn for painkillers. Why don't you search in here?"

"I'd rather you do it. I don't want to leave her side."

"Fine." Frank almost sounded annoyed. "I was just tryin' to save time. Seems to me, the sooner she gets something, the better."

He crossed the threshold and then slammed the door shut, leaving

Gabriella alone with the young woman.

***

Frank re-entered the barn. The resident livestock had been frantic for food and fresh water when Frank had entered previously with their own two horses. Now, the barn was filled with the contented munching of animals, oblivious to the horror that had befallen their humans, as they focused on filling the emptiness in their bellies.

Frank ignored the animals and went directly to a promising cabinet. And there it was; enough medication to down a horse. He snatched it up and returned to the relative warmth of the farmhouse.

***

It hadn't taken long for the water on the stove to heat enough for Gabi's purposes. She poured some of the steaming liquid into a cup and then used the rest to wash the woman as best she could. She had just covered her with warm blankets when Frank returned with the medicine.

The woman was beyond help, especially as it was twenty miles to the nearest town in a terrible snowstorm. Both Gabi and Frank knew that it was only a matter of time, and that time was running out fast. But if Gabi could get even some of the painkiller into her, it would make her passing a little easier.

Frank mixed a dose into the cup, stirred it, and, along with a cloth, brought it over to the bed.

Gabriella smiled her thanks as she took the cup and dipped the corner of the cloth into the liquid. She pressed it to the woman's lips and, surprisingly, got a response. She moved her lips and took in some of the medicated water, then licked her lips and groaned. Gabi resoaked the cloth and continued with her ministrations.

Frank found the family Bible sitting on the table and opened it in search of information.

"Family name is Winters," he read. "Jeffrey and Margaret. 'Maggie for short'. Married June 14th, 1889." Frank puffed. "Hardly long enough to get bored with the marriage bed."

Gabi frowned. "Frank, can't you show even the least bit of respect and compassion for this situation?"

"What? Just sayin' they were still happily married. I figure that's a good thing."

Gabriella shook her head but didn't respond. There were some things Frank was never going to understand.

Then Gabi's attention returned to the woman as the warm water and meds seemed to revive her. She did not open her eyes, but once the water relieved the dryness of her throat, she did manage to speak.

"Jeff …" It was little more than a breath from her lips.

Gabi leaned closer. "What was that?"

"Jeff," Maggie repeated. She lifted her arm as though to reach for him, and a soft smile tugged at her lips. "Jeff. It's all right. I love you. You look so fine in your Sunday best …"

Frank and Gabi exchanged a sad look. She was delirious, and perhaps that state was the best thing for her. Or maybe she was seeing things more clearly than either of them. Frank lacked the imagination to consider the spiritual anything more than nonsense. But Gabi hoped there was more to life than the suffering they endured on this Earth. She knew that her daughter, Ella, had come to visit on more than one occasion, and the cynicism of others would never deter her from that knowledge.

Maggie's grip was weak as she clutched Gabriella's hand. She opened her eyes to slits, and though her expression was distant, she saw Gabriella and focused on her. "One more Christmas . . ." She sucked in a rasping breath. "We were looking forward ... our first married Christmas . . ."

Gabriella smiled softly. "How did you meet?"

Maggie's eyes flickered closed. "I've known Jeff all my life."

Gabi squeezed the hand that held so desperately to hers. "Can you remember anything about the person who attacked you?"

Maggie groaned, lolling her head from side to side as her breathing increased.

"Snake …" she murmured, then a sob escaped her lungs, and she drew in a shuddering gasp. "No . . . Jeffrey . . . no . . . a snake . . ."

"A snake?" Gabi repeated as she heard Frank step in closer. "What about a snake?"

"A snake." She gasped again as her face crumpled into overwhelming grief. "A snake on his arm … evil. The Bible speaks of evil . . ."

Gabi gulped down the knot in her throat. "You're tired, try to rest."

"Don't go!" Maggie's whisper was desperate as she refused to relinquish Gabi's hand.

"I'm not going anywhere. I'm staying right here with you, Maggie. You're not alone."

Maggie gave a little nod, and then her painful, labored breathing became her only movement. The muscles around her throat stood out whenever her chest rose, her body desperately gulping in air. The gaps in between the breaths gradually widened, and Maggie slipped deeper into unconsciousness, the air sometimes catching the vocal cords like a murmur of despair.

***

Gabi sat with her until the end. It was about three o'clock in the morning when she finally stood up and gently pulled the blanket over Maggie's face.

Frank stirred on his bedroll. "She's gone?"

"Yes," Gabi sighed. "We've got to find him, Frank. I reckon we're closing in, but he's still about two days ahead of us."

"All for a fresh horse," Frank murmured, glancing at the covered form on the bed.

"At least she was able to give us something. The snake can only be the tattoo on his arm. We'll report this to the law in the next town, and they can send someone out to deal with the particulars. I don't think there's any doubt he's the same man who attacked Penny. We have to stop this insanity and find out why."

"We'll get him, Gabi." Frank lay back down and turned on his side. "Get some sleep. We need to get going as soon as this storm passes.

***

Waterville, Kansas

It was a good ten days before the doctor deemed Gus well enough to let them head out onto the trail again. Then it was granted only on strict instructions: the patient must keep taking his medicine and stay warm and dry. Good luck in this miserable climate!

Malachi hovered like a mother hen, and Gus grumbled like an old bear, but they still managed to get on the road and put some miles between themselves and the town that had given them nothing but headaches. They'd managed to get some more money out of that lawyer fella, and they hadn't even had to lie about why they needed it!

Unfortunately, just as when they had first arrived in this town, when they finally headed out again, the weather wasn't the only thing that was still cold. Harris had completely disappeared, and the two friends were back riding in circles, hoping to find some lead to follow.

Trotting into Lehigh, Kansas, the fellas' spirits were feeling just as damp and unfortunate as the town that surrounded them. They dismounted, stiff and slow, in front of the livery stable. The plan was to get the horses settled and tended to, then get some hot food. But even this basic plan got sidetracked, and a soft bed, accompanied by a hot meal, would come to them at a price.

The two men lingered for a few minutes, stamping their cold feet and looking around for the liveryman, but that fine gentleman was nowhere to be seen. The horses stomped and snorted their warm breath into the cold air, while Gus tightened up the collar around his throat and began to cough, then curse the fact that he was coughing again.

"Where the hell is that lazy, no good ... don't he know he's got a business ta run?"

"Mabee, he's gone off ta git his own supper." Malachi was always willing to give the other fella the benefit of the doubt.

Gus snorted. "Take these." He handed Malachi the reins to his horse. "You wait here, and I'll go send that telegram to the Kid. Let 'im know where we are.

"Yeah, okay."

Gus stomped his feet one more time and coughed into his coat sleeve, then, with a disgruntled sniff, he trudged across the street toward the telegraph office.

Malachi gave a dejected sigh as he watched his friend walk away. He stomped his own feet and began to pace around in a circle with his hands, still holding the double sets of reins, tucked into his armpits to warm them up.

The two horses stood patiently, sitting down on a back hoof, and playing with their bits.

Malachi began to search the street, up and down the block, hoping to catch sight of the liveryman. He took note of the other people strolling about on this chilly afternoon, but none of them stood out as being of any importance to him. He dismissed them. It was then, when he took his attention away from the far distance to focus on things in closer proximity, that he locked eyes with the very man who had been so elusive until this instant.

Harris had been trotting his horse up to the entrance of the livery when he found himself staring into the startled blue eyes of a familiar face. He pulled his horse up in surprise and did a quick scan of the street before he faced forward again and acknowledged the former convict.

"Hey, Cobb." Harris's greeting came out as a snarl. "Sure didn't expect to see you in these parts."

"Oh yeah ... hi ya, Harris." Malachi felt his nerves jangle; he didn't care much for confronting Harris all on his lonesome. "How ya doin'?"

Harris was suspicious, taking note of the two horses Malachi was holding, and knowing that where Malachi Cobb stood, Gus Shaffer wasn't far away.

"What you doin' around these parts, Cobb? And where's your partner?"

"Oh, we're just on a job down here fer some lawyer fella." Malachi was never good at lying, so he tended to fall back on some semblance of the truth. "Gus is over there, sendin' 'im a telegram."

"Oh yeah?" Harris responded, though his attention was no longer on the little man. He was looking around and over his shoulder, not wanting to allow Shaffer to come up on him from behind. He pulled on the reins, getting his horse to back away from the livery and out to the street. "See ya around, Cobb."

"Yeah, ah ... take care 'a yerself."

Harris continued backing until he reached the street, then he turned his horse's head north and nudged him into a trot.

Malachi breathed a sigh of relief and began to search in the direction of the telegraph office, hoping to see Gus returning. The cold trail had turned piping hot.

Malachi had just enough time to catch a flash of movement out of the corner of his eye when he heard the thumping of the horse's hooves coming at a run through the snow and then onto wood. A loud crack and a flash of fire grabbed his senses. A bullet slammed into the wooden door right behind the ex-convict. Malachi ducked, and clutching his head, he dashed forward to get in between the two, now dancing, horses.

Another rifle shot quickly followed upon the echo of the first, and the already nervous and blowing horses reared backward, trying to pull away. But Malachi had a strong hold, and he went back with them, hoping to use them for cover. This plan backfired as the horses panicked further, and Malachi found himself in real danger of being trampled. Then Harris's horse was on top of them, plunging headlong into Ky's little bay and knocking the animal off its feet.

Malachi went sprawling into the muddy snow, just barely making it out from under the falling animal and saving himself from being crushed. The air filled with panicked yells and screams from townsfolk, while thrashing hooves scrambled for a foothold in the slippery muck. Gus's horse pulled away from Malachi's grip and reared up, then overbalanced. The hind feet slid out from under him, and he toppled over backward, hitting the ground so hard that he managed to break the tree of his saddle, rendering it useless.

Harris pulled his horse out from the fray, then, bringing his rifle to bear, he aimed at the little man struggling to get to his feet and draw his own handgun.

Fortunately for Malachi, Gus had heard the ruckus and was coming, at the run, with his revolver in hand and taking aim at the largest target in his sights. He pulled the trigger, and Harris's horse let out a quiet snorting squeal and instantly ducked away from the burning pain caused by the bullet nicking him across the top of his neck.

The action wasn't much, but it was enough to spoil Harris's aim, and he had to scramble simply to bring his injured horse back under control.

By this time, Malachi had his revolver out and was taking potshots in Harris's general direction, so that, along with Gus coming at him, made the fugitive decide to head elsewhere. He pulled his horse around and, taking a shot at Gus to slow him down, he spurred his frantic animal into a gallop and headed for the outskirts of town.

Gus carried on across the street, cursing as he came. He grabbed his partner and pulled him the rest of the way to his feet.

"Dammit, Ky! Why'd ya let 'im see ya?"

"Wull—I didn't know he was there, Gus. He come up on me afore I knowed he was there."

"Now he knows we're after 'im. Dammit! C'mon, stop wastin' time. Let's go."

"But, Gus . . ."

And Malachi gestured toward the two horses that were standing in the middle of the street, looking woebegone. Both animals were wet and covered in mud. Gus's chestnut was favoring his right foreleg, with the broken saddle still strapped to his back. Neither of them looked inclined to go for a gallop anywhere.

Then, wouldn't you know it, the crowd of curious citizens gathered around the horses, parted down the middle to make way for the angry scowl sporting a tin badge, who had his eyes set on the two bedraggled transients.

"What in tarnation is goin' on here?" came the snarling, clipped accent of the man behind the badge.

Malachi shifted, avoiding eye contact. "Wull ... ahumm . . ."

Gus started to cough.

***

The sheriff strode into his office and sat in the chair at the desk without even offering his guests a warming cup of coffee.

Gus and Malachi dragged their feet along behind him and, knowing the drill, stood at the front of the desk to face the lawman.

Malachi felt the chill from the still-open door and scurried back to close it, thinking of his buddy's health issues. When he returned to the desk, the conversation was well underway.

"No, sir, Sheriff! —cough, cough, cough— we were hired to track that man, and the longer you keep us here, jawin' about it, the more of a head start yer givin' 'im."

The sheriff sat back in his chair and scrutinized the two vagabonds standing before him. "Really, Mr. Johnston?" was his skeptical response. "So, you're bounty hunters."

"No, sir—cough, cough—we ain't no stinkin' bounty hunters." Gus looked truly disgusted. "That man is an escaped convict from Wyoming, and we've been hired to track 'im down, cause ya see, he's also wanted fer questioning in some other matters."

Malachi grinned through the mud and jerked his head up and

down in a nod, hopefully emphasizing his partner's words.

The sheriff looked from one man to the other, then snorted in disbelief. "You got any proof of this?"

"Well, ahh ... not on us," Gus was scrambling. "Ah, but if ya send a telegram to that lawyer fella, who hired us, I'm sure he'll back us up. But still, ya know the longer you hold us here, the less chance we got of catchin' up with 'im."

"Yeah, well, you just hold your horses," the sheriff told them, "'Cause I'm gonna check out your story, and you ain't leavin' town until I get down to the bottom of this. You're both damn lucky that none of our citizens here got hit with any stray bullets. As it is, the livery is gonna need some repair work done, and if this lawyer fella don't back ya up—and even more to the point, send money to cover the costs, then you fellas will be guests of the jailhouse here, until you can work off the debt."

The smile on Malachi's face dropped to an open-mouthed frown as the thought of being stuck here in a jail cell sank in.

Gus puffed himself up with frustration. "Ahh, well now, Sheriff, there ain't no call fer that. We got enough money on us ta pay fer any repairs. There weren't none that were too bad. Ain't no call fer us ta be stickin' around town now. You just tell us what you need, and we can be on our way."

"Uh-huh." The sheriff was skeptical. "Fine. I will ask Cecil how much he reckons it'll cost, and I'll let ya know. But, in the meantime, you fellas ain't goin' nowheres until I can substantiate your story."

"Oh now, Sheriff, there ain't—"

"NOWHERES!" the sheriff reiterated. "Yer horses ain't fit for travel, and if I get wind of you tryin' ta buy new ones from Cecil, I'll throw ya both into a cell for the duration. Do I make myself clear?"

The partners exchanged looks, and Gus started to grumble, then cough, but they couldn't think of any way out of this. If they pushed the sheriff too hard, then he just might do some real digging and find out that Mr. Johnston held an uncanny resemblance to a wanted highwayman who was supposed to be dead. The fact that they were in the heart of Kansas, where chances were good that no one had even heard of Gus Shaffer, did not help the deceased outlaw feel any less anxious.

"Yessir, Sheriff," Gus relented. "We'll just get us a room at the hotel and wait ta hear from ya, tellin' us we can go."

"Fine.' The sheriff was content with this. "I will send a telegram to your lawyer friend, and we'll see what he has to say."

***

Wet snow fell from a slate-grey sky as the grumpy partners made their way to the hotel.

"What are we gonna do, Gus?" Malachi whined. "This is the closest we come ta Harris all year, and now we's gonna lose 'im again!"

"Don't ya think I know that? Cough, cough. There's nothin' we can do about it! If our horses was fit, we could leave tonight, but as it stands—well, I don't think the Kid would want us stealin' horses, so we're just gonna have ta wait."

"Yeah, okay. I guess a night or two in town won't be too bad." His sentence trailed off as he sent a sidelong glance to his partner, thinking how pale he looked, and how that cough was getting bad again.

Meanwhile, Gus walked on ahead, mumbling to himself. "Damn. Kid don't seem ta want us ta steal nothin' no more ... just 'cause he's up and got his precious pardon, he thinks we all need ta live by his rules ... grumble, grumble, grumble . . ."

***

Harris was in a foul mood. What the hell were Shaffer and Cobb doin', followin' him halfway across the goddamn country?

Can't a man go about his own business without having to put up with unwelcome company? Dammit! What the hell was that about? But Shaffer and Cobb? Shaffer is an old grouch, and Cobb is such a dimwit he's more of a nuisance than a threat. But they're a nuisance I don't need. Bet ya Nash is behind this, somehow; that bastard always did have it in for me. Made my life a misery in prison, and here he is, doin' the same thing now that we're both out. What the hell is his problem, anyway? Damned busybody!

And a traitor, too. Harris's eyes squinted as his memories clarified. *Makin' friends with that damn guard, and gettin' all chummy with the prison doctor. When push came to shove, every inmate in that hellhole knew which side Nash was on. Yeah! Sidin' with the law, damn him! He probably was a spy all along, just like Boeman said.*

Harris cursed the bad aim when he'd ended up hitting Nash's horse rather than Nash himself. That would have been one less damn thorn to worry about.

Oh, it had been so tempting when he had that whole cozy little picnic in his sights. He could have taken Nash out, right then and there. But no, he'd been hired to take out the woman, so he'd had to let his own desires take a step back and do what he'd been paid to do.

Harris grinned with malicious satisfaction. It had been a clean shot; there was no way that pretty little thing could have survived it. It was a shame, in a way. Harris would have enjoyed takin' that beauty and having his way with her. She probably wasn't still a maiden, considering she was with Jack Kiefer, and maidens were the best. Most of 'em fought like hellcats. Yeah, he liked it when they fought back; it made the ride all that much more exciting.

He growled. Even with this perpetual wet, cold snow coming down, and his persistence in keeping his tired horse moving at a steady clip through the slush, he felt his need take hold. Just thinking about what he would have done to that Marsham gal before he'd had to kill her was makin' him feel mean.

***

A day and a half later, the sheriff was satisfied that the two transients were telling the truth, and, even more of a surprise, that the lawyer had wired enough money to their local bank to cover the cost of a new barn door. Cecil couldn't have been happier; it was going to be even better than the door he'd had in the first place.

Then, considering Cecil was now in a good mood, he ended up selling those two fellas a couple of nice horses, fully tacked out, for quite a bit lower than he would otherwise have accepted. Of course, he still made sure he received a tidy profit from the exchange—would be no kind of businessman if he didn't. But everyone parted on good terms, and the partners headed out of town, still frustrated by the delay but overall optimistic, especially since it wasn't snowing yet.

***

On the first day out, Gus and Malachi pushed the horses hard, knowing they had a lot of ground to make up. Harris was running scared, or mad, or both, 'cause he sure wasn't doing much to cover his tracks.

"look'it here," Gus stopped his horse and pointed to sloppy tracks in the mud. "That idiot tried ta backtrack and then rub out the tracks with wet grass. Nash always did say that Harris was none too bright."

Malachi spit out a stream of chewing tobacco, then grinned. "Yeah. He's mean, but even in prison, he needed someone ta point him in the right direction ta be of any use. Just plain luck that he was the only one who got away durin' that prison break."

"Hmm." Gus pushed his horse forward through the wet and slippery grasses. "Lucky for him. Ain't lucky for anyone who crosses his path."

Malachi sobered at this reminder of the fates. "Yeah, but he do make mistakes, Gus. Mabee his luck is about ta change."

"It sure will if I got somethin' ta say about it."

***

That evening, they made camp out on the trail, and though the wind was chilly and the air damp, no precipitation fell upon them. With their nice new ground sheets and bedrolls, they were able to spend a relatively comfortable night. The next morning, they saddled up at first light and hit the trail again, following Harris's tracks with very little trouble, and only twice having to circle back and re-establish the route.

By mid-morning, they arrived in Florence, Kansas, and found the whole town in an uproar. Some drifter showed up the night before and, after some drinks and a little poker, had paid for the sexual rights to a pretty, little blonde-haired gal. Well, she used to be pretty. Nobody really cared too much about the whore, but afterward, that bastard had gone out and found someone else to abuse. Apparently, once hadn't been enough to satisfy his needs.

If he had stayed with using the upstairs or crib gals, it wouldn't have mattered so much, but he stepped across the line and committed an act so atrocious that it turned the stomachs of all the locals.

He'd made his way out to one of the finest homes on the outskirts of town and found which bedroom window would give him access to the fourteen-year-old girl who slept there. He waited patiently until the town quieted, then he crept in through the window and knocked the girl out while she slept.

He didn't rush through this experience—he saw no need. He jammed a chair up against the door, bound the young girl hand and foot to the bed, gagged her nice and snugly, then, using his knife to cut the cloth, he stripped her naked. He sat on the chair in the room and waited, admiring her pretty, little, adolescent body. He waited until she awoke; she had to be awake. How else could she appreciate everything he had planned for her?

He was gone before the first light of dawn bled across the horizon. Gone before he could hear the mother's anguished screams and the father's enraged cursing. Gone before her blood-spattered little body was even cold.

This outraged town is what Gus and Malachi rode into. They didn't hang around to get details; they knew enough to know that they were on the right track and were closing in on him. Harris had taken the time to hide his trail just enough to get this town's small posse heading in the wrong direction. But it wasn't enough to fool the partners.

Gus snorted with disgust when they came across the simple ruse that had confused the posse, and he and Malachi booted their horses onwards. Both men could feel the anticipation now; they knew they had Harris on the run, and today would be the day they'd get 'im!

But what they didn't know was that they left Lehigh, where they'd had the previous run-in with Harris, too soon. They were so anxious to get after their quarry that they hadn't thought to check the telegraph office again, so they missed the warning from Jack not to apprehend Harris.

Nor did they know that Gabriella and a Wells Fargo detective were also on the hunt.

But even if Gus and Malachi had received that warning, after what they'd heard in Florence, neither was inclined to sit back and watch from a distance. They both wanted to get that bastard—and no damn telegram would have stopped them.

CHAPTER TWENTY-THREE
FULL CIRCLE

Arvada, Colorado
Winter, 1889

Jack walked out of the telegraph office as he read the new message from Kenny. By now, he should have figured out that walking and reading at the same time is not a healthy practice. He still got a chuckle about Leon knocking himself out on a low-hanging tree branch because he had been so absorbed in his book while riding that he hadn't been paying attention. Yet, Jack was now doing much the same thing. It almost always caused a mishap, and this time was no exception.

"Jack!"

"Oh! I'm sorry." Jack looked up into Miranda's dark blue eyes and instantly felt guilty, though why he should, he had no idea.

Miranda noted his embarrassment. "That's quite all right. No harm done."

Jack smiled and tried to relax. "How are you? It's been a while."

"Yes. I thought it best to stay away," she admitted, as she twitched an awkward smile. "How is he? I worry about him, you know."

"Yeah, join the club," Jack mumbled, then sent her a friendlier look. "He's all right, Randa. Just, still feeling a little uncertain about things."

"Oh." Miranda's brow creased. "I thought Mrs. Tanquay had left. I thought, perhaps ... there had been some resolution."

Jack sighed; there was no side-stepping this. "Not yet," he admitted, and Miranda's expression fell. "Gabi has tried ta end it only 'cause she thought that you and Leon were together. Then you ended it 'cause you thought she and Leon were together. Now, neither of ya want ta see 'im 'til he makes up his mind, and he just ain't able ta do that, right now."

"Oh." Miranda perked up and smiled, albeit a little sadly. "Actually, in a way, that's good news."

"It is?" Jack was confused.

"Well, yes," Miranda said. She took Jack's arm and they walked on together. "I know that Gabriella had left, so I thought that meant things were over between them. But when Napoleon didn't come calling, well then, I thought that he didn't want to be with me, even if he and Gabi had called it off. But now, obviously, he simply hasn't made up his mind. So, there's still hope."

"Oh." Jack was silent for a moment, trying to digest feminine logic. But then, it did kinda, actually, make sense. "Have you been seein' anyone?"

Miranda sighed. "Oh no. Not that there haven't been offers. I'm not really interested in getting involved with anyone yet. Napoleon caught me by surprise."

Jack laughed. "Yeah. He has a way 'a doin' that."

The pair continued walking in silence, but then they both felt the strain, so Miranda brought up a new topic.

"Have Jean and Penny returned home yet?"

"No, not yet."

"Oh. It's getting close to Christmas. Are they likely to be home for the holidays?"

"I don't know, Miranda. I doubt it."

"So, it's just going to be you three grass-widowers alone during the festivities?"

Jack shrugged. "I suppose so. I haven't heard anything about Caroline and Steven comin' out. The weather is so unpredictable this time 'a year, and I know that until we get to the bottom of all this, Cameron would prefer they stay away. Especially with Rosa. I think it's gonna be a quiet Christmas."

"Oh no! You can't have that." Miranda was adamant. "I know David and Trich often come out to the Rocking M for Christmas, why don't we make it a definite? Trish and I can put on a nice spread for you gentlemen!"

"Oh, I dunno." Jack hesitated, wondering how Leon would feel, having Miranda there. "I think David and Trish are gonna spend

Christmas Day with her folks this year."

"Plans can change," Miranda pointed out, but then she noticed Jack's discomfort and guessed quite easily where it was coming from. "Why don't you ask Napoleon if it's all right with him? If not, we won't come. But if he's okay with it, there's no reason why the three of you should spend that day alone. It would be rather depressing, don't you think?"

"Yeah, probably would," Jack agreed. He, for one, was disappointed at the timing of all this. Like Cameron, he had hoped this Christmas would finally find them all together again. "I'll ask him."

"Good." Miranda patted his arm. "And assure him that there's no pressure from me for him to make up his mind. It would just be nice to spend Christmas with people you like, especially if the ones you love can't be there."

"Yeah, all right. I'll discuss it with 'im, and I will give 'im your assurances."

"Good! Now, I must be off. I didn't come into town just to talk to you, you know."

Jack laughed and kissed her hand. "It was still a pleasure."

"Oh, you men!" Miranda teased, kind-heartedly. "You all love to flirt!"

"Yes, ma'am!" Jack saw no reason to deny the accusation.

"I'll see you later, Jack. Let me know what he says."

"I will."

Miranda carried on in the direction they had been going, while Jack turned and went back toward the telegraph office, since this was where Gov was parked and patiently waited for him. When he got to his horse, he gave the youngster a rub on the forehead, then opened the telegram to read it again and decide if he should be worried about it.

K and N. Carson fired from Arz. Ter. Prison. Suspected of beating an inmate to death. He's disappeared. K.R.

Just as he was finishing this for the second time, he felt the presence of another horse coming up beside Gov, and he glanced up to meet Karma's dark red face. He smiled and looked up further to see his partner in the process of dismounting.

"Hey, Leon. Did ya have a good visit?"

Leon shook his head, looking regretful. "No."

"Why? What happened?"

Leon sighed. "I couldn't do it. I got as far as the front gate to the cemetery, and I couldn't go any further."

"Oh. Well, maybe ya ain't ready yet. You got time; I don't think Doc Palin's goin' anywheres."

Leon sent him a half-hearted smile. "No, I don't suppose so."

"Here, what do ya think 'a this?" Jack asked as he handed over the telegram.

Leon took it, and his face darkened as he read the short note. His jaw tightened in anger. "That bastard! Doc said he'd do it again. Dammit!" Then, he sighed deeply, shaking his head with regret. "I don't suppose there's much I can do about it though, not with all these damned restrictions on me."

Jack smiled, having gotten used to his partner referring to the deceased doctor as though he were still a living, breathing entity. "Kenny don't even know where he is," he pointed out, "and it would be foolhardy ta go tryin' ta find 'im this time 'a year."

Leon looked his nephew in the eye, then nodded in agreement. "Yeah, I know. It's just—dammit!"

Jack put a reassuring hand on his uncle's shoulder. "I know. C'mon, Leon, let's go home. I was just talkin' to a mutual friend, and I got somethin' else ta discuss with ya."

***

"You saw Miranda?" Leon asked as he tried to pull the knife out of his heart.

"Well, yeah. It ain't that surprisin'. She does live here, ya know."

"Yes, I suppose," Leon mumbled as Karma picked her way along the icy road. "I haven't seen her since Thanksgiving. And then she danced with everyone but me!"

"She was tryin' ta give ya room," Jack reminded him. "She's been worryin' about ya. She asked how you was doin'."

"Oh." Leon's tone turned cynical. "And then invited herself out for Christmas dinner."

Jack sighed, feeling frustrated with Leon's attitude. "She offered that they all come out, hopin' ta make the day a little more festive for us. She did say that if you weren't comfortable with it, they wouldn't come."

"Hmm."

"I was kinda hopin' that David and Trish would come out," Jack commented. "It would be nice ta have somethin' other than stew for Christmas dinner."

Leon scowled, and his angry tone showed his frustration. "Jeez! First, you told me to give Gabi another try and practically forced me into it. Now, you're pushing Miranda at me. Just whose side are you on, Kid? Who are you rooting for?"

"I'm rooting for you, Leon," Jack yelled back at him, really getting fed up with his attitude now. "I just want ya ta stop avoidin' the whole thing. Neither of them ladies deserve that. How are ya gonna make up your mind, if'n ya keep avoidin' 'em?"

"Maybe I don't want to make up my mind!" Leon yelled back, causing Karma to startle and start mouthing her bit; she didn't like it when her human got angry. "Maybe I don't want either of them. Did ya ever think of that?"

Booting Karma forward, a little harder than he needed to, the pair took off down the icy road at a cautious gallop, leaving Jack behind. Gov fidgeted, trying to go after his friend, but Jack held him back, not wanting to risk his legs on the slippery surface.

"Aww, jeez, Leon," he mumbled as he watched the mare and his partner disappear down the road. At least he was heading towards the ranch, and not taking off cross-country. Jack sighed and gave his dancing gelding a reassuring pat on the neck. "This is gonna be one hell of a Christmas."

***

By the time Jack arrived at the ranch, Leon had had time to not only cool Karma down from the slippery gallop home but to cool himself down as well. Jack came trotting up to the barn just as Leon was leading his mare towards the field, and the two men stopped and stared at each other.

"Jack, I'm—"

"Yeah, I know," Jack responded with a touch of exasperation, as he swung his leg over and stepped down from his saddle, "you're sorry."

"Yes." Leon looked contrite. "I know you're trying to walk a fine line here, and everybody's bending over backward to help me adjust. I suppose that is what's frustrating; everybody's trying to be so nice. Even Miranda. She's just being helpful. Even though it would probably be hard on her to come out here for Christmas, she still offered to do it, to try and make the day a little nicer for us."

"Yeah. I think that's all she was tryin' ta do. She did say that if you weren't okay with it, she wouldn't come out. I don't think she's tryin' ta pressure ya."

"I know. Like I said, that's what's so frustrating!"

Jack looked at him, his eyes asking the question.

Leon frowned and shook his head. "Miranda is just so nice. If she were being petty and hen-pecking, it would make all this so much easier. But she's being nice. She knows I've got history with Gabi, and yet she still offers to come out to make dinner for us. Why couldn't she be mean and irritating? Why does she have to be so nice?"

Jack grinned. "Yeah, I can see why mean and irritating might be preferable." Leon's shoulders slumped; he looked wretched. Jack clapped a hand on his shoulder. "Ahh, c'mon, Leon, cheer up! It's not every man who has two beautiful women in love with him."

Leon groaned. "You're not helping."

"Sure, I am," Jack countered. "And one day, you'll be forever grateful, on top of all the other debts you owe me."

"You're going to be insufferable about this, aren't you?"

Jack's smile grew into a full grin. "How often do I have you in my debt?" he asked, as he started to lead Gov into the barn. "I just might start makin' a list of all the things I've done for you over the years. Things like, harassing the governor—or should I say, governors. Not to mention takin' the train to Wyoming every month—sometimes twice a month! Oh, and we can't forget . . ." And so on, and so on, as Jack and Gov disappeared into the barn, and Jack's voice faded away.

Leon sighed and turned to look at his mare.

Karma stood and looked back at him.

"You have my permission to kick him," he informed her, "any time you like."

Karma swished her tail and, flicking an ear, thought about this for a moment. She wasn't sure that she wanted to kick the other human. They hadn't always seen eye to eye, but lately, they'd been getting along fine. And besides, she liked Gov, and he might take exception to her kicking his human. No, she thought, she didn't want to kick him.

Leon nodded as he turned, and they continued to the field. "I suppose you're right," he agreed. "He'd never let me live that one down."

***

Florence, Kansas

Frank and Gabriella finally arrived in Florence, Kansas. They were cold, wet, and tired, but knew that checking in with the local law was going to happen before anything else got tended to.

They sipped hot coffee, standing near the stove to take the chill off while exchanging information with Sheriff Andrews.

"He left here the day before yesterday?" Frank's mustache reflected his spreading smile as he gave Gabriella a meaningful nod. "So, we're right on his tail."

"Yeah, but not before that bastard did some real damage. Damn! I shoulda locked him up after he beat up that upstairs gal." Sheriff Andrews darted a look at Gabriella before he scratched pensively at his chin. "Sorry about the language, ma'am, but what that man done has got everybody riled up. If ya don't mind my askin', what do you folks want 'im for?"

"He's suspected of the attempted murder of a young woman in another state. Her family brought me in to track him down." Frank gazed across the road towards the undertaker's office. "The description Mrs. Winters gave was an exact match for the man we've been tracking."

"Good luck findin' 'im," Sheriff Andrews snarked. "He's leavin' a blood trail on the wind, but ya can't track the wind. We went after 'im for what he done, but he just up and disappeared."

Frank huffed, "You went after him for beating up a whore?"

Gabriella sent Frank a look of daggers, then was even more incensed when the sheriff snorted.

"No! We went after 'im 'cause he raped and murdered a young

girl here. The whole town was set ta lynch 'im."

Gabriella's mood darkened. "We'll find him, Sheriff. My associate and I are both excellent trackers. There will be no lynching, though. As I said, he's wanted in Colorado and Wyoming, and we've been hired to take him back there. Alive."

The sheriff chewed his lip and glanced at Gabriella, wondering why this woman was taking the lead. "It ain't usual to bring a woman on a job like this. Hell, it ain't usual or decent for a woman to be trackin' an animal like that in the first place." He narrowed his eyes and focused on the detective. "I will have to check out that identification, Mr. Carlyle."

"He'll check out," Gabriella told him. "I agree, it's not usual to bring a woman, Sheriff Andrews, but I'm an expert shot, at least as good as you are, and I have a vested interest. Mr. Carlyle didn't want me around, but as a private detective, he had no choice. It was a good job I was there; Mrs. Winters needed a woman's touch."

"I couldn't agree more, ma'am. God forbid anything like that should happen to any of my womenfolk. But I'd like to think there'd be a gentle hand to help 'em, if it did." He stood, looking out at the street, full of bustling activity and chattering groups. "Bringin' in something like this has set the town afire. I won't have any trouble gettin' another posse together. Our last attempt ta track 'im down was disorganized. This time, we'll be better prepared. We'll find 'im. You're welcome to join us, Mr. Carlyle—provided the Wells Fargo agency confirms your identity."

Gabriella stiffened. "And me?"

"The law's on his trail now, ma'am. You can stay here or leave on the next train. You're free to go."

Her eyes narrowed, sensing there was little point in arguing. She gave a curt nod and turned on her heel to stride out into the street.

She'd hardly gotten two yards when she heard footsteps clattering up behind her, and a hand grabbed her arm.

"Where are you going?" Frank demanded.

"To get my horse. I'm going after him."

"Gabi, there's no need. The law's on his trail now. We'll get him."

"Yes. But their interests are for the Winters couple and that little girl, so Harris won't be questioned about why he shot Penny. Nobody will care because this double murder is a hanging offense.

We'll never know why he was after Penny, or even if it was him at all. I need to get to him first."

"The horses need rest, and so do we. I'll stay with the posse. I'll question him. I'll find out."

She cast thoughtful eyes down to the ground. "Yes. That's a good idea. People are angry. The sheriff is right; if they catch him, they could lynch him on the spot. If you're with the posse, you'll make sure they keep him alive."

"You're giving up too easily. Don't you even think about going after this animal alone!" Frank's beady eyes narrowed with suspicion. "Go back to the Rocking M. Wait for me to tell you what he says when I've questioned him."

"I have no reason to go back there."

Frank frowned, sensing a deeper meaning behind the bleakness lacing her words. "But what if something needs to be followed up on, after we get him?"

"Then I'll do it. In the meantime, there's no reason for me to go all the way back to the ranch."

Frank laid a hand on Gabi's arm. "What happened between you and the boys? Why are you doing this if they're so hostile towards you?"

Gabi patted his hand; in some ways, she was beginning to like Frank. He was an intellectual misfit, much like her. "I'm here for the Marshams, Frank. I know how it feels to lose your daughter to a criminal, and I'll do whatever I can to prevent that from happening to anyone else. Although I guess we're too late for the girl here." She gave him a sad smile, watching his face register the gravity of her words. "And, if stopping Harris means I have to put up with a bit of attitude from Napoleon Nash, and the law in this town, then I'll swallow it down and carry on." She turned and continued along the sidewalk, turning to give Frank a reassuring nod. "I'll give my horse a few hours' rest, and then I'm going to head out. I'll see you on the trail. I'm sure you'll catch up to me."

Frank took off after her. "I can't let you go on alone."

She stopped again and shrugged. "It's not your call, Frank. It's best that you stick with the posse, so you can be part of the questioning if they get to him first."

Frank didn't like it. "What kind of man would I be if I let you ride out of here on your own?"

"A professional one. The posse will soon catch up with me; we both know that, and the only way I can stay involved is if it's too much bother for them to take me back. Go with them, Frank, I'll be fine."

Frank growled but then nodded. "Okay. It does make sense in a backward kind of way. If we get split up, I'll send a telegram to Nash, and you do the same. We'll get in touch again that way."

Gabriella chewed her lip.

Frank cocked a brow at her. "What?"

She shook her head. "No. I'd rather not get in touch with them. I'm done there. If we lose touch, we can both contact the Wells Fargo branch and meet up there. We've been tracking 'Mitch' for twelve days. We can't fail at the last hurdle."

"We're gonna get him, Gabi. He's not going to get away from us now."

Gabi nodded, then she surprised the hell out of Frank by leaning forward and giving him a quick kiss on the cheek. "Bye, Frank. See you soon ... hopefully!"

***

It was cold and damp as winter slid in. No new snow had fallen, but the snow that was there insisted on hanging around, turning the ground into a slushy, mushy mess. The chilly breeze, that kept up a constant fluttering, didn't help to make the scene any more pleasant or endurable. Indeed, the only good thing about this situation was that Harris's tracks were plain as day to those who knew how to read them, and Gus and Malachi not only knew how to read those tracks but also knew they were catching up.

By early afternoon, they spotted the speck in the distance, moving away from them at a steady pace. Gus took his spyglass from his saddlebag and zeroed in on the gradually diminishing object. More than once, they had thought they'd caught up with Harris, only to find that it was some deer or stray cow, and they didn't want to get their hopes or adrenaline up before they knew for sure. The land out here was mostly flat with only a few rolling hills, so they could see for miles. It was easy to mistake one moving object for another.

Sure enough, as Gus focused on that distant speck, it developed into a man and a horse. The casual way they moved suggested that the rider had not yet realized they were being scrutinized.

Gus lowered the spyglass and smiled. "Yup. It's him."

Malachi grinned while he continued to chew, and then he spat out some of the brown juice. "So, what's the plan, Gus? We can't exactly sneak up on 'im."

"You got that right," Gus agreed. "Why don't we hang back here a bit, wait and see what he does? If'n he don't spot us, maybe we can come up on 'im when he's makin' camp."

***

Twenty minutes into the slow-motion chase, the two pursuers noticed the speck change direction, then, turning back onto its original course, it started to move off again. Since the speck was moving directly away from the hunters, there was nothing to indicate an increase in speed, so it took a moment for them to realize that their quarry had spotted them and was on the run.

Once this fact had been ascertained, all need for discretion was gone. They roused their horses from the casual jog and booted them into a gallop.

They knew they were on fresher horses, and probably better ones as well, so it didn't surprise them to find the distance between pursued and pursuers diminishing. Their blood was up, and the excitement of the chase took hold to the point where Gus forgot to cough. They encouraged their horses to run faster, despite the mud and snow-covered ground that often caused them to slip and lose traction. The horses gave it their all, and Harris's lead grew shorter.

Then Harris made an abrupt turn to the right and headed at full speed towards a stand of trees, such as they were, in this bleak landscape, obviously hoping for some cover. This instantly put pressure on his pursuers to pick up the pace. If Harris made it to cover, then he could turn and start taking potshots at them while they were still stuck out in the open.

They pushed their horses harder, but even then, they knew that Harris would make the trees before they could catch up with him. They kept at him in a straight line until he plunged in amongst the foliage, and though they could see him inside the sparse branches, he still had the advantage of cover. They saw him dismount and get ready to make his stand, and the partners split up so they could come at him from both sides, rather than straight on.

Gus had an eerie feeling of déjà vu, only from the opposite side, as he remembered Morrison and his posse attempting to trap him with the same maneuver. Hopefully, he and Malachi would be more successful than that posse had been. Then his musings were cut short as Harris's rifle barked from the cover, and Gus experienced that knot of anticipation of a bullet hitting home. But Harris missed his shot, and Gus's horse kept going. Then Gus was inside the cover of the trees as well, and he pushed through the low-hanging branches, causing wet droplets to shower down upon him. He didn't notice. He was too focused on his intention.

Having missed Gus, Harris turned to bring Malachi down, but he was too late, as that horse also jumped over some deadfall and disappeared into the jumble. Harris cursed and quickly made a run for his horse. He could hear them coming, one on either side, and if he'd been smart, he would have stayed where he was. At least, in this spot, he would be able to see them, and he had some cover. But Harris was not smart. He panicked.

Gus had drawn his revolver right after entering the woods, so he was ready as soon as he had a target. It didn't take much weaving between the sparsely spaced trees before he caught sight of movement up ahead. He levelled his revolver and fired. He missed his mark, as a tree branch took the hit, but he did succeed in spooking the horse. That animal lunged back and tried to get away from the brutal human who held him.

Harris became so preoccupied with trying to hang onto his horse and level his rifle to get a shot off at Gus that he completely forgot about Malachi coming up on him from the other direction.

Malachi didn't bother with any of his firearms, as the quarters were too close, and he didn't want to take the chance of hitting Gus by accident. He aimed his horse straight at Harris, and just as the fugitive heard him coming and spun to face him, the animal's chest hit him, full force, and sent him sprawling into the cold, wet mud.

Harris had the wind knocked out of him, but he still tried to scramble to his feet, and, having dropped his rifle, he went for his handgun instead.

Malachi spun his horse around again and ran the fugitive over, and probably would have done some damage if it wasn't for the mud cushioning the impact.

Harris tried to push himself up and out of the mire, coughing muck out of his mouth, but by then, Gus had jumped down from his horse and, running over to the barely recognisable Harris, kicked him in the ribs and sent him rolling onto his back.

Harris started to curse while still spitting mud, but before he had a chance to recover, Gus was standing over him with a cocked revolver staring him in the face. Harris stared up at him and snarled.

"What the hell you doin', comin' after me?"

Gus grabbed him by the shirt and hauled him to his feet. "Shuddup!" Gus was disgusted with all the carnage this man had left in his wake and was in no mood to be genial. "Tie 'im up, Ky!"

Malachi ginned with glee; finally seeing this malicious bastard at a disadvantage made his day. "You betcha!" He hurried forward with the leather straps, got Harris's hands behind his back, and tied them together.

Harris cursed and snarled throughout this procedure, but he didn't take his eyes off the gun in Gus's hand. He was a dangerous bully when he had the advantage, but he preferred to do his fighting from behind, and certainly not when he was outnumbered.

"You fuckin' bastards!" he continued to rant. "What are ya doin'? I thought we was all on the same side, here!"

"I ain't never gonna be on the same side as a man who treats ladies the way you do!" Gus snarled at him.

Malachi snickered as he gathered the three horses and secured them. "Yeah. You got some s'plainin' ta do."

Harris glanced from one, back to the other. The sneer wasn't leaving his muddy face. "What are you talkin' about?"

"Well, ya see," Gus explained as though he were speaking to a child, "we got some friends up Colorado way who really wanna have a word with you."

"Colorado?" Harris repeated, but even through the mud, they could see the blood leave his face. "I ain't been near Colorado."

"Well, whether ya have or ya ain't, is no mind ta me," Gus continued. "But there're still certain folks who wanna talk to you, real bad, about somethin' that happened at that prison in Wyoming. Yeah," Gus smiled, "they're real interested in havin' a few words with you."

Nervousness settled over the prisoner, and he shifted on the fallen tree they had him perched on. "You don't know what yer talkin' about. You got nothin' on me."

"Hell, that don't matter none," Gus told him. "We ain't the law; we don't need nothin'. All we need is you, and that's what we got, ain't that right?"

Harris snarled again, and he made a lunge for his captor.

Gus got his hands up to block him, and Malachi grabbed his arms before he'd taken a single step.

"You bastards!" Harris yelled at them as he was unceremoniously shoved back down onto his perch. "What the hell game are you playin'! Nash put ya up ta this, didn't he? That fuckin', sanctimonious bastard! I should'a kilt 'im when I had the chance—"

Harris didn't see the blow that thudded into the side of his head, momentarily stunning him.

"Who ya callin' a bastard—you bastard!" Gus had him by the front of his shirt, shaking him in his anger. "We seen what you done to those ladies! And we heard about worse, so don't you go callin' Nash a bastard!" Then Gus sent him a sneering grin. "And since you mentioned it, when did you have the chance ta kill Nash? Colorado, maybe?" He snorted in disgust. "You idiot. You don't have the brains ta get the better of Napoleon Nash."

"Yeah?" Harris challenged as soon as his head stopped ringing. "I tell ya, I had that son-of-a-bitch in my sights, more 'n once! I ever get him there again, I'll kill 'im!"

"Big talk fer someone in your situation," Gus growled back. "If I was you, I'd start givin' some serious thought to answerin' whatever questions are put to ya, if'n you have any desire ta be seein' daylight again. You think on that."

"I ain't tellin' you nothin'," Harris snarled, then spit at his captor.

Gus stepped out of the way but then landed another blow to the other side of the captive's head, nearly knocking him to the ground.

Malachi was worried that his partner was becoming too wrapped up in his role.

"Hey, Gus . . ." Malachi commented with a chew on his lip, "don't ya think you oughta stop hittin' 'im, so's he can answer the questions?"

Gus glared at his partner, then snorted and backed off. Malachi was right; Gus had been gettin' ready to beat the living daylights out of this snake, and then he'd be no good for anything.

Harris smirked, thinking that these two worthless outlaws were no match for him. This was going to turn into a waiting game; sooner or later, they'd slip up and he would slit their throats. Everything was going to be all right...

CHAPTER TWENTY-FOUR
COMBINED FORCES

Gabriella picked her way through the undergrowth. She was disappointed but not surprised that she had tracked “Mitch” down before the posse had. Right now, is when she really could use their backup.

She had noticed the tracks of two other horsemen, and this caused her some concern. Had the fugitive joined up with his buddies to create even more havoc? If this were the case, it would really be too dangerous for her, on her own, to attempt an arrest. But that fact didn’t stop her from securing her horse just inside the copse of trees and silently making her way into the heart of the foliage.

Where the hell was that posse? She knew any group was only as strong as its weakest member, and the ground they covered would be dictated by horses and men more used to working fields than tracking felons. Finding the fugitive and leading the posse to him might have to suffice if he had met up with buddies.

She crept forward, stalking cautiously now that she could hear the murmur of voices in the copse of trees. She moved like a cat until she could peer through the branches of a mulberry bush. It was stiff in its winter armour, with prickly, harsh stems now devoid of leaves, but it would give her cover if she remained still and didn’t draw the eye.

What she saw surprised her. A smile twitched on her lips. She knew two of these men, and they knew her.

***

“What we gonna do, Gus?” The smallest of the group kept his rifle, held in the crook of his elbow, pointed at the man sitting on the rock. “We was told ta find ‘im, but that lawyer fella never said what ta do when we did.”

"Yeah. It ain't like we can go handin' 'im over to the local law," the larger man considered. "They would start askin' questions we can't answer. We'll make camp here and send that lawyer a telegram."

"Ya mean, one 'a us goes back ta town ta send it? But we're gonna have ta keep goin' back ta town fer the answer." The smaller man shook his head, doubt and concern showing on his face. "You ain't fit ta be campin' out in this weather, Gus. How are we gonna fix this?"

Gabriella stood, making her way into the clearing. "Maybe I can help."

Gus and Malachi turned, their weapons pointing straight at her.

"Hands up!" Gus barked.

Gabriella gave him a reassuring smile and raised her hands. "Don't you remember me? We've met before. I spent some time in," she glanced at Harris, "well, let's not give too much away to him. Remember that place you used to live?"

Malachi's eyes narrowed as his toothy mouth widened. "Eh, it's Nash's lady. That sure was some fine weddin', weren't it?" His face morphed into a frown. "Weren't you workin' fer that Wells Fargo agent? Who've ya got with ya?"

"A Fargo agent?" Harries shuffled anxiously.

"You! Keep still!" Gus snarled at his prisoner. He eyed Gabriella cautiously. "Yeah, it is her ... not that you'd know it in them clothes. What've you done to yourself? Why're you done up like some kind 'a buckaroo? You can get shot real easy, got up like that, and wanderin' into a man's sights."

"You need to watch him," Gabriella cautioned, "he'll stab people just for fun. Have you searched him well?"

"Sure have." Malachi chewed lazily at a gob of tobacco, "and we got no worries about 'im knowin' who we are, ma'am. We were in prison together, ain't that right, Harris? He knows me real well."

Gabriella's eyes widened. "Harris? So, you were in prison with Mr. Nash?"

"And he broke right outta there too, ma'am." Malachi spat messily onto the snow. "He's wanted."

"Why're you here, and who's with ya?" Gus demanded. "I can't believe you're dumb enough ta waltz in here alone."

"I guess I'm that dumb. I really am here alone."

"If you expect me ta be stupid enough ta believe that, you must think I was made by a finger," growled Gus, before breaking into a gut-wrenching cough.

Gabriella walked forward slowly; her arms still raised. "I'm here alone because they wouldn't let a woman join the posse. They're behind me, but I don't know how far away they are. We've been looking for a violent man called 'Mitch', who's suspected of taking a shot at Penelope Marsham. On the trail, we came across the body of a man he had killed, and his dying wife." She stared at Harris. "You raped her, didn't you? It took her days to die. And after what you did to that little girl, you should be thanking your lucky stars that we caught you before that posse did."

Malachi's eyebrows flew up. "What do you think yer doin', settin' off after an animal like this, alone? Yer plumb loco!"

Gabriella gave Harris a cold stare. "So, you're Harris, and you were in prison with Napoleon Nash. Why would you shoot Penelope Marsham?"

"Go to hell, you slut!" Harris snarled at her. "You got nothin'!"

Malachi stepped forward and cracked Harris on the jaw with the butt of his rifle. "Don't talk to her like that! D'ya hear me, Harris?"

Harris fell to the ground, muttering oaths and obscenities all the way down.

Gus glanced uneasily at Gabriella. "How far ahead of that posse were you?"

"Relax, Mr. Shaffer. I have no interest in turning you in, and I believe I can help you hand this piece of trash over to the law without exposing yourself to the risk of arrest."

"He might be able ta say what really happened when Doc Palin was killed," Malachi said. "That's why this lawyer was payin' us ta find 'im."

Gabriella nodded. "You seem to be around a lot of violent incidents, Harris, and you have a whole lot of questions to answer." She turned back to Gus. "I'll let your lawyer know he's been caught, so he has the chance to ask the questions he needs to."

Gus lowered his gun, gesturing for her to drop her hands. "Just what are you proposin', ma'am?"

"I had intended to track him down and make sure I led the posse to him, but now you've got him, I'd be better taking him their way, back to Florence."

Gus shook his head. "Nope. You ain't goin' anywheres alone with him."

"I can handle a gun, Mr. Shaffer. Tie him to his horse, and I'll be fine."

"I don't care, ma'am. I ain't lettin' no woman go off on her own with a murderin' rapist." Gus narrowed his eyes. "Even if she is the law."

Gabriella gave a wry smile. "Just because I've worked with the law occasionally doesn't mean I am the law."

"Yeah, but you knifed us in the back." Gus reminded her. "Two fellas died 'cause a you, and two more went ta prison. Nash may have forgiven ya for it, but I ain't so sure I do. And I doubt Bess and Mary would have either, if'n they'd known you was ta blame."

"Mr. Nash knew I hadn't intended things to go that far. Do you think he would have forgiven me if he hadn't known that?"

"How should I know?" Gus snarked. "Nash did lots of things back then that didn't make no sense. All I know is that you've sided with the law before and you could be doin' it again, right now."

"You know my history with Nash, and you know what happened. The law isn't any friend of mine."

Gus focused on the trampled snow at his feet. "I suppose ya got a point about that." Gus met Gabriella's eyes again, determination turning them hard. "I don't quite trust ya, not after them things that happened at the Elk, but we ain't handin' this bastard over to you. You can join us, and if we run inta that posse, I'll pay real close attention to what you tell 'em."

Gabriella smiled. "Thank you, Mr. Shaffer. As far as I'm concerned, you're a pair of hired guns who were sent to track down an escaped felon. It being the truth makes it all the more believable."

"But, ma'am," Malachi piped in. "If'n you ain't got no likin' fer the law, what you doin' out here trackin' this mean son-of-a-bitch?"

"Because I'm helping the Marshams. Their daughter was shot in the throat. She's engaged to Jack Kiefer, you know."

Gus and Malachi exchanged a look.

"He shot Kid's fee-on-cee in the throat?" Malachi growled, rolling the word around his mouth like hot marbles. "He kilt her?"

"She's alive. But I need to know why he did it."

"Like hell she lived!" rumbled Harris. "That was a clean shot!"

All three of his captors looked at the prisoner.

"Well, nice ta meet ya there, 'Mitch'!" Gus sneered at him.

Harris scowled, realizing that he had just admitted his guilt.

Malachi grinned. It wasn't often he met somebody who was slower on the uptake than he was.

"If'n there weren't a posse on the way, I'd make 'im talk," grumbled Gus, getting back to the business at hand. "But helpin' you ta hand 'im over is our best chance." He fixed Gabriella with a glare. "You'd better be tellin' us the truth. If yur lyin' ta me, Nash's lady or not, I'll make sure I get away, just ta meet up with you again."

"Such a suspicious mind, Mr. Shaffer. Stay like that, and you should keep ahead of the law." Gabriella nodded towards Harris. "He's a violent moron, and you're so much better than the likes of him. Let's go. I give you my word that I won't turn you in."

***

Gus stiffened at the sight of the posse cresting the ridge.

Gabriella noticed the change instantly. "I made you a promise, Mr. Shaffer, and I meant it."

The posse stopped as the lead riders noticed the small group approaching. After a momentary pause to hide their disbelief, the lawmen angled their horses down the slight decline and approached them at a hand gallop.

Sheriff Andrews frowned when he recognized the one woman among the three scruffy-looking drifters.

"You!"

Gabriella looked up into the angry grey eyes of the sheriff from Florence.

"Sheriff Andrews. You're here." She gave him a conciliatory smile, knowing that she was now dealing with a posse of bruised male egos.

The sheriff was fuming. "What do ya think you're doin', comin' out here on your own?"

"I realized I couldn't wait." She decided that amiability would work better than indignation.

The sheriff found this woman unsettling, so he turned his angry eyes to the captive.

"We got you, you bastard." He glared at Gabriella again. "Do you have any idea what he could 'a done to you!"

"I told you, I have a vested interest in catching this man."

"That's not an answer!"

Gabriella clenched her jaw. So much for being amiable. "You know damned well I'm aware of what that man has done. Don't ask stupid questions unless you want a stupid answer."

Andrews narrowed his eyes. "Lord preserve me from meddlin' women." He turned to his posse. "Duke, Bishop! Go get 'im." He glared again at Gabriella. "Lady, unless you do as you're told around here, you'll be treated the same as him, and you'll end up in my jail. I'm in charge. You got that?"

She nodded meekly. They needed to keep this man on their side if Frank was to have access for questioning. "Yes, sir, I've got it. It's reassuring to know that there are competent lawmen such as yourself to take care of us."

Andrews' eyes mellowed. "Just leave this to us, will you?" He raised his gaze to look at the man snarling between two deputies. "He ain't too impressive." He moved his horse closer to Harris. "You're under arrest for the murders of the little Johnston girl, and Jeffrey and Margaret Winters. You ain't worth the dirt they spent their lives diggin' in."

Gus felt secure enough in this situation to speak up. "Not ta mention the deputy in Superior, Nebraska." He sneered at Harris. "You've left a real wide trail of dead bodies behind ya, ain't ya?"

Deputies in the posse glared at Harris, some fingering their ropes. This was getting personal.

"He also needs to be questioned about two attempts on the life of Penelope Marsham and the murder of Doctor Palin," Gabriella put in. "There's a lawyer who needs to interview him, as well as my detective. There are issues in other states we need him to answer for. The governor will have to be informed."

"Your detective?" chuckled Frank as he came forward. "Since when was I 'yours'?"

"Arrest them!" Harris yelled. "That there is Gus Shaffer and Malachi Cobb, from the Elk Mountain Gang. Shaffer's alive, and he's still wanted. Cobb is breakin' his parole by bein' with a criminal. Arrest them!"

Sheriff Andrews' attention turned to the two strangers.

Gabriella noted Gus shifting in his saddle and was quick to jump to their defence. "Nonsense! They were hired by the lawyer I mentioned to track down Harris. He's a fugitive from the Laramie Penitentiary in Wyoming, and he needs to answer for crimes committed during that escape. These men did everything they could to help me. Why would members of the Elk Mountain Gang do that?"

"Don't listen to her," Harris said. "She's practically one of 'em. Hell, she even lived at Elk Mountain for a spell. You can't trust a word she says."

Frank turned to Andrews. "Sheriff, I'm taking custody of this prisoner. I don't give a damn who these men are and what petty crimes they might or might not be wanted for. If Mrs. Tanguay says these men helped to bring Harris down, then that's fine by me. Harris is who we're after, and I'm willing to leave it at that."

Andrews paused before nodding toward Gus and Malachi. "Yeah, he's right. You can go, and thanks for helpin' out, fellas."

"But . . ." Malachi spat tobacco juice, "we's gettin' paid ta bring 'im in. What about—"

Gus rolled his eyes.

Andrews glared at the indignant little man. "You just be thankful I ain't takin' you and your partner in for questioning. I already got the feelin' there's more ta this situation than you're tellin' me."

"Yeah." Gus slapped Malachi on the arm. "C'mon. Let's take the sheriff up on his fine offer and get gone. That lawyer is still gonna pay us."

"Oh. Yeah, okay."

Gus threw Gabriella an almost imperceptible smile. "Much obliged." He touched the brim of his hat. "You take care, ma'am."

Gabriella returned the smile to both men. "You, too. You've done a good thing today, and I'm very grateful."

Gus gave her one last enigmatic look, then, picking up his reins, he rode back into the trees with Malachi.

***

Florence, Kansas

Gabriella looked up from her book, her brows gathering in curiosity. Who was knocking on her hotel room door? Frank was at the jailhouse, trying to get the chance to question Harris, just as he had been every day this week. She hoped it wasn't that sheriff coming back with further reprimands.

"Who is it?" she called out.

"It's Jack."

Gabi dropped her book in surprise. Scooting off the bed, she hurried over and opened the door. "Jack? What are you doing here?"

He smiled, dropping a light kiss on her cheek. "I came to see you. We've been worried about you. We didn't even know how to get in touch until Frank sent the telegram." He held her face in his hands, searching for any trace of the injuries he'd been told about. He flinched at the newly healed scar on her eyebrow. "How have you been? Did it all go smoothly?"

She glanced into the hallway. "You're alone?"

"Yup," he said, watching her. "Were ya expectin' Leon?"

Her eyes became guarded. "No, not at all. Have you just arrived? You must be hungry after that journey."

"I sure am. I'm all checked in here. You fancy joinin' me for lunch?"

She smiled. "Of course. Let me get my jacket."

***

They sat facing one another over the red-chequered tablecloth. Jack observed her with a careful scrutiny before pouring them both a glass of water. "How ya been, Gabi?"

She shrugged, smiling at him. "Fine. Gus and Malachi send their regards."

"You saw 'em?"

She nodded. "They were a big help. They'd found Harris and were debating the best way to hand him over to the law when I came across them. They were very sweet; they wouldn't leave me alone with him, and only headed off when Harris had been turned over to the posse." She sipped her water. "They took quite a chance, and I won't forget it."

Jack smiled. "I'm glad to hear it. Gus would hate a man like Harris." He frowned. "I read about the Winters couple in the newspaper. Terrible . . ."

"It was," Gabriella agreed. "It took nearly three days for that poor woman to die." She sighed, shaking her head with regret that she couldn't have done more. "Let's talk about something more cheerful. You met Hannah?"

Jack grinned. "She's beautiful. A real, special, young lady." He paused. "I did wanna talk to ya about her. Leon needs ta meet her."

She nodded. "We've spoken about that. I told Napoleon that I would arrange it when this is all over. It shouldn't be long now—now that we have Harris."

"Yeah, I read your letter. Leon showed me." Jack sat back, waiting for her to respond, but she merely smiled benignly at him. He eventually gave in. She was as stubborn as Leon, and if he didn't break the silence, they could sit here all afternoon. "It was a real sad letter."

"It was a real sad meeting," she replied, paraphrasing him with precise attention. "I truly regret going to the Rocking M."

Jack reached out a hand, clasping hers. "He's sorry, Gabi."

"I know that." She pulled her hand away as the waitress brought their meals over.

The young woman placed the plates down in front of them. "Do you folks need anything else?"

"Not for me," Gabi answered. "This all looks great, thanks. Jack?"

"Nothin' else for me, miss."

Jack waited until the waitress had moved away, then started in again. "I don't think you understand what I mean. He's sorry he treated you so badly. Real sorry."

"I know that, too. He and I have already discussed this." She poked idly at her fried chicken as her appetite diminished with this conversation. "I don't know how long it will take for Frank to get the chance to interview Harris. He's been trying for the last three days."

"Don't change the subject. You know what I want to talk to you about."

She flicked up sad eyes, fixing him with a hard stare. "I don't want to fall out with you, too, Jack, but there's nothing left to say."

"I don't agree. I made the point 'a comin' all the way out here ta see ya about this. He's been confused. He was completely broken down in prison. His head ain't settled and seein' you took 'im right back to the last moment you were with him. He regrets that and wants ta see ya again."

"I accepted his apology. I'm not angry with him. The timing isn't right, that's all. There's nothing more to be said about it."

"You used to confuse him, even when he was at his best. He never really knew where he was with you."

"Where he was with me? I had exactly the same problem. He said he loved me. We had two beautiful children together, and we even got married, in a way. And yet, he refused to leave the outlaw life. Even when the governor offered him a way out, he wouldn't take it. I should have left him then. I should have known it would not end well." She poked at her chicken, afraid to take a bite in case her tightening throat caused her to choke on it. "It's better this way. Obviously, you're both still dangerous men to know."

"And I made the same choice with Haley," Jack pointed out. "We were all so young then. Things have changed."

"And yet, you both still draw danger. Why should I risk my safety, my daughter's safety, for him?"

"But we got Harris," Jack persisted. "Frank will get the answers out of 'im. Once we find out who hired Harris, this will all get cleared up, and we can get back ta livin' again."

"I don't know. This could just be the first of many who come to seek revenge upon you two. There were a lot of angry people when you got off. Then Leon was released early . . ." She shook her head. "This whole situation is wrong."

Jack took a mouthful of chicken and stuffing and used the chewing time to decide on a different tactic. He swallowed and chased it down with water. "Well, if'n that's how ya feel, Gabi. He does forgive you. He understands now why you had to leave.

"You and Hannah had a lot ta do with us acceptin' the governor's offer. I remember him sayin' that maybe, if we got our pardons, you would come back."

"Then why didn't he get in touch? I had no idea you made that choice. I thought you'd gone to ground or left the country. If he'd wanted us back in his life so badly, he could have tracked us down."

"Yeah." Jack shrugged. "I dunno. Maybe because the deal with the governor was just as risky as outlawin', or maybe he wanted to wait until we actually had our pardons before contactin' ya. Clean slate and all. But then, he ended up in prison before that could happen. He's ready to try again now, though."

"Really?" She snorted. "Better late than never, I suppose. He seems to think that I was especially hard on him."

"Other folks were hard on 'im, too, and they managed to stay friends. He's close ta Kenny, the warden."

"I suspect the nature of our relationship is different."

Jack grinned. "No argument there. Kenny's married."

Gabriella fixed him with resigned eyes. "What do you want,

Jack?"

"I want you to come back with me. There are a lotta things you two need ta talk about."

"I'm not going back, Jack. I'm sorry you wasted your time."

"Gabi, you have unfinished business."

"My business with Napoleon is about as finished as anything can be."

"No, it ain't. You have a child together. That's a life-changin' event."

"Oh, Jack, come on. It's a life-changing event for a woman, but men are free to simply walk away. It happens all the time."

"But Leon ain't the one who walked away."

"Oh, please. He did walk away, repeatedly. He wouldn't leave that life. He'd come and stay with us for a few months and then be gone again. What kind of a father is that? What kind of a family is that?"

"He can't change that, Gabi. All he can do now is try to make it better. He was shattered when you left with Hannah. And I know darn well, he ain't gotten over Ella. His heart was broken, and then you left. It hit 'im hard."

Gabriella set her knife and fork down, her diminishing appetite completely gone.

"Jack, please leave this, or I'll walk out. He's found someone else now. He needs to stop living in the past; he needs to let this go. Has anyone thought about the effect all this has had on me? I can't take any more."

Jack reached over to hold her hand. "I have, Gabriella. You lost your daughter in the worst possible way. I understand why you left. And I understand why you went after Dicks."

Gabriella cocked a brow at him. "I don't know what you're talking about. Dicks committed suicide."

Jack snorted. "Yeah, okay." His smile dropped, and he squeezed Gabi's hand until she looked up to meet his gaze. "Let's just say that I know what it does to ya, takin' another's life. It don't matter what the reasons are. It takes a piece of your soul, no matter what. I appreciate that, Gabi. So does Leon. Apparently, Frank does too, or he would never 'a let you get away with it.

"We both understand why you took Hannah away. You were right ta do so; it was best for her. But you wouldn't have ta hide anymore now, or lie about who he is. You might have a real chance." He stopped and looked directly into Gabi's soul. "How are the dreams?"

She gasped in exasperation. "Are there no secrets between you two?"

Jack patted her hand. "Some. But he told me you helped. He also told me how low you got, Gabriella. I'da helped. You could have found me if you'd wanted to."

"You come as a pair. Contacting either of you wouldn't have helped. It would have made things worse."

He looked deeply into her eyes, willing her to understand. "Gabi, you were so alone you wanted to kill yourself, for god's sake! I didn't know you were so desperate. Didn't you think we'd look after you no matter what, but especially at your lowest point?"

She looked down at the tablecloth, her lashes forming perfect crescents against her pale skin. "No . . ." She tugged at her hand, but he held firm. "You look after him. I'm on my own. I know that now, more than ever."

Jack groaned. "You're not, Gabi. You can ask us for anything."

Gabriella snatched her hand away, shaking her head as she stood. "He'll meet his daughter; I promised him that much. But there's nothing else between us, Jack. Maybe there never was. Maybe I was just another challenge for him to conquer, like a new, state-of-the-art safe." She tossed her napkin down. "I'll see you around, Jack . . ."

Jack watched her stalk from the restaurant and pursed his lips. Why was he the only one who could see how stubborn they both were?

CHAPTER TWENTY-FIVE
KIDNAPPED

Great puffs of steam blasted out from the train, obscuring Gabriella's skirts as she walked along the platform. She looked sharply up at the whistle, its shrill scream grating on her nerves. The swirling, opaque cloud faded, gradually revealing Jack Kiefer's long legs and leather jacket.

He smiled, bright blue eyes cutting through the wisp of gray vapor before it dissipated into the cold, winter air.

"Frank told me where to find you."

She raised her eyebrows. "I'm shipping Cameron's horses back to him. I've just signed the manifest."

"You had Berry, didn't ya? He's a nice colt. Tucker ain't bad either. Are they settled in? It's gonna be a long journey for them."

"They're fine. I've just checked, and they have plenty of fresh water and hay. They'll be checked again at the next stop, about 5 hours from now. There's another horse in there with them, so everyone has company."

Jack smiled. "Can I see them?"

"The train's due off any moment."

Jack scanned the platform. "Most of the doors are still open; we've got time. I just wanna be able ta tell Cameron that I saw them settled in and comfortable, that's all."

Gabriella consented. They strolled along, passing the freight cars, until they reached the open stock car. "They're in here." Gabi made a nickering sound before calling out to the horses. "Berry, Tucker, we've come to say goodbye again."

One of the horses nickered back, and they could hear shuffling from inside the car as the horses put their heads over the makeshift stalls inside the stock car.

Jack walked in, stroking Berry's velvety nose before stretching over and patting his neck. "Good boy. Yeah, you look all right for the journey." He looked around at the two other heads, reaching out to see why Berry was getting so much attention.

"Aww, they want some fuss, too," Gabi murmured, rubbing her face on Tucker's soft muzzle, then reaching over and giving the third horse a scratch. "They've got company here. They'll be fine."

"Yeah," Jack agreed as he wandered further into the car, looking around. "It ain't good ta be lonely. Is there another horse comin'? The stall at the end is empty."

"I very much doubt it. The train is due off at any moment." As if to confirm her words, the voice of the conductor calling "All aboard!" echoed around on the platform, followed by the shrill blare of his whistle. The loud rattle and clang of freight car doors rolling shut came closer to the stock car as the yard crew secured the train for travel. "We'd better get off. It's leaving."

Jack nodded. "Yeah, it is."

She looked at him, standing between her and the door. "Seriously, we need to go."

Jack gave a heavy sigh. "I'm sorry about this, Gabi."

She arched her brow in surprise. "Sorry about what?"

He strode forward and wrapped an arm around her, lifting her off her feet while clamping his other hand firmly over her mouth. He quickly dragged her into the end stall, falling on top of her, and pinning her to the ground.

She fought, overcome with disbelief and shock, but she was no match for the strength of a man who had at least fifty pounds on her.

"Shh!" Jack hissed in her ear.

She heard the ramp being dragged away from their open door and kicked out, hoping to attract attention, only to find Jack clamping her into immobility with his legs. She tried to scream, but the muffled cry was lost amid the slamming of the train car door and the excitement of the horses, who stomped around their confined area trying to assess whether the humans were playing or fighting. Should they be worried about this turn of events? In the face of no actual confirmation, they decided to snort and roll their eyes, their hooves clopping and banging on the wooden floor, ready to flee if things took a turn for the worse. The fact that they could not flee hadn't entered the equation yet.

Gabriella's muffled cries were utterly lost in the excitement.

“Clear!” someone shouted from the platform.

She struggled harder. What the hell was going on? This train was about to leave.

“Wriggly little thing, ain’t ya?” Jack chuckled. “I’ll let ya go in a minute, once we’re on our way.”

She squawked in frustration, but the train had started to move, chugging slowly out of the station. Jack relaxed his hold, still keeping his hand firmly clasped over her mouth. “Not long now, Gabi. We just need ta get up ta full speed. We’ll be well outta the station, then you can scream your head off, as much as ya like. Nobody’ll hear ya.”

He felt her groan in vexation, hearing the station slip further out of earshot. The engine's rhythm and throb grew until it settled into an even beat. He released her and scrambled to his feet against the wall of the stall, waiting for the inevitable explosion.

She climbed to her knees, and with eyes filled with rage, she lunged at Jack, pummelling his chest with her clenched fists. She kicked at him, aiming for his most vulnerable parts, but he was quick to protect that area, and besides, the train's motion kept her from lifting her feet high enough without risking a fall.

She realized the futility of her attack and, bracing her legs against the rocking motion, she stood, fists still clenched and glared into those eyes. The fact that all she saw there was amusement infuriated her further.

“What the hell do you think you are playing at?”

“Ya wouldn’t talk ta me, Gabi. I need ta speak to ya someplace where you can’t scuttle out in a huff.”

“Scuttle? Huff? This is kidnapping!”

He tilted his head. “Yeah. I guess I’m gonna have ta throw myself on your mercy there.” He gave her his most glittering smile. “I ain’t as good with words as Leon; I’m more of a doer. If you’d been Leon, I’d have cracked ya on the jaw. But I can’t do that with you.”

She sniffed and crinkled her nose as she tried to brush soiled straw from her hair. “What did you push me into? Urgh!” She looked around as the reality of the situation sank in. Far from amused, she snarled at Jack with the sharp glare of her eyes, leveled at Jack like gun barrels. “What are you thinking?”

“You’ll have regrets for the rest ‘a your life, if’n ya don’t talk to him.” He raised his eyebrows to echo his smile of appeasement. “One talk—one chance.” He gave her his most innocent look, but the underlying glint of humor shone through. "Gabi, I'd never have done that to ya if it weren't important. Ya gotta give it one last try. Both of ya do. How can I persuade ya? Don't this show how desperate I am?"

"Desperate!" She growled her frustration. "There are some things you can't force. You know that."

"Gabi, I only wanna talk. At the next stop, we'll go wherever you wanna go. I'll make sure you're safe, and I give ya my word of honor, I'll take ya wherever ya wanna go."

Gabi sighed as her anger dissipated to be replaced by bitter disappointment. "You, of all people. I trusted you, Jack."

"And ya still can, Gabi. C'mon, let's sit down before we fall down. Standin' in a moving train ain't exactly conducive to conversation."

To prove his point, Gabi nearly fell over as the train made a sudden lurch to the left.

Jack leaned back against the wall and sank into the straw. He sent her a disarming smile and patted the spot beside him. "C'mon, Gabi, sit."

Gabi growled, then sighed and rolled her eyes. He was right about one thing; the train's movement made it impossible to keep her balance and her dignity intact. She stumbled over to the wall and slid down beside him.

He rested his arm on his raised knee. "Can you honestly say you wouldn't have regrets, in the wee small hours of the mornin', if ya don't give it one last try? You're free ta do that now, for the first time in your lives."

Gabriella fixed him with anguished, dark eyes. "He's moved on, Jack. Even if he can't admit it, I can. Why won't you listen to me? It's over."

His eyes softened. "Gabi, he and Miranda have called it a day. They both knew he had unfinished business with you."

Her brow knotted in curiosity. "But I'm willing to bet it was she who ended it. Not him."

Jack nodded. "Yeah, but only because she beat 'im to it. It seems everyone can see this, but you."

"Me? How come I'm the only one who can see that he's moved on? He was happy with Miranda before I blundered back into his life. I'm trying to get out of this situation with some dignity." She tugged at her hairdo, lopsided and full of straw. "You just don't want that to happen, do you?"

"Dignity?" Jack sighed. "It only takes a few minutes to say goodbye to someone, but it takes the rest a your life ta try and forget 'em. Where's the dignity in regret? I've never found any, and God knows, I have enough regrets ta build my own jail cell."

Gabi shook her head. "I know all about regrets, and the one thing I don't want to do is add to them. I don't want a man I have to chase and fight for attention." She let her head drop back against the wall and closed her eyes. "I don't have the energy for this anymore. Why can't I have a normal life, like any other woman?"

"'Cause you ain't like any other woman, Darlin'. You don't fit into the peg holes that life gave ya, so ya went out and made your own. So did Leon. Maybe that's what keeps pullin' you two back together." He looked at her. Trails of tears were running over her pale skin, and her chest heaved in silent sobs.

He watched her, noticing for the first time that her defenses were crumbling; she was always so guarded, so emotionally reserved. But that was breaking down before his eyes. Was she weakening, or had their relationship changed along with their circumstances? Jack reached over and stretched a comforting arm around her. "What are ya scared of, Gabi? You can tell me."

Gabriella dropped her head, taking in gulps of air, hesitating to vocalize her worst fear.

"Gabi, yer as bad as Leon. You're too scared 'a bein' hurt ta open up, so you're hidin' from life. Stop it. Ain't ya learned that don't work?" He gently brushed away a tear. "Ya know, for real smart folks, you two have a way of reinventin' dumb."

She spoke but was unable to hold Jack's gaze. "I'm afraid I'll find out that it never mattered at all ... if I don't go back, I'll at least have our memories . . ."

"Aw, Darlin', is that all?" Jack held her close, rocking her gently in time to the motion of the train. He smiled softly. "I can promise ya that ain't the case. I don't understand what you and Leon had, but it was as true as the day is long. I wish all I needed to deliver was that assurance, but I gotta do things the hard way; I decided to deliver you.

TO BE CONTINUED

Preview

Book Seven: Family Ties

Jean clasped Eli to her, huddled under the stairs to keep out of range of any shots fired through the door. She lifted the glass to Eli's lips, allowing him to sip the cordial. He had quickly picked up on his mother's anxiety, clinging silently to her and staring at his big sister, the whites of his eyes catching the light.

Hannah leaned over, patting the young child's hand. "You're being very brave, Eli," she whispered. "A real man. Aunt Helèna says we need to be quiet."

Helèna glanced at the child and nodded at Hannah. She was vivacious but read people well; she knew she had to be quiet. Elijah was an unknown quantity; the boy's bottom lip was starting to quiver. This was a danger. The poor child could burst into tears at any time.

The doctor sucked in a breath, following the minuscule sounds out to the area where the coal was dropped into the cellar. She stood, staring up at the coal hatch. Was that a twig snapping? Was somebody there? Helèna raised her gun, pointing it at the hatch. It was bolted from the inside, so if anyone tried to get in that way, they were likely to get their head blown off through the doors.

She dropped her arm. The sounds receded. Or did they? They were practically inaudible, and Helèna began to doubt if she had heard anything at all. She walked back into the main part of the cellar.

"Was there—" Penny asked, anxiously, but a piercing look from Helèna instantly cut her off.

Penny began to suck in tight breaths. Were they here? Had they come for her again?

Hannah was quick to grab her hand, clasping it to her chest.

Penny looked at her in surprise; the dark eyes no longer swirled with mischief; they seemed to transmit wisdom beyond the girl's years.

Hannah smiled, nodding gently, before she pulled Penny's hand up to her lips, kissing it softly and hugging her close.

Penny felt Hannah's breathing against her; calm, regular, and even. She either trusted her Aunt Helèna or hadn't grasped what was going on. Penny closed her eyes and hoped beyond hope that she could trust her life to this strange, middle-aged woman. How she wished Jack were here. Why hadn't he stayed with her?

Helèna had changed focus. Was that the sound of a door opening? She had moved over to another area of the cellar and was aiming above their heads. She was now holding the gun in a two-handed grip, pointing straight up. If anyone walked over the floor above them, they could be dispatched by a shot through the floorboards.

Penny hugged Hannah to her and braced for the explosive shot.

It was clear that Helèna believed someone was up there.

Penny caught a breath at the squeak from a floorboard above her, and her blood turned to ice water. Somebody was up there. There was no room for doubt anymore; someone was walking in the hallway above them.

Penny screamed silently in her head. Why didn't Helèna shoot? He was there, creeping about. Penny's hand went up to her mouth, her teeth clamping into her knuckles, and her stomach turning over in fear.

The door rattled, and every nerve in Penny's body jangled, alight with terror; memories flooded back of lying on the ground, drowning in her own blood. Her breath came in great rasps of panic.

Why didn't that mad woman shoot?

List of Characters

- Andrews: Sheriff in Florence, Kansas
- Baird, Isabelle: Lives in Arvada. On the hunt for a husband
- Bill: Bartender in Arvada
- Carlyle, Frank: Wells Fargo Agent. Leon's watchdog
- Carson, Floyd: Former senior guard at the Laramie Prison
- Clayt: Telegrapher in Arvada
- Cobb, Malachi: Ex-Con. Former member of the Elk Mountain Gang. Buddy to Gus Shaffer
- Dion, Heléna: Gabriella's older sister. Doctor. Served in the Civil War as a spy
- Gibson, David: Doctor in Arvada, Colorado
- Gibson, Nathan: Son of David and Tricia
- Gibson, Tricia: David's wife
- Granger, Rosie: Infant daughter of Steven and Caroline
- Granger, Steven: Defence lawyer for Leon and Jack. Now married to Caroline
- Hardcastle, Agnes: Runs the boarding house in Arvada
- Harris, Karl: Escaped convict, murderer. Uses the alias "Mitch'"
- Jacobs, Carl: Sheriff in Arvada
- Janson, Josephine: A professional companion. Childhood friend of Leon and Jack
- Jefferies, Beth: Adopted daughter of Sam and Maribelle
- Jefferies, Maribelle: Sam's wife
- Jefferies, Merle: Sam's mother
- Jefferies, Sam: Ranch hand at the Rocking M Ranch
- Jefferies, Todd: Adopted son of Sam and Maribelle
- Johnston: Young girl raped and murdered by Harris
- Kiefer, Jack: Leon's nephew, business partner and best friend
- Lisa: Waitress at the Laramie Café
- Marsham, (Granger) Caroline: Oldest daughter of Cameron and Jean. Married to Steven Granger
- Marsham, Cameron: Rancher in Arvada, Colorado
- Marsham, Elijah: Son of Cameron and Jean. Youngest

child

- Marsham, Jean: Cameron's wife
- Marsham: Penelope: Second daughter of Cameron and Jean. Middle child
- Mitchell, Mason: Former warden at the Laramie Prison
- Molly: Prostitute at the Black Rose in Arvada
- Nash, Napoleon: "Leon" . Ex-outlaw, ex-convict. Former leader of the Elk Mountain Gang
- Palin, Ben: Deputy in Arvada, Doc's nephew
- Palin, Walter: "Doc". Doctor at Laramie Prison. Deceased
- Pearson: Senior guard at the Laramie Prison
- Rawlins, Hershal: Lives in Arvada
- Reece, Alex: Kenny and Sarah's youngest son
- Reece, Charlie: Kenny and Sarah's middle son
- Reece, Connar: Kenny and Sarah's eldest son
- Reece, Evelyn: Kenny and Sarah's daughter and youngest child
- Reece, Kenny: Former guard at the Laramie Prison, now warden.
- Reece, Sarah: Kenny's wife
- Schulmeyer, Eric: Runs the livery stable in Arvada.
- Shaffer, Gus: Former leader of the Elk Mountain Gang. Buddy to Malachi Cobb
- Sorenson, Frans: Runs the General Store in Arvada
- Tanguay, Ella: Leon and Gabriella's youngest daughter. Deceased
- Tanguay, Gabriella: Leon's former lover/wife. Mother to his two daughters
- Tanguay, Hannah: Leon and Gabriella's oldest daughter
- Thornton, Miranda: Love interest of Leon's. Tricia Gibson's cousin
- Winters, Jeffery: Man murdered by Harris
- Winters, Margaret: Woman raped and murdered by Harris

WYOMING GOVERNORS

In order of term

- Hoyt, John Wesley: 1878 – 1882
- Hale, William: 1882 – 1885
- Morgan, Elliot: 1885.
- Warren, Frances: 1885 – 1886
- Baxter, George: 1886
- Morgan, Elliot: 1886 – 1887
- Moonlight, Thomas: 1887 – 1889
- Warren, Frances: 1889 – 1890
- Barber, Amos: 1890 – 1893
- Osborn, John: 1893 – 1895
- Richards, William: 1895 - 1899
- Richards, DeForrest: 1899 – 1903

About the Author

I have always been a cowgirl at heart, even though I have lived my whole life on the West Coast of Canada and the USA. But our road trips always draw us east and south. Montana, Wyoming, and Colorado; these are places where my imagination runs wild.

In 2021, we made a change and moved to Selah, a small town in Central Washington. The lifestyle here suits me better than on the coast, and it didn't take me long to settle in and make new friends.

I've been an artist/writer all my life, painting and writing about my first passion: the West. I also found a niche with painting pet portraits and animal studies. Now that I am retired, I can indulge in the things I love the most: my husband, my animals, my art, and my writing. I'm busier now than I have ever been before, and I wouldn't have it any other way.

Visit my blog at: www.twoblazesartworks.com and enjoy my free novel "Dinner at The Elk" about Leon and Jack's early years.
Click on Writing Blog on the left, then scroll down until you find the link.
Dinner at the Elk is also available for free on Inkedin and for sale on Amazon.

Visit my blog at: **www.twoblazesartworks.com**

www.ingramcontent.com/pod-product-compliance
Lightning Source LLC
LaVergne TN
LVHW041057080826
845145LV00007B/1610